Masters' Mysterium

NIAGARA FALLS

R. R. Reynolds

Masters' Mysterium
Niagara Falls

Copyright © 2019 by R. R. Reynolds

ISBN 978-0-9886797-1-9

Masters' Mysterium Press

The Lord is not slow in keeping his promise, as some understand slowness. Instead he is patient with you, not wanting anyone to perish, but everyone to come to repentance.
— 2 Peter 3:9.

FOR MAGGIE

CHAPTER ONE

Bailey Tannahill sloshed through the muck that threatened to crest the top of her knee-high rubber boots and inundate her toes with cold, slimy water. The spring-fed pond was crystal clear near its source but became a reed-filled, muddy mess on the far side. She had been hired by the Millers to remove a pest from their property—the muskrat.

The Millers said they would pay her five dollars a muskrat and she could keep the hides and meat. Bailey had just turned sixteen and the money sounded good. The pelt market for muskrat had tanked over the last couple of years, but she could still make three dollars a hide. Not good, but with the bounty offered by the Millers, it would fix her up with gas and ammo for quite a while. She might even be able to put on layaway that sweet Winchester 94 Trapper she had her eye on at the gun shop in Niagara Falls.

Stopping for a moment near a willow, she reached into the pocket of her camo jacket and pulled out her phone. Cranking up iTunes, and popping in her earbuds, she felt the reassuring full volume blast of Crowder's "Run Devil Run" rattling her skull.

Bailey surveyed her surroundings. Several areas appeared to have deep muskrat runs, and although she couldn't see the lodge, there were a couple push-ups nearby. It looked promising—she should have brought help.

She did ask her brother Ian if he wanted to tag along and help her set Conibear traps, and was even willing to cut him in on part of her windfall, but he declined with some stupid excuse about having something important to do. She was sure that it had to do with his new girlfriend, Ruth-Ann Wilkens, but she didn't press the point. Ian was nineteen years old but still awkward around the girls—they probably hadn't even kissed.

Bailey couldn't criticize him too much as she was just as uncomfortable around the opposite sex. Although she didn't consider herself a girl, she wasn't yet a woman either. "Tomboy" used to be the proper word for her, but that had gone out of fashion. She was attracted to boys but was also so much like them that she doubted any would ever be interested in her. Ian told her that he heard comments from some of his friends wishing that she'd let her fiery red hair grow out and put on makeup, she might even be cute. But, she had no desire to be cute or to change. Her hair was cut short, so it didn't interfere with hunting. Her clothing was practical and straightforward—if a boy didn't like her baggy jeans and camo ensembles, then that was their loss. Just the thought of wearing a dress made her gag.

At least the late March weather was brisk, but not too cold, and much better than the previous few months New York State had just been through. Her family's compound wasn't far from Youngstown and Old Fort Niagara. Being sandwiched between Lake Erie and Lake Ontario meant that the lake effect snow could be brutal, and there was always the possibility of a late-season blizzard, but for now, it looked like life was returning to the land.

She found a sweet spot with a clear muskrat slide that entered a narrow channel under the water. It was deep enough that she could probably get away with a leghold trap and drown the unsuspecting rodent, but she didn't want to take the chance, as the water level fluctuated in the marsh. If the muskrat didn't drown, they were known to twist their legs off to escape. Her father raised her to take sustenance off the land—she even planned to help her mother cook muskrat meatloaf with her catch; so, while she had no qualms about killing an animal if necessary, she had no wish to be cruel.

Pulling a Conibear trap out of her pack, she set it and lowered it down into the water in the spot most likely for a wandering muskrat to happen upon. She pushed a wood stick through the chain to hold it in place. When the unsuspecting vermin traipsed down its favorite trail, it would come upon the trap and hopefully try to pass through it. The trap would, in most cases kill it instantly, and the animal would be waiting for her, just like a hairy chuck steak in the Aldi meat aisle.

A bright light flashed above her head, causing her to look up, as she felt what could only be called an electric shock pass through her body. Was she just hit by lightning? She didn't see any clouds, and it didn't hurt—more of a static shock that startles but does little damage.

Looking around, she couldn't locate any cause for what just happened, but the wind started to shift sharply to the west, causing her to scan across the Millers' field.

Bailey gasped and quickly knelt in the marsh water, trying not to be seen. She cursed herself for not bringing her rifle or even a handgun along on this expedition, but she didn't expect to need one on her muskrat hunt. Her only weapon was a Buck skinning knife at her side that she doubted would help her in this situation.

In the distance, two creatures seemed to be made of mist—she could see completely through them. The ghostly beings were moving through the reeds of the adjacent marsh, heading towards the ten acres of young winter wheat that the Millers had planted as a cover crop on an outlying section of farmland.

As she watched, the beasts transformed from a fog into solid beings. They were huge, their bulk supported by four sturdy legs; both of them with mottled gray hide covering bony, emaciated flesh. They each displayed four tattered bat-like wings sprouting from their feline bodies. A large, spiked tail reminiscent of a Stegosaurus lashed from side to side as they slunk through the marsh towards the wheat field. What gave Bailey the shivers was that each beast had four heads upon one stalk of a neck. The heads swiveled around as they scanned their surroundings. One of the heads looked like that of a vulture; another, a pox-ridden saber-toothed tiger; the third, a bull with glowing eyes and razor-sharp horns; and the scariest of all—the one that stopped and looked in Bailey's direction—a rotted human corpse of a head.

She decided to lay as flat as she could in the water while attempting to keep her phone dry, and hoping that the creatures had not seen her. She was shivering but not sure whether from the chilly water or fear.

The beast appeared to lose interest and continued with the other towards the field. When they reached it, they stood next to each other for a moment, then separated; one moving straight ahead and the other veering away in an arc. Both swished their tails back and forth through the young wheat like twin scythes, tearing it out by the roots and ripping into the soil as they went.

She stayed low and tried not to make a sound as the creatures went about whatever they were doing. As she lay there, a muskrat swam up and looked at her in a way that suggested the rodent was upset at her blocking its path. It then started chewing on her rubber boots.

Bailey swore under her breath and hoped the confused critter wouldn't end up chomping on her instead of her boots. She was the one supposed to be eating the muskrat, not the other way around.

The beasts, having appeared to complete their ritual, moved off towards the north, their solid forms reverting back to mist.

When they were out of sight, Bailey shook the muskrat off of her and stood up. She was cold and wet and worried about possible hypothermia but needed to see what the creatures had done. Walking towards the field, she stopped and gasped.

She had seen these types of creatures before—the entire world had. A similar one was torn apart by angels on the main street of Creekside, Wisconsin. That's when everyone knew that the world had changed forever.

In front of her, prints the size of an elephant's with foot-long claw marks sunk deep into the earth showed her the way. They led to a circle more than a hundred feet in diameter. Within the circle, straight lines—carved out by the beast's tail—ran back and forth, dividing it into triangles; within the five triangles was a pentagram.

———

Ian Tannahill sat on a cot in one of his parents' underground bunkers. The scratchy wool blanket with its bright plaid colors was out of place in the bland concrete and steel room. The shelter was designed by his father as a backup if the secondary bunker failed—which meant that the primary had already been compromised. Redundancy was his father's middle name; if this one was overrun, there was a crawl tunnel to the next.

There were four cots: one for each of his parents, his sister Bailey, and himself. A weapons locker took up one side of the cramped room, with a toilet and sink hidden behind a shower curtain on the far side. He had to admit that his father was inventive. Each bunker from the first to the fifth got progressively smaller and less elaborate but provided everything needed to survive for an extended period. This, the third one, had a cook stove, filtered ventilation, running water piped in from a spring, and several months' worth of canned food and bottled water in case the spring became contaminated. When this one became too rank, they could always move on to the next.

While he found the bunkers depressing, the buildings above ground were no better than the ones below. His mother tried to add a homey touch to their nineteenth century farmhouse with tchotchkes and bright curtains, but that didn't extend to the other buildings—not to the massive corrugated metal barn that housed their bug out truck and other vehicles, nor to their twelve high cube cargo containers that had been welded together and covered over with dirt, making them into a nineteen-hundred-square-foot command center and storage facility ready for any disaster.

Ian didn't inherit his father's love for the outdoors or his predisposition to paranoia. Those traits seemed to have fallen to his sister Bailey. She was, at sixteen, a mirror image of her father. At first, Brian Tannahill attempted to change his boy—make him into a man. His father would take him fishing and hunting, but Ian never performed up to expectations. On projects around the compound, the elder Tannahill would look at Ian with a frustrated grimace and take whatever chore it was away from him and do it himself. He'd hear comments his father made to neighbors about his son's klutziness; about how far below par he was compared to their boys—that he'd never be a man. Eventually, his father gave up and concentrated on showing Bailey the skills that would help her survive in a post-apocalyptic world.

Instead, at a young age, Ian fell in love with the theater when his mother took him to a recreation of an old-time melodrama. It was a simple story with a hero, a villain, and a damsel in distress, overacted and heavy on the cheese factor—he loved it.

Thanks to his mother's lobbying, when he turned eighteen, he was able to escape to a yearlong theater arts program in the Catskills. He learned a lot and was eager to move to Manhattan and start a career as a stage lighting technician on Broadway. He realized that a certificate would probably not be enough to land him a job unless it was as a stagehand or rigger Off-Off-Broadway, but he was willing to try.

The phone call two months ago from his father was devastating. Brian Tannahill needed his son back on the compound to help prepare for Armageddon. The business with the angels destroying a town in Wisconsin—and then wreaking havoc on the Las Vegas Strip—had spooked him. No amount of persuasion would change his father's mind, not even the calming words—broadcast internationally—of Senator William "Bill" Stevenson, of Nevada, the man who had proven himself by his death, resurrection, and abundance of good works to be the savior of this screwed-up world.

His father cut off his funding, as a theater background wouldn't help him survive in a world where angels and devils fought in the streets. Ian didn't even have enough money of his own to relocate to New York City, so he dutifully drove his aged Ford Bronco back to Youngstown and began his existence as a lonely mole man, cut off from civilization.

He tried to make it work, doing everything assigned to him. On the few occasions that he was able to leave the compound, he ended up in fights with some of the local guys he'd grown up with. They liked to mock what they considered his sissy ways and humiliate him. When he tried to stand up to them, he usually ended up decorating the sidewalks with his blood.

Things started looking up when he met Ruth-Ann Wilkins. He had known her since high school; although they had been in several classes together, he was too scared ever to try to talk to her; she was pretty, popular, and out of his league. After running into her at the Niagara Falls Walmart, he worked up the courage to ask her out—surprisingly, she accepted.

The relationship lasted about a month before he found her making out with one of his so-called friends that had once put the impression of his graduation ring on his forehead. He tried calling her multiple times to see if there was a misunderstanding but she would never answer.

He gave up yesterday.

His father sent him down to the bunker to inventory the firearms. On his lap sat a Beretta 9mm pistol. He had dutifully checked it off on the inventory sheet and inspected it. It appeared to be oiled and in proper working order. He loaded a full magazine into the pistol and chambered a round.

Raising it to his temple, he pulled the trigger.

The Beast loped down the middle of East Vegas Valley Drive, unconcerned by the screams of local homeowners and the ever-increasing volume of the screeching sirens. Seeing the frightened looks of the humans before they ran into their shelters was proving quite entertaining.

Two uniformed humans in white vehicles with flashing lights pulled in front of the Beast to block its way. It was annoyed as the pathetic creatures got out and started yelling and waving ineffectual weapons.

Tucking its four bat-like wings close to its feline body and swiveling its bull head forward to face the humans, it charged.

The stings from the weapons pointed at it were mere annoyances, while the squishy sensation of its right horn piercing soft flesh felt decadently sensuous. And the scream that emanated from the dying flesh was quite satisfying to the Beast's eight ears.

Making quick work of the other human it proceeded to stomp on each vehicle, flattening their roofs until their cursed sirens stopped blaring and the flashing lights went dark. Remembering that it needed to reach Valley High School as quickly as possible, it continued down the road. It dare not anger the Imperator.

Corson sat just behind the podium at Valley High School in Las Vegas. The gym was filled to capacity to marvel at the resurrected Senator Stevenson, who would outline the bold promises of the new paradigm that was unfolding. Television news crews lined the west wall of the building while Secret Service agents flanked either side of the dais.

Brushing a speck of lint from his pressed slacks, Corson waited impatiently as the mayor of Las Vegas droned on. The Imperator, looking regal in the late senator's body, sat beside him, pretending to be going over some notes. The Imperator wouldn't consult with him as to his speech, which he found infuriating. In Corson's previous position he had full control of a rogue nation, and now he sat, totally demeaned, in front of a bunch of pimply high schoolers.

Finally, the mayor waved a hand towards the senator and invited him to stand. The applause from the humans was deafening as it reverberated off the cinderblock walls. Senator William Stevenson winked at him and stood.

Raising his arms as he approached the podium, he motioned for the crowd to be silent. "Thank you for the warm welcome and for inviting me to speak here today," the senator boomed. "Everyone in Las Vegas has heard of the outstanding Academy of Hospitality and Tourism that Valley High operates to train those who will one day run the resorts of the rebuilt and re-imagined Las Vegas.

"That is why I wanted to make my announcement here because it is the next generation"—he looked around the room, gesturing with a broad sweep of his outstretched arms— "that will do marvelous and miraculous things, and change this world forever.

"I have blessed myself with tremendous wealth, and I have already given millions of dollars to help rebuild our city after the destruction brought upon us by the demons." He paused and raised his index finger for dramatic effect. "But, I plan to do more—"

Before he could continue the double doors from the hallway blew inward as a Beast squeezed its bulk through the narrow opening. The Beast was similar to those seen by the crowd on television during the battle of Creekside, Wisconsin. The sight of it threw everyone into a panic as they started to claw their way over each other to find an exit.

Once inside the gym, the Beast spread its four ragged wings. Its demonic heads swiveled, taking in the entire room of terrified humans while its feline body slunk down to pounce.

Corson watched in boredom from his seat as the senator jumped off the dais and jogged over to stand before the Beast.

"I command you to stop!" Stevenson yelled loud enough so the students in the cheap seats at the back could hear, even as they continued to climb over each other and tumble down the bleachers.

The Beast stood silently regarding the senator as the humans started to quiet down.

"Leave us!" Stevenson said. "Return to the pit of hell where you belong. I command this in my name!"

Corson watched as the Beast lowered its heads in submission and backed its bulk out of the double doors. The crowd stood there in stunned silence.

"They will come for you," Stevenson warned the students. "Mark my words, they will kill every last one of you." Turning towards the cameras, he continued: "They wait for those watching on television as well. Even the angels will not be able to stop them."

Stevenson waived a scolding index finger at the Secret Service personnel that stood nearby with their guns drawn. "Weapons are ineffectual against such abominations. You would have been killed as well."

Stevenson walked up the steps and returned to the podium. "They come in their vile demonic forms to terrorize, but they also live amongst you now as possessed humans. Your friends may be inhabited by one such as we have seen here today. Your family may be taken over so completely that they do horrible things to those they love." He milked a long pause for all it was worth. "They may even take you!"

Corson tried not to smile as the crowd looked on in fear.

"I was going to hold off announcing this," Stevenson said as he assumed a solemn air. He paced in front of the assembly with his arms folded Lincolnesquely behind his back. "I came here only to speak on the improvements coming to Las Vegas. But this is too important; I cannot keep it from you.

"I can teach you the power to cast out demons, just as I have today. I can give you control over the creatures of the earth and the demons below. I can give you the knowledge to become wealthy, the same as myself. Each of you are capable of performing amazing feats. We've all seen the woman, Emily Iverson, who can manipulate matter, and the young man, Gavin Young, that can heal just by the touch of his hand. I offer you the same. I have the power to grant this to everyone in this country *if* they follow my direction.

"I know that I have been mentioned as a potential presidential candidate. I am indeed flattered and honored, but this announcement is so much more important: I will be constructing an academy where every right-thinking citizen may come and learn the hidden secrets and the lost arts that will save this world, now that the supernatural walk among us."

Stevenson raised his hands in the air, as if in a blessing.

"I have risen from the dead for this purpose and this purpose alone. I promise that I will save you."

———

Ian had closed his eyes. He didn't want his last view to be one of the bunker, but he felt his grasp around the pistol loosen just as he pulled the trigger. He couldn't believe that he had botched his own suicide.

Opening his eyes, he looked around to see where he dropped the gun. It wasn't on the bed; it wasn't under the bed; it wasn't anywhere.

While he was rooting around the bed, he spotted an old *Playboy* magazine he had hidden there at one time. He went to pull it out from between the mattress and the springs, but when his fingers brushed it, it disappeared.

Ian jumped in surprise. His back hit the shelving that stored some of their food rations. A box of rigatoni and a can of Hormel Chili fell off of the shelf and slapped his hand, only to disappear as well.

"What the hell?"

He ran over to the ladder and climbed out of the bunker. The light almost blinded him as he sat there on the rim with his feet dangling. He couldn't comprehend what was happening. Did he succeed in killing himself, and this was some kind of weird heaven or hell—perhaps the last delusion of a dying brain?

Violet, their chocolate lab, ran over and dropped her chew bone next to him. He reached for it to give it back to her but it, too, disappeared as soon as he touched it.

Violet stood there wagging her tail like it was some new kind of game. He wanted to push her away but was afraid to touch her for fear she might disappear too.

Ian contemplated his next move. He could go back down into the bunker and pull another pistol out of the weapons locker and give it another try, or he could attempt to figure out what in the hell was going on. He wished there was some way to know what to do—some sign that there was a future for him.

His phone rang. Pulling it out of his pants pocket, it surprisingly didn't vanish in his hand. "This is Ian," he answered.

"Are you the kid that applied for a job as a lighting tech at the Pantomime Theater?"

"Uh…yeah," he replied, not sure of anything at the moment.

"Great. Can you drop by tomorrow for an interview?"

"Sure," Ian said, trying to mask his enthusiasm. He'd submitted dozens of resumes, and this was the first time anyone had called him back.

"Okay, be here at ten," the man said.

"Who should I ask for?"

"My stage manager is out tomorrow. Just ask for the Amazing Ahti."

———

"You don't believe me," Bailey said to her family as they gathered around the kitchen table.

Her father leaned against the counter wearing faded jeans, camo T-shirt and a Git 'Er Done baseball cap—making it clear which side of the family Bailey got her fashion sense from. "I've never known you to lie," Brian Tannahill said. "But it just doesn't make any sense. Have you been feeling ill lately, or have you been taking something you shouldn't?"

"I'm not crazy or on drugs," Bailey huffed, "or lying. I know what I saw. They started out looking like two patches of fog, but they became solid and looked just like that demon thingy that was killed in Wisconsin—the one they kept showing on television."

Her mother looked up from the table. "Sweetie, why would they be here? There's nothing remarkable about the Millers' farm."

Linda Tannahill was a successful real estate agent in the Niagara area before meeting Brian Tannahill. It was love at first sight, so she said; she'd been obliged to give up her profession to stay on the compound and prep for the end of the world. She was one of the most down-to-earth and gentlest human beings on God's green earth, and Bailey had no idea how she fell in love with a paranoid doomsday prepper with obsessive-compulsive disorder.

"Nobody in the area has reported seeing anything unusual," her father said. "Why would you see them and nobody else?"

"I don't know," Bailey said as she plopped down at the table. "All I know is what I saw. I think something bad is going to happen."

This got her father's attention, as he was always focused on the worst-case scenario: the world-ending apocalypse, be it by nuclear war, civil unrest, natural disaster, or now—demons. She knew the recent events in Wisconsin and Nevada had spooked him, and Bailey had just squirted lighter fluid on the flames of his paranoia.

"Okay," her father said. "We're bugging out at the end of the week."

They all stared at him.

"Brian, is that necessary?" her mother asked.

He stopped leaning and stood up straight. "The Millers are only five miles away. If they're that close, it's no longer safe here. We have cameras, motion sensors, and trip wires around the perimeter, but how do we guard against demons that can move like clouds? Guns are useless; bunkers are useless; it would only be a matter of time before the compound is compromised. We'll take the bug out truck and the bus and head someplace safe."

"But I have an interview tomorrow with the Amazing Ahti," Ian protested. "This is a big opportunity."

"To shine lights on some magician?" the elder Tannahill said. "Wasn't he the guy in the center of that whole mess in Vegas? That's another reason why we need to get out of the area."

Bailey added, "Yeah, Ahti popped Senator Stevenson in the melon. That was a pretty impressive shot. Did you see the way the senator's head just exploded?"

Her mother put her hand on Bailey's. "I worry about you, Sweetie."

"The senator didn't press charges," Ian observed. "Besides, how do you charge someone for killing a guy that came back from the dead? Working for Ahti would be a sweet gig."

"Out of the question," Brian said. "We're stronger as a unit, and I'm not leaving you here to be corrupted by that hack magician. I'll start on the checklists to make sure that we're supplied."

Linda Tannahill looked up at her husband. "But where will we go?"

"My theory," he said as he bent over and kissed his wife on the top of the head, "is that you fight demons with angels, so we should go where the angels are."

Bailey furrowed her brow. "Heaven?"

"It's heaven only if you're a compulsive gambler," her father said. "Las Vegas."

CHAPTER TWO

Trudy Masters-Young attempted to brush her hair. It was never an easy task even under the best of circumstances, but the lack of humidity in southern Nevada had turned her bobbed brunette mop into something resembling straw.

There was a knock at the door of her drab motel room, which allowed her to admit defeat and toss her brush onto the sink counter. She looked at herself in the mirror and sighed. She had always heard that pregnancy brought out a woman's inner beauty and would make her look radiant. Trudy was four months pregnant and looked like shit—felt like it too.

Walking over to the door, she steadied herself and opened it. Rachel stood on the other side wearing a Cluck and Grunt T-shirt: a joyous pig and chicken dancing upon a plate of bacon and over-easy eggs.

"Ready for girls' night out?" Rachel chirped.

Trudy pointed at the hideous shirt. "Did Bill make you wear that?"

"He's got one for you too," Rachel said as she handed her a plastic bag.

"Not a chance."

"It's a favor to Bill," Rachel pouted. "His concourse restaurant at Kim's casino resort will be opening soon. We'll get new shirts when the Mysterium is finished and his other restaurant opens."

Trudy waved her petite friend inside. Rachel's long blonde hair was getting lighter under the Nevada sun, while her freckled face was starting to tan. Reluctantly she pulled the shirt out of the bag, inspected it, and then tossed it on the bed.

"I'll pass. There's no way we're going into Vegas wearing matching shirts—especially *these* matching shirts."

"That's okay, we'll still have fun," Rachel said. "I made an itinerary for us."

"I can't wait to hear it," Trudy said as she considered what could be on an angel's itinerary for a night out in Sin City. "I can't drink or be around smoke so that should limit our options."

Rachel took a deep breath. "First, we can watch the fountains at the Bellagio."

"I hear that's closed due to the removal of the Eiffel Tower's debris—the debris, I might add, that almost smushed my hubby and me into the payment."

"Well, then, we can go see the Pirate Show at Treasure Island."

"That's drained because of a demon crashing through the manmade lake bottom."

"New York, New—"

"Shut down due to the destroyed roller coaster that caused considerable structural damage to the building."

Rachel looked utterly deflated. "There's a famous ice cream parlor at Caesar's Palace."

"Now you're talking," Trudy said as she ushered Rachel to the door.

Emily was waiting in the idling Jeep wearing a Harley-Davidson T-shirt and jeans. "Hey, Trudy," she said as they got in. "So, Rachel didn't talk you into wearing the Cluck and Grunt T-shirt?"

Trudy laughed. "No! It's enough to make me go vegan."

"So, what's the plan?" Emily asked.

"Rachel knows of an ice cream parlor on the Strip," Trudy said.

Emily looked let down. "That's it?"

Rachel cleared her throat from the back seat. "I hear they have a banana split that is large enough for us all to share." After no response, she added, "Sharing is important."

Emily rolled her eyes at Trudy. "Okay, but we'll need to figure out something more than that to make it a proper girls' night out."

"Will Maggie be okay?" Rachel asked in a worried tone.

"She's fine," Emily said. "She has the run of the house. Hopefully, your German shepherd won't eat all of my shoes by the time we get home."

———

Trudy could barely see Rachel, who was hidden behind an enormous sundae glass filled with three flavors of ice cream, whipped cream, nuts, sauces, and two whole bananas.

"Well, there goes my diet," Trudy moaned.

Emily dug at the mountain of calories with a long spoon. "It's not bad—in a sickening sweet sort of way."

Trudy peered around the mammoth dessert. "Rachel, aren't you eating? This was your idea."

Rachel leaned in and whispered, "There's a demon at a table on the other side of the room."

Trudy tried to nonchalantly glance over to where Rachel was pointing. "You mean the big guy in the Dust Bunny Ranch T-shirt?" The tag line was "we don't multiply" along with a phone number.

"Yeah, that's him," Rachel said.

"You're not going to do an angelic smackdown in here and scare the kids are you?" Trudy warned.

Rachel looked flustered, realizing where they were. "Not unless he starts something."

Emily took another spoonful of ice cream. "Let's chill out with our ice cream. If he wants to cause a ruckus, I'll stop him."

Trudy groaned. "Too late, he spotted us and is coming over."

When he was still ten feet away from the table, Trudy could smell him. It wasn't the smell of brimstone and sulfur, though—more like cheese nachos and sweat.

"Hi, I'm Sal," he said, stopping tableside. "That's a mighty tasty looking banana split you gals have."

Trudy looked over at Rachel, who was glaring at Sal. "You're a rebel," Rachel said to him.

"Why, yes ma'am, I am. That was very nice of you not to use the D-word."

Sal picked up Rachel's unused spoon, took a big scoop of ice cream, and shoveled it into his mouth. "This is one of my favorite places."

"So," Emily said, "not to be un-neighborly, but why did you come over to our table?"

"I can't remember," Sal said as he licked the spoon and put it back down in front of Rachel. "Oh, yeah, that T-shirt you're wearing." He pointed to Rachel. "That's Bill's place, isn't it?"

"You know Bill?" Rachel said.

"I have trouble with my memory. It is Bill, isn't it? He's the guy that was making those tasty ribs at the Mysterium groundbreaking." Sal broke into a wide grin and pointed at Trudy. "I know you too! You're the funny-looking girl."

Trudy groaned. "Thanks. Have we met?"

"Yeah, I was told to take you someplace safe when the event turned sour." He looked suddenly dejected. "I could have eaten those ribs all day."

"You're the one that flew me up the Strip and dropped me under the Eiffel Tower?" Trudy recollected.

"Yeah, that was me. I'm sorry about everyone pointing at you and screaming; people are rude in this town."

Trudy wanted to push her way out of the booth to confront the demon, but Emily wouldn't budge. "You dropped me under the Eiffel Tower, and then it almost fell on me!" she practically screamed. "That's not what I'd call taking me to someplace safe!"

Sal looked perplexed. "I didn't know it would fall. After all, nobody can see the future. It looked shady, and the senator wanted you someplace out of the way."

"I knew," Emily said, "that the senator would come up at some point."

"Just be glad you never met him," Trudy said. "What a scumbag."

"Yeah, but it worked out," Sal piped up. "His soul is gone, and now the Imperator can use his body. Who healed him anyway? I missed that part."

Trudy looked down at her strawberry sauce-smeared napkin. "My husband did."

"Ah, so that's why he wanted you kept safe." Sal wagged his finger at her. "You're on our team!"

"I'm not on *your* team!" Trudy snapped. "Would I be sitting here with an angel if I were on your team?"

"Hey!" a guy several tables away yelled at them. He was wearing a Stevenson For President T-shirt and didn't look happy. "You're the ones that destroyed the Strip. I lost my job at the Luxor because of you assholes." He pointed at Rachel. "You're that friggin' angel that they keep showing on television—you can go to hell if you ask me."

Other patrons started gawking. The guy's three fellow louts laughed and punched each other in the arm. Trudy thought they could be linebackers for the Green Bay Packers.

Emily slid out of the booth and stood up. "I've got this."

Sal held out an arm to block her. "The funny-looking girl is under the Imperator's protection. I'll take care of the rude people over there. You should leave."

With that, Sal walked over to the loudmouthed lout and punched him in the nose.

The new and improved Senator Stevenson had been in office only six months but was already on the short list of candidates for President of the United States. His death and resurrection didn't hurt any, and he had all the campaign finances in the world—literally.

Many senators tried to live on their meager $174,000 income without success. They kept their houses in their home states and ended up sleeping in their offices or grouping together with other lawmakers in a congressional version of a frat house. Stevenson would have none of that. He decided to move into a 12,000-foot Romanesque estate with nine bedrooms and fourteen bathrooms near the naval observatory in Washington, DC.

The trip back from Vegas had been excruciatingly slow via human air transport; Stevenson was happy to be home.

"Corson," the senator said as he sat in his home office. "Do you have any updates from Niagara Falls?"

"No, Imperator," Corson replied as he distractedly texted on his phone.

"No, Senator," Stevenson corrected.

"Excuse me," Corson replied, not looking up. "...Senator."

Corson was Stevenson's assistant and replacement for Alastor Hiisi, who now occupied the pit. Corson had voluntarily removed himself as the oppressor of North Korea to take this assignment, but the rebel sometimes didn't focus on his current duties and, to Stevenson's annoyance, kept trying to offer direction to his replacement, half a world away.

Corson stopped texting and looked at him. "I haven't any updates as yet."

"I need someone who can focus, Corson. Why are you distracted?"

"My replacement had a question on how best to expend their growing nuclear arsenal. He is leaning towards a direct attack on South Korea."

Stevenson cocked an eyebrow. "You did inform him of my displeasure if that should happen before I command it?"

"I advised him that he is getting ahead of himself. Until their plutonium processing increases and they complete further missile testing, they are better off using that threat to destabilize the region. Besides, the blowback of nuclear fallout would devastate the North's croplands and livestock as well, sending them into starvation—if they were not obliterated by the United States first, that is."

Stevenson glared at Corson.

"Yes," Corson added, apparently realizing that he had missed a key element in the senator's question, "I did mention your displeasure of any armed conflict at this time in human history, but I can understand his confusion. Humans have conducted war throughout their miserable existence; they have never known peace."

"But I am the bringer of peace and harmony to the world, Corson," the senator said. "War will become a thing of the past—for a time."

"I will make sure that he understands."

"It sounds like he doesn't possess the same patient attitude as you and—"

"Plus," Corson interrupted, "any strike would be met with the total destruction of North Korea. We would lose a key ally in the region. Why lose a nation that happily oppresses millions of their people only to gain a radioactive wasteland?"

"Would you like to return to North Korea?"

"No... Senator," Corson said. "He is capable but anxious to prove himself. Valefar was one of the rebels involved in spreading the Black Plague in medieval Europe. He is skilled at mass annihilation but will need to learn restraint. Besides, I exist only to serve you."

"You should have put that last sentence first," Stevenson grumbled. "In any case, I need you to assist me in constructing the Stevenson Academy of Peace and Justice."

"Is that why you have the wanderers searching for a location in New York? I find that humans have no patience in learning dark arts and strive to have power without the appropriate experience to back it up."

"It is also a flaw that many rebels possess," Stevenson jabbed. "Be that as it may, humans are flocking to our cause. We need a facility that can suitably indoctrinate them. We must instruct them on how to properly worship me, as well as how to control their fellow humans. I'm modeling the academy after Heinrich Himmler's Wewelsburg training facility for the Nazi SS. Humans do have some excellent ideas."

Corson nodded begrudgingly.

"Did you spend any time in Germany during World War II?" Stevenson asked.

"I regret that I did not," Corson said. "I was in Singapore." Then, in an apparent attempt to bolster his reputation, he added, "I was the motivator in the Alexandra Hospital massacre."

"I heard about that," Stevenson said with a smile. "Hundreds of so-called innocent staff and patients bayonetted by the Japanese—but we all know that no human is truly innocent.

"I must admit that I had my doubts about you when you first came on board, but our little discussion shows me that you can avoid becoming another Hiisi. We all enjoy the kill, the ability to destroy what the Tyrant has created, but his bloodlust was unrestrained, and that is what caused his downfall."

"May I ask a question?" Corson said.

"Granted."

"Why Niagara Falls? Wouldn't someplace closer to Washington be more convenient, or perhaps your supposed home state of Nevada?"

"Niagara has always had a fascination with the paranormal, as shown by their numerous supposedly haunted locations. Many of those who attempted to overthrow my rule I have condemned to that tourist trap. What can be more pathetic for a rebel than being forced to pretend that they're some human's dearly departed great aunt? I aim to capitalize on this gullibility. Plus, there is someone there who is capable of assisting us from a logistical standpoint."

"Who?"

Stevenson smiled. "The Amazing Ahti."

———

"Why are we here?" Daeva asked Antero Ahti.

"To put on a magic show," he said. "I thought we'd gone over this a few times before; like, just after I saved you from getting sent to the pit by the loyalists."

"Not the concept of a show," she said, waving her hands around. "But why here?" She yanked on her hip-hugging miniskirt before sitting down in the front row of the theater and crossing her legs. It had been built for a Chinese acrobatic troupe that had their visas revoked, then some mimes bought it, but who could say why that deal fell through? Finally, Ahti was able to purchase it with a generous donation from Senator Stevenson, she imagined, in gratitude for the hack magician killing him. The world was getting too strange—even for a rebel.

"What's wrong with it?"

"Did you notice," she continued, "what side of the river we're on?"

Ahti stared at her blankly, the stage floods bouncing harsh light off of his beaklike nose.

Daeva tried to simplify it for him. "You know how if you have railroad tracks and someone says they live on the wrong side of them? Well, that's us."

"It's a nice theater, and it was cheap."

"It's cheap because nobody wants to be on this side of the Falls! Our neighbor across the street is a wastewater treatment plant. Did you look over at the Canadian side? That's where you brought us, and I bought into this thinking that we're going to be on that side—you know, the side with nice hotels and lots of tacky attractions."

"That's not very patriotic of you," Ahti said.

"Okay," she said, raising her hands. "Don't blame me when you get rolled by some homeless guy in our parking lot."

"We open in a couple of weeks," Ahti said. "Can you try to be a little more positive?"

"I'm just sayin' if mimes couldn't make this work, what hope do we have?"

Ahti ignored her. "I've got an interview this morning with a potential lighting technician. Try not to scare him away."

"Can we afford one?"

"He's some kid fresh out of school. I think I can throw minimum wage at him and he'll take it."

Daeva stood up. "I'm going to my hotel—on the Canadian side—to get a massage. I'd hate to get in the way of the great theatrical impresario."

"Impresario—I like that."

Reverend Jay Masters stood in the dirt just beyond the construction fence of the Las Vegas Masters' Mysterium. The slow progress was torturing him the way few things could. So far the basement level, the concrete pad of the first floor, and some steelwork were all there was to show since the ground-breaking ceremony over four months ago. Granted, the ceremony was interrupted by an angelic/demonic war that leveled a third of the Strip—but still.

"Admiring your baby?" Kimberley Kali said to him as she walked up.

"What little there is of it," he groused. Kim had the gray business-suited executive look down pat. He tried to imagine her dressing like Holly complete with a short skirt, sky-high heels, and a low-cut top, but the picture was just too disturbing. "Were they this slow when your casino was constructed?"

"Honestly, quite a bit faster," she said. "But my casino is pretty much cookie-cutter, along with some distinctive trim. Your Mysterium is a one-off filled with some extremely expensive technology."

"I'll need to talk to Denise," he said. "Let her know what a quick opening means for us."

"Us?"

"Well, what else is going to draw tourists into your roach motel? Certainly not your restaurants, now that you have Bill cooking for you."

"For your information, Kimberly Kali's Diamond Resort and Casino is at 100 percent occupancy. And I sampled the menu for the new Cluck and Grunt—it's heavenly."

The idea of Kali's resort being full only deepened his moroseness as he thought about all that potential revenue being left on her craps table and not spent at his Mysterium.

"Why don't you stop fretting about something you can't change?" Kim said. "Go and spend some time with your daughter."

"I'm on her shit list," Masters said. "I doubt she'd want to hang out with her father."

"So, have you apologized to her?" Kim said.

"For what?"

Kim shook her head. "Let's see, you cut a deal with Satan behind Trudy's back and almost got her and everyone else killed."

"It was to help them and their motley gang of inbreds from Wisconsin."

"You almost got me killed too."

"Yeah," Masters said. "I've straightened that out with the senator. You're on his protection list now, just like Trudy and Gavin—although I'm guessing you'll be just as ungrateful as they are."

"Yep, we're so totally ungrateful for you putting us under the protection of Lucifer. We should be kissing your feet."

"Sarcasm isn't your forte, Kim; don't try it around an expert."

"Look, all I'm saying is that you can't live the rest of your life separated from your daughter."

"I spent her first twenty-one years separated, and it seemed to work out okay."

Kim gave an audible groan and started to walk off. She called back at him: "In this business, I've learned to work with all sorts of morally bankrupt individuals, but you're one of a kind."

Masters pointed at the construction site. "As long as I'm not monetarily bankrupt, I'll do just fine."

———

Trudy stood in the middle of Emily's backyard. It was almost dawn, with just the slightest hint of pink light coming from the east. It was in the mid-fifties in Nevada on this brisk March morning, and she drew her cotton robe tighter around her. Looking down, Trudy noticed that she was wearing a pair of muskrat fur slippers. Their glass eyes looked up at her expectantly.

She wondered why she was here. Was this another vision, or did she sleep-walk from the motel over to Emily's? Neither prospect was very appealing—and how did she end up with Rachel's slippers?

She felt a hand on her shoulder. Rachel was standing next to her, giving her the crooked smile and dimples, which only annoyed Trudy more.

"Why am I here?" Trudy grumped. "Is this a vision?"

"Not a vision," Rachel replied. "We need your help—and your son's."

"I don't understand. I'm only four months pregnant."

"True, he is young," Rachel said, patting Trudy's slightly protruding belly. "But his service is required now."

She noticed others walking into the backyard—Uriel, Jonathan, Nate, Tomas, and Koda. Koda didn't speak, which was unusual for him. Instead, he took her by the hand and led her to the spot she knew, but could not see, was the center of the angelic ladder to heaven and had her kneel.

The other angels stood in a circle around them and transformed. No matter how many times she had seen a transformed angel, her response was always the same: awe mixed with a healthy dose of terror. They stood around her, glowing brightly. Rachel and Nate with their shields of spinning lightning giving off a deep hum that shook the ground, their wings of polished daggers spread behind them. Jonathan, in his flowing robes of light, with soft, gentle, but no less impressive wings spreading forty feet across Emily's yard. Tomas, the cherub, a graceful, four-winged feline being of molten gold, his four heads—lion, eagle, bull, and man—rotating upon one neck until the face of the man looked at her with gentle eyes, even as his massive diamond claws dug into the Nevada dirt. And then there was Uriel, the archangel, towering above the rest, his halo of lightning sparking above him.

More angels appeared in the air about twenty feet above the rest. They floated in a circle around her and the rent in space-time that she could not see. Trudy recognized them as seraphim, like Edwin. They burned as fire above her, two of their six wings extended, the others covering their heads and feet.

Koda, the angelic Inuit, remained in human form and knelt beside her. He softly said, "Please close your eyes, young mother, as God's spirit will descend upon you and this town. Do not open them until I tell you it is safe."

"Safe?"

"You tremble in fear before an angel, but we are nothing compared to the One who comes with the morning light."

Trudy closed her eyes and waited. She had no idea what to expect and wondered why Gavin wasn't here with her, and why Emily hadn't come out of the house with the racket they were making in her backyard. She at least expected Maggie, Rachel's ever-growing German shepherd puppy, to be barking her fool head off.

The seraphim started chanting, "Holy, holy, holy."

Trudy screamed.

Even with her eyes closed, the light blinded her. She put her head to the ground and cried. She felt like she was being ripped apart and put back together dozens of times over in a matter of seconds. She was in agony—a pain so immense she didn't think she could stand it. The pain felt like she was being carved like a jack-o'-lantern, her insides being scooped out and tossed aside. She prayed that her child would survive what was happening to her.

Just when she thought she could stand no more, the pain vanished, and something far more intense had taken its place—a feeling of joy. Not only the happiness of everyday existence or special occasions but euphoria so complete it filled her to overflowing. The hollow space in her soul that the pain carved out was being filled with pure joy. In some ways, it was worse than the pain, as she realized she couldn't hold it all in and knew that it would soon dissipate. The thought of that loss caused her to bawl like a child.

She felt a flutter in her abdomen and wondered if her son felt it too.

There was a sound that reminded her of a roaring waterfall that surrounded her.

Koda put a hand on her shoulder and shouted, "You may open your eyes!"

Trudy raised her head off the ground and wiped her eyes. She was kneeling in a column of light that she realized was the ladder. Up to now, her husband was the only human on earth that could see an angelic ladder. *How was this possible?*

She stood as Koda took her hand. Around her, the ladder was nothing like she imagined. Instead of pure white light, it was a tumultuous river of charged particles that interacted with each other, sparking and tumbling as they cascaded around her. The noise, too, was unexpected; she always imagined that something she couldn't see would be silent as well.

Koda turned her so that she could make out that some areas of the ladder were indented. She didn't know what that signified, but the little Inuit started moving her towards one of them.

Before she knew what was happening, she was outside of the ladder, and a chill wind hit her. It was literally freezing as she looked around. She was no longer in Emily's backyard in Nevada, but in a rocky and barren setting with snowcapped mountains looming hazily in the distance.

She held out her hand to the ladder and could feel the static discharge from it as the column of light rose into the sky and spread out branches of lightning every fifty feet or so, for as far as she could see.

Koda was nowhere to be seen. He had dumped her into a frozen wilderness and taken off—nice.

A middle-aged woman walked around the corner of an upturned dingy and into view. She was dressed in a parka and jeans with sturdy boots. "Hej!" she said. "Velkommen. Kan jeg hjælpe dig?"

"Uh…" Trudy stammered. "Where am I?"

The woman smiled. "Oh, you speak English. My name is Rania," she said, holding out a hand.

Trudy looked around her new surroundings. A couple of dozen houses dotted a moonlike landscape of barren rocks that rose up to a rocky hill. The buildings were small but all brightly painted in reds, blues, and bright greens.

A fjord of cold-looking water with several icebergs separated them from the mountains on the far shore.

"Where am I?" Trudy asked again while shaking her hand.

"You are about three kilometers outside of Aasiaat."

"Where?"

The woman chuckled. "You're in Greenland, child!"

"Whoa! Greenland—really?"

The ladder flared, and Koda walked through—dressed now in a parka. He gave a big smile. "Sorry to have left you, young prophetess, but I realized I forgot my jacket."

"Koda," Trudy said, "what just happened? I can see the ladder now."

"You and your child have been blessed. It is as we thought: your son is bonded to the ladders, even more so than his father. You now share in his gift."

"How did I wind up in Greenland?" Trudy asked.

"We need your help to know what should be done," Koda said.

"Done?"

"Let's go inside," Rania said. "You are not properly dressed for this climate."

Trudy pulled her robe closer around her. "I'm from Wisconsin," she said. "I'm used to it."

"Even so," Koda said, "we need to speak for a few minutes. It would be more comfortable indoors."

"My house is just up the hill, near Koda's," Rania said as she wrapped her arm around Trudy. "I can't wait to hear about the exciting things happening in the United States."

"Are you an angel?" Trudy asked.

"For heaven's sake, no!" Rania laughed and pointed at Koda. "I hope I am never as annoying as an angel," Koda replied to her good-natured insult with a sheepish shrug.

Trudy nodded. "Yeah, I've got one of those."

The path to Rania's house twisted its way up the hill past woodsheds and tarp-covered snow machines. She could tell that this was a working community, one that was busy all summer just to survive winter.

"Welcome," Rania said as she opened her front door. "It's nothing elaborate, but I try to make it comfortable."

The house was small, tiny compared to even Emily's bungalow, but it was indeed a cozy and welcoming environment, with wood-paneled walls and an electric heater in the corner keeping the chill at bay. Paintings of spring flowers decorated the walls.

Rania pointed to a sofa. "Have a seat, and I'll get some water boiling."

She sat down next to Koda. "It is quite an honor to have you here with us," he said. "We do not get many visitors."

"I don't understand what just happened," she said. "What did Rachel mean by my son being needed now?"

Koda patted her knee. "You are needed as well. We need you to see into the future and tell us what is to come."

Trudy stammered, "There's no on/off switch I can just flip and have a vision."

"Rachel has been working with you," Koda said confidently. "I'm sure we will be impressed with your abilities."

A short silence ensued. Koda sat there, staring at her expectantly.

"What?" Trudy said. "I said I can't just do that..."

Trudy found herself standing in a parade ground surrounded by the ubiquitous mobile classrooms favored by over-enrolled but poorly financed school districts. Behind the buildings, footings with protruding rebar marked the outlines of what would become more permanent structures.

To her right was an old farmhouse with a garden behind it. Nearby a three-story metal garage or warehouse cast a shadow over the house and driveway.

A man came out of the metal building, which seemed familiar to her. The man was in a nice suit that looked out of place as he stood on the gravel driveway. He had the same over-dressed, pompous demeanor of a demon she once knew back in Wisconsin. Rachel had sent Mr. Azael into the pit, hopefully for eternity, but she knew he was not the only evil being that walked the earth in pinstripes.

Even though she knew that she could not be seen, she turned and walked up the wooden stairs and into an open doorway of one of the classrooms. It was sweltering inside—apparently air conditioning clashed with demon sensibilities—but the students that sat at their desks were dripping sweat onto their pressed military uniforms.

They wore matching gray uniforms with an ominous patch on their shoulder—a single "S" in the shape of a lightning bolt. Everyone was facing forward, studying a whiteboard where the instructor had scrawled "The Eleven Satanic Rules of the Earth" by Anton Szandor LaVey, the founder of the Church of Satan. Most of the rules she thought her father would heartily agree with, but they still made her cringe, especially the one that said you should treat someone nicely unless they annoy you, then you should utterly destroy them.

"The Revealed One," the instructor said, "has commanded us to peace—but as you know, peace is nothing without justice. That is why he blessed us with being the first faculty and students at this facility. It is our duty and honor to give peace to those who obey him, along with justice when required. Greet all in peace, but if they disrespect the Revealed One or dishonor you—kill them slowly so that they die knowing it was because of their evil ways."

Trudy couldn't take any more of the lecture and walked back outside.

Three flags fluttered in the wind on the far side of the parade ground. One was the American Flag. The other she couldn't identify, but it was blue, with two women and a bird perched on a globe. It also had the word "Excelsior" at the bottom. The final flag was blood red with black wording that spelled out "The Stevenson Academy of Peace and Justice."

Feeling the hair on the back of her neck rise, she turned to see the man in the pinstripe suit standing just behind her. He couldn't see her—could he?

He looked so damn familiar.

Then it came to her. She had seen him for a couple seconds on television. He was the one from the senator's funeral who shot her father's business partner on the sidewalk—the business partner who just happened to have been possessed by Satan.

CHAPTER THREE

"Wake up, young prophetess," she heard a reassuring voice say. "It was only a vision. You are safe with us."

Opening her eyes, she realized she was on a bed, with Koda and Rania looking down at her.

"What happened?"

"We were hoping you could tell us," Koda said.

"How long was I out?"

"About an hour," Rania said. "Have you ever passed out during a vision before?"

"Never," Trudy said as she sat up in bed and clutched her head. It felt like someone had been using a jackhammer on her skull. Besides being scary and annoying, she could now add painful to the list of side effects of seeing the future.

"What did you see?" Koda pressed.

"I was at Stevenson's academy. It looked like a nice place at first, but it kept getting worse. The senator will brainwash people into doing his bidding—they'll even kill for him."

"This is troubling," Koda said as he took Rania's hand. "We've been talking about closing this ladder to relocate it someplace closer to Stevenson's plans. Did you happen to see where this academy was located?"

"I did see a state flag that had the word Excelsior on it. I'm not sure what state that is."

Koda shook his head and looked at Rania, who pulled out a smartphone and Googled it. "New York State," she said.

"That's a big place," Trudy grumbled as she slowly stood up.

Koda helped her into the living room. "I'll make sure that every one of my kind in the New York area is alerted and on watch. We will soon know what the senator's plans are."

"Would you really close this ladder?" Trudy lamented. "It seems so welcoming here. It would be a shame to lose what you built up over the years."

"Three hundred years," Koda said. "Although Rania hasn't been here as long."

"Thank goodness," she said. "I'm originally from Copenhagen, Denmark. I'm still not used to living out here—I miss the shopping."

Trudy watched as Rania gave Koda a big hug as if to counteract her vapid statement. "But Koda saved me from early death and we've been friends ever since."

"We must be getting back to Nevada," Koda said, looking slightly embarrassed. "Do not worry on the return trip. I will not let go of you. There are five other ladders around the world that you have not experienced. We would not want you wandering off to Africa, Asia, or someplace even more interesting."

"More interesting?"

"If you should make a wrong turn, you may end up in heaven."

———

Trudy awoke and found herself in the functional but somewhat drab motel room that she called home, with Gavin snoring beside her. Looking at the clock, it was seven a.m. She sat up and gently slapped herself a couple of times on the cheek to try to dispel the fog that persisted in her brain.

"Are you getting up?" Gavin asked as he awoke and rolled over to face her.

"You wouldn't believe the dream I had," Trudy said as she sat there. She bent over and kissed him on the cheek before she resumed the challenging process of standing while pregnant. "I can't drink because of the baby, but I'd be hitting the bottle right now if I weren't."

"Was it a vision?"

33

"Nah," she said, standing up. "In my dream, Rachel told me it wasn't a vision."

Walking over to the chair that she'd hung her robe on before going to bed, she stopped. Neatly tucked under the chair, four rodent eyes stared back at her—Rachel's muskrat slippers.

Grabbing her robe and reluctantly putting on the footwear that she despised, Trudy opened the door. The street below was filled with townsfolk, all pointing towards the sky. From her vantage point on the second floor of the motel, she could easily see what the commotion was about. New Creekside had grown over the last several months as a continuous stream of pilgrims made their way to live near the angels. They all seemed to be gathering in the streets to point excitedly at the wondrous weather formation that now covered the town.

Four tornados, one at each point of the compass, rose from the desert floor. Lightning flashed from within them as they tightly spun up to about a thousand feet and then spread out a canopy of cloud cover over Calamity and New Creekside, shading them from the sun. Where the clouds met, there was a spinning vortex of clear air, just like the eye of a hurricane.

Then it began to rain.

Trudy held out her hand to catch some of the gentle showers and put it to her mouth. It was the most refreshing liquid she ever tasted.

Gavin stumbled out onto the porch while rubbing his eyes. "What's happening? It wasn't supposed to rain today—and why are you wearing Rachel's slippers?"

"Long story, champ," Trudy said. "I need to see something, or at least try to see something."

Walking to the end of the motel's balcony to get a better view, she had to grab the railing when she looked towards Emily's house. Rising above Calamity like a mighty sequoia, a column of pure light rose into the sky, punching through the cloud cover. Thick branches of lightning spread out every hundred feet or so, looking like a ladder to heaven, and causing Trudy to gasp.

"Are they comfortable?"

Trudy turned to see Rachel next to her. "What?"

"My slippers," Rachel said. "I didn't want you to get cold last night."

"So it was real?"

Rachel smiled back at her. "Of course, silly! I told you it wasn't a vision."

"Then where were Gavin and all the others?"

"They were all sleeping. It was a special night, just for you and your child."

Trudy was starting to become worried. If the events happened, what did that mean for her and Gavin—and their son? She knew that at some point they would be of no use to Stevenson and would undoubtedly be killed by his over-eager students.

Attempting to mentally change the subject, she said, "So, I can see the ladder now because of my baby?"

Rachel grinned. "He's a gifted child. You might surprise yourself with what you can do now."

"So, what am I supposed to do with these gifts I'm reverse-inheriting?"

"I'm not sure. Perhaps because of your visions, you might find out before any of us."

"Great," Trudy sighed. "Most of my visions are of death and destruction."

"Then you will help us fight the plans of Senator Stevenson," Rachel said. "Remember when you said you wanted your son to grow up to be a man? And what was the feeling you had when the Spirit came down upon you? Was it one of joy? That is what you will fight for."

Trudy looked once again at the ladder while holding her belly. "I'll duke it out with Satan himself if I can protect Gavin, and my son can grow up to be a man like his father—and not like my father."

———

"Why is this taking so long?" Reverend Jay Masters groused as he sat in the conference room at Paradise Museum Design in Las Vegas.

"Need I remind you that much of the Strip was destroyed just a few months ago," Denise Sullivan said. "It's difficult to get the engineers and designers needed for a project the scope of the Mysterium. We've got subcontractors from coast to coast working on the show elements, but we could use more local resources. Besides, you keep adding to the design but expect to have the same timeframe."

"Are you saying that you're not up to the task?" Masters complained. He was well aware of the events on the Las Vegas Strip and that he was asking for the moon—but he was, after all, Jay Masters, and fully expected the moon to be delivered to him, on time and gift-wrapped.

"The additions will be wonderful," she said. "I think that the memorial to those who died is touching and—"

"Will draw additional suckers with fat wallets," Masters finished. "So, what's the problem? When I'm out at the site, all I see is a concrete pad, steel beams, and a crew that always appears to be on their lunch break. When I'm at the warehouse, I see bits and pieces—a plastic demon here, a plywood angel there. Nothing is put together. And the guy that's programming the anima-tronics has a rod up his ass bigger than his robot's."

"Reverend, you're talking about a twenty million dollar addition to the facility. It's a big project just by itself, not counting the ninety million going towards the Mysterium proper. As I said, it's taxing all of the contractors to supply that kind of manpower and equipment to a project of this size, consid-ering what's happened."

"I thought that's why we had the miraculous Senator Stevenson helping us? He was more useful when his brains were splattered all over the stage at our groundbreaking ceremony."

Denise winced. "You might want to keep those thoughts to yourself, Reverend. The senator is a very powerful man, and I'm told he does not look favorably upon anyone criticizing him."

"The senator and I have an understanding," Masters said as he tapped his fingers on the desk. "Perhaps you're the one dragging your feet. Maybe I should discuss this delay with him directly?"

"No!" Denise held up her hands. "That's not necessary. I'll see what we can do to fast track the project."

"Every month we're not open is a month I'm not making money," Masters said. "I'm getting rich off of the Wisconsin Dells Mysterium, but I'll soon have a grandson to spoil, not to mention a wife that can max out a credit card before breakfast. I'll need to be filthy rich as soon as possible."

"Understood," she stammered.

"For updates that are as useful as this one, you should be communicating to Kim and not wasting my time," he said as he stood and moved towards the door. "She can weed out the useless chatter and give me the CliffsNotes version."

"Yes, Reverend," she meekly replied.

Masters left the meeting and headed towards his limo. He knew Denise was doing the best she possibly could under the circumstances, but yanking her chain never grew old.

His phone rang as he was getting into the limousine for the drive back to Kali's Resort. "Yeah," he said.

"Hey, it's your daughter."

"Which one?"

There was a pause. "Should I be concerned?" Trudy replied.

"Nah, you're my one and only," he said. "I just got done busting someone's non-existent balls, and it's hard to come down from the high."

"Listen," Trudy said, "take your fancy new helicopter and get over to Calamity; you've got to see this."

"So, I'm back in your good graces?"

"Not even close," Trudy said, "but this will be on the news before long; it's better that you see for yourself, as I'm sure you'll get questions about it."

"I don't know why you're holding a grudge. Look at all the good my deal has done, not to mention the full funding of the Mysterium—which I might add; you're part owner of."

"Yeah, lucky me. You couldn't do a deal with just any old demon like Azael, you had to go and hit up Satan for financing—nice."

"How sharper than a serpent's tooth it is to have a thankless child."

Trudy made an irritated sound. "Now you're quoting Shakespeare at me? Just get out here. Oh, and tell the pilot to stay below a thousand feet as he nears the town."

"I'm not following," Masters said.

"I can't explain it; you have to see it."

"Okay, I'll get my pilot to meet me at Kali's, and I'll be right over."

He looked out the window as he cruised down South Las Vegas Boulevard. Demolition had mostly been completed on the structures destroyed by the angelic battle that had taken place a few short months ago. Over five hundred people had died, but the toll could have been much worse if it weren't for his son-in-law Gavin's healing power. Kim hadn't lied to him—what hadn't been destroyed had become so popular among those wishing to see the area for themselves that occupancy was 100 percent across the board. Kimberley Kali's Diamond Resort and Casino hadn't suffered any damage other than to her pride—and a few singes to her parking lot asphalt—and she was raking in the money.

The circumstance annoyed Masters even more as he didn't have an attraction open to capture some of that windfall. Now, he was in a swift competition with those rebuilding and those wishing to add to their facilities quickly. He even heard rumors that the Wynn Resort was going to build its own exhibit on angels and demons.

He picked up his phone again and dialed.

"This is Kim," he heard.

"Hey, get my helicopter prepped for a quick trip to Calamity."

"Last time I checked," she said, "I was the owner of this resort and not your slave. Get Holly to do it."

"She's in Wisconsin for a couple weeks to visit her mother and check on the Mysterium. I had Edwin tag along to see how the attraction operates. I want you to come along with me to Calamity; it'll be worth your while. Something is happening, but Trudy's tight-lipped about it. Also, I want to talk to you about a business idea I have."

Kim groaned.

"I heard that," he said. "Look, it will be well worth taking an hour or two from your busy schedule of…whatever the hell it is you do."

"You know how to endear yourself," Kim said. "Okay, I'll be your gofer this time, but this better be good."

———

"Hey, where's Mom?" Ian said to Bailey as she sat at the kitchen table, oiling an AR-15. It never ceased to amaze Ian that his sister was only sixteen but had fully bought into their father's doomsday scenario. He knew that despite her short hair and gruff manner, several of his so-called friends were trying to work up the courage to ask her out. She needed to smile or do something that showed she was interested because the local boys were simultaneously smitten and scared of her.

"She's in the garden," Bailey said as she rammed the oilcloth down the barrel of the rifle. "She's fixing the fence; some rabbits got in there last night. I told her I'd shoot them for her, but you know how she is."

"Yeah, they might be someone's mother," he laughed. "I'm going into town for my interview and wanted to see if she needed anything."

"Dad told you not to go," Bailey said as she slammed a thirty-round magazine into the rifle, gave it a slap, and stared at him.

"This is the chance of a lifetime," Ian said. He knew his dad would be furious when he found out that he went to the interview, and even more so if he got the job, but it was the sign he was looking for—a sign that kept him breathing for another day.

Baily put the weapon on the table. "Can I come along to watch you crash and burn?"

"Thanks for the support, but it's that vacant theater on Buffalo Avenue. There isn't much for you to do around there while I'm being interviewed. Plus, it's a bad neighborhood. You might end up hurting some gang member."

She wiped her hands and stood up. "I'd kind of like to meet this Ahti guy. The news said he used a Barrett 82A1 to pop the senator, but they didn't mention what scope he used. It'd be nice to find out."

"I'm sure he doesn't want to talk about that," Ian frowned as he grabbed the keys to the Ford Bronco off of the peg. "But I do need to talk to you about something—in private. Let's go ask Mom what she needs from town and I'll let you tag along."

"Sweet!" Bailey said. "Give me a second to find that copy of *Soldier of Fortune* that had the article about Ahti. I want to see if he'll sign it for me."

———

Emily Iverson inspected the new chain-link gate that she had installed on her backyard fence. There was now so much traffic in her backyard from the angelic ladder that was placed there; she was getting tired of angels traipsing through her living room each time they came or went.

It was also essential to keep Rachel's dog Maggie in the yard, as the eight-month-old German shepherd hadn't yet learned to obey anyone. The overgrown puppy was right now digging up something in the yard, and she wasn't sure she wanted to know what it was.

Emily glanced up at the pillars of clouds that now shaded the town. It'd take some getting used to, but it did cut down on the afternoon heat, and the occasional light rain might even allow her to plant a backyard garden in the future.

"Hello, young warrior," Koda said as he walked up to the gate. He wore blue jeans and a T-shirt but carried a parka over his shoulder, which seemed odd for southern Nevada. "I am off to Greenland for a few hours. Is it okay for me to try out your wonderful new gate?"

Emily had to smile at the little Inuit. "Come on in, you can be the first."

Koda raised the metal prong and paused before opening it. "This is a great honor."

"If you say so. Why are you off to Greenland, if you don't mind me asking?"

Koda looked at her with sad brown eyes and shook his head slowly. "We will have a meeting to determine if the Greenland ladder should be closed."

"Closed? Why?"

"It is very upsetting. We've had the ladder for over three hundred years, but the world has changed with the risen Senator Stevenson. We may need to position a new ladder closer to where world events are taking place."

"I hope it doesn't come to that," Emily said.

Koda's smile returned. "I will be sure to bring you back a treat from Greenland. Have you ever had smoked reindeer heart?"

"Uh, no."

"Some find it a little pungent, but it is delicious, thinly sliced on some hard bread with butter."

Emily was trying to think of some way to politely decline when she noticed Maggie running up to them with something in her mouth.

"Hey, girl," Emily said. "Whatcha got there?"

It only took a second for Emily to realize what it was. Having been in the Army, she was very familiar with what the shepherd had in its mouth: a Beretta M9.

———

"Bailey," Ian said as he drove the 1996 Ford Bronco towards Niagara Falls, "I've got to tell you something."

"Yeah, so what's this big secret?" she said. "Other than sneaking behind Dad's back and catching hell for it later."

"Something odd has been happening to me."

"Odd? What kind of odd? Are you growing back hair? That's a common Tannahill trait. You can get waxed."

"I'm serious! Something weird is going on, and I don't know what to do about it."

"Okay, big brother," Bailey said as she put her feet up on the dash. "What's got you freaked?"

"I touch things—"

She held up her hands and scrunched up her face. "Okay, too much information. I don't want to hear about that. Gross!"

"Get your mind out of the gutter and let me finish. I touch things, and they disappear."

"Disappear?" Bailey said, suddenly showing some interest. "Like how? What do you mean?"

"They just vanish—*poof!*" he said. "I don't know where they go, and I can't get them back."

"Yeah, right, David Copperfield. What kinds of things?"

"Anything—sometimes I have to think about them vanishing, and other times it's by accident. I can't seem to control when and where it happens. So far I've lost, among other things, Violet's chew toy, a box of noodles, a can of chili, a magazine, and—a Beretta."

"You lost a pistol? Dad's going to be pissed when he finds out."

"Yeah, I know. It's got me afraid to touch anything because I don't know if it's going to be transported to the land of lost socks and pens."

"Pull over," Bailey said. "Show me."

"No."

"Show me!"

"I don't want to get in the habit."

"Call me a doubter."

"You don't believe me?"

"Yeah, like you believe I saw demons at the Millers."

"I never said I didn't believe you."

Bailey sighed. "Look, Ian, considering all the shit that's been going down with this demons and angels business, I'm willing to check my doubts at the door. So, show me already, and then I'll help you figure it out."

Reluctantly, Ian pulled over onto the gravel shoulder and came to a stop. "What do you want me to make disappear?"

Bailey took her feet off the dash and opened the glove compartment, pulling out an old roll of Life Savers. "How's this?"

"That'll work—I guess," he said as she put it on the seat, only to watch it roll down towards the crack between the seat cushion and the backrest.

They both reached for it at the same time. The Life Savers vanished.

And so did Bailey.

Uriel stood next to Emily's coffee table, looking down at the pistol. "This is worrisome," he said in his thick Ethiopian accent that Emily always found endearing, even when he was speaking of serious issues. "Weapons are not allowed within the town boundaries."

Emily picked up the Beretta; it had a nice heft in her hand. "Quality one too. Not something you want to leave in the dirt. It had a round in the chamber, and the safety was off; it's a miracle Maggie didn't shoot herself, or someone else. We have a lot of people moving to New Creekside. Could it have been missed when they immigrated?"

"Not a chance," Nate said. His helmet-like dome of slicked back hair and white polyester jumpsuit called to mind a Vegas-era Elvis—or one of the scads of Elvi that impersonated him. "I hate to brag, but protecting angels never miss a thing."

"Except a good fashion sense," defrocked priest Tony Abbadelli chimed in. "What's the big deal anyway? Most of my parishioners back in the day were packing heat."

"Human's don't always see the big picture," Uriel said. "Having weapons in town only makes a mistake more severe."

"Yeah, Tony," Nate said. "Don't you remember when you took a shot at me?"

Tony threw up his hands in frustration. "I'll never hear the end of that, will I? I was Tom Ruxton back then, and you blew my cover. Technically, it was Tom who tried to shoot you."

"I found a few other items in the backyard," Emily said as she watched Maggie chomp on a rawhide. "That dog chew, for instance. I also found a box of rigatoni, a *Playboy* magazine, and a can of chili."

"Do you still have the chili?" Tony asked. "Maybe it's mine."

"You dropped a can of Hormel Chili in my backyard?"

"Did it have beans?"

"Yes."

"Wasn't mine then," Tony said. "Fiber makes me gassy. But the magazine *is* mine."

Nate walked over to the sliding glass door. "I'll have a protector stationed to guard the ladder. Perhaps we can find out who our Secret Santa is.

"Then again"—Nate pointed towards the yard—"we can just ask that girl."

"Girl?" Emily said. "What girl?"

"The one that just popped into existence next to the ladder."

They all turned to look at the teen that wasn't in the yard a few seconds ago. She looked frightened as she stood there in jeans and a camo T-shirt.

"Hello," Emily said as they all walked up to her. "Don't be afraid. I'm Emily Iverson. What's your name?"

"Bailey." Her voice shook. "Bailey Tannahill. Where am I?"

"You're in Calamity, Nevada," Uriel said. "Where were you before you arrived here?"

"I was in the Bronco," she stammered. "Ian was going to show me how he could make a roll of Life Savers"—she held up the candy in her trembling hand—"disappear."

Emily went over and put an arm around the girl, who looked like she was going to faint. "Where's the Bronco? Is it nearby?"

"Nearby?" Bailey looked at her and then at the backyard and surrounding desert. "No, at least I don't think so. My family lives in Youngstown, New York—near Niagara Falls."

"You're a long way from home," Nate said.

Emily turned to Uriel. "Wasn't Trudy's vision of her son at Niagara Falls? That's a big coincidence."

"This isn't a coincidence," Uriel said. "Nate, go find Trudy."

———

Ian was in a panic. The disappearance of a handgun was nothing compared to the vanishing of his sister. He didn't even know if she was still alive—she could have been vaporized. As much as she liked to give him grief, he still loved her and didn't want anything terrible to befall her. He thought that the way he felt now was the same as Bailey would have felt if the Beretta hadn't disappeared when he pulled the trigger. He pushed the morbid thought aside as he debated what to do.

He could call his dad, but what would/could he do? Assuming he even believed him. The police were out, as a wild story like this would land him in jail or a psych ward.

He was ten miles from the theater. Ian decided that he would continue to the interview and try to figure out some solution to this catastrophe later.

About fifteen minutes after he pulled back onto the highway, his phone rang. He fumbled for it in his pocket and answered.

"Hey, it's Bailey," he heard. "Glad you have your phone on for once."

"Bailey!" Ian shouted as he slammed on the brakes, nearly causing another car to rear-end him. He ignored the irate driver's cursing and horn honking. "Oh my God, you're alive! Where are you?"

"You're not going to believe this: I'm in Nevada."

"Nevada?"

"I'm in that town of angels, just south of Las Vegas. Oh, and I found the Beretta and your chili. I'm not going to attempt to get Violet's rawhide back, though, and some old dude took your magazine—not that I was going to touch it. Eww!"

"What can I do?"

"They're very nice here, so don't worry about me. Worry about how you're going to explain this to Dad—along with the interview, you shouldn't be going to."

"Okay, I'll explain to him what happened, but I don't know if he's going to believe me. Stay by your phone, so I can get in touch with you, and he can hear you're all right. If I tell him that I made you disappear and reappear in Nevada, he might agree that I have a future in the magic business."

———

Trudy and her husband Gavin stood in front of what would soon be their home. The residents of New Creekside didn't think it was proper for them to stay in the cramped motel room and deserved an appropriate abode. Right now it was just wood framing, but it was far enough along for Trudy to envision what it would look like. Several residents were volunteering their time and purchasing materials to make the site into a quasi-Victorian house with a shaded porch and a view of the only paved road through Calamity.

"We're spoiled," she said. "They shouldn't spend their time and money on us. There are plenty of other priorities in town. What about the Community Hall or the Welcoming Center?"

Gavin put a hand on the back of her neck and gently rubbed. "You're four months' pregnant. You've started showing that you have a bun in the oven, and they want to make sure that little Jay will live in a good environment."

"What do you mean, I'm showing?" Trudy sucked in her stomach. "I'm as svelte as ever. But I will like having a safe environment for the baby. Right now, we live in a rundown motel owned by an archangel slumlord."

As she looked down the dilapidated asphalt, she noticed Rachel heading towards them with a big smile on her face.

"What's up?" Trudy asked.

"It's a miracle!" Rachel said.

Trudy pointed up. "You mean the clouds? We kind of guessed it wasn't a natural phenomenon."

"Not that, silly," Rachel said. "Salazar's tent that Gavin turned into the arboretum has a new feature—a spring!"

"Really?" Gavin said. "I still feel bad for destroying Salazar's revival tent."

"So now," Trudy said, "besides the trees and plants, it's muddy?"

Rachel shook her head. "It comes up right under the altar and flows out of the tent and across the road. It's working its way through town. New Creekside will have a creek!"

Trudy said, "Wow, with all our new amenities, we'll have a better rating on Trip Advisor."

"So, did you pick out a room for me?" Rachel asked.

"Don't worry, sissy," Trudy said. "You and Maggie will be living with us, but you may need to share a room. And shepherds have sensitive hearing, so you probably should get the dog some earplugs to block out your snoring."

"I don't snore!" Rachel huffed, adding mildly: "Do I?"

"Like a banshee," said Trudy.

"Hey," Gavin said as he pointed down the street to a figure in a white polyester jumpsuit. "Here comes Tony Manero—or is that Nate?"

"Did my father show up?" Trudy yelled over to Nate.

"I haven't seen him," he answered as he walked up to them, "but there is a guest in town. Someone who would like to meet the three of you."

CHAPTER FOUR

Ahti sat in his dressing room surrounded by cardboard boxes full of props and costumes, along with an open bottle of Maker's Mark bourbon. He didn't have any furniture other than two cheap folding chairs. The kid that sat before him seemed clueless.

"What was your name again?" Ahti had received the boy's resume but lost it somewhere in the surrounding clutter.

"Ian Tannahill," the kid said.

"My stage manager is out today, so I'm not sure what he did with your resume," Ahti lied. He didn't have a stage manager and doubted he'd have the budget for one anytime soon. This kid would have to be a self-starter to survive. "So, tell me something about yourself that won't put me to sleep."

The kid stared at him for a moment. "My parents are survivalists and live on an armed compound in the middle of the woods."

Ahti laughed. "That's a good one." Then he realized the kid was dead serious. "Really?"

"I grew up in an underground bunker surrounded by freeze-dried ice cream."

"Well, I wasn't expecting that, but do you have any experience as a lighting technician?"

"I've worked with a light opera company for a season, and before that some local stage productions."

"This will be a big production and an excellent opportunity for someone reliable and creative. We'll need someone that can multi-task. I'm not sure a light opera company represents the required experience that will be needed for our elaborate stage productions."

"I'm willing to learn," the kid said. "I looked up the show that you had at Kimberley Kali's Diamond Resort and Casino. The lighting rigs all look like something I can handle. The ETC Congo control panel is the same one that I trained on for my certificate. I'm sure I can handle it—plus, it would be an honor to work for the Amazing Ahti."

Why'd the kid have to use flattery? It got him every time. "Let's go take a look at the theater."

Ahti led the kid out the door. As they walked down the center aisle to the stage, he could see that the kid had already spotted the problem.

"Where's the lighting?" the kid said.

"The mimes who previously owned the place sold them off in a silent auction," Ahti said. "All we have are the four floods up there."

"That's it? How are you going to put on a magic show with just floods?"

"That's where my new lighting tech comes in. You'll also need to handle the purchasing and installation of all of the stage lighting and effects. In other words, you'll have complete control—as I said, it's a big opportunity."

"What kind of budget are we looking at?" Ian asked. "I have some contacts that can probably get us a sweet setup for a song."

"The song better be something by Boxcar Willie. Three grand tops."

"Three grand?" The kid scratched his head, a nervous habit, Ahti surmised. "A used dimmer board of any quality will cost half of that—if I can find one."

"Ever watch *MacGyver*?"

"Sure, but I was never a fan," the kid said as he continued to survey the theater. "I have no idea how this can be done."

"*MacGyver*," Ahti continued, "was a television show about a secret agent that devised clever solutions to complex problems using everyday items."

"So, you want me to make spots from tin cans, duct tape, and a can of Sterno?"

Ahti smiled. "You're starting to think like MacGyver. Are you up to the challenge?"

The kid stood there dumbfounded. "I can try."

"Good, you're hired. We'll start you out at minimum wage, and I'll give you a raise in six months to a year if it works out. Now, close your right hand and make a fist."

The kid did as instructed.

"Now open it."

The kid stared at his hand with a WTF expression on his face. "What's this? How'd you do that?"

"Magic, kid, magic." Ahti pointed to the object that appeared in the kid's palm. "It's something to help you solve all of your problems—a Swiss Army knife."

———

Bailey stared at the medals in the wooden display case on the wall. "Are those real?"

Emily walked over to the wall next to the kitchen. "Yep, Bronze Star and Purple Heart."

"That's so cool!" Bailey said. "Well, maybe not the Purple Heart—that must have hurt—but the Bronze Star, that's pretty awesome." Bailey gave Emily the once-over. "Where were you injured?"

"I lost a leg in Afghanistan," Emily said casually.

Bailey looked down at Emily's two good legs "Huh?"

"Long story," she said. "The Bronze Star was for pulling two of my wounded buddies to safety while under fire."

Bailey looked gobsmacked like she'd just met a rock star. "Wow…"

"You do what you have to in battle."

"My dad," Bailey said, "he's always talking about how to behave when under fire. He has an area in the compound where we can practice moving between buildings—it even has pop-up targets, but nothing is shooting back at us. I'm not sure if I'd chicken out if someone were trying to kill me."

"You don't do it because you're brave," Emily said. "You do it because those are your brothers that are hurt and you need to help them—you *must* help them. I was scared to death, but it didn't matter at that point. My left shinbone was already shattered, so I figured the pain couldn't get much worse. And if they killed me, then my pain would be over. There wasn't much of a downside at that point."

"You fought those demons in Vegas too," Bailey said. "My dad can't stop talking about that. He says that's a sign that the end is near."

"So, seeing me on television makes him think of the end of the world?"

"Yeah, but in a good way. It's hard to impress my dad, but you did."

There was a knock on the door, and Emily shouted, "Nobody knocks around here—come on in!"

The awestruck look Bailey had been giving Emily dialed up to eleven as she saw a familiar trio coming through the door. "Oh, my God! It's them!"

"Hey, guys," Emily said. "I'd like you to meet your biggest fan. This is Bailey Tannahill, direct—and I do mean direct—from Niagara Falls."

She noticed that Trudy looked shocked, which didn't surprise her. After all, Trudy's vision of her future three-year-old son took place under the famous falls. Uriel was right: there was a plan here that Emily couldn't quite figure out, but somehow, she knew that God hadn't allowed Bailey to be brought here by accident. But why drop a sixteen-year-old doomsday prepper into a town of angels?

Trudy held out her hand. "Nice to meet you, Bailey. I'm Trudy Young, and this is my husband, Gavin."

"Hi, I'm Rachel!" the petite angel squeaked, giving Bailey a beatific smile.

Bailey looked like she was going to faint. "You're an angel," she said in apparent awe. "I can tell from your glow—but I've also seen you on television."

Trudy put her neglected hand down. "She's also a so-so waitress—wait, what glow?"

"All of the angels are glowing," Bailey said. "Uriel and Nate were glowing. That's how I could tell they weren't human."

"I've never seen them glow," Gavin said.

Bailey put her hands on her hips. "Maybe you're not looking hard enough."

"What does the glow look like?" Trudy said as she stared at Rachel. "Maybe it's light refracting off her dimples?"

"She's right," Rachel said. "We do have a slight aura while in this form, but no human has ever been able to see it."

"Until now," Emily said. "We have a special young woman here."

Gavin spoke up: "So, Bailey, what brings you to Calamity?"

"My brother made me disappear."

"I'm an only child, but I hear that happens," Trudy quipped.

"Then I appeared here"—Bailey pointed out the window—"right next to that big column of light."

"Wait," Gavin said. "You can see the ladder?"

"Is that what it's called?" Bailey said. "Sure, I see it. Doesn't everyone?"

"You did what?" Ian's father screamed in his ear. They stood in the aluminum paneled barn that contained their bug out truck. His father had never hit him—yet.

"I got a job as a lighting technician for the Amazing Ahti."

"No! Not that—."

"Oh, I made Bailey disappear to Nevada."

"Yeah, that's the part. What the hell are you talking about?"

"I can make things disappear, and they materialize in Nevada in that community of angels."

"Son," his father said as he sat down on the running board of the truck and ran his fingers through his graying hair. It looked like the wind had been knocked out of him as he put his head in his hands. "First, Bailey says she sees demons, and now you say that you can make things—and people—disappear. It's just not normal."

"But they reappear in Nevada," Ian said in his defense. "She's perfectly safe." He took his phone out of his pocket and dialed. "Bailey, can you talk to Dad? Let him know you're okay before he has a stroke?"

Ian put Bailey on speaker and handed the phone to his father.

"Bailey, are you all right?" Brian Tannahill said.

"Hi, Dad, don't panic. I'm okay."

"Where are you, honey? Ian says you're in Nevada."

"Yep. I'm in that town of angels south of Vegas. You're not going to believe who's here with me. Here's Emily, the one who fought that demon." Ian heard rattling as the phone was handed off. "Emily, say hi to my dad."

"Hi, Dad," Emily said. "Don't worry about your daughter. She's safe and sound, and we'll figure out a way to get her back to you."

"Keep her," Brian said.

There was an awkward pause before Emily spoke again. "Excuse me? I think the reception is bad."

"Keep her there," he said. "We were heading to Nevada anyway. No sense in her traveling thousands of needless miles. She's a good girl, and I'll pay for any expenses."

"Don't worry," Emily said. "I have room here, and she's more than welcome. But why are you heading to Vegas?"

"We're bugging out," the elder Tannahill said. "Bailey has seen demons making pentagrams in the fields not too far away from us. I designed our compound to withstand attack from humans—but not from demons. I saw you on television. It's clear you know how to fight them, but I hate to admit that I'm totally unprepared. Bailey will be safer there with you for the time being."

"Glad you see it that way," said Emily. "We'll take good care of her until you get here."

Bailey got back on the phone. "Thanks, Dad. I have one of the Berettas here as well, with a full magazine. Ian made it disappear earlier."

Ian's father gave him a scowl. "I've been wondering why bunker three's inventory is off."

"Oh, and Dad," Bailey added, "Ian's clueless on how his newfound power works, so don't let him touch you or Mom."

Ian, who had overheard, grinned sheepishly. His father instinctively inched away from him.

"So what are we going to see?" Kim asked Masters as the helicopter lifted off her resort's convention center roof.

"I told you all I know," he said. "But it might be something we can use for the mini-Mysterium we'll be opening in your main ballroom."

"Hold on," Kim said. "What about my ballroom?"

"I just thought it would be nice to borrow it for six months or so until the Mysterium opens."

"You mean Joshua Tree? That room is already fully booked for the next year."

"You can cancel the reservations."

"No, I can't!" Kim shouted over the noise of the helicopter. "I've got deposits already from an insurance company, a bank, some tech firm, and a group of cosplayers."

"What the hell's a cosplayer?"

"Nerds that dress up as characters from sci-fi films, cartoons, comics—that sort of thing—and do role-playing. Weird kids, but inventive."

"Will they have a Wonder Woman?"

"Most likely, several of them."

"I love a woman who knows how to use a rope, so don't cancel them—but move them to another ballroom closer to my suite."

"Misogynist," Kim huffed.

"Look," Masters said, "I'm losing...*we're* losing money, as long as that crappy design firm you found dawdles."

"They're doing the best they can."

"You owe me."

"I owe you a swift kick out the door of this helicopter at two thousand feet up."

Masters held up his index finger. "That reminds me." He hit the intercom button to the pilot. "I was told you'll have to stay under a thousand feet when approaching Calamity."

"Yes, Reverend," said the pilot. "May I ask why?"

"Don't know, but I'd take it seriously. You understand where we're going, right?"

"Yes, Reverend. I'll keep us under one thousand."

Masters turned his attention back to Kim. "So, what was I saying? Oh, yeah, you're missing out on your percentage of revenue from the Mysterium, because right now it's a big vacant lot in that dustbowl you call overflow parking."

Kim crossed her arms. "You're a pain in the ass."

"I'm not going to hurt your precious ballroom. I just want to move some of what *is* finished over to the space and make it sort of a preview of what to expect when we're open."

"So, just a preview center is what you're saying?"

"Yeah," Masters continued. "But something we can charge admission for, along with a gift shop to funnel them through."

"Sounds kind of cheap and tacky," Kim said, "right up your alley, but not necessarily right for my resort."

Masters waved a dismissive hand at her. "We'll give it some production values. I'll call the senator and see if he can get me some demonic items for display."

"If you call him, it's off! I don't want anything to do with him. He tried to kill me."

"I told you that you're under his protection now. Besides, it was Daeva, that demon who moonlights as a female magician, that wanted to kill you—the one you, need I mention, hired."

"She took her orders from Stevenson."

"Do your employees normally try to kill you? If so, I'm impressed."

The intercom broke in: "Reverend," the pilot said, "I'll be slowing for the inspection, but you should look out the window. I see now why we have a ceiling of a thousand feet."

The inspection had become old hat to the pilot of the Sikorsky helicopter. New Creekside not only had protecting angels every hundred yards or so around the town—with cherubs stationed further out as a deterrent to all but the most foolhardy—but the airspace was also patrolled.

Kim looked out her window and gave a little wave, wiggling just the tips of her fingers, to the protecting angel that glowed mere feet from the fuselage. The angel improvised a gesture something like a salute.

"Getting used to them?" Masters said.

"No, and I never will. In fact, I think I just peed my pants."

Masters tried to slide his hand under her thigh and felt the sting of Kim's swat. "Hey, watch it, buster!" she scolded.

"Just checking the upholstery. We're good."

The angel's shield of lightning hummed and flashed nearby. Its wings of swords spread further, and the being banked away to the left.

"Holy shit…" Masters said.

"You're impressed too."

"Not with the angel," Masters said as he pointed out the other window, "with that."

Four tornados of clouds mixed with lightning spun up to the altitude that Trudy told him to avoid and spread out into dark clouds that completely covered the town. As the helicopter came under the canopy and prepared to land on his new helipad, Masters could feel the cooler ambient temperature even from within the cabin.

"I see why Trudy couldn't explain," he said in a croaking whisper.

———

Trudy's father bought them a golf cart so they could zip around Calamity and New Creekside without her having to exert herself. A plot of land near what would become the new Welcoming Center had been set aside as a helipad for the Mysterium helicopter. Her father was on a buying spree after what had become known colloquially, and in the media, as "The Battle of Las Vegas." The increased attendance at the Wisconsin Dells Mysterium only added to the windfall that befell him in the form of interviews, speaking fees, and even a book contract. Now he had a shiny new black Sikorsky with the Mysterium logo on the side. It was a nearly fifteen-million-dollar aircraft with an interior befitting a Rolls Royce more than a helicopter. Life was good and getting better all the time.

The perimeter was still guarded by protecting angels, but it seemed like every week they moved further out as the town within the boundaries continued to grow. The Welcoming Center would be a facility where potential new residents could be interviewed and inspected. The angels were quickly able to discern who genuinely wished to join the community, from those with ulterior motives—such as the media, or government infiltrators. Until the residents and angels gave their thumbs up, newcomers were not allowed to pass beyond the angelic border patrol.

Trudy pointed to the sky. "Here comes Daddy Dearest."

As Gavin drove them down to the helipad, they pulled up near Josh Barber, who was futzing with some stakes in the ground.

"Hey, Josh!" Trudy sang out. "What are you up to?"

"Hey, Trudy, Gavin," Josh Barber said as he whisked off his baseball cap and wiped his brow before putting it back on. "I'm working on what will become the new Barber Gas and Towing. The town is growing so fast we really need a garage and gas station. Since we'll no longer be allowing vehicles into the town, we'll have a parking lot over there, near the Welcoming Center, and I think you've started a trend with the golf carts." He waved his hand to a patch of desert. "We'll have cart parking over there, covered from the elements, complete with solar-powered charging stations."

"That convenience store you run with Tony must be doing well," Trudy commented.

"It's doing okay," Josh said, "but I got my reimbursement check from the government for my gas station last week. In typical government fashion, they overpaid for it. It hurt when I found out that the Army bulldozed it into rubble, but the check makes me feel a little better—although I'm sure they'll tax me on it."

"Yeah," Gavin said. "From what I hear, what was left of the town after everyone was removed has been leveled by the Army. My parents are supposed to receive a check for my Aunt's house since they were the only ones listed in her will. I think the government would prefer that Creekside, Wisconsin, is forgotten about as soon as possible."

They watched as the black copter came in for a landing.

Josh pulled his cap down to shield his eyes from the dust being blown in their direction. "Trudy," he yelled over the *whop-whop-whop* of the giant chopper, "can you ask your father to move his damn helipad a bit further down the road? All the crap that thing kicks up is going to damage the paint on the cars!"

"I'll see what I can do," she said. "But you know how deep his concern is for other people."

Josh held up his thumb and index finger, spaced a half-inch apart. Trudy laughed and closed the gap on the digits to make a big zero.

The helicopter spun down and Trudy's father, with Kim in tow, walked over to greet them.

"I see why you were so secretive," Masters said. "It'd be hard to explain these weather phenomena over the phone. Is it permanent?"

"I believe so," Trudy said. "God is showing His favor on our town."

"I'd wish He'd show some to the Mysterium," Masters grumbled as he looked down at his Corthay calf leather shoes, which had set him back a cool two grand. He stepped away from the blow and dabbed them dry with his Brooks Brothers handkerchief. "What's with the water—someone leave a faucet on?"

Trudy hadn't noticed, but a thin trickle of water was working its way down from New Creekside—and, she presumed, Salazar's revival tent. "Oh, that's just our new creek."

"Is Koda here?" Kim asked as she stepped over the newly forming creek.

"No," Trudy said. "I hear he's in Greenland at the moment."

Kim's deflated look confirmed that the Inuit had made an impression on her.

"I'll tell him you were here," Trudy said. "I'm sure he'll be back in time for the grand opening of the new Cluck and Grunt."

Masters looked around. "So, what else is on the tour?"

"We have a new visitor to town," Gavin said. "She's from Niagara Falls."

"Where I had my vision of my son," Trudy remarked. "Only it must have been a mistake because his name was Jay."

Masters stared at her. "We're not going to do this again, are we?"

"You put my son, your future grandson, in jeopardy," Trudy said stiffly. "Although, it wouldn't be quite as bad if you seemed the slightest bit concerned or sorry about it."

"I don't know how you think my doing business with Satan is going to hurt my grandson."

Trudy looked at Kim and made a theatrical gesture at her father as if presenting the Missing Link. "You see? That's just what I'm talking about."

"If you ask me, you should focus your hostility on your husband over there," Masters said. "He's the one that healed the senator, the host body that Lucifer now inhabits."

Gavin looked pained. "I'm sorry that I did."

Masters snorted. "Yeah, well, sorry and five bucks will get you a pair of fuzzy dice at Kim's casino gift shop."

Kim put a hand on Masters' arm. "Maybe we should be going."

"No, I'm tired of my kid blaming me for trying to help her."

"Help?" Trudy laughed. "You only know how to help yourself. Everything you do is for you."

"Look around." Masters waved towards town. "All of this wouldn't be here if it weren't for me. Your shitkicker Creekside residents and their angel buddies would be back in Wisconsin under the military's thumb if I didn't get them out of there and set them up with housing, electricity, water, and sewage to flush all their crap."

Trudy's eyes were two glowing coals as she spat, "That's because Satan was manipulating you and you're too full of yourself even to recognize it! As you said, Senator Stevenson was sacrificed so Lucifer could inhabit him. But the only way that could happen was if Gavin healed the fallen politician. Gavin couldn't heal him unless his power was amplified, and that couldn't be done unless the ladder flared. So he wanted the residents, both human and angel, to arrive here in one group from Wisconsin—which, I might add, couldn't be done until you did your deal with the devil for the land this town sits on."

"That's all conjecture," Masters said.

"You were being played," Trudy said. "Gavin, let's get out of here. I don't want my baby around this man."

Trudy and Gavin got back on the golf cart. "Do you know the sad thing?" Trudy said. "Your grandson is already working miracles and you're not here to see them."

"What miracles?" Masters asked.

Trudy pointed towards the center of Old Calamity. "Thanks to your grandson, I can see the ladder now."

———

Brian Tannahill loaded the last of the supplies into the bug out truck. The disappearance of Bailey had moved his schedule up, along with the need to get Ian away from his new employer. His converted AM General M923A2 5-ton truck would provide them with a secure living space behind armor plating and a somewhat uncomfortable ride on knobby 48-inch tires.

"Hey, Ian," Brian said as his son came into the barn. "Can you check the spare and double-check that the compressor is working?"

"Sure," Ian said.

Brian looked at his boy, who was staring at the ground. "Is something wrong? Don't worry, we'll get to Bailey in a few days and you can apologize for zapping her across the country."

"I'm not going."

Brian walked over to stand before his son. "Well, you're not staying here with all hell breaking loose. I'm also not letting you work for that murderer Ahti."

"He didn't kill anyone—permanently."

"We need you," Brian said. He awkwardly placed a hand on the boy's bony shoulder. Ian wriggled out from under it.

"No, you don't," he said hotly. "You need Bailey. She's like you. She's capable of helping you—I'm not."

"Son—

"Bailey's the son you wanted. Go get her! I'll stay here and take care of the compound. I'll also get a chance to do what I enjoy doing—working as a lighting tech. I might even be able to put my newfound skill to work in Ahti's magic act."

"It's too dangerous to stay here," Brian said. "And you should never tell him about your, uh, powers. I don't trust him."

"We have the most secure compound in the lower forty-eight," Ian said. "Who the hell builds five underground bunkers anyway? If things get worse, I'll move into Youngstown or Niagara Falls for a while."

Brian tried to touch his son again; the boy backed away. "Ian, I've worked my ass off my entire life to make sure that my family was secure and now it's being torn apart. Bailey's in Nevada, you want to stay here, and your mother and I will be traveling in the middle. Have you thought about what this will do to your mother?"

"Brian Cody Tannahill!" Linda shouted from the doorway. "Don't use guilt to make Ian change his mind. He's a grown man. Let him stay on the compound if that's what he wants."

"It's too dangerous," Brian said. "He's right; he's not Bailey. He's a klutz. He'd get himself killed."

"That's right, Dad," said Ian, "talk about me like I'm not even here."

"Brian!" Linda scolded, as she walked up. She put her arms around Ian's shoulders; he didn't protest. "You didn't raise weak children. Bailey *is* like you, but that doesn't mean Ian isn't able to take care of himself. He needs to be the man that he was meant to be."

"You don't want me living in your bunkers my entire life do you?" Ian said. "I need to be able to stand on my own."

Brian knew when he had lost a fight. "Like you said, we have five bunkers; I guess you could have a different one Monday through Friday and move to the house on weekends."

Ian smiled. He could already taste his independence. "I'll take good care of them. Go have angel food cake in Nevada with your angelic buddies. I'll be fine."

———

Emily smiled as she peeked in on Bailey. The dog had taken a liking to the girl and wouldn't settle down in her crate for bedtime, so Emily let her stay out. Now, Bailey and the shepherd were fast asleep in the guest bedroom. Bailey had her arm around Maggie as both snored in unison.

Quietly closing the door, Emily headed towards the kitchen to make some coffee. It was six in the morning and a gentle rain was falling—at least she didn't have to go out to water her plants.

She heard the "shave and a haircut" knock and walked over to open the front door, giving the appropriate "two bits" response. "Come on in, Uriel," she whispered. "Bailey is still sleeping."

"I won't be long," he said as he came in out of the rain and held out a green plastic trash bag. "A couple of the New Creekside residents have girls about Bailey's size, and when they heard she didn't have time to pack a suitcase before her trip they donated some clothing."

"That's wonderful," she said, taking the bag and putting it on the kitchen table. "I can remember when there weren't any kids at all in Calamity. We're becoming a real community and not a hangout for the antisocial, the elderly, and people in the witness protection program."

Uriel gave a hearty bellow before remembering he had to be quiet. He whispered, "Sorry, I just thought that Tony Abbadelli fit all three categories."

"Yeah, I think he's a lot happier now that he's come out of the FBI closet, gone into business with Josh, and has Nate to insult at every opportunity. Want some coffee?"

"I'd love some. Did you know that Ethiopia was the birthplace of coffee?"

"No, can't say I did. Hey, that's right—you're from Ethiopia. Well, not *from* there, but you've lived there for a long time."

"Hundreds of years," Uriel said. "I still try to get back there occasionally. I can take you sometime to show you the breathtaking beauty of the highlands. It's very different from Nevada or Afghanistan."

Emily grabbed a couple coffee mugs off the shelf. "It sounds lovely. Is that where the coffee is grown?"

"The coffea arabica, or coffee plant," Uriel pontificated, "is indigenous to Ethiopia and the largest producer of coffee in Africa, and the livelihood for millions of people. The highlands have, in my humble opinion, some of the world's best beans."

"The Ethiopian tourism bureau should hire you as their spokesman," Emily said. "You can point out all of the attractions, and who's going to doubt an angel? And speaking of attractions," she added, "what's with the new clouds? Not that I'm complaining, but it's like something Moses would be more comfortable with."

"The clouds are a sign to the world."

"A sign? We're pretty much forgotten about out here. We're like Area 51 with a few fanatics camped miles away, pointing supersized zoom lenses in our direction."

"When Calamity faded to almost ghost town status, this area seemed forgotten and alone. It is a sign that we are not forgotten—that we are cared for and watched over. There have been points in human history where the realities of heaven and earth intersect—this is one of those times.

"There have been other signs recently," Uriel continued, "but not as obvious: Gavin and his healing power, the spring that flows now from the revival tent's altar, Trudy being able to see the ladders and move through them, you and your ability to manipulate matter. And then there's Bailey and her brother."

"What about me?" Bailey said from the guest room doorway. She was wearing an olive drab U.S. Army T-shirt that was much too large for her and shorts that Emily loaned her.

"You're a special young woman," Uriel said. "You can see the ladder. Previously only Gavin could see it; now Trudy has received the same gift, and you as well."

"The best things come in threes," Emily said.

Uriel continued, "You also possess a talent that even they do not have: you can detect angels and demons by their aura."

"And I can see them before they materialize," she added. "I saw some at a neighbor's farm. First, I could see through them, but then they became solid."

Uriel looked at Emily and commented, "Talented indeed."

"It's cool and all, that I have a superpower," Bailey said, "but it's scary too. It creeps me out thinking that demons have been walking around for who knows how long and I've never noticed."

Emily motioned for Bailey to have a seat on the stool next to the counter. "Maybe you've had this gift your entire life but have never seen anything before, because there never were any demons or angels around."

"No," Uriel said, "I believe if she can see us in our non-material forms that this is a new gift, as angels have been near her before. We're a little more numerous than humans give us credit for. Bailey will see what I mean when she begins to explore her new world."

CHAPTER FIVE

Masters sat on the patio of the bungalow Kim had lent him. The three thousand square-foot residence was on the resort property but tucked away in a secluded area near the tennis courts. Room service had just provided him breakfast that he picked over while reading the *Las Vegas Sun* newspaper.

The top story above the fold was Nevada Senator William Stevenson's likely run for the presidency. Due to his miraculous resurrection and silver tongue, he'd been filling up the news cycles with everything from diffusing a terrorist standoff near the Capitol to kissing babies.

The local news wasn't much better. The lead story was about how the senator was pouring his own money into rebuilding the Strip and helping local charities fulfill the needs of families that have lost loved ones in the battle or were now unemployed due to the destruction of their workplaces.

A short article about the unusual cloud formations over New Creekside caught Masters' eye. The angels weren't allowing the media to venture close enough to verify their nature, the article said, but their resemblance to nuclear mushroom clouds had prompted concern that they could be giving off harmful rays, presenting a health risk. Authorities were advising the residents of Calamity and New Creekside to vacate the area as soon as possible until the government inspectors could investigate.

Just a few short years ago a phenomenon like that would have been front page news around the world. Now it was buried toward the back of the paper next to a small display ad for a Vegas church. The Sunday sermon was titled:

"Do you recognize the Antichrist?" *Well, at least someone doesn't have their head up Stevenson's ass.*

Tossing the paper on the empty chair next to him, he picked up his phone and dialed.

"Jay?" Holly said. "How are you?"

"I'm fine. How's my Mysterium?"

"It's fine. I'm fine too, in case you're wondering."

"Great, so everything and everyone is just fine. Is Edwin staying out of trouble?"

"Edwin has already made several suggestions on how we can improve the facility."

"Unless those include jacking up the admission price, I'm not interested."

Holly made an exasperated noise in her throat. "Don't be such a prick, Jay. He's thought of a use for that room in the back. We can set it up as a lecture hall. Edwin thinks he can get some of his angel friends to give talks there and answer questions from the curious."

Masters mulled this over and said, "You know, that's not a bad idea. We can upsell that in our ticket packages. Have your photo taken with an angel—or breakfast with an angel—there are a lot of possibilities."

"I think Edwin is hoping that, instead of a media circus, people can ask intelligent questions and receive answers to the important matters of life."

"Holly, honey, you've been hanging around angels too long. Anyway, I called because I want you and Edwin to hop a flight back to Vegas."

"But we've got a lot of work left to do here," Holly protested.

"Have Edwin delegate the project to one of his angel buddies."

"I also haven't seen my mother yet."

"Lucky you. So, buy her a ticket to Vegas. But tell her that people in Nevada, unlike where she lives, wear shoes, so she might want to stop at Walmart first. There's the slight possibility that they'll have some clown shoes for her."

"Hey, that's my mother you're talking about! And what's the big hurry anyway?"

Masters stared at his phone. What he was about to say sounded so weak and pitiful that he didn't want to utter the words. He was sure that the constant bickering with his daughter must have emasculated him at some point. How else could he end up in such a pathetic situation?

"Well?" Holly said.

Masters sighed. "I miss you," he said, as he hung up and tossed his phone across the tabletop.

———

Holly scratched her head and looked over at Edwin, who stood next to a workbench covered with drawings. Looking more professional than anyone else at the Mysterium, he wore a suit and tie, and his hair was neatly combed.

Her brain still spinning from Jay's "I miss you" comment she asked Edwin, "Did hell just freeze over?"

Edwin smiled. "I prefer the idiom 'when pigs fly.'"

"Well, I think there's a whole flock of them circling Las Vegas right now."

Holly walked over to see what Edwin was working on. The table had several pencil sketches of Calamity and the people who lived there.

"You never told me you were an artist," she remarked.

"Using a pencil and paper is new to me. My kind enjoys art in all its forms. While we cannot create matter, we can manipulate it. My canvas is usually the blackness of space, and my pencil is the super-heated gas of a nova; it's a little more abstract than this. I noticed that the Hubble space telescope had taken some nice photos of my work. I was going to order a print."

Holly noticed a drawing of a limousine in the middle of a road; she was standing next to it. "Hey, that's me!" Remembering her express trip back to Creekside where her limo became an air taxi thanks to Edwin, she added, "At least you didn't draw me throwing up."

He pulled a drawing out from the bottom of the stack. "Here's Nate and Tony, when Tony used to be Tom, in front of the rock shop. And this is the ladder in Emily's backyard."

Holly picked up the paper. "So that's what it looks like. Pretty awesome."

"Thanks. It would be better in color; pencil doesn't do it justice."

"I'll get you some colored pencils or watercolors."

"I would appreciate that. I was thinking we could make a display area that shows Calamity and New Creekside with humans and angels living side by side. We could even have video interviews from the residents."

"That's a good idea, but Jay wants us back in Vegas as soon as possible."

"Is there something wrong?"

"No." A pleased little smile played upon her lips. "But I think the bastard is getting lonely."

Edwin picked up his pencil and started drawing.

"What are you drawing now?" Holly asked.

"A flying pig."

———

Brian and Linda stood next to their oversized bug out truck as their son, Ian shut the rear hatch of his Bronco that was parked nearby. Their destinations were different, which didn't please the elder Tannahill. Ian's Bronco was filled with old lighting equipment that belonged in a scrap yard, while *his* truck was filled with everything necessary for survival in a cold, cruel world.

"It's not too late to come along with us," Brian said to his son. "You want to get into the theater business? Well, there's no better place than Vegas."

Ian shook his head. "This is what I'm meant to do. I was in a pretty dark place for a while because nobody was calling me back… and other things. When I was ready to give up, I asked for a sign, and then Ahti called. This isn't just a job; it's something that I'm sure Senator Stevenson orchestrate since he's friends with Ahti. The senator gave me the sign I asked for—and a job."

"Have you considered that we're going to a town of angels?" Linda said. "That's better than Disney World. Not many people get that chance."

"I don't believe in them," Ian said as he grabbed his baseball cap from the Bronco's dash.

"Don't believe?" Brian said. "How the hell can't you believe in them? You see them on television practically every day."

"I believe they exist, but how do we know that they intend good for us? Every time they're on television they're surrounded by death and destruction. It doesn't look like they have our best interests at heart if you ask me."

Brian said icily, "So, you want them to be more like that phony Stevenson?"

"Be careful where you say that, Dad," Ian warned. "Many people have already been helped by him. Some of his followers don't like to hear him criticized. But in answer to your question: why not? He's doing some good in the world, not holed up in some town in the middle of the desert. If angels cared, they'd be out helping people instead of destroying cities—they've been doing that since Sodom and Gomorrah, and it hasn't worked so far. If you ask me, they're the real devils."

Brian glanced over at his wife, who looked like she was going to cry. "Come on, Linda, let's go."

"If there is anything you need," she said, "check in with our neighbors, I know they'll be willing to help." She went over and gave Ian a hug and kiss on the cheek. "My prayer is that the angels will watch over you."

"Thanks," Ian said. "But I can take care of myself."

"Hey, Koda," Emily said as he came in from the backyard. "How was Greenland?"

"It was enjoyable to be back with my friends in that community—not that I do not love this one as well.

"Here"—he plopped a wax paper-wrapped item on the kitchen counter—"as promised, a delicacy from Greenland."

Emily used her thumb and index finger to lift one side of the butcher paper and saw blood seeping through onto her counter. "Reindeer?"

"I'm sorry, but they didn't have any smoked reindeer heart. This is muskox."

"Shouldn't angels be vegan?"

"We have a small garden, and there is a grocery store a few miles away from our community, but most items are imported and expensive." He grabbed a banana from a fruit basket on Emily's counter and began to peel it. "Therefore, fish, fowl, and various mammals, along with seasonal berries, are the predominant Greenlandic cuisine. Protein-rich meat is not a choice; it is a necessity for survival. You should try Suaasat sometime. It is a hearty soup made with either seal or whale meat."

Emily's stomach churned in protest; she changed the subject. "So, does it look like you're going to have to close the ladder in Greenland?"

"It has already begun. My family that I love is dispersing throughout the world. It is sad, but it must be done—and quickly."

"What's the hurry?"

"Events are moving rapidly now that Senator Stevenson has been inhabited by the Father of Lies. We must be prepared to act."

Emily unwrapped the slab of muskox that Koda had brought her. As she studied the dead flesh, she thought back to what Uriel had once told her about ladders.

"I thought ladders were living things, just like a tree. Must you kill it?"

Koda rubbed his forehead. "They are very much like a tree, without a soul but alive nonetheless. It pains the entire community that the ladder must be sacrificed, but one death can save millions."

"Why not just add more ladders?" Emily suggested. "God created everything, so He can add more, right?"

Koda smiled. "I wish it were that easy, young warrior. The ladders depend upon the behavior of physics that human theoreticians have yet to discover, along with dimensional space-time laws that were set down at the creation of the universe. To be honest, it is very complicated, and even we angels are unable to comprehend most of it. God is the composer and can change anything He wishes, but I doubt He would want to throw away the entire symphony over one note."

"So where are they going—the Greenland community?"

"They will disperse both human and angel, maintaining their bonds of friendship," Koda said. "Some will move to Nuuk, Greenland's largest city; others will make the journey to ladders throughout the world. Some, like my dear friend Rania, will be moving here. Because of the clouds and cooler weather, this ladder is more inviting to them now."

The front door opened. Bailey came in, followed by Trudy and Rachel.

"Hey, guys," Emily said. "How was the grand tour?"

Rachel plopped on the sofa, quickly grabbing the remote before her dog could get to it. "You've gotta be faster on the draw, pooch," she chided Maggie.

"It was good," Trudy said. "I think Bailey was surprised that so many angels live here."

"Yeah," Bailey said. "It's like every other person is glowing. Then there are those big angels around the perimeter. Rachel says they're protecting angels."

"Like me!" Rachel added as she found *The Andy Griffith Show* on TV Land.

Bailey said, "There were also some that didn't have a form but were like ghosts. I could see through them the same way I could see the demons."

"Those," Koda said, "are angels in spirit form; very few of us take a material form."

Emily spoke up: "I'm sorry, this is Koda," she said to Bailey.

"You're an angel too," Bailey said as she stared at Koda.

"You are quite right, young lady," Koda replied. "I do have a material form, but sometimes I wonder if I should have been a little taller."

Bailey's phone began blaring out a rock song as she fumbled in her pocket to find it.

"'Great White Buffalo'?" Emily questioned.

"Yeah, that's the ringtone I assigned to my dad. He loves Ted Nugent." She found the phone and picked up the call. "Hey, Dad! Hold on; I'm gonna put you on speaker." Bailey put the phone on the counter and pushed the speaker button. "What's going on?"

"We're on the road heading towards Nevada," Bailey's father said. "We're taking back roads to stay off the grid, so it's going to take a while before we get there."

"Is Ian there? May I talk to him?"

There was a long pause.

Bailey stuck her face closer to the phone. "Hello?"

"He's not with us," Linda Tannahill said. "He wanted to stay behind and work for that theater in town."

"He got the job?"

"Yeah," Brian said. "Minimum wage from that hack magician. I told him he could do better in Vegas, but he wants to be on his own."

"Wait," Rachel said as she turned off the television. "What magician?"

"Ahti," Bailey said. "He's the guy who popped the senator. Why?"

"What?" Emily said. "He's going to be working for Ahti—the Amazing Ahti?"

Brian said, "Who's that speaking?"

"Emily"

"Oh, okay. Ahti's starting up some magic show in Niagara Falls, and Ian is going to be the lighting technician."

"No!" Emily shouted at the phone. "You need to turn around now and get him!"

"He won't come with us."

"You've got to get him now!" Emily said frantically. "Ahti is a demon. He's the one who tried to kill me in Vegas."

"He was that big glowing thing they caught on camera?"

"Yeah, and like Bailey said, he's the one who killed—didn't kill, whatever—Senator Stevenson."

"We knew about the assassination attempt," Brian replied, "but since the senator didn't seem overly concerned about having his brains blown out, Ian didn't think that was going to be an issue with his employment."

"Yeah, well, it's a big issue," Emily said. "I tossed Ahti out a twentieth-floor hotel window after he shot the senator. If he learns that Bailey is staying with me, he's not going to be pleased—he might take it out on your son. Plus, Ahti doesn't like humans who have a power like your son does. He considers it competition to his failing magic career. If he learns that Ian can make things disappear, he'll kill him."

"Oh, God!" Emily heard Bailey's mother cry. "Brian, we have to turn around."

"Wait!" Koda said. "Let me go and watch over young Ian. I will not let anything happen to him."

"And you are?" Brian Tannahill said.

"I am Koda."

"Uh, okay..." Brian gulped.

"Dad, he's an angel."

"But," Trudy said, "you're not a protecting angel. Perhaps Nate should go."

"That is true," Koda agreed. "As a ministering angel, I would be able to help Ian, but I would be no match for Ahti in a fight."

Emily said, "I don't think Nate and Ahti are the best of friends, so that might escalate the situation."

"I can go," Rachel said, "if Trudy and Gavin promise to stay in New Creekside where they'll be safe—and stay out of trouble."

"Trouble? Little old us?" Gavin deadpanned.

"Good idea, Rachel—but I'm going with you," said Trudy. "My hubby here needs to stay close to the ladder so he doesn't start having his headaches again."

"Hold up!" Gavin said. "I'm not letting you go into a dangerous area without me, especially not in your condition."

Trudy wrapped an arm around his waist. "I'll be safe because Rachel will be with me—just like the old days before my super stud muffin showed up and swept me off my feet."

"Oh, boy…" they heard Ian's father groan. "Well, *somebody* go and rescue my son!"

"Don't worry," Emily said. "We'll get the logistics figured out—won't we, Trudy?"

Trudy let go of Gavin. "I know just how to get us there."

"The Amazing Ahti, featuring Daeva," Ahti said as he waved his arms with a flourish at the theater marquee. "How's that sound?"

Daeva looked up at the currently vacant white plastic marquee. Rebels never worked well together, and Ahti was already getting on her nerves. "Why do I get second billing?"

"Because it sounds better, and because I'm the star, my name is the one people know."

"Kim Kali tossed you out of her theater. Why was that? Oh, yeah, because you *destroyed* it."

"But I'm the one that got you the gig to replace me, and the theater needed updating anyway. Then you try to kill her. That doesn't get you promotions, you know."

"I don't—"

"Plus," Ahti reminded her, "I saved you from the pit."

"Okay, fine!" Daeva said. "I'm sick of hearing about how you saved the day."

Ahti pointed to a black Bronco heading their direction. "There's the kid I hired as our lighting technician."

Daeva put a hand up to shade her eyes. "He looks like he's truant from high school."

"I can't discriminate because of age—it's some law. The upside is his salary expectations are pretty low," Ahti said as he motioned Ian to pull over in front of the theater.

"Hey, kid," he said as Ian got out of the Bronco and went around to open the rear liftgate. "I'd like you to meet my assistant Da—"

"Assistant?" Daeva protested, hands on hips.

"Opening act?"

She glared at him. "Watch it, buster."

Ahti closed his eyes and shook his head. "I'd like you to meet Daeva—my co-headliner."

"Pleased to meet you. I'm Ian Tannahill" The boy held out his hand.

Daeva gently held his hand for an extended moment. "Well, Ian, it's nice to finally have a *real* man on the payroll."

"So, kid," Ahti said as he peeked into the Bronco. "What did you find us?"

Ian finished opening the back of the Bronco. "It's the best I could do on our budget, but it will give us some basic lighting that we can add to later."

Daeva held her tongue, but she considered the equipment a pile of crap that might have been halfway decent thirty years ago but was landfill-ready now.

Ahti was equally unimpressed. "We'll make it work somehow, but I was expecting more from you, kid."

"Hey, be nice to this handsome young man," Daeva said. She put her arm around Ian, making sure her left breast was firmly up against his arm. "He just saved your ass by finding this stuff. You should be more grateful."

"Well, if you're so enamored by this crap you can help the kid take it into the theater and set it up," Ahti said as he walked off.

"I didn't want to disappoint him," Ian said to Daeva. "But there's not a lot you can do for three thousand bucks."

"Don't mind Ahti, he's always grumpy until he's had his breakfast bourbon. Oh, look at the time," Daeva added, not even looking at a watch. "I have a meeting. Be a dear and set up the equipment, okay?"

"Uh...okay, sure."

She gave Ian a peck on the cheek that made the boy blush, confident that would be enough to keep him coming back for more of Ahti's abuse.

———

Masters sat in front of his laptop in his suite going over the financials that Holly had e-mailed him. She was due back later in the afternoon; he couldn't believe he was excited about that—and not just because of the prospect of getting her in the sack.

He did congratulate himself on turning a former stripper from Bug Tussle or wherever the hell she was from into a decent manager of a growing enterprise. It validated his ability to transform even the dimmest bulb into a spotlight under his wise tutelage.

His self-congratulation was interrupted by a knock at the door.

"Hey, Pops," Trudy said as he opened it. She was standing there in ragged jeans and a T-shirt, with sunglasses pushed up on top of her equally ragged hair. He vowed to get his daughter a fashion consultant as soon as possible.

Behind her stood Gavin and Rachel. Rachel gave him a dimpled smile while Gavin rocked back and forth on his heels, looking like he was ready to bolt.

"Well?" Masters said, not making a move to invite them in.

"I want to bury the hatchet," Trudy said.

"Yeah, in my skull most likely."

"You read my mind," Trudy said. "But we need to make amends and move forward. It's for everyone's good, and especially for my son."

"You mean little Jay," Masters said.

Trudy pushed her way inside as Gavin and Rachel followed. "Let's not get ahead of ourselves. Okay, here's the deal. You need another Mysterium."

"I do? I haven't even opened the second one."

"Holly manages the one in Wisconsin, you have this one in Vegas; if you're a chain, where would be the next logical place to put a Mysterium?"

"Branson?"

Trudy shook her head. "Niagara Falls."

Masters motioned them towards the sofa. "Take a seat." He could already figure out why Trudy had Niagara Falls on her mind, but he wanted to hear her out. In truth, he had already put an offer in on a parcel on International Drive in Orlando, Florida, for the third Mysterium.

The three of them sat on the sofa, looking like the three wise monkeys of see, speak, and hear no evil fame. "So, what's your idea?" Masters asked.

"Well, you wanted to get me into the business," said Trudy. "Like I said, Holly is managing the Wisconsin Mysterium, and you have the Las Vegas one. I thought that I could manage a Niagara Falls satellite."

"Hmm, I seem to remember you telling me that the Mysterium promotes evil and you didn't like the deal I cut with Senator Stevenson, aka Lucifer, to build this one in Vegas. You know I'd have to go back, hat in hand, and ask for more cash to expand that quickly."

"Okay…" Trudy said.

Masters crossed his arms as he leaned against the writing desk. "No, not okay. You'd never agree to that unless something else is going on. I'm not going to ask your husband over there because he'd probably tow the party line. Rachel,"—he pointed to her—"I know you can't lie to me, so tell me the truth of why we need a Mysterium in New York State."

Trudy looked doubtful. Rachel grasped her knee reassuringly and told her, "He's your father and should know." She turned to Masters and explained: "There is a girl in Calamity that can see the ladders and angels and demons as well, even if they are not in material form. Her brother has the gift of being able to transport things and people to the Calamity ladder, and he sent her there accidentally. Her parents are coming to get her, but the brother can't come because he's working for the Amazing Ahti. If Ahti finds out that Ian can make things disappear, he'll kill him. We need to rescue—"

"Hold up," Masters said, raising his hand. "I can't process this angelic stream of consciousness. What's Ahti got to do with this?"

"He's starting a magic show in Niagara Falls," Trudy said.

"So, this whole pretense about a new Mysterium is just to rescue this kid and kick Ahti's ass?"

Gavin finally spoke up. "You've condensed the essentials, yes, but we also think that there is more going on there beyond a failed magician's desire to get back in the limelight. The girl, Bailey, saw demons in the Niagara area that looked like they were hunting for something. Trudy also had a vision of a school that Stevenson will set up in New York State. Rachel and Trudy will go to find out what the demons are up to."

Masters considered his options. Trudy was under the Senator's protection, and Rachel could take care of herself. Still, it would be safer for everyone if it was not generally known that they were in Niagara Falls.

"Okay," he finally said. "Go pack your bags. I'll get you on a private jet." He noticed that Rachel looked a little peaked. "Oh, that's right, the angel afraid to fly. I'm not sure of a way around that. You could take the bus."

"I'll fly along," Rachel said. "Alongside the airplane, but not in it. I still need to be close enough to protect, but it is just too nerve-racking to be in the aircraft."

"I think," Trudy said, "that you may draw a little too much attention that way. Plus, I don't think you're FAA certified. You'll just need to tough it out with me in the jet. They have barf bags."

"Well, that's settled," Masters said. "I don't know how long it will be before the senator finds out. I'll think of something to tell him if he gets suspicious—the guy is pretty gullible."

Rachel stood up and went over to him. Putting her hand in his, she looked at him without the goofy smile she usually maintained. "Be very careful around the senator. He's the most dangerous being in this universe."

"Don't worry about me, kid," Masters said. "I've preached about him back in my faith healing days—red outfit, pointy tail—he takes sinners to hell unless they repent and drop some cash in my basket."

"You don't understand," said Rachel. She then quoted from Revelations: "'But woe to the earth and the sea, because the devil has gone down to you! He is filled with fury, because he knows that his time is short.'"

"He does seem to be a bit on the cranky side," Masters quipped.

"This isn't funny," Rachel said, stamping her foot. "Imagine a being whose beauty surpassed all others, whose intelligence was second only to God

Himself. Who walked before the throne in holiness until iniquity was found in him.

"The war that was fought went far beyond any human war. What takes up a few words in your Bible seemed for us to stretch into eternity. I lost family during that time; those that I loved, rebelled. After they were cast down, we knew there would never be redemption for them—our sadness seemed unbearable. Their minds are now so corrupted that they would never bow to the One they hate.

"Then we were given the task of protecting you from our fallen brethren—even from yourselves. We will battle anyone to protect you, but there is one spirit that gives us pause—even Uriel would hesitate to battle Satan by himself. If your business partner instills this feeling of trepidation in an archangel, shouldn't you be concerned as well?"

Masters lowered his head and closed his eyes. He needed a moment to think about this. The chances of Trudy running into the senator were increased if she went to Niagara Falls. It was better if his daughter and future grandson were in Calamity and safe. Masters had seen the news when the senator decided not to press charges; he was even seen on television giving Ahti a hug, letting the world know that he was a man of peace and held no ill will against anyone. Something was going on, as the senator would have happily thrown Ahti under the bus if he weren't of some further use.

He looked up at them. "I'll go," he said. "Trudy, you'll need to take over the work on the Vegas Mysterium while I'm gone."

"Wait, what?" Trudy said. "Why you?"

"Because I've danced with the devil before; I have a better chance of finding out what's going on in Niagara. I'll go under the pretense of scoping the place out for a future Mysterium, which is more believable than sending you guys. I'll find the kid and talk some sense into him and figure out what the demons are up to. Piece of cake!"

Rachel frowned. "Were you paying any attention to me at all?"

"Not really," Masters said. "Look, I know they're dangerous. Ahti's a seraph, right? I'll take my seraph buddy Edwin along in case it gets ugly. I'll also bring along Holly, for some reason that escapes me at the moment."

He put a hand on Rachel's shoulder. "I understand the danger—I'll be careful."

———

Ahti had just chucked an empty Maker's Mark bottle into the trashcan from ten feet away. He congratulated himself on his perfect three-point shot, even as his head pounded in protest at the grating sound of glass on metal.

He had spent the last evening at the Seneca Casino on the United States side of the Falls. He couldn't understand what Daeva was complaining about. The facility was beautiful, the gaming rooms well maintained, and the smell of smoke and booze comforting.

Unfortunately, their perk of providing drinks at the games caused Ahti to overindulge, and now he was paying for it. A little hair of the dog didn't seem to help either.

The sound of his phone chiming made him cringe. "Yeah," he said.

"Ahti, this is Bill Stevenson."

"Senator, what a pleasure."

"You sound terrible! Have you been hitting the bottle?"

"No, it's been hitting me."

"We'll have to work on that, but at least you didn't call me Imperator. It shows that even hungover you keep your wits about you."

"Thanks," Ahti said, wishing he could hang up. He wasn't used to speaking directly to the Imperator, as he was too far down the totem pole. The man on the other end of the phone sounded like the senator and even disapproved of his drinking the way the senator did, but the corrupt politician was long gone and his body now inhabited by Lucifer. This new senator could crush him whenever he wished—send him to the pit, torture him for a thousand years, or force him to possess the body of a teetotaler.

"I decided to honor you by entrusting you with a vital task," Stevenson said. "You'll be working directly with Corson, and I expect this to be as successful as your work in Las Vegas."

"Certainly, Senator."

"Your service to me in Vegas has not gone unnoticed or unappreciated. This is truly an amazing opportunity for the Amazing Ahti."

Ahti knew that any honor given to a rebel came at a high price. He was perfectly happy having a magic show and pickling his liver. He didn't want a new job at the potential cost of ending up like Hiisi, whom he assumed was now in the pit. Still, he could not turn down the offer, both because his ego was shouting at him to take it and the stark terror of what saying no would mean.

"I'd be honored," he stammered.

"Good," Stevenson said. "First on your agenda is to locate a suitable location for my new academy. The Niagara area has always been a favorite playground and prison for our kind. I'm sure we'll have rebels fighting over who will work on this project. As for the facilities, I've had a few wanderers marking various potential locations, but the infrastructure required to build from scratch will take too long."

"Academy?"

"Many humans are ready to worship me, but we need to be able to train those that are most promising. They, in turn, will train others. Along with the core courses on how to properly venerate me, we'll also instruct them on subjects such as insurrections, military coups, desecration of holy sites, torture, genocide, et cetera, along with firearms training, hand-to-hand combat, and survival skills. It will be wonderful!"

"Survival skills…"

"What's was that, Ahti?"

"I might know of the perfect spot, but I'll need to check it out."

"I knew you could handle the job," Stevenson said. "Keep in touch."

CHAPTER SIX

Bailey needed to take a walk by herself. Her brain was still spinning around in her skull as she attempted to make sense of everything that had been going on. Plus, she wasn't used to being around so many people. She much preferred the tranquility of the natural world, and the opportunity to become one with nature that hunting and fishing provided. Emily's house was particularly hectic, as her living room was also Calamity's unofficial town square. A constant stream of visitors, both human and angelic, made it practically impossible to think.

The desert landscape was foreign to her, as were the clouds that churned overhead and the angels that guarded it. The gravel road in front of Emily's house stretched about a quarter-mile to the east before petering out. At the end, two protecting angels stood about a hundred yards apart. Everyone was telling her how terrifying it was to be around a transformed angel, but she couldn't see what the big deal was. They were big and glowing and visible. The ones that gave her the willies were the nearly invisible ones—the gossamer wisps floating past her from time to time.

One moved in front of her now, as if trying to block her from walking further into the desert. The two visible protecting angels turned to face her as well.

"Nothing to see here!" Bailey shouted. "I'm just taking a walk."

"The desert is dangerous, little one," one of the Protectors said in a voice that cascaded around her, bringing back memories of Niagara Falls.

"I can handle myself," she said and proceeded to walk forward—and through—the apparition that stood in front of her. But instead of leaving her alone, the vaporous being started following her.

"Go away!" she said. "I want to be alone."

The angel came around and blocked her again.

"I can handle myself," Bailey said. "I've been around snakes and spiders before. I want to be alone for a while." Then, once again, she walked through the apparition.

The angel came around and stopped in front of her.

Bailey sighed. "Okay, tag along if you want, but I don't need you watching over me."

She kept walking into the desert, not sure what she would find. It looked like the nearest mountain was miles away, and the ground in front of her was pool table-flat. There weren't even any cactus like she'd seen in old Western movies, just scrub brush and fist-sized rocks. There was nothing to hunt, even if she had one of her rifles.

The thought of Ian being in Niagara Falls alone with a demon, the very one that Emily had fought in Vegas, scared her. She had tried to call him several times already and left vague messages in case Ahti was listening in. He hadn't called back, but that was normal; he often forgot to turn on his ringer and unlike most guys his age, seldom looked at his phone for missed calls or texts.

She prayed that he would be safe.

Turning around, she was able to get a better view of Calamity and New Creekside. They were probably the most interesting small towns in America, or perhaps the world. The clouds could be seen as tightly formed only over the towns. Lightning coursed through them as they swirled unnaturally overhead. Also, the glow from the ring of angels that protected them was blinding even at this distance and in full daylight.

While she was admiring the view, she heard a deep raspy growl that sent a shiver down her spine. Slowly, she turned around and found herself face to face with a mountain lion. The cat was easily Bailey's weight and stood as high as her hips—and it was only ten feet away.

Cursing herself for not bringing the Beretta, she spread her arms and tried to make herself bigger in the hope that it would dissuade the feline from eating her.

The cat growled again and moved its red-brown body to a position to pounce.

"If you're going to help me," Bailey said to the angel, "now's a good time."

The angelic apparition didn't move. It stayed behind Bailey as the cat crept closer.

"Please, help me," Bailey asked again. "I'm sorry I said I can handle myself—okay, I admit I can't."

The mountain lion perked up its ears and purred. Then the big cat padded over to her and rubbed its head against her leg.

"Um…" Reaching down, she scratched the cat behind the ears. "Good kitty?"

Looking towards the angel, she said, "What just happened? I thought I was lunch for sure. You guys were right about the desert. I think I'll be heading back to town now."

She started walking back but noticed that now she not only had an angel following her but the mountain lion as well.

"Shoo!"

Bailey picked up the pace, but the lion stayed with her.

"Tell it to go away."

As she reached the protecting angels she had previously scoffed at, she looked at them and shrugged. "What do I do now?"

"Wildlife," one angel said, "are coming closer to town because they smell the water from the new stream. We welcome all of God's creatures. Take your cat to the spring to drink."

"It's not my cat."

"Your feline has a different opinion. He has obviously adopted you."

Feeling that it wasn't worth responding to the angel's comment, she continued down the road towards Emily's house. As she approached, she stopped in front of the chain link fence. She wasn't sure how Rachel's dog and her new pet would get along. The column of light that everyone in town referred to as the ladder was glowing as usual between the house and the horse barn. To her, it looked like some kind of giant alien death ray that would destroy the world. It was an amazing sight, and she wondered why she was one of the few that could see it. She also vowed to stop watching the Syfy channel.

The ladder suddenly brightened for a moment, something she had already come to know as indicative of an angel moving between dimensions. It was a common occurrence, and it took a while for her to be able to sleep as the phenomenon flashed right outside her bedroom window.

She decided to keep walking down the road and towards what the towns-folk had been referring to as the Arboretum. Supposedly, it was a revival tent at one time, but when Gavin healed the sick, the land also responded; now trees instead of tent poles supported a tattered canvas that let enough light through for the plants that grew there to thrive.

Bailey neared what looked to be the entrance, only to find a fair size stream flowing out and eroding the road in front of her. It was too wide to jump, and she doubted her cat would follow her, so she ducked through a ripped portion of the canvas only to wind up interrupting a meeting.

Three men sat around a card table. She knew one of them, the old guy that took Ian's *Playboy* magazine; the others she hadn't met before.

A man in a weird purple suit stood up and smiled at her. "Hello, I'm Sergio Salazar. You must be the young lady that Tony has been telling us about."

"Hi, I'm Bailey Tannahill. I didn't mean to interrupt."

Another man with a bald head and thick glasses stood up. "I'm Reverend Brustad, nice to meet you. You're not interrupting at all."

They seemed to notice the mountain lion at the same time, and each took a step back.

"My cat," she said. "I haven't named him yet."

The old guy, Tony, spoke up. "Siegfried and Roy could have used you in their show."

The mountain lion walked past them to drink from the stream emerging from the ground near what she assumed was once an altar.

"We're all ministers," Salazar said, "so we gather once a week to discuss the spiritual health of our community."

The old guy must have noticed the way she was looking at him.

"Yeah, I'm a priest," he said. "What about it?"

"Bailey," she heard from behind.

A man stood just inside the tent. "Hello, Bailey, I'm Jonathan. I'm the one who accompanied you into the desert."

Bailey gave the angel the once-over. Clad in a Route 66 T-shirt and blue jeans, he was tall, lanky, about the same age as her father—and, like his brethren, gave off an ethereal glow.

"Why didn't the cat eat me?" she asked.

"The mountain lion was never going to eat you. He knows that you are someone it can feel safe around."

She furrowed her brow. "I'm a hunter. I've never had wild critters think I was safe," she said as she glanced over to the mountain lion, which was contentedly licking its paws nearby.

"The cat senses that you are a friend to all wildlife," Jonathan said. "And he's taken quite a liking to you."

"A friend?" Bailey scoffed. "Crazy cat."

The mountain lion padded over to her and gave her booty an affectionate head-butt, much like a housecat. "I wonder how introductions will go with Rachel's dog?" Bailey said while steadying herself, "I hope they get along."

Reverend Brustad smiled. "'The wolf will live with the lamb, the leopard will lie down with the goat, the calf and the lion and the yearling together; and a little child will lead them.'"

———

Masters stood on the tarmac at the executive airport in Henderson, Nevada, as the jet taxied up. He had several bags with him and had already notified the charter company that he would need the plane ready for a quick turnaround to Niagara Falls. The two replacement pilots stood by, having a clandestine smoke in the shade of a parked fuel truck.

Masters raised his hands towards them and mouthed the words "What the fuck?" since he had no intention of being blown up by the hired help.

As the engines shut down and the cabin door opened, he approached the plane. Holly and Edwin climbed down the fold-out stairs and walked over to him.

"Turn around," Masters said. "Get back on the plane."

"What do you mean, get back on the plane?" Holly screeched at him as he attempted to peck her on the mouth, which she turned her head to avoid.

"We're going to Niagara Falls," he said as he watched the new set of pilots putting out their cigarettes as the jet fuel truck pulled up next to the aircraft. "You're always bitching at me to take you to someplace romantic."

Pointing to Edwin, then at his luggage, he barked: "Don't just stand there, put my bags on the plane."

"Don't touch them," Holly said. "You don't talk to an angel that way."

"He's also my employee, so I was exceptionally polite."

Edwin dutifully picked up the bags and headed back to the plane.

"What's wrong with you?" Masters said. "I thought you'd be happy to go on a vacation."

"You had us fly all the way from Wisconsin to Nevada just to turn around and fly back to someplace close to where we left from?" Holly complained. "Plus, my mother will be flying out tomorrow."

"You know, most people would enjoy a flight on an executive jet," Masters said. "Not to mention the added perk of missing your mother."

"What's the big hurry anyway?" Holly said. "At least let me have a night's sleep here, and then we can fly out tomorrow."

"I have a reservation for us tonight at the Sheraton, with a view of the Falls."

"But—"

Masters moved closer to her. "Niagara Falls is known as the honeymoon capital of the world."

He could tell from her besotted expression that he had her hooked; now he just needed to reel her in. "They're becoming known for their weddings as well."

Holly's eyes narrowed to menacing slits. "You're not shitting me, are you, Jay? You better not be."

"I planned this entire trip just so that we can be together. Why else would we be going to Niagara Falls?"

Holly dug her cell phone out of her purse. "I'll call my mother and re-schedule," she said. "Don't disappoint me Jay, or I swear…"

He smiled as he turned her around and back onto the Gulfstream.

———

Ian congratulated himself on installing the dimmer board in the musty tech room at the back of the Pantomime Theater. It sat on an unused door, which in turn sat on two wooden sawhorses. He was exhausted from stringing cables and pulling lighting rigs up to the rafters.

He rested on a chair while watching Ahti on stage, trying desperately to set up a crappy sound system he found on eBay. According to Ahti, the artist knows what sounds best; he refused to employ the services of a professional sound technician.

Ian knew a guy at the theater arts school that knew all about sound systems. He pulled out his phone to see if he could offer some advice, as Ahti looked like he was drowning in a sea of spaghetti. Ian was surprised to see that he had a lot of missed messages from Bailey. Dialing her number, he and waited for her to pick up.

"Ian!" Bailey said. "Where are you?"

"I'm at the theater," he said. "Sorry I missed your calls; I had the phone on mute. What are you up to?"

"I'm watering my mountain lion."

"Huh?"

"Never mind. Is Ahti there?"

"Yeah. Why, do you still want to ask him about the scope?"

"No." Her voice dropped to a whisper. "I need to tell you something. Can he hear you?"

"Nah, he's on the other side of the theater."

"Good. Ahti isn't what he seems. Don't tell him that I'm in Nevada with Emily and the angels. Especially don't tell him anything about you being able to make things disappear."

"Why not? I thought he might want to use it in his act if I can perfect it."

"If he knows about it, he'll kill you."

"Yeah, right, I know magicians are competitive but…" He noticed Ahti walking up the aisle towards him. "Got to go, I'll talk to you later."

"Wait—"

He put the phone back in his pocket as Ahti opened the door to the control booth.

"Hey, kid," Ahti said. "I've decided to give you a promotion—you're now our sound tech and stage manager. Oh, and you may need to handle the concession stand before the show. Do you know how to pop popcorn?"

"Promotion?"

"Sure. I like what you did with the lighting, and it's time for you to move up in the ranks. I'm sure you can handle it. We'll talk about a raise sometime."

"Thanks…" Ian muttered somewhat sarcastically.

"No problem, kid," Ahti said as he grabbed a metal folding chair and sat down next to him. Pulling out a handkerchief, Ahti wiped the sweat off his brow. "I'm surprised you could get that crap to work."

"It should hold together until we can get something better," Ian said. "I may need to swap things around once you start rehearsals."

"Do you live far from here?" Ahti asked. "I'm just wondering how long your commute is, since I may need you to be here at a moment's notice."

"It's not too bad. The compound is isolated but still close to major roads."

"Compound…I'm picturing something with barbed wire and machine gun nests. Are you part of one of those militias I hear about?"

Ian laughed. "No, but my dad's paranoid. He prepares for any eventuality. We have underground bunkers, an armory, food and water supplies, a large garage and maintenance shed, storage buildings—you name it."

"You must have a big family to manage a place like that."

"Just my parents and my sister, but they all moved out," Ian said. "It's just me trying to keep up with the place."

Ahti stood up. "Just you on that big compound? Are they coming back?"

"Maybe someday, but no time soon."

"Well, I'll let you get back to work," Ahti said as he moved to the door. "I already did most of the work on the sound system, so you should have that finished by end of day."

With mingled dread and excitement, Ian looked out the control booth window at the serpentine pile of cables on the stage. "I'll get right on it."

"Good," Ahti said. "And thanks for the talk. I pride myself on getting to know my staff."

————

Emily and Trudy sat on lawn chairs sipping tea in front of the ladder. Emily always loved the early morning as the sun started peeking over the mountains. It used to be the best time to be outdoors and not be blasted into submission by the heat. Now with the clouds overhead, she expected the coming summer months to allow her to sit outdoors even at midday.

She imagined that Trudy was enjoying the view of the ladder that, to the eyes of a chosen few, glowed just a few yards away.

"So, you can see it now?" Emily asked.

"Yep, and I've got to say, it is pretty impressive. It's nice of you to invite me over."

"It's nice to have company. Bailey's a teenager, so I don't expect her to be up until noon."

"So, how did it go with the whole cat versus dog thing?"

Emily laughed. "They actually got along. When I checked in this morning, Bailey was sleeping with the dog on one side of her and the mountain lion on the other—good thing it's a queen bed."

Emily held her hand over the ground, and a few rocks started to glow greenish-blue as sparks jumped between them. She raised her hand, and the rocks followed along through the air. Moving her fingers, she twirled them around above her palm. Then she tossed them from hand to hand before winding up and chucking them towards where the ladder was located. They vaporized in an instant when they hit, but in doing so created a very pleasing light show that resembled a small fireworks display.

"How does that look?" Emily said.

Trudy took another sip from her mug. "Not bad. But you only see half of the light show in our world. Trust me, it pops when you can see the other side."

"So, it's your baby that's giving you this power?"

"That's what Rachel and Koda have been telling me. I wonder if I'll still have it after he's born?"

"Yeah, I wonder how that works," Emily said. "Have you tried going through the ladder again? Could you bring another person with you?"

"Another person?"

"Like, if I held on to you when we walk through, would you take me with you?"

"Sort of like a trans-dimensional conga line?"

"Maybe just holding hands," Emily said. "If your son is giving you that power by being inside you, maybe it would transfer to another person as well."

"I haven't thought about that. Gavin can see the ladder, but he isn't supposed to touch it—Jonathan told him that it might be dangerous."

"What about someone who can't see the ladder...like me?"

"Koda said it was possible to get lost. There are seven ladders around the world; we could even end up in heaven."

Emily smiled. "I'd want to bring my camera for that." Putting her cup on the ground, she slapped the arms of the lawn chair and added: "Want to give it a try?"

"Now? What about Bailey?"

Emily stood up, holding her hand out to Trudy. "It's a safe town; besides, Bailey has a mountain lion, a German shepherd, and a loaded handgun for protection. It'll be fun. Nothing ventured, nothing gained."

Trudy took her hand, and they walked over to the ladder. "I only know how to get from here to the Greenland ladder. We should probably get our coats."

"Nah," Emily said. "Just a quick trip to prove it's possible, then we'll head back."

———

Trudy didn't know what to expect as they took another step into the ladder. She felt a thin veil of static electricity pass through her as they walked forward. Emily was still with her; so far, the experiment was a success. She thought about walking backward and returning to Nevada, but Emily now pulled her along.

"Can you see this?" Trudy shouted.

"Yes!" Emily yelled. "But not before I stepped into it. I guess it works."

In front of them, Trudy could make out what looked like another circle of light. She didn't believe that was the correct one, as Greenland was further north, but Emily pulled her towards it.

"Wait!" Trudy shouted over the din of the ladder. "You don't know where that goes!"

"Guess we'll find out!" Emily yelled in her ear. "This is fun!"

As they stepped through, they found that instead of it being early morning, it was still nighttime, with nothing but a full moon for illumination. It looked like a pleasant enough area from what Trudy could see, with well-maintained houses around a central square overlooking a pasture and the ocean. Nobody was out and about, so Trudy couldn't ask where they were.

"Look!" Emily pointed out to sea.

Trudy's eyes were adjusting; she could make out a possibly red and white passenger ship not far off shore. *Spirit of Tasmania* was emblazoned in bold letters across its hull.

"Well, this isn't Greenland," Trudy said. "Let's go."

"What's the hurry? I've never been to Tasmania. I wonder why they have a ladder here?"

"An abundance of Tasmanian devils?"

Emily laughed. "That's right!"

"Maybe I can bring a couple back for Reverend Brustad to practice his taxidermy skills on. Rachel could use new slippers." Trudy squeezed Emily's hand. "Well, we're burning moonlight. Let's give it another try."

———

Emily let Trudy guide her back into the ladder. The column of light was disorientating; it wasn't like a spotlight—more like standing in the middle of a freeway, with beams of light whizzing past her. It wasn't silent either; it brought back memories of Afghanistan. The Army had a small detachment of M1A2 Abrams tanks in the country, and their turbine engine-powered roar rumbling past was almost as deafening as the ladder.

Other ladders invaded the circle of the one they were currently in—equally bright semicircles arranged around the perimeter.

"Which way?" Emily shouted. She couldn't tell which was the Nevada ladder, or the Greenland one, or even the one they had just left. Other ladders remained to be explored, but she dutifully followed Trudy. If her guide got lost, they could keep bouncing between ladders for quite some time.

"This is it!" Trudy yelled in her ear.

They exited into a brisk cold that Emily had never experienced before. It looked to be late afternoon, but this cold was worse than nights in a tent in Afghanistan. She started to regret not taking a jacket along.

"I wonder where everyone is?" Trudy said.

"Koda told me they were moving everyone out of town as quickly as possible. Maybe it's a ghost town now?"

"I don't think they had a lot of residents to start with," Trudy said. "Did he say where they were going?"

"All over the world, even a few to Calamity."

Trudy looked up the hill. Rania was making her way down the rough path towards them, the furry hood of her parka bouncing up and down behind her head.

"That's Rania," Trudy said. "Her house is the green one at the top of the ridge."

"Koda told me about her. She's going to be moving to Calamity."

As Rania jogged down to meet them, her expression didn't look happy. "I wonder what the problem is?" Trudy said.

"Trudy!" Rania panted as she ran the last few yards to her. "What are you doing here?"

"Just thought we'd drop by for a visit." Trudy pointed to her friend. "This is Emily."

"You shouldn't be here," Rania said. "The ladder could collapse at any moment."

"What do you mean?" Trudy said.

"We've all moved down to the capital of Nuuk before we disburse. I was just picking up a few last things and then I was going to leave. Koda told me that the ladder will become unstable once the majority of people have left and could close without warning."

Trudy turned around to examine the ladder. "It does look smaller than I remember. Also, the color is changing from a bright white to the color of autumn leaves."

She jumped back as the ladder suddenly expanded out about five feet. Lightning started to rain down from the branches above that had previously spread out at regular intervals—just like a traditional ladder.

"What is it, Trudy?" Emily asked anxiously.

"Uh-oh, it's flaring. Rania's right, we need to get out of here or we'll be stuck a helluva long way from home."

Emily grabbed Rania's arm. "Koda said you were coming to Nevada. Come with us now."

"I—"

"The trip is amazing, and it'll save you a plane ticket," Trudy said as she took Emily's hand.

Trudy could tell they didn't have time for Rania to make up her mind. She grabbed her with her other hand and pulled both women towards the ladder.

"Go! Go! Go!" she yelled.

———

"We have a busy day ahead of us," Masters said to Edwin as they sat in his suite at the Sheraton. He had booked a room for Edwin just across the hall. Rachel's warning had spooked him, and he wanted Edwin nearby in case anything happened.

The door to the bathroom opened and Holly came out holding a copy of *Brides* magazine. "We need to hire a wedding planner."

"You were in there so long, I was going to call the coroner," Masters said. "Why pay for a wedding planner? Do it yourself."

"I don't know the area," she protested. "I need help since I'm certainly not going to get any from you."

"I can help you," Edwin volunteered.

"No, you can't!" Masters snapped. He had far too much on his plate try-ing to find this kid Ian and check on Ahti. He needed Edwin's help—and protection.

He looked over at Holly, who stood there with the magazine rolled up like she was going to whack him on the nose like a puppy that had peed the floor.

"So," he said, "you can run a multi-million-dollar tourist attraction, but you need help buying a cake? I've got more important things to do."

"There's a helluva lot more to planning a wedding than that, you dumb-ass!" Holly shot back. "And what's so damn important that you can't spend time with me like a normal engaged couple? Look out that window. What a view! It's so romantic. You were romantic—once."

Masters didn't even turn his head towards the spectacle of the Falls just outside the window. "I promised Trudy I'd check on something for her," he said. "It shouldn't take long, so set up some appointments later this week for the cake, or planner, or whatever the hell we need, and I'll be all yours."

"You promise, Jay?" Holly huffed and pointed to Edwin, "Promise in front of an angel."

"Have I ever lied in front of an angel?"

Edwin held up his index finger and looked like he was going to speak.

"There!" Masters cut him off. "Glad we have that settled."

———

Trudy could feel the Greenland ladder collapsing in around them as they ran towards what she hoped was its Nevada equivalent. While the column of light looked only about twenty feet across from the outside, it was much larger from the inside.

She hoped she hadn't lost her direction as they ran the last few feet to-wards the semi-circle of light that hopefully was home.

She knew she had chosen correctly when they stepped out of the blazing light of the ladder and saw Emily's Harley sitting under the covered carport. "Glad we're not in Tasmania," she muttered.

Rania looked stunned and didn't say anything, while Emily went over and kissed her bike on the gas tank. "I'm home, dear," she said. "How's my Fat Boy?"

"Emily's very passionate about her motorcycle," Trudy said, trying to relieve some of Rania's tension. She seemed confused by everything around her—an environment much different than her home.

"This is Nevada?" Rania said. "It's almost as barren as Greenland, but instead of green it is all brown."

"It took some getting used to for me as well," Trudy said. "I'm from a part of Wisconsin where it's all pine and birch forest, so this is completely new to me." She patted Rania on the arm. "But I got used to it. You will too."

"Is Koda here?" Rania said.

"We'll find him and let him know you're in Calamity. He'll be thrilled."

"No need," Emily said. "Here he comes now."

Koda didn't even take the time to open the gate that Emily installed in her fence but jumped over it—no small feat for the diminutive Inuit. He ran over to Rania and gave her a big hug.

As they stood there embracing Trudy looked at the ladder. It seemed to have sparked a bit and grown a little brighter when the two of them were reunited.

She smiled. Another addition to the family…

CHAPTER SEVEN

Ian sat on the living room sofa watching the *Mystery Science Theater 3000* presentation of *Santa Claus Conquers the Martians*. The movie was crap, but the banter by the robots was priceless. Crow T. Robot was in the middle of reciting "A Patrick Swayze Christmas" when the alarm sounded, warning that the perimeter sensors protecting the compound had been tripped.

He grudgingly grabbed the remote and brought up the security cameras on the television. A car was barreling down the gravel road towards the house. He wasn't sure who it was, or why they ignored the sign at the entrance to use the intercom and wait for the okay to enter. The car was going too fast, and he didn't have time to disengage the spike strips that ran across the road. He couldn't hear it, but his imagination filled in the sound as the car's four tires blew out almost simultaneously and the vehicle skidded into a tree.

"Oh, shit!" Ian said as he grabbed a shotgun off the wall and ran out the door.

He hustled down the road, jumping over the laser sensors as he went. The car's grill was crushed; radiator antifreeze streamed onto the ground. The driver's side door opened. A man fought his way around a deflating airbag and fell to the ground.

"Ahti?" Ian stammered as he approached.

"Hey, kid, can you give me a hand up?"

Ian reached down and grabbed Ahti's arm, pulling him to a standing position. "I'm so sorry," Ian said, hoping he wasn't now unemployed. "I wasn't expecting you."

"That's quite some defensive system you have," Ahti said as he looked up and pointed to a machine gun twenty feet up a tree with the muzzle directed towards him.

"It follows movement. Don't worry, it won't fire unless someone from the command bunker clears the safety. Although, my sister has been known to use them during deer season."

Ahti reached in and popped the trunk. "Help me with my bags."

"Bags?"

"I'll be bunking with you, kid. I thought we could ride-share to work, although it would have been easier when my car had inflated tires."

"You don't have a place to live?" Crap, his boss was destitute!

"When I was out in Vegas I had a suite at Kali's hotel. Her place was a shithole, but convenient. Being an owner-operator is a new adventure for me. I'm piling all my funds into the theater—and your salary. I'm sure that's worth a guest room for a few months."

"Uh," Ian said as they walked around to the trunk. Ahti motioned for him to start unloading the suitcases.

"Speaking of convenience," Ahti said, "where's the closest bar?"

———

"Okay, so here's the deal," Masters said to Edwin as they sat at a Burger King across the street from Ripley's Believe it or Not! Odditorium. "I bet you're thinking that I'm clandestinely looking for a site for a new Mysterium and that I'm lying to Holly about getting married, just to get us out here."

"The thought has crossed my mind."

Masters took a bite of his Whopper, critically examined what remained, and put it down with a frown. "Pickles. I hate pickles. They always put too many of them on their burgers. Guess I should have asked for it my way, huh, like on the commercial?" Edwin returned a thousand-yard stare. "Never mind. Rest easy, pal, I'm not here scouting for a new Mysterium, so that hack museum of oddities over there has nothing to worry about."

"Are you lying to Holly about the wedding?" Edwin asked. "Because she loves you, and I don't want to see her hurt. And frankly, it's hard enough for her to be around you when you're not lying to her."

"It's for her own good."

"Lying seldom benefits the person being lied to."

"This does. We need to find a young guy who's working for the Amazing Ahti before Ahti violates labor laws and kills him. While we're at it, we need to check out what mischief Ahti and the senator are getting into."

"So why should Holly not be made aware of this? And why didn't you leave her someplace safe like Calamity?"

"I might need her to satisfy my manly desires."

Edwin rolled his eyes.

"Wow, I didn't know angels could make a face like that."

"Really, why did you want her along? At least make an attempt at being honest."

Masters felt the words coming up his throat like vomit and being forced into his mouth and over his tongue like a bad pickle.

"I want her close because...I love her."

———

"I hate him," Trudy said to Rachel as they walked into Kali's hotel lobby.

"He's your father," Rachel countered.

"Wasn't my choice," Trudy said. "We could have handled things in Niagara. What's he going to screw up now for his own greedy purposes when he gets around Ahti and the senator?"

Rachel stopped and looked up at her. "He's protecting you."

"I thought that was your job?"

"Well," she said, "I am better at it, but I also know when someone is trying to protect someone they love. It's what I do."

"Okay, Miss Know It All, should I just forget how he screwed the entire human race for his own selfish gains and make nice to the scumbag?"

"Yes," Rachel said.

Trudy turned away. "Wrong answer."

"You need to forgive him."

"Argh!" Trudy shook her closed fists in the air, causing hotel guests to stop and stare while some started pointing at Rachel in recognition. "No, I don't. I'm not an angel. I can't just forgive and forget. I especially can't forgive him for jeopardizing his grandson."

"Trudy, he didn't know you were pregnant. He did what he thought was right to keep you and Gavin safe."

"He left me," Trudy softly said. "He left me before I was born. Why wouldn't he do that with his grandson if he did it to his own daughter?"

Rachel grabbed her by the arm and steered her over to a quiet part of the lobby.

Trudy started crying as she looked around at all the happy tourists that had come to see the destroyed Vegas Strip where hundreds of people had recently died. "He left me and didn't show up for twenty-one years."

Rachel caught Trudy's eyes. "You were too distraught to notice when you were telling us your vision of Niagara Falls that when you said your son's name will be Jay, your father collapsed in shock. All he could do was repeat his name. I've never seen him that way before."

"So, what does that mean? He likes the idea of a little mini-me named Jay?"

"All humans have an opportunity for redemption. Trust that his mistakes with you will not flow over to your son."

Trudy shook her head. "He'll have to prove it. I'll give him enough rope, and he'll hang himself—probably along with the rest of us."

She had to look away as Rachel continued to stare at her with a sad expression. Rachel was her best friend and the purest soul she had ever known. Anything she said had to be taken with great seriousness.

"Okay," Trudy finally said. "I'll forgive the asshole. Just stop looking at me with those sad puppy dog eyes."

Rachel broke into a wide grin. "It worked!"

Ahti pushed his fingers into the mattress of what was supposed to be a teen girl's bedroom but resembled something belonging to Rambo. It felt soft enough, and his hand didn't get snared in a booby trap, so he assumed it was okay.

"Your sister has an odd way of decorating," Ahti said as he looked around the room. A large poster from the movie *American Sniper* was plastered over the closet door. On a wall by the window was a display of Bowie knives. Several specialty firearms magazines were spread out on the small desk along with a pair of brass knuckles as a paperweight. "No boy band posters?"

"My sister's not into girlie stuff," Ian said, pointing to a *Band of Brothers* poster on the far wall. "She's more of a guts and glory kind of gal. By the way, I removed all the live ammo and grenades, so you don't have to worry about anything exploding while you're sleeping."

"Thanks," Ahti said, shuddering. "If the rest of the compound is as formidable as your sister's room, I don't think you'll have any problem keeping out the riffraff once our show at the Pantomime becomes famous."

"Do you think it will?"

"Sure, I had the best act on the Strip, and that whole thing with the senator just added to the public's curiosity. They'll eat it up."

"Oh, that reminds me," Ian said as he walked over to the desk and picked up a well-read copy of *Soldier of Fortune* magazine that Bailey had left in his truck. Ahti's smiling face was on the cover with the tag line MAGICIAN, MERCENARY, OR MURDERER? "Can you sign this for my sister? She's a big fan of yours."

Ahti smiled. "Certainly, kid. What's her name?"

"Bailey."

"Like Baileys Irish Cream?"

"Yeah, but no 's' on the end. Just plain Bailey."

Ahti pulled a pen out of his pocket and signed it. He was flattered that he even had the teen girl audience—or at least one of them. "Glad to make the kid's day. Where's she at now?"

"They decided to go out west for an extended hunting trip," Ian said.

"Deer?"

"Mountain lion to start with, I hear."

"Mountain lions," Ahti said. "Mean animals. I hope she bags one."

Ian smiled. "I'm sure she will."

Rachel took Trudy's hand as they walked down the third floor of the concourse that wrapped its way around Kali's hotel lobby. Her closest human friend was still upset, and she hoped that where they were going would cheer her up.

"We haven't seen Bill for months," Rachel said. "This is a big day for him."

Hearing Bill's name seemed to calm Trudy. "Yeah, it's not every day you get to open a restaurant on the Vegas Strip. I just hope they don't make fun of him. He gave us jobs when we needed them. His chili may be toxic, but he has a big heart."

"Koda has been watching over him," Rachel said. "He made sure that Bill—and his patrons—are protected; someone else is doing the cooking."

Just beyond the Prada store, they found it. The hot pink neon sign on the storefront proudly proclaimed Cluck and Grunt in classic script letters, with the tag line "Heavenly food at down to earth prices" underneath.

"Look at all the people!" Rachel said, noticing what must have been a hundred tourists waiting patiently outside for the grand opening.

"Poor saps," Trudy said. "I hope the gift shop stocks Imodium."

All the people in line started talking amongst themselves and pointing at her while taking out their phones to snap photos. She still wasn't used to her newfound celebrity and could only smile and give a little wave as they approached the security guard protecting the front door.

"We're here to see Bill," Rachel said to the man who towered over her.

"Are you on the guestlist?" the guard said, apparently not recognizing her, as he pointed to his clipboard.

"Former employees," Trudy spoke up. "Not that we're proud of it."

The door opened, and Koda stuck his head out. "It's okay, young protector, they are with me."

The guard waved them inside. The seating area was done up like a Fifties diner with a black and white checkerboard floor, pendant lighting, and shiny chrome galore. A way-cool Wurlitzer bubbler jukebox against the far wall, blasting out Buddy Holly's "That'll Be the Day." Photos of Fifties icons—Elvis, Marilyn Monroe, Marlon Brando, James Dean—decorated the walls. Formica and chrome tables and plush, red leather booths completed the illusion of having stepped back in time.

"Well, Bill has finally gotten his wish," Trudy said. "He always wanted a traditional diner."

"He is very excited," Koda said. "He's speaking to the media now in the kitchen. I will let him know that you are here."

Rachel went over to one of the Formica tables and pulled a plastic covered menu from the metal clip that held it in place near the plastic yellow and red condiment bottles.

Trudy looked over her shoulder as they scanned the menu.

"Bowl of Red," Trudy read aloud. "Himalayan Yak Chili and Iron Skillet Corn Bread, twenty-seven dollars. Yikes!"

Rachel laughed at an appetizer item: "Angels on Horseback—Delta de l'Ebre Oysters Rolled in Pancetta. We never had that on the menu before. Why is it called that?"

"Diner lingo doesn't always make sense, but Bill likes it." Trudy pointed to another one: "Noah's Boy with Murphy Carrying A Wreath? Iberian Ham, La Bonnotte Potato with Cabbage—I don't get it."

"Ham was one of Noah's sons," Rachel explained.

Trudy pulled the menu out of her hands and tossed it on the table. "At thirty-five bucks, I still wouldn't get it."

Rachel noticed Kim walking towards them with a big smile on her face. "Thanks for coming," she said. "Bill will be done with the interviews in a couple minutes. So, how do you like the place?"

"It's a lot fancier than the one in Creekside," Trudy said, "and it doesn't have that lingering odor and grease buildup of the original. I guess that takes time to perfect."

"Trudy," Kim said, "your father told me that you will be taking over as the Mysterium point person in Vegas. Congratulations!"

"Yeah, lucky me," Trudy said.

Rachel poked her elbow into Trudy's ribs. It was an old Masters communication method that she had learned from Holly. "She'll love the chance to be involved with her father's dream and help people learn more about angels."

"From my viewpoint," Kim said, "it will be nice to work with someone that's—"

"Not an asshole?" Trudy filled in.

"To put it mildly," Kim said. "The good news is that Denise has pulled out all the stops. We have new construction crews being added every day to the site. The building exterior should be completed in a few weeks. She has also sub-contracted a dozen additional fabrication firms for the interior. I expect we'll start the load-in in a month, and if testing goes well, we'll be ready to open most of the facility in two months tops."

"So, what changed?" Trudy said. "My father was having a conniption the other day about the delays."

Kim's smile evaporated. "I'm sorry, guys, but Denise called the senator."

Rachel blew out her cheeks. While she welcomed the Mysterium revealing the world of angels to the populace at large, she didn't like that Lucifer was involved. She also needed to protect Trudy from the ramifications of this further cooperation with Satan. "What did he want in return?"

"Nothing, as far as I know," Kim said. "The senator is quite enamored with the good reverend."

"Birds of a feather," Trudy mumbled.

Rachel spotted a man in a white chef's jacket walking towards them. "Bill?"

"Rachel! Trudy!" Bill said as he came over and gave them a big hug.

Rachel was surprised that Bill didn't have his typical unwashed smell that usually preceded him. Also, his chef jacket was sparkling white, without a stain to be seen. Bill was clean-shaven and sported a trendy haircut. He'd also lost some weight.

"I hardly recognize you," Trudy said. "Vegas *has* been good to you."

"It sure has," he said. "Thanks to Kim here, and Koda, I've learned a lot. I'm leaving in a few weeks to study at Le Cordon Bleu in Paris—oh, and the Food Network is asking me to host a show for them."

"And," Kim added, "he's looking forward to the classic Cluck and Grunt that will be in the Mysterium on the recreated streets of Creekside."

"I sure am," Bill agreed. "It's nice here, but I'm looking forward to having my old place back, even if it's only a... uh, what is that word you use, Kim?"

"Facsimile?"

"Yeah, that," Bill said. "I miss my old cook stove and pots. I'm working with the designers to show them exactly how everything used to be."

Rachel noticed that Bill had started to tear up. "Are you okay?" she asked.

"Trudy," Bill said, "will your father be around? I want to thank him."

"Thank him?" Trudy said. "Why?"

"If it weren't for him, I wouldn't have this opportunity. I wouldn't have this Cluck and Grunt or the one being built at the Mysterium. I would never have friends like Koda and Kim to help me. I'd just be a fry cook in a little town in the middle of nowhere."

Rachel noticed that Trudy was unusually quiet.

"I'll be sure to tell him," Trudy softly replied.

"This must be the place," Masters said to Edwin as they pulled their rental car into a pot-holed parking lot next to the Pantomime Theater. He had a hard time finding the theater because he assumed it was with all the other attractions on the Canadian side. Fortunately, there was a mime attempting to extricate himself from an invisible box on a plaza near the Ferris wheel. He knew exactly where it was but wouldn't break character in front of his small audience of bored tourists to tell him. Instead, his white-gloved hands pointed frantically across the river to indicate that they were in the wrong country.

They found the theater on Buffalo Avenue, directly across from a waste-water treatment plant.

"Are you sure this is the correct location?" Edwin said. "It doesn't seem to be in current use."

"That's what the girl at the gas station said. Let's go have a look."

On the far side of the theater, there was a ladder up against the marquee. A mini-skirted woman whose thighs looked oddly familiar to Masters stood on a rung ten feet in the air. He walked directly under the ladder and looked up.

As he continued to stare up the woman's skirt, she looked down at him.

"Reverend Masters! What perfect timing. Can you hand me the lower case 'i,' please?"

"Daeva?"

"You know this demon?" Edwin said, moving closer.

Masters held an arm out to stop him. "Yeah, she's pretty handy with a pitchfork."

"I'm sorry about that, Reverend," she said. "I was under orders not to kill you, but I needed to get you out of the way so I could kill Kim Kali."

"Oh, in that case, my sore back was worth it. Too bad it didn't work."

"Reverend"—she pointed to the box with large plastic letters— "the letter 'i,' please."

Masters looked down at the box. Rooting around, he found the letter and handed it up to her.

"Thank you," Daeva said. as she finished the lettering and climbed down the ladder.

Standing back to admire her work, she asked, "What do you think?"

Masters looked at the marquee, which now read: DAEVA, THE MISTRESS OF DARK DELUSIONS PRESENTS A DEMONIC JOURNEY THROUGH DEPRAVITY, WITH COMICAL INTERLUDES BY THE AMAZING AHTI.

Masters snickered. "I like it! But more importantly, what will Ahti think?"

Daeva smiled. "He'll be pissed when he sees it. Which, knowing his usual level of intoxication, might be a month from now."

"Oh," Masters said, realizing he'd forgotten something. "Have you met Edwin?"

"We may have met many eons ago," she said. "I think I've seen him groveling around the Tyrant's Throne from time to time. He's remarkably restrained, this one. Most loyalists would be turning all big and sparkly right about now."

Edwin spoke up. "My friend the reverend doesn't wish it. If it were not for him, I would send you to the pit this very moment."

"Well, then, I must thank the reverend," Daeva said. She sashayed over and planted a big wet kiss on his mouth.

"I'm engaged," he muttered through the lip-lock.

"What a pity," she said, patting his chest. "So, what brings you to Niagara? Did you hear about our show?"

"Actually," Masters said, "I'm looking around for a suitable spot for a new Mysterium."

Daeva imitated the mime by pointing to the other side of the river. "Smart people build over there."

"But not you?"

"Ahti's a dumbass."

"That's a given," Masters agreed, "but the land does appear to be less expensive over here."

"Since when do you have money problems?" Daeva huffed. "The Imperator will pay for anything you desire. Ahti gets this shithole as his only reward, and I get stuck here with him. I used to have a nice gig in Vegas—a beautiful suite and reserved tables at the best restaurants. Now look at me. It's pathetic." She pointed towards Edwin. "I can't even get into a good fight with a loyalist nowadays."

"I have an idea," Masters said. "Why don't you work for me?"

"Reverend," Edwin cautioned, placing a hand on Masters' arm, "that's not wise."

Daeva gave a little chuckle. "Well, your pet loyalist isn't turning all sparkly, but he is taking on a pleasant shade of red. So, Rev, what do you have in mind?"

"We can have a theater as part of the Mysterium that you may operate as you like," Masters said. "You can show off for the tourists, along with the special perk of sticking it to Ahti. Until it's completed, I'll help you find a vacant theater to perform at."

Daeva crossed her arms under her inviting bosom. "That's an interesting proposition, but where will we be located?"

Masters made his best pantomime point across the river.

Daeva looked up at the sign. "I know exactly where to leave my resignation notice."

———

"She's a rebel," Edwin said as they got back in the car. "You can't trust her."

"She can trust me even less," Masters said. "Ever hear the phrase divide and conquer?"

"It' a translation of the Latin maxim, *divide et impera,* or divide and rule," Edwin said. "Uriel taught me that in his course on human history that he has been giving to new community members. It's quite an interesting phrase that has been used to both empower a sovereign by breaking down the factions that, together, might be able to defeat him, and, in equal measure, to destroy that very same sovereign."

"Whatever," Masters said. "In this case, the point is that Daeva is the brains of this misguided magic show, and we just stole her out from under Ahti. It'll drive him nuts!"

"You have a very unusual thought process," Edwin concluded as they pulled out of the lot. "We still need to find this boy, Ian, so that he doesn't fall victim to Ahti's wrath."

"Well, we have the address of where he lives. Let's drive out there and talk to him. It sounds like it's secluded, so we can have a conversation without the chance of Ahti seeing us talking to the kid."

———

Ahti sat on the camo bedspread in his borrowed room while dialing the senator. He never dreamed it would be this easy. The kid's parents were going to be gone for a while, and by the time they returned, they wouldn't recognize the place.

"Ahti," the senator said. "Good news, I hope?"

"I found the perfect place for your academy, and it's already partially built out as a fortification."

"You found something that quickly?"

"It belongs to my lighting technician's family, the Tannahills. They are full-on doomsday fanatics. This place has underground bunkers, its own water and food supplies—not to mention an excellent perimeter defense system, as I, unfortunately, found out the hard way."

"Is the family on our side?"

"I think the kid is," Ahti said. "The rest are out on some extended hunting trip."

"How big is this family?"

"Just the kid, his parents, and their heavily armed teenage daughter."

"It's important to find out exactly where they are. If the boy is on our side, you should be able to acquire that information without too much difficulty."

"Uh," Ahti said, "I'm not sure the family is going to be delighted at having their property seized. It might turn the kid against us, although I'm more afraid of his little sister."

"I am the master of persuasion, Ahti," the senator said. "And I always get what I want."

"I never doubted that for a moment, Senator," Ahti brown-nosed.

"See that you don't. Good work, Ahti. Despite Corson's whining, I knew my faith in you wasn't misplaced."

"Thank you," Ahti said as he heard the line disconnect. He reached for a bottle of Wild Turkey that he had brought along and guzzled it down. Now he needed to go find the kid and try to explain what was going to happen before the construction crews showed up and were shot dead.

"I'm bored," Bailey said as she sat on a lawn chair in Emily's backyard. Emily sat next to her, tossing glowing rocks into the ladder, as Maggie and Bailey's mountain lion chased each other around the yard.

"We could go into Goodsprings," Emily suggested, "but the only place there is the bar, and you're too young."

"Any gun ranges around?" Bailey inquired. "I've got a little money on my debit card. We can fire off a few mags—it'd be fun to go up against an Afghan veteran."

Emily looked like she was going to agree until a pink Cadillac pulled up near the fence, and two women she hadn't met before got out and waved. Bailey could see that one was glowing and the other wasn't.

"Hey, guys," the blonde woman said, "we wanted to stop by and welcome our new resident to Calamity."

Bailey and Emily stood up while the visitors came through the gate. The human woman looked friendly enough, although she resembled a real estate agent with her perfectly styled hair and expert makeup.

"Hi, I'm Kris," the woman said, casting a worried glance at the mountain lion. "I heard you had quite a trip."

"Didn't even pack a toothbrush," Bailey said.

"Annie here," Kris said, "is an angel."

"I could tell from her glow," Bailey said, looking Annie over. "Nice to meet you."

"Since you didn't have time to pack," Kris said, "I was wondering if you'd like to go into Vegas with me and find you something to wear."

Bailey's eyes lit up. "Do they have a Bass Pro Shop?"

Kris gave a bewildered look. "Uh, why don't you just relax and let me do the shopping, honey."

Annie spoke up. "I'll be attending a community meeting, or else I would have loved to come along." Looking over at Emily, she asked, "Would you like to join them?"

Emily gave a barely perceptible grimace. "I'll stay right here and watch the critters. I get claustrophobic in crowded malls."

———

Trudy sat on a bench in Salazar's tent waiting for Gavin to finish healing a group of new residents that had arrived the previous day. She liked that they didn't need to venture into Vegas for him to perform his miracles. It was much safer and less taxing for him to stay in New Creekside, close to the ladder—which, aside from being the source of his power, protected from harm. He was doing what he loved, and she envied him for having an actually useful gift.

Rachel was off to some angelic meeting at the nearly finished Community Hall. The angels had to put up with a lot, being around annoying humans twenty-four hours a day. It was good they got some alone time where they could do angelic things—whatever those might be—as she imagined some heavenly version of Sheepshead or beer pong.

Three coyotes came into the tent and started lapping up water from the stream. They seemed entirely unconcerned about the nearby humans as they drank. One of them padded over to Trudy and spun around twice before lying down at her feet.

Trudy went back to reading the Mayo Clinic Guide to a Healthy Pregnancy when her vision started to blur. She tried to shake it off, but when everything came back into focus, she was no longer in the tent.

She found herself sitting on a bench in a glass-enclosed cabin that was she guessed about ten stories up. Looking around, she realized she was in a giant Ferris wheel that towered over the surroundings and offered a spectacular view of Niagara Falls.

Trudy was looking towards the Falls, but something in her felt she needed to turn her head. Down below and across an open plaza, and a crowded street, a group of perhaps a thousand people stood in a vacant lot.

The wheel stopped for a moment, she assumed to load/unload another cabin, and she was able to observe a few more details. There was a stage in the middle of the construction area with a rack of gold shovels on one side and several rows of occupied chairs on the other.

She recognized the distinguished-looking man behind the podium with the silver hair and signature custom-tailored suit: none other than Senator Bill Stevenson. The crowd clapped enthusiastically at what was obviously an intro-duction. Stevenson gestured towards the dignitaries on the dais; she saw her father and another, much younger man stand up and walk to the podium. The unknown man, who looked to be in his twenties, hung back while Stevenson gave her father a big handshake and hug.

She guessed that the vacant lot was a new site for a Mysterium. He was supposed to use a Niagara Mysterium as a cover story—not cut a deal.

Trudy felt her stomach churn, which could have been due to several things: the motion of the wheel turning again, the height, being pregnant—or, most likely, the disgust she felt that her father was being praised by Satan.

She wanted to pound on the glass and get her father's attention and flip him off, but the vision cleared, and she was once again sitting on the wooden bench in Salazar's tent.

The coyote lying at her feet must have sensed something was wrong as she sat there shaking in anger. It pushed her ankle with its muzzle and looked up at her.

Trudy reached down and scratched it behind the ear.

––––––

Ian was attempting to make Ahti a ham sandwich as requested when the alarm went off. He turned on the kitchen television and brought up the entrance security camera. Two men were standing next to their car; he recognized one of them from his many TV appearances: Reverend Jay Masters.

"What was that, kid?" Ahti said as he walked down the stairs. "That's not going to be echoing through my skull every afternoon, is it?"

Ian quickly turned off the television. "The security alarm must be buggy. I think you broke a sensor when you drove in. I'll go take a look."

He handed Ahti his sandwich. "Hopefully it's something simple. I'll be back in a few minutes."

"Sure, kid," Ahti said as he opened the refrigerator door. "Got any beer?"

––––––

"I see someone," Masters said.

"Odd," Edwin said, "that he's coming to us and not simply allowing us to drive in."

"Looks like a young guy. I bet he's the one we're hunting for."

The boy trotted up to them. "Reverend Masters, I'm Ian Tannahill. I guess Bailey told you how to find me."

"Yeah, she said you were out in the middle of nowhere, and this certainly qualifies."

"Let's move over here," Ian said, waving them down the road fifty feet. "There're no cameras on this spot. Ahti is staying with me. My sister was talking some nonsense about him being dangerous. Is that true?"

"Very dangerous," Edwin said. "He's a demon and would kill you without a moment's hesitation."

"This is Edwin." Masters jerked a thumb at his angelic assistant. "He's an angel, so I'll take his word for it. Personally, I think a bottle of bourbon has more to fear from Ahti than you do."

"What your sister was attempting to tell you," Edwin continued, "is that Emily fought Ahti in Las Vegas. He doesn't believe that she, or any human, should be able to perform miraculous feats. That is why he attempted to kill her. If he finds out that you can move objects through space-time, he will certainly attempt to kill you as well."

Ian stood there for a moment before saying, "My sister's a freak but she knows everything about survival, and if she's saying Ahti is dangerous, that's good enough for me.

"But what do I do? He's moved in. I'll be around him a lot, and I can't control when I make things disappear. If I do it in front of him, and he notices, I'm toast."

Masters thought back to Emily being roasted alive by Bill's BBQ stand that Ahti threw at her, only to be healed by Gavin. "You don't know how accurate that statement is," Masters said. "Just play it cool, kid."

"Don't call me kid," Ian snapped. "Ahti always calls me kid. I hate it."

"Okay, okay! Ian, you do the lighting for that fire trap theater, right?"

"Yeah, but it needs a lot of work. I'm also the sound tech and stage manager—and concession stand cashier. Want to buy some Goobers?"

Masters smiled at hearing that. He wished he could cut his staff down as thin, but Holly would screech at him nonstop, and no amount of monetary savings was worth that torture.

"Here's what I'm thinking, ki—uh, Ian. Let Ahti stay here in the lap of hick luxury and you'll move to the theater. Tell him that you have so much to do that you need to work nonstop 24/7. Throw some shit in a suitcase, grab a sleeping bag, and move out. Trust me, he'll gladly toss you the keys to get more work out of you, and also have his own bachelor pad."

Ian looked at his feet. "Ahti is friends with the senator. I can't go against the senator; he's a good man. He's done so much for the world already."

Edwin started to speak, but Masters waved him down. "Listen, Ian. Ahti shot the senator. Ahti may say he's the senator's friend, but I'm sure the senator must hold some grudge, no matter how forgiving he is. Unlike Ahti, I'm a true friend of Bill Stevenson. I've been to his home many times. He's bankrolling my Vegas Mysterium to the tune of over a hundred million dollars, and I expect he'll do the same with the one I'm planning for Niagara Falls. He's looked after my daughter and son-in-law like they were his own children. If you want to hitch your wagon to someone who is respected by the senator, then you'll choose me over Ahti."

This seemed to cheer Ian up as he stopped examining his shoelaces and looked at him. "I trust you. I'll go pack."

CHAPTER EIGHT

"I trust you?" Edwin snorted as they drove back towards Canada. "Oh, you're so trustworthy."

"Was that angelic sarcasm?" Masters said, "or were you just imitating my daughter?"

"I was sent here to be your friend and inspire you to be a better person, and all you do is dig yourself a deeper hole."

"This is like fracking in the Dakotas," Masters said. "Pump some crud into the holes until what was solid shatters and reap then the rewards."

"Rachel warned me about you."

"You trust the word of someone who wears muskrat slippers? And why would you be mad at me?"

"You're misleading the boy," Edwin said. "Telling him that you are the senator's friend when you're not...are you?"

"Wow, I must be good if an angel can't tell when I'm lying." Masters smiled. "No, I'm not Lucifer's buddy, but this Ian kid is obviously star-struck by the senator. I needed to transfer his loyalty from Ahti to me to get him out of there. It was for his own good."

"You could have told him that Satan inhabits the senator now."

"He wouldn't believe it at this point. You saw how enamored he is of the senator. I've seen a lot of that lately. Everyone has started following him because he came back from the dead. Sounds sort of familiar in a way—"

"He imitates true miracles," Edwin said. "He is a fraud. You, of all people, should know that."

"That's my point. My son-in-law did the grunt work in healing the senator's body, and Satan takes the credit. Now he's a messiah to multitudes of people, including that Ian kid. We have to be careful when we crush his idol. I'll know when the time is right."

Masters looked over at Edwin for a moment. "So, do you trust me now?"

Edwin gave an audible sigh.

Masters smiled. "I'll take that as a yes."

———

Bailey stood in front of the Dillard's department store at the Fashion Show Mall, holding a bag containing a sundress that Kris had picked out for her. She hated the thing before she even tried it on. It was so flimsy and short, she felt nearly naked standing before the dressing room mirror; she hadn't even shaved her legs. Kris told her that it made her look cute and complemented her red hair—even more reason to despise it.

Kris had wandered off to try to set up an appointment for a manicure for the two of them. Bailey couldn't think of a single reason how having pink nail polish would improve her marksmanship or deer-gutting ability. Still, Kris was kind to her, so she decided to go along with it, although she did want to stop at a Walgreens for some nail polish remover before returning to Calamity.

As she waited, she felt the hair on the back of her neck stand up, causing her to turn. An elderly man was strolling towards the Dillard's entrance. At first glance, he didn't appear any different than the other old men she had seen walking around Vegas. He was skinny, liver-spotted, and wore a cotton sweater to keep himself warm in the mall's cranked-up air conditioning.

What made her look again was the mist that surrounded him from head to toe, flowing around and through him. Even though it was only vapor, it seemed to weigh him down, causing his whole posture to slump so that his face was pointing towards the ground. Every so often the fog would condense into a spear-like apparition and jab itself through his chest, causing him to wince. She alone seemed to be privy to the phenomenon; other customers paid no heed.

She followed the man into the men's clothing aisles as the mist continued to swirl around him. Unsure what was going on or what she could do to help, she decided to cut him off in the underwear aisle and ask.

"Excuse me, sir," she said.

The man looked up at her. "Leave us."

"Pardon?"

"Leave us be. We live here."

"You live in Dillard's?" Figuring the old dude was senile she thought about leaving him alone, but something caused her to stand firm. "I'm Bailey. What's your name?" she said. "Is there something I can do for you?"

"Many names," he said, his eyes darting nervously about for an escape route. "Many names that we will not tell you. Leave us alone. We know what you are. Don't make us leave."

"You know what I am?" Bailey said, not sure she wanted to hear the answer. "What am I?"

"*Exorcista!*" he shouted at the top of his lungs. "*Maledicti exorcista!*"

The man finally met her eyes, and his expression of terror cleared for a moment. "Help me," he gasped as his pupils dilated as if he were in the dark.

Bailey stepped back as the man broke eye contact and started to wail. "Leave us!" he shouted as shoppers stopped to stare.

Bailey dropped her shopping bag. She had no idea how to help the man, but her hands rose in response to his cry. The mist touched her palms, and she realized that the feeling wasn't one of vapor like when she walked through Jonathan, but a material presence—one she was able to grasp and hold on to.

Taking a firm grip, she pulled as hard as she could, and the mist followed with her. The man cried out in pain as she continued to rip the cloud away from him, pulling hand over hand like a rope.

"You're hurting us!" he shouted.

The mist gave way and separated from the man, causing Bailey to fall backward into a shirt rack, knocking it over.

The old man collapsed to the ground as the mist that only she could see broke into many individual clouds; one of them moved closer until it was just inches from her face. It solidified until she was able to make out some details. A visage that she knew would haunt her dreams for the rest of her life materialized. Although its features were not well defined, the searing hatred the demon held towards her was palpable. She had never seen such anger in a being.

Bailey screamed as the now separate entities, including the one that was near her, scattered, causing every display rack throughout the men's clothing section to crash to the floor.

People came over to kneel by the man. Before her view was cut off, she saw him look at her and mouth the words "thank you."

Bailey felt herself being lifted from under the shoulders and brought to a standing position. Instead of letting go, the strong grip of two store detectives ushered her away to a back room.

"Hey, Dad," Bailey spoke into the office landline, which was on speaker. "Got any bail money?"

"What? Bailey, where are you?"

"Hello, Mr. Tannahill. This is Kris, I'm with the New Creekside community. We're at the Dillard's in Vegas. Bailey had a little misunderstanding with mall security. I think we have it all cleared up, but the police would like to have something in writing from Bailey's legal guardians saying it's okay for her to be released into my custody."

"Thanks for the explanation, whoever you are," said Brian. "Bailey, you tell me in your own words what happened."

Bailey looked around at the two police officers and a store detective that stayed with her in the back office. She didn't want to say too much in front of them. "A man was having a medical issue, and I tried to help him. I think I did, but it would have been easy for someone to get the wrong impression."

"Mr. Tannahill," one of the policemen said, "I'll e-mail you the form for your signature and the number to fax it to. It's purely for our records. I understand that Bailey is staying at the angelic encampment, so I have no issues with her safety."

"Okay, we're in Oklahoma right now," Brian replied. "We should be able to find a place with a fax machine. What do you know about the situation, officer?"

"We reviewed the store video and Bailey never touched the man, so despite how strange the incident was, we have no reason to hold her any longer."

"Strange?" Brian said. "What do you mean?"

"Every display in the men's clothing area was either knocked over or crushed. Several patrons had minor injuries. There was no visible cause for the destruction."

"Okay, that *is* strange."

"Considering where your daughter is staying, it doesn't seem all that unusual nowadays. But I would advise that she not come back into town. We'd hate to see her or others get hurt."

"Don't worry Mr. Tannahill," Kris said. "I'll take her right back to New Creekside and wait for your arrival."

"We'll step up our pace," Brian said. "Bailey, take care of yourself. We love you."

"Love you too, Dad," she said. The store detective pressed the speaker key, ending the call.

"Well," Kris said, "I guess no manicures for us today."

Bailey breathed a sigh of relief.

Ahti lay in the backseat of Ian's Bronco with a towel over his eyes. His head pounded, and the kid's driving wasn't helping.

"Can you manage not to hit *every* pothole?" Ahti asked.

"Sorry," Ian said, and then dumped his right front tire into a Grand Canyon-sized crevice.

Ahti groaned.

His dreaded talk with the kid about the compound went better than he expected, as he was able to avoid the entire subject. The dedicated lad wanted to move into the theater to work twenty-four hours a day. Smelling overtime, Ahti quickly changed him over to salaried. Meanwhile, he welcomed the chance to get the kid out of his hair and out of the compound.

116

A tow truck had been summoned to take Ahti's vehicle into the shop for repair, so even these friendly carpools would soon be over.

"You got everything you need, kid?" Ahti said.

"I have my stuff in the back. Thanks for this opportunity."

"Sure, whatever," Ahti said. "I like your enthusiasm. You'll need to unload the truck that arrives tomorrow with my stage gear from Vegas. Do you happen to know where I can buy a couple sharks?"

"Sharks?"

"Yeah, eight to ten feet long, big teeth, nasty disposition—*sharks.*"

"I have no idea."

"Well, call around today. Ask the humane society."

"We're almost to the theater," Ian said as the Bronco slowed.

"Do you see Daeva's car?" Ahti said. "We need to hit the ground running today."

"Uh, no car... and I don't think we'll be seeing her today."

"What do you mean?"

"Take a look at the marque," Ian said as he pulled the Bronco up to the curb.

Ahti removed the towel and sat up. Looking through the windshield, he sighed. Daeva, using exclamation points, created a fair representation of a hand—middle finger extended. The message next to it read: FUCK YOU AHTI. I QUIT. LOVE DAEVA.

———

Trudy sat in a conference room at Paradise Museum Design. About a dozen people were at the meeting, with Rachel sitting to her right. Her mind was elsewhere, and the speakers had the muffled mumble of grownups in those old Charlie Brown TV specials.

"What's your opinion, Trudy?" Denise said, snapping her back to reality.

She had no idea what the question was or even what the topic pertained to. All she kept seeing was her father hugging the senator and knifing everyone else, including her, in the back.

Rachel patted her hand and spoke up: "We're a bit concerned with the theoretical hourly ride capacity for the Battle of Creekside attraction. It seems that it is overly optimistic, as it doesn't take into consideration e-stops and slowdowns related to assisting handicapped riders. You mention 3,200 per hour, but it will most likely be closer to 2,900, at least in the beginning, with a longer cycle time."

Denise looked at her notes and then at one of her designers, who nodded back. "We'll recalculate that and let you know the updated figure. Thanks to the reverend, we're not planning a soft opening so I won't lie, the first few weeks will be difficult."

"If," Rachel continued, "my calculations are correct, then we'll have to expand the number of other attractions so that our guests are not milling about on Creekside's Main Street. My suggestion is that we use the banquet area of the Mysterium's Cluck and Grunt for hosting speakers from New Creekside. This will allow several hundred people at a time to interact with angels, and also be taken out of the traffic flow down the shopping corridor."

"That's an excellent idea, Rachel," Denise said with a smile. "Are you sure you haven't worked before in the theme park industry?"

Rachel blushed. "No, but I've always wanted to go to Disneyland."

Bill Stevenson took advantage of the Senate's typical three-day weekend to fly over to Niagara and check on his future academy. His original plan was this: with the cooperation of the governor and local government, he would start eminent domain proceedings, which would pretty much allow him to do whatever he wanted as long as he provided fair compensation to the displaced owner and that the facility he was constructing was a public facility. The academy would indeed be public...although perhaps it would not serve the public good.

Now that he stood on the grounds of what would become one of his most notable achievements, he wanted the compound even more—despite the site's current state.

"Kind of run-down, isn't it?" he muttered to Ahti. "I assume this is the best you could do."

Ahti responded in an injured tone. "It took a lot of work to find this property; it's not on the Multiple Listing Service, it has several built-in infrastructural advantages. I hope you're pleased."

"That remains to be seen," said Stevenson skeptically. "So, you said there is a young man that lives here, and his family is on vacation?"

"Yes, but we don't have to worry about him. He's sleeping over at the theater, so we have the place to ourselves."

"Have you watched the news today?" the senator asked.

"Never do—too depressing."

"There was an interesting piece on something that happened in Vegas yesterday. Apparently, several rebels had an unfortunate meeting with a teenage girl. She displaced them from their cherished human abode."

"Why should I be concerned about some lowlifes that can't afford to get an apartment?" Ahti said.

"Because the exorcist was a Bailey Tannahill from Niagara Falls, and she is staying with the loyalists at New Creekside." The senator saw that this caught Ahti's attention. "Odd coincidence that this is the Tannahill compound, isn't it, Ahti?" he added.

Ahti stammered, "I knew the girl had a violent streak, but I didn't think she'd attack rebels—or even had the power to do so."

"More is going on here than I anticipated," the senator said. "I would hate to fall into a loyalist trap because of your carelessness, Ahti."

"I had no idea—"

"Drunken fools seldom have ideas," the senator said as he patted Ahti on the back. "Show me around the place. Perhaps I'll change my mind about you."

As they strolled down the gravel entry road, the senator scanned the area. "Machine gun nests and spike strips. I am impressed."

"They work, too," Ahti said, "although I have them disabled at the moment. The nearest tire store is ten miles away."

At the end of the drive was an open area with a farmhouse on one side and a multi-story metal barn on the other. Towards the back was a manmade hill that covered all but the front of one of the cargo containers.

"Very nice," Stevenson said. "I see that behind that bunker is open acreage. Does that belong to this property as well?"

"I believe so. They do a bit of farming when not preparing for Armageddon."

"I can see that land being used for our barracks and classrooms. To the right, just behind the barn, would be an excellent location for my temple to myself." He smiled a barracuda smile. "Okay, Ahti, you've convinced me. This is the perfect place, after all. We'll have a construction crew out here as soon as possible."

Ahti breathed a sigh of relief. Just then, five matte green busses pulled up. "What's all this?" he said.

Stevenson watched the "troops"—some of the personnel were advertised as having paramilitary backgrounds—exit the busses and head towards the various buildings. "I've arranged for you to have some company, Ahti," he said. "The boy and his family accomplished a lot on a limited budget, but we need to strengthen the security. I've brought in my private security detail to control access. The company I contracted with will bring it up to my standards. I have Corson rounding up all the rebels in the area, even the disgraced ones, and having them meet here."

Stevenson looked at Ahti. "You don't mind sharing a bed, do you?"

———

Bailey brushed the coat of one of Emily's mares as the sun started to dip behind the nearby mountains, casting shadows across the concrete floor of the stable. Helping Emily with her animals made her feel less of a burden, especially after her run-in with the law. Everyone was curious about her newfound "gift" for exorcism, but Calamity was demon-free and she had no one to practice on.

Her mountain lion padded its way into the barn but, surprisingly, created no concern amongst the horses. Bailey felt no tension in the horse she was grooming, even as the big cat entered the stall and curled up next to her.

"You know," she said to her cat, "not that long ago if I saw something like you, I would have shot and skinned you for your hide."

In response, the mountain lion rolled over for a belly rub. A paw the size of Bailey's hand batted her leg persistently.

"Still might…"

"So, what has changed?" said a voice from the barn's entrance. She turned to see Jonathan walk over and stand next to her.

"Everything," Bailey replied. "This whole place is weirding me out."

He smiled and bent down to scratch the feline. "You have a way with animals—and demons too, I hear. It would be odd if you weren't 'weirded out.'"

"I just don't know what to do with these superpowers," she said. "Do I become a demon hunter or open a zoo?"

Jonathan laughed. "Sometimes it takes a while to discover your gift, and even longer to know what to do with it. Tell me, do you know how Rachel's dog received her name?"

"No," Bailey said as she put down the brush. "We have a dog named Violet. I gave her the name Violet after the teenage girl from the movie *The Incredibles*."

"I haven't seen the movie," Jonathan admitted.

"She has superpowers…" Bailey stopped.

"And?"

Bailey was unsure why the naming of her dog now gave her goosebumps. "She…she didn't know what to do with them or how to be normal."

"Some things that may be considered coincidence," Jonathan said, "may also have meaning. You should watch the movie again. You might gain insight into your own condition."

"You were telling me about how Rachel's dog got its name," Bailey prompted.

"Ah, yes. Her human namesake, Maggie, is a dear friend. She no longer resides in this world, but I do get a chance to visit her from time to time. When I first met Maggie, she was a little older than you but just as confused as to where her life was heading." Jonathan sighed deeply. "Unfortunately for her, she made wrong choices and almost paid with her life. I met her in Nepal when she tried jumping off a cliff."

"Is that where she died?"

"No, that was much later. Did you see on television the funeral that was held in Wisconsin? The one the vice president attended?"

"The one with all the angels?" Bailey said. "I think everyone in the world saw that."

"That was Maggie's funeral."

"I'm sorry," Bailey said. "I've never been to a funeral. I can't imagine how sad it must be—to lose a friend."

"I was the one who greeted her after her transition. She knows now the joy that she was always searching for."

Bailey squatted down and scratched her cat's ear. "Wasn't she a war hero or something?"

"She was—and is—a warrior," Jonathan said solemnly. "Everything that happens now was set into motion by her. That is why a drug-addled prostitute that tried to committed suicide was given a funeral worthy of a world leader. The man who loved her most, Sheriff Winston—who also lives here in Calamity—named Rachel's dog Maggie in her honor.

"As all angels eventually do when we live in community, we befriend humans that we instinctively know to be trustworthy and honorable. That bond lasts throughout life and into eternity. For me, Maggie was that person on earth. That was the bond that created the Wisconsin ladder."

"Emily told me that Uriel was there when this one was created," she said. "That he is her angelic friend."

"That is correct," Jonathan acknowledged.

Bailey stood up and wiped her hands on her jeans. She realized that she didn't really have any friends. She had always been the loner—the outsider that never fit in at school. "I wish I had an angel friend," she said wistfully. "You say you go on being friends with your human companion, even after they kick—I mean, die?"

Jonathan nodded. "When humans transition to eternity, we do not stop being their friends and family, but we are free to form new bonds." The angel regarded her affectionately for a long moment with his soulful eyes. "I would like to show you how to develop your skills and the proper use of them. I'd love to be your friend."

Bailey didn't know what to say. After she was about eight years old, she never had anyone say that they "wanted" to be her friend.

"Well," she said, "I don't think I'll be able to yell at the canine Maggie after this."

———

"We should let this kid fend for himself," Masters grumbled to Edwin as they pounded on the glass doors at the entrance to the Pantomime Theater. "What's he to us, anyway?"

Masters could see a figure coming to the door. "Shit, it's Ahti."

Ahti popped the lock on the front door and opened it. "Reverend Masters, what an unpleasant surprise."

"We were just in the neighborhood and thought we'd drop by."

"Come on in," Ahti gestured, "but leave your loyalist leashed outside."

"Reverend," Edwin protested.

"It's okay," Masters replied. "Go get a cat out of a tree, or help some elderly grandma cross the street. This won't take long."

Ahti patted Masters on the back as they walked through the lobby. "You demean an angel?"

"I treat him like any employee," Masters said. "Speaking of which, although I'm sure you've seen your marque, I wanted to tell you in person that I stole Daeva from you. She'll be working for me now—with the senator's approval, of course."

"Well, we can't go against the Imperator, now can we?" Ahti waved Masters into his office. "I didn't realize that the Mysterium was in the magic show business or I would have applied."

"Sorry, but Daeva is more...interesting. Anyways, I'll be building a Mysterium in Niagara Falls—on the Canadian side. Daeva seems to have a preference for nice hotels and low crime rates."

"She's an ass."

"With a big heart-shaped ass," Masters said appreciatively. "Got any other staff I can steal?"

"Just a kid fresh out of school, but I imagine with your connections to the Imperator you wouldn't need a minimum wage intern."

"Am I sensing a little jealousy?" Masters said. He went over to Ahti's desk and shook an empty bourbon bottle. "You did blow the senator's brains out. That's quite an honor, from what I hear. I can't imagine you need any more recognition than that."

"And it relegated me to this turd of a tourist trap town. Can you believe that humans want to watch water falling over a cliff?"

"Natural wonder or some such nonsense," Masters agreed. "Give me a bar, a casino, and a good titty show, and I'm happy."

Ahti brightened. "Exactly! We understand each other, Reverend. Sometimes I wish the Imperator would lower his lofty goals of world enslavement and destruction. Why have academies for humans when you can create a pleasure palace dedicated to every carnal delight?"

"I'd book a room," Master said. "That academy—is that the one the senator was droning on about in Vegas?"

"I don't have cable yet," Ahti said, "but yeah, he's going to construct it here in the Niagara area. He'll instruct humans on how to be evil as if they couldn't figure that out on their own."

"Maybe I can talk him into locating it near my Mysterium."

"Too late, he already picked out a spot—with my help." Ahti leaned in conspiratorially and added sotto voce: "The kid who works here has a compound out in the woods. The place is like a fort. Anyway, we're taking the property and have already started moving rebels in. It means I have to share the house with the Imperator's motley rabble, but I'll talk them into cooking and cleaning."

"I'd like to meet this kid," Masters said. "I might need a retreat in the woods to get away from my fiancée."

"He's out picking up my breakfast from Dunkin Donuts."

"Perhaps another day then," Masters said. He picked up the empty bourbon bottle again and waved it in front of Ahti. "Let's hope he brings you plenty of black coffee. Well, I should probably be going before my angel craps on the sidewalk."

"Drop by anytime," Ahti said. "And if you see Kim, say hi for me."

Kim Kali and Koda sat in a corner booth at the Cluck and Grunt watching Bill make his rounds and delighting tourists with stories of having an angel as a waitress in Wisconsin. He patiently posed for photos and scribbled his autograph as best he could.

"He's come out of his shell," Kim said. "I'm happy to see him do more than grunt at guests."

"It is because of you," Koda said. "I knew that you had a good heart."

Kim smiled. "I thought you said that I only do things for my own benefit?"

"You could have easily made Bill a figurehead with little involvement in the actual business. Instead, you gave him confidence and a purpose." Koda put his hand on hers. "You are a very nice person—but I still would not have him cook."

"It helps to have a patient angel instructing me."

"I will have even more time now that the Greenland ladder has closed."

"Aren't you sad about that?"

"Very, but we have a greater need at present for a ladder in another location. Which reminds me, may I borrow your phone?"

"Sure," Kim said, handing him her iPhone. "I can show you how to work it if you like."

Koda smiled. "Despite common misconceptions about Greenland, we do have modern technology."

"I was thinking about the angelic part of you. There's no shame in admitting to being technologically challenged. Even I get a little confused sometimes."

"Not to worry," Koda said, "the operation, as you humans say, is a piece of cake." He stared bewilderedly for a moment at the device's array of icons. "Do you tap once or twice?"

Kim was enjoying his predicament. "Here, let me—"

"Never mind, I've got it."

Dialing a number, he waited a moment. "Hello, Reverend Masters, this is Koda. Yes, I am the Eskimo smartass that you refer to. Although in Greenland we prefer the term Inuit, so I would be an Inuit smartass. Is it possible to speak with Edwin for a moment?"

Koda looked up at Kim. "The reverend is very happy to hear from me," he commented, then held up his index finger. "Hello, Edwin, this is Koda. The ladder has closed. Yes. Thank you. Bye."

"What was that all about?"

"Edwin would have no way of knowing that the Greenland ladder had closed if he were not told. In some ways, angelic communication lags behind human innovation."

"Oh, did I tell you?" Kim said. "We're doing the load-in today of the temporary Mysterium exhibit in my ballroom. I told Denise that I don't want anything demonic on display—only angelic. I'm sure I'll hear crap from Masters about needing to include all the goodies that Stevenson has been giving him, but he can go to hell. I know Trudy is on board with a strictly heavenly display."

"People think that the senator is on the side of angels," Koda said. "We know better. He only pretends to be an angel of light but is filled with deceit."

"Why doesn't Uriel or someone say something to the public? Let them know that he is not the real senator but Satan."

"Those who see clearly already know. That is why New Creekside is expanding so quickly. Those who wish to blind themselves see the senator as their savior. Even the words of an angel will not convince them otherwise."

"That seems a little defeatist. There are always people who haven't been following the news. They need to know."

"We will protect those who do not have understanding, as we always have. But it will not be by word, but by action."

"So what's the plan?"

Koda gave a gentle laugh. "I do not know, Trudy hasn't told us yet."

CHAPTER NINE

Masters stood in the plaza next to a Ferris wheel and took in his surroundings while Edwin bought some fudge from a candy store.

Across Clifton Hill Street, he stared longingly at a motley cluster of attractions anchored by a Travelodge.

Edwin came up to him and stuck out a paper sack that contained some gooey caramel fudge covered in angelic fingerprints.

Masters waved it away. "Do angels get cavities?" he asked rhetorically. "Never mind," he added when Edwin ventured to reply.

Masters continued to stare across the road. He started this journey with no intention of looking for new properties until the Vegas and Orlando branches were in full operation, and he could slowly wean himself off the senator's deep pockets. *But damn, look at the view!*

"Time to shake the tree," Masters said as he dialed the senator.

Edwin grabbed the phone away. "That is not advisable at this time."

"Hey!" Masters grumbled as he deftly snatched the phone back and dialed. "I thought angels were quicker than that." He put the senator on speaker. "Stevenson, it's Jay Masters."

"Reverend," he heard. "What a pleasure to hear from you. How are your lovely daughter and son-in-law?"

"They are safe and sound."

"My wrath would be severe to anyone who hurt them," Stevenson warned. "But enough unpleasantries. How may I help you?"

"I'm over in Niagara Falls scouting out a spot for a new Mysterium. I've found the perfect plot, but there are a few obstacles."

"Obstacles?"

"Nothing major, just a few buildings."

"How many constitute a few?"

"A couple haunted houses and several other tourist traps, a pizza place, and a Travelodge."

"I see. But why Niagara? I thought we were going to build out the Vegas Mysterium and then concentrate on Orlando?"

"My fiancée thinks this place is romantic or some such nonsense, so we're going to tie the knot on my noose here, but the trip has gotten me thinking that I can easily crush the surrounding so-called attractions. Besides, Ripley's is only a block away. I can easily bankrupt them."

"I'm in total agreement with you," Stevenson said, causing Edwin to scowl. "My Academy of Peace and Justice is going to be constructed in the vicinity, and I think we can create a unique synergy between the two. Would you be willing to add a section devoted to my academy? Perhaps a recruiting center on-site?"

"I'm sure I'll get the normal angelic pushback to an idea like that," Masters said, glancing at a visibly angry Edwin.

"That's inconsequential. Send me the address of the properties you're looking at, and I'll see what I can do."

As Masters hung up, he could feel Edwin's eyes boring into him. "What?"

"You just did business with Satan," Edwin stammered. "Again! And in front of an angel!"

"Yeah, so?" Masters said. "You're the one who insisted on standing there. You shouldn't eavesdrop on other people's calls—it's bad form."

"I..." Edwin waved his paper bag of fudge at him, visibly exasperated. "I don't know how to reach you. You can't do things like that."

"I just did," Master said. "Stick with me, Edwin my boy, and I'll teach you the ropes."

———

Corson stood on the gravel shoulder of Warner Road at midnight as a ghost tour from Niagara Falls entered the Screaming Tunnel. Fear and trepidation were etched on the dozen tourists' faces as they walked into the graffiti-covered stone tunnel.

Legend had it that a young girl had escaped from a fire in a nearby farmhouse, her nightclothes engulfed in flames. She burned to death in the drainage tunnel. At midnight—so the story goes—if you light a match, you will hear her scream as the match mysteriously extinguishes itself.

Corson knew it was all a load of crap. About a hundred years ago, there was a death in the tunnel: a young woman was raped repeatedly, and her corpse burned to cover up the crime. But there was no ghost, although a spirit did live in the tunnel. A spirit adept at blowing out matches and providing girlish screams—seven times a week."

About five minutes later, the tour group ran screaming from the tunnel. Another successful night.

Corson straightened his tie and walked inside. With his weak human eyes, it was hard to see anything in the blackness. The space was about sixteen feet wide—too small to transform and use his real senses—so he decided to wait until his protégé made himself known.

"Corson!" A whisper floated around his head. "Is that you?"

"Pythius," Corson said, "stop hiding! I'm not some tourist from Buffalo."

"Did you come to release me from this cursed bondage?" the formless voice echoed off the dank walls.

"Release you? I thought you enjoyed your little haunting career. Although, you may think about opening a gift shop at the tunnel exit."

"You know that the Imperator imprisoned me here."

"You shouldn't have tried to rebel."

"He failed us."

"He freed you from the Tyrant, and you were so ungrateful as to try to stage a coup. Many have tried to rebel against the Imperator, and all have met terrible fates. What made you want to try something so foolhardy?"

"I was ignored," Pythius said as his voice floated around the tunnel. "He didn't see the greatness in me, the ability; the right to command legions—the right to rule. Why should someone so blind be allowed to lead us?"

"You have only lived in this tunnel for a few decades, yet you whine like it has been an eternity. The Imperator could have condemned you to a far worse fate. If you remember, the previous haunter of this tunnel now resides in the pit. The Imperator was most generous to you; he must see something in you after all."

"Do…do you think his eyes have been opened to my value?" Pythius's voice seemed hopeful, just as Corson expected.

"These are interesting days, my friend," Corson said. "Those that have value will be called and you, I am happy to say, are one of those. I have been sent to command you to accompany me on a vital mission for our leader."

"What service may that be?" the voice said as it swirled around Corson. "Is it worthy of my magnificence?"

"I think our opinions of your magnificence differ, but you will find this service very enjoyable. A rebel who runs a campground in Arizona has located a human of great value to the Imperator. We must bring the human back to bow before him in submission."

"Why should I accompany you, Corson? You are nothing but the ruler of a failed nation that is despised by all."

"I have moved onwards and upwards. I now am the right hand of the Imperator. Follow me and achieve greatness."

"Hiisi used to utter such nonsense. Where is he now?"

"Fortunately, he has transitioned to an existence in the pit—with a little help from the Reverend Jay Masters."

"Who?"

Corson shook his head. "You need to get out of your tunnel more often. I will bring you up to speed on what has transpired while you have been terrifying teenagers."

The tunnel grew cold. "I do not appreciate being mocked," Pythius said.

"You will obey my will."

"And if I don't?"

"Then you will meet the same fate as your eager student, Saloth Sar. I'm sure you remember that he ruled Cambodia as Pol Pot, killing hundreds of thousands of humans. For all his supposed greatness, his decomposed corpse now lies in a shabby grave of dirt surrounded by rotting wooden fences; his magnificence has faded to nothing."

Corson's booming voice reverberated down the length of the empty tunnel. "Obey my words and do as the Imperator commands, or you will meet the same fate as your apprentice. You will also be forgotten."

———

Brian Tannahill pulled into a campground near Kingman, Arizona, for the night. He wanted to push on, as Las Vegas was only another hundred miles up U.S. 93, but Linda would have none of it. She wanted to be awake and savor the moment of seeing her daughter again and catching up on all the news. Like any good survivalist worth his salt, Brian knew when it was better to concede defeat and live to fight another day.

The campground manager gave him a curious look as he pulled his massive and militarized truck up to the check-in shack. Apparently, the guy regarded him as a potential troublemaker and gave him a parking spot at the far end of the campground, well away from the more conventional vehicles.

He had spent several hours inside the truck, trying to get an Internet connection, but to no avail. Slamming the laptop shut at three a.m., he remembered that he hadn't connected the hookups to the campsite.

He climbed down the ladder, hefted Violet out of the truck, and placed her on the ground. The chocolate lab could take her time doing her business while he hooked up the sewer line, so he and Linda could do theirs. Violet ran around the truck, nose to the ground, examining all the new and strange scents of the desert.

He started pulling the water and sewage lines out of the truck to hook up the utilities. As he worked, he surveyed the flat, barren land that was so different from the lushness of upstate New York. Although the campground wasn't overly busy and there didn't seem to be any sign of so-called civilization for miles, he still felt exposed. The drive across country that would typically take a tourist only a few days had stretched over two weeks as Brian had taken every back road and Jeep trail his vehicle would fit down. Even the off-the-grid routes seemed crowded (in Brian's paranoid view) at times, as he happened upon one or two other vehicles a day. At those times he would reach down and pat the sawed-off shotgun that was under his seat, and motion to Linda to climb in back in case they needed to seal up the truck and hunker down for a fight.

Right now, Linda was getting the queen bunk ready for bedtime. For dinner, they had an Army-quality MRE (Meal, Ready to Eat), which left her in a foul mood. She had been grumbling that they hadn't had anything but canned goods for weeks and was looking forward to finding a farmer's market when they reached their destination. They avoided restaurants like the plague. Brian hated even stopping at green markets due to the number of people knocking about and getting their germ-contaminated hands on the produce. Besides, Brian didn't think that fresh broccoli was any better than freeze-dried broccoli that had been adequately cleaned and sanitized. It all tasted the same to him—nasty.

Brian put on his rubber gloves and started screwing in the adapter for the sewer line to the campgrounds inlet while trying to ignore the stench. As he was kneeling down working on the line, a shadow covered him as Violet started growling.

Turning his head, he looked up at two men. One of them was in a suit and tie, which seemed out of place in the campground. The other wore overalls and looked like he hadn't bathed in decades.

"Are you Brian Tannahill?" the man in the suit asked.

Brian started to stand while reaching into his pocket and hitting a remote panic button with his thumb. The remote was for seniors who had fallen and couldn't get up, but he had modified it to set off an alarm in the truck to warn Linda of danger.

"What if I am?" he said.

"The father of Bailey and Ian Tannahill?" the foul-smelling one asked.

"Leave them out of it," Brian said. "If you have a problem, then have it with me."

"No problem at all," the man in the suit said. Suddenly Brian doubled over in pain. His head felt like it would split open, the agony blinding him, as he fell to the ground. Through the pain, he could feel another consciousness enter his mind. He no longer had control of his own body as his vision slowly cleared.

The presence wouldn't speak to him, but he knew instinctively who it was. His head rose but not of its own volition. Looking to where the two men had stood, there was now only the refugee from *Deliverance* in the dirty overalls.

"Just don't stand there," he heard himself say. "Take care of the female—and silence that infernal dog!"

The disgusting shitkicker flashed a gap-toothed grin. Picking up a rock, he hurled it at Violet, who yelped in pain and limped off. Brian couldn't move but hoped that Linda had sealed the truck and armed herself.

The man in the overalls disappeared. A few moments later, screams came from the truck. The vehicle rocked back and forth as Linda's wails of agony continued unabated. Brian wanted to fight—wanted to *kill*—whatever was in his head and protect his wife, who was enduring God knew what.

He understood that they were too far away for anyone else in the campground to hear his wife's shrieks of terror. If Linda was going to be saved, he must be the one to do it. Struggling, he finally managed an internal cry of anger that only caused the being that now controlled his body to laugh inwardly at his weakness.

All he was allowed to do was kneel there in horror as the crashing of pots and pans and his wife's pleas for mercy faded into silence.

———

The spirit controlling Brian's body drove his truck out into the desert. The smelly man now sat beside him in the passenger seat that Linda always occupied. He hadn't heard anything from the back of the truck; he hoped that she was still alive.

"There's a good spot," the smelly one said.

"Yes, Pythius, this will work," the spirit said as he pushed Brian's foot onto the brake and turned off the ignition.

Jumping down out of the truck, he walked with Pythius to the back of the vehicle. He felt himself opening the door as Pythius reached in and pulled out something that landed with a thud at his feet.

The spirit that controlled Brian's head looked down.

Linda was clearly dead. Her broken body stripped naked and desecrated with a knife. Her neck broken, and her head at an impossible angle.

Brian cried in agony towards the spirit that didn't care.

"Roll it into the gully," he heard his voice say. "The animals and carrion fowl will clean up the mess. Only he matters."

———

Emily lay in bed having a perfectly lovely dream about riding a Harley Night Rod motorcycle to Sturgis when her door burst open and a mountain lion, German shepherd, and a teenage girl jumped onto her bed.

"Today's the day!" Bailey shouted into her ears as Emily tried to shake off the assault.

"What day?" she asked groggily, rubbing the sleep from her eyes.

"My parents will be here today," Bailey pouted. "You remember, don't you?"

"Oh, yeah… sure," she said, having totally forgotten.

"We need to go into town and get some balloons and a cake."

"Is it somebody's birthday?"

"I want to make it special for them," Bailey said. "We can dress up their new trailer."

"Yeah, maybe we can order a camo-frosted cake with missile launchers for candles," Emily suggested facetiously as she extracted herself from the pile and stood up. "Have you heard from your father? Did they say what time they'd be here?"

"No," Bailey said, pulling her phone out of her pocket. "Last time I heard they were in Arizona. Let me call Dad."

As Bailey dialed, Emily went over to her closet to decide what blue jeans and T-shirt she would be wearing today.

"Hi, Dad!" Bailey chirped.

"Is this Bailey?" she heard as the phone switched over to speaker. Her father's voice sounded more formal than usual—colder than the warm greetings he usually gave her.

"Well, it's sure not Ian," she said. "When will you and Mom be here?"

There was a long pause. "There's going to be a little delay. We need to do something first."

"How much of a delay?" Bailey complained. "You're supposed to be here today."

"It's important. It's going to help millions of people," her father said.

"But you're supposed to be here *today*," Bailey repeated dejectedly.

"It's an important assignment for Senator Stevenson. You know how much I respect the senator."

Emily could see from Bailey's expression that something wasn't right.

"I don't understand," Bailey said. "Can you put Mom on?"

"She's in the bathroom. We ate at a Denny's, and something didn't agree with her."

Bailey scrunched up her forehead. "Since when have you started eating at restaurants?"

"Sorry, I've got to concentrate on my driving. We'll talk to you later… honey." The line went dead.

Bailey shook her head. "Something's wrong. For one thing, my dad hates the senator. And he would never go out of his way to 'help millions.' The compound was designed to keep *everyone* out, even those who might come asking for help if the world was going to shit. He'd bend over backward to help his family or those close to him, but he always said that everybody else had made their bed and they could lie in it."

"Try to get a hold of your brother," Emily said as she quickly grabbed some clothes. "Have him call your parents and see what his opinion is. I'm going to get dressed and find Uriel."

———

Stevenson invited the press to witness his grand announcement. Thanks to Corson, and even the traitor Pythius, he was now able to move ahead with his ambitious plan for the Academy of Peace and Justice. He had a plane ticket waiting in Phoenix for the physical Brian Tannahill to fly to Buffalo. Corson would squawk about it being in coach, but he never wanted his subordinates to become too comfortable in the human world. It sounded like the human caged and under Corson's control, had been putting up quite a fight the entire way. He expected Corson to add a migraine to his list of complaints when he arrived.

The venue Stevenson had chosen enjoyed a certain notoriety in the Falls area: the Echo Club. Formerly a mansion built in the middle 1800s, it had since undergone several incarnations, the latest being a restaurant club that catered to private events and bus tours.

Several rebels had been "haunting" the building for years. The point was to instill in the public a fascination with the occult that they would twist and pervert into something dark—not to mention the added perk of scaring the shit out of them.

The senator sat at the bar nursing a martini until Corson arrived. "About time," he said as his servant wrapped in Brian Tannahill's flesh walked into the room. "The press is growing restless."

Suddenly, Corson put a hand to his forehead and pounded his other on the bar top. "He's a fighter," he said with a pained expression. "He's hasn't accepted his fate yet."

"The papers are ready for the signing," Stevenson said. "Let's do this, and then you can be free of our doomsday prepper."

Trudy, Gavin, and Rachel stood in the back of Emily's crowded living room. They had heard that Senator Stevenson was going to make an important announcement from Niagara Falls, and most of the old-timer Calamity community had shown up witness the event.

Trudy studied Bailey, who sat on the couch next to Emily. The girl was clearly worried about her parents. Since Bailey's father suggested that he was doing something "important" for the senator, they thought it best to watch the pompous blowhard's broadcast on television.

"Another announcement from the illustrious senator," Trudy huffed. "That bastard seems to be on TV constantly. They sure give him a lot of free air time!"

"Hush, it's starting," Emily shouted to the standing room only crowd behind her.

Stevenson was speaking in the banquet room of the Echo Club. A small group of dignitaries, outnumbered by the press, was in attendance. Amid polite applause, Stevenson walked up to the microphone-studded podium with a phony mega-watt smile plastered on his face and addressed the phalanx of cameras. "Welcome, all. Today I wish to announce my dream for an Academy of Peace and Justice is becoming a reality, thanks to the generosity of an exceptional individual—Brian Tannahill."

Trudy could hear Baily gasp as her father walked into the shot and shook Stevenson's hand.

"Is that your father?" Trudy asked.

Bailey turned away from the television; her face showed not shock or fear, but anger. "That's not my dad," Bailey said. "You can't see it but there's mist flowing around him, just like the demons at the mall."

Their attention was drawn back to the screen as the senator outlined his vision for the Academy of Peace and Justice.

"It will be a beautiful institution," the senator was unctuously saying, "a cherished repository of knowledge and hope for generations to come. Brian Tannahill has generously made this possible by deeding his property to my foundation. The Tannahill estate is a labor of love for Brian and his family. I know it pains him to part with it, but he understands the grand work that I am attempting and chose to honor me by placing his compound at my feet as a gift."

"Oh, come on," Trudy mumbled.

"My father would never do that," Bailey complained. "He loves our compound more than life itself."

"Brian," the senator continued, "would you care to say a few words?"

"Certainly," the spirit holding Brian hostage said as he walked to the microphone. He looked directly into the camera, his face expressionless. "This would not be possible without the love and support of my lovely wife Linda, who unfortunately could not be here today. I also wish to acknowledge my son Ian, who is employed by the Amazing Ahti, and my beautiful daughter Bailey. Bailey, if you're watching, enjoy your stay in Nevada. You may be certain that the senator will come for you—to thank you for your service to the angels."

"What does he mean by that?" Bailey said.

"A threat," Uriel said. "He attempts to intimidate us into submission."

Trudy noted Brian Tannahill's glazed eyes and ghostly pale skin. He grabbed his head with both hands as if in pain.

Removing his hands, Brian grimaced into the camera. He was having difficulty speaking, almost as if he were having a stroke, his hands shaking at his side. "Desert RV Park, outside Kingman, Arizona…north five miles…dirt road. Into the desert. Dry wash."

Stevenson patted Brian on the back and smiled. "Already planning for the next academy, I see. Let's have you sign the deed over on the current project and then we'll get to work."

They watched as Brian Tannahill—or at least his body—sat down at the table. Stevenson handed him a pen. Quickly signing, he dropped the pen on the desk, rose, and walked quietly out of the room.

"Like I said, he loved the compound more than anything," Bailey stammered. "He lived there for years before he even met my mother. He would never give it away of his own free will."

"It wasn't him," Rachel said. "You saw the mist Bailey. A rebel controlled what just happened—except for that part about Arizona. I could see the internal struggle. Your father was trying to communicate with you."

"I got that, but what he was trying to say?" Bailey asked. Her bottom lip began to tremble. "Mom, she wasn't with my dad…why not? He was trying to tell me something about Mom!"

"We do not know that, Bailey," Rachel said softly. "I think it would best if you would leave us now." Bailey hesitated; Rachel walked over and placed her hands on Bailey's shoulders. "Please, Bailey."

The young girl departed, still stifling her tears.

"I did not want Bailey to hear our plans; she is too close to this," said Rachel. She turned towards Trudy. "Come with me. I may need your gift."

"Wait!" Gavin said. "Where are you going, and what about me?"

Rachel took Gavin's hand. "We need to find the location Mr. Tannahill was pointing us to. Trudy may be able to provide additional knowledge about what is happening."

Trudy sighed. "A vision, you mean."

"Well, I'm coming too," Gavin said.

"No," Rachel said in a whisper to both of them. "What we will find might very well be beyond healing."

———

"It's not right, Jay," Holly said as she gazed out the hotel window at Horseshoe Falls. "We shouldn't get married here."

"Why not?" Masters said, wondering why he was now the one pushing to get married in Niagara Falls. "The wedding planner is maxing out my credit card as we speak."

"Our friends and family aren't here," Holly pouted. "It's taken years to get you this far, and I'm not about to have a wedding that's more like an elopement when we can have something special." She crossed her arms as she turned to glare at him. "I'm not going to settle."

"We have Edwin here, and I'll fly Trudy and Gavin out."

"What about Rachel and Nate, Koda and Uriel, Tony and Kris, Emily and—"

Masters flung up his hands. "I'm not chartering a flight for the entire town."

Holly continued to give him the stink eye. "They're my friends. They should be your friends too. What's the saying? 'Happy wife, happy life.'"

Masters groaned, "Just shoot me now."

He turned away from Holly's gorgon gaze before he turned to stone. Now somebody was pounding at the door to the suite. "What!" he yelled, flinging it open.

Ian burst in. "Have you seen the news?"

"No, I've been too busy getting my ass chewed by my fiancée."

"My dad was on television with Senator Stevenson," Ian said as he grabbed the remote off the dresser and tried to find a news station. "It was a press conference from here in Niagara. He signed away the compound to the senator's foundation. Something's not right, he'd never do that!"

"Is that your phone?" Holly said to Ian as "Ride of the Valkyries" from *Apocalypse Now* blasted through the room.

"My sister's calling, that's her ringtone," he said as he pulled out the phone. Ian put Bailey on speaker. The siblings said in unison: "Have you seen the news?"

"Yeah, I've seen it," Ian confirmed. "I was just trying to find it on TV to show Reverend Masters and Holly." He looked around the room. "Where's Edwin?"

"He said he had some important project to work on," Masters said. "I think he may be in the bathroom."

"Why would Dad do that?" Ian asked Bailey. "He always called Stevenson a son of a bitch. And he would *never* give up the compound."

"It's not Dad. Or it is, but not totally—"

"What?"

"He's possessed by a demon," Bailey said. "You've got to help him."

"Possessed, are you sure?"

"Somehow I've become the world's leading expert on possession," Bailey said. "Yes, he has a demon in him."

"So, what can I do?" Ian said.

Masters stepped up. "We'll find him. I'll make sure that the senator has his lackey let go of him."

There was a rustling sound, and then Trudy came on the line. "Hey, Pops," he heard her say. "Rachel and I are going to do a little investigative work on this side. If things get intense out there we can get the A-Team in the van and come out to help you."

"Thanks," he said, then turned to Ian. "Did they say where the press conference took place?"

"Yeah," Ian replied. "The Echo Club. It's on the American side, not too far from here."

Masters walked over to the closet to grab his jacket. "Well, let's pay them a visit."

"Find Edwin first and make sure he's with you," Holly said. "I don't trust you not to do something stupid if you're on your own."

"Thanks for the vote of no confidence," Masters grumbled. "Come on, kid—I mean Ian. We've got this covered."

———

The drive from Calamity, Nevada, to Kingman, Arizona, took a little over an hour and a half. Rachel could have gotten them there in about five minutes, of course, but Trudy was pregnant and already prone to nausea, even without flying the friendly skies tucked under Rachel's wing.

Kris's pink caddy was more comfortable, and Trudy made a mental note that maybe she should look into this Mary Kay business. Of course, all she needed to do was tell her father that she wanted a Cadillac and she'd have a shiny black one blazoned with the Mysterium logo delivered to her the next day, but she didn't want to be a rolling billboard for the Mysterium, even though she was now an executive with the company.

Trudy looked over at Rachel, who was uncommonly quiet.

"You know," she said to her friend as she surveyed the scrub brush that went on for miles, "Emily has been trying to tell me the desert is beautiful. So far, I'm not seeing it."

She expected some rebuttal from Rachel about all of God's creatures that make the desert their home, but she continued to sit there stoically in the passenger seat.

Trudy looked over at her friend. "So, what do you expect we'll find?"

"We know where Mr. Tannahill is, and Ian and Bailey," Rachel said. "We don't know where Bailey's mother is."

Trudy swallowed hard. "Maybe she's back in Niagara Falls?"

Rachel pointed at a dirt road. "We know they got as far as Kingman. Demons show no mercy and have no desire to keep anyone alive that doesn't fit into their plans."

Trudy felt herself tearing up and wiped her eyes so she could focus on driving. "So Bailey was right, something has happened to her mom," she said. "And that's why we probably don't need Gavin's healing power."

Rachel nodded slightly and pointed again to the dirt road. "That may be it."

"Let's give it a try. Mr. Tannahill didn't really give us a lot to go on."

"He is a strong man to fight against a demon enough to even say what he did," Rachel said. "Whatever he was trying to communicate was important to him."

"There's a gully up ahead on the right," Trudy said. "I'll pull over."

"No, not there. Trudy, do you see the birds up ahead? Vultures, if I'm not mistaken."

"Rachel," Trudy said quietly as she slowed the car, "I'm not sure that I'm up to seeing what's out there."

"We have to. We owe it to Bailey to find out."

Trudy drove further down the road until they were near the spot where the vultures were circling. Turning off the engine, she opened the door and got out to stand on unsteady legs.

"Stay here," Rachel said as she started walking over to the dry wash that during the rainy season could quickly turn into a torrent, hurtling through the desert.

"Do you see anything?" Trudy shouted as the desert faded into white. She was no longer in Arizona. She was enveloped in a cool mist that clouded her vision, while the roar of Horseshoe Falls nearly deafened her as she stood on rocks just feet from the base. Trudy had only seen the Falls in visions like this one, but it was no less spectacular as she looked up at the massive sheets of water cascading over the rocks. She could feel the mist on her face and the rush of the water as thousands of gallons a second poured over the cliff. Nobody was there, and she wondered why she was being shown this vision.

Looking across the river, Trudy noticed an abandoned power plant, its massive concrete walls dark and moldy as it hugged the bottom of a cliff on the Canadian side. She could tell that it had not been used for years.

A light pierced the sky. It started on the roof of the building and shot several hundred feet upward. The roar was overpowering; even the mighty Falls fell silent as the sky buckled in on itself, twisting around a central core. Trudy realized that a new ladder was forming just on the other side of the river. It flared several times, casting lightning down the canyon as it ripped the fabric of space-time and melded dimensions into a singularity. Rachel had once tried to explain how it all worked, but since she didn't even see the ladders until recently, she didn't pay much attention. But she knew that a ladder in Niagara Falls was divine intervention. Perhaps as Koda once told her, there was hope.

"Trudy! Call 911!" Rachel's shout brought her back to Arizona. The angel knelt near the drop-off to the dry riverbed and bowed her head for a moment. "We found her."

CHAPTER TEN

"I wonder if they're still at the Echo Club?" Masters said. "He'll be tough to track if he's already left."

"Track—wait!" Ian pulled out his cell phone. "My whole family is set up with the Find My iPhone app. Dad didn't like the idea of being tracked, he said he wasn't a game animal, but Mom goaded him into it. Let's see…"

"Well?"

"Hold on," Ian said. "Okay, got it. He's not at the Echo Club, but at a park near the falls."

"What would he be doing out there? There's nothing to look at but water."

"Yeah, he was never that interested in it. He called it God's tourist trap."

Masters snickered. "I kind of like your father." He made a right turn to head back towards the park and added: "How was he dressed, the last time you saw him?"

"He was wearing a suit at the press conference," Ian mused. "That's not like him. I didn't even know he owned one."

Masters veered into a parking spot, cutting off a white van with a handicap tag hanging from its rearview mirror. "Well, it should be pretty easy to spot a guy in a suit amongst the tourists."

"According to this"—Ian held up the phone—"he should be over by the observation tower. Let's go!"

They got out. As they walked down a path, with the sound of the falls wafting through the trees, Masters looked over at Ian.

"What's wrong?"

Ian shook his head. "I was just thinking about the last time I saw my dad. We didn't leave things in a very good place. He was mad that I was going to stay here and work for Ahti and not bug out with the rest of the family. Guess he was right."

"Over there," Masters pointed. "I see a guy in a suit on the platform over the river."

The observation tower consisted of steel trusses about twenty stories tall with a walkway suspended between it and the cliffside. On the far side of the tower, the walkway extended out even further, giving tourists a dizzying view of the river and falls over two hundred feet below.

"That's him!" Ian said. He started to trot towards the entrance.

"Slow down," Masters huffed. "He's not going anyplace. He'd have to pass us to exit the observation deck."

"Hurry!" Ian shouted and took off at a full run towards the far edge of the observation deck.

"Kids…" Masters grumbled to a man wearing a Dollywood T-shirt as he worked himself up to a slow jog.

When Masters reached them, he stopped at stared. Something wasn't right. Ian had made an attempt to hug his father but was pushed away. Brian Tannahill's eyes were not filled with fear or panic or even concern for his son. They were cold, calculating eyes that he had seen before in Alastor Hiisi. They were the eyes of a killer.

"Hello, Ian, nice to meet you," Brian Tannahill coolly said. "In the interest of full disclosure, yesterday I had an associate kill your mother." He pointed a thumb at himself. "Only he mattered; he was the only one on the deed. She was nothing but a piece of meat to be slaughtered and discarded."

"Dad…I don't understand," Ian said. "Mom's dead?"

"Human skin is soft, easy to shred and gouge. The vultures won't have to wait until her body decomposes to enjoy a good meal."

"That's not your father talking." Masters put a hand on Ian's shoulder. He could feel the boy shaking. "Which one are you?" he called out to the demon. "What's your name?"

"Why, Reverend Masters, I have wanted to thank you. My name is Corson. Because of you, Hiisi now resides in the pit, and I was able to assume his place at the right hand of the Imperator."

"So you're Stevenson's minion?" Masters said. "If I were you, I'd watch my back, or you'll end up on permanent retirement, like Hiisi."

"Stevenson?" Ian said. "What does the senator have to do with this?"

Brian Tannahill's body chuckled. "Is the boy really that clueless?"

"Yeah, pretty much."

"Well," Corson continued, "let me enlighten you, young man. The senator stopped being the senator when your employer Ahti blew his brains out. Now, in part thanks to the good reverend's son-in-law, he is someone I'm sure you've heard of. We servants call him the Imperator; you may know him as Lucifer."

Ian looked visibly pained. Turning towards Masters, he said, "Why didn't you tell me?"

"Don't be angry with the reverend," Corson said. "He was probably trying to save you, or some such nonsense. The rumor is he's going soft. Personally, I don't believe it. I've heard stories about the reverend; how he would photograph a friend being disemboweled just to make himself famous. Now that's the Jay Masters we all know and love."

"Let me speak to my father!" Ian demanded.

"I'm afraid not. I'm not one for sentimental moments."

Brian Tannahill closed his eyes, and both hands grasped his head as if he were in pain. When he opened them again, the killer was gone, and the real Brian Tannahill briefly emerged.

"I love you, son..." he said in a voice that shook with emotion.

"I love you, Dad," Ian said, his voice trembling, too.

In a flicker, Brian Tannahill was banished, and the demon regained control.

"Well, that was embarrassing," Corson said while taking out a handkerchief and wiping his forehead. Glancing at his watch, he continued. "Look at the time. Got to go." And with that, he jumped over the railing and fell twenty stories to his death.

Trudy and Rachel started the long drive back to Calamity in silence. The police and ambulance personnel were all professional, and when they recognized Rachel, they still managed to perform their duties—albeit with some trepidation at being so close to an angel. They also heard that the Tannahill's' dog, Violet, had been found injured at a campground and was being treated by a vet.

"I can't tell her," Trudy said, tearing up. "I can't..."

Rachel patted her leg. "I'll do it."

"Do the police understand that it wasn't Bailey's father who did it?" Trudy asked. "They seemed to jump to the conclusion that he is involved."

"Bailey will know that her father didn't do it. That's what matters most."

Trudy's phone rang. "Can you take it and put it on speaker?" she asked Rachel.

"Trudy?" she heard her father say as Rachel held the phone.

"Hey, Pops, where are you?"

"Watching the cops scrape Ian's dad off some boulders."

"Oh, God..." Trudy said.

"A demon named Corson made him jump off the observation deck on the American side of the Falls. The tourists finally got to see something interesting fall off a cliff."

"Dad!" Trudy scolded. "I hope Ian isn't standing next to you."

"No, the poor kid is down there with his father."

"We have equally bad news," Trudy said. "We found Mrs. Tannahill—mostly."

"That doesn't sound good."

"It isn't."

"The demon, Corson, told us that he had an associate of his kill Ian's mother. So Ian is aware of her death, but I don't think he's fully processed it."

"As far as we know," Trudy said, "Bailey doesn't know that either parent has died. I'm not sure how she's going to take it."

Rachel piped up: "What is Ian's mood, besides mourning? Is he showing signs of anger?"

"He knows that Stevenson is involved, so when he starts dwelling on it, he's going to be pissed."

"That's what I'm afraid of," Rachel said. "I understand Bailey is better trained than Ian, but they both have military-level training that can make them dangerous to others and themselves. Keep a close eye on Ian. Don't let him do something foolish."

"I'm going to have him stay with Edwin at the hotel," said Masters. "I don't want him to be alone right now—that is, if I can find Edwin."

Trudy thought for a moment. "I think I know where you might find him."

Senator Stevenson was taking the opportunity while in Niagara to stop by the Pantomime Theater. He realized that the former Tannahill compound was too remote for effective advertising, so he planned to use Ahti's theater to create a welcome center for prospective recruits. The place was a dump; he'd have to throw some money at it to avoid being laughed out of New York State. But it was convenient—and, at 30,000 square feet, large enough to provide a suitable venue.

He only had one problem: he hadn't informed Ahti that he was being cast aside.

As his chauffeur opened the door and he stepped out, he couldn't help but laugh at Daeva's obscene termination notice. The local constable had taped a half dozen, probably ignored by Ahti, pink notices to the front door demanding that Ahti clean up his signage.

Stevenson rapped on the glass front door hoping to rouse the drunk or at least find his young assistant there to let him in.

Eventually, Ahti stumbled his way through the lobby and unlatched the front door.

"You look terrible," Stevenson said.

"I hear that a lot," Ahti replied.

"Where's your intern?"

"Beats me. He's been hanging around Masters, so I expect him to ditch me like Daeva did."

"While we're on the subject, clean up the sign out front. It presents a bad image, having Daeva continually flipping you off in plastic punctuation. I assume that you're sober enough at least once a week to safely climb a ladder."

"Yes, Senator," Ahti said, taking the insult without rebuke.

"One other thing," Stevenson said. "I'm taking the theater for myself. You'll have to find someplace else to practice your so-called magic."

"What? Taking the theater?" Ahti seemed genuinely surprised, which pleased Stevenson. Ahti had fully believed he was going to be taken care of, in reward for his excellent aim back in Vegas.

"Yes, it's nothing personal. Properly built out, this will be the perfect place for my recruitment center. The theater itself can show an informational film, and the side rooms will process individuals that meet my standards. I may even imitate Reverend Masters and install a gift shop."

"Where am I supposed to go?"

"I don't care, Ahti, as long as it isn't here," Stevenson said. "Also, you will need to vacate the compound since you are now nonessential personnel."

"Why don't you just send me to the pit?" Ahti moaned.

"If I cast aside every rebel who has displeased me, or not lived up to my expectations, I'd have no one left."

"When have I displeased you?" Ahti said. "I shot the senator. I found the compound for you."

Stevenson smiled and grasped Ahti by the shoulder. "It's not personal— this time. You have been useful, but the needs of my vision require tough decisions to be made. You are simply...what's the word? Expendable."

As he turned to leave, he added: "Corson needs to clean up a messy situation and will be along later to pick up the keys. Make sure you take care of the marquee and have your personal items out by then."

———

Bailey sat in her room with tears streaming down her face. Maggie sensed her pain and was nuzzling her in an attempt to cheer her up. All she could think about was that her parents were dead, and the senator was to blame.

Trudy and Rachel hadn't returned yet, but the news apps on her phone filled her in on what had happened both in Kingman, Arizona, and Niagara Falls. Emily had also tried to console her, but she couldn't deal with it and ran to her bedroom and locked the door.

Usually, the authorities and news media wouldn't be releasing names of victims until their families had been notified. But because Brian Tannahill had just been seen on television with Stevenson, it was easy for the press to identify him and link him to the woman found dead in Arizona—at the location he mentioned on television. Wild speculation was rampant, with the pundits suggesting that Linda Tannahill must have fought with her husband over his decision to donate the compound to the senator's grand vision. After killing her and making his way back to Niagara, he completed his life's work of honoring the senator but afterward was so distraught at murdering his wife of twenty-three years that he took his own life.

Bailey knew it was a load of shit and was shaking with anger and anguish.

She debated what to do, as there wouldn't be much time left before Trudy and Rachel returned, making it more difficult to escape. Walking over to her dresser, she pulled out the top drawer and picked up the Beretta. She popped out the magazine and inspected it. She had good aim and had more than enough ammo to do what she intended.

She stuck the gun between her belt and back and covered it up with her shirt. Putting on a grey hoodie, she grabbed her wallet, wiped her eyes, and walked towards the living room.

"Hey, Emily," Bailey said, scanning the room for any nosy loiterers.

Emily was in the kitchen, trying to scrape a failed cooking experiment into the trash. "Bailey," she said, wrinkling her nose at the stink in the air, "do you mind taking this trash out? I think I'll confine myself to the microwave from now on."

"No problem," she said, then hesitated. Emily was her friend; she'd taken her in and fed and clothed her, but she needed to get past the angels and out of New Creekside to accomplish what she knew she had to do. "Hey, Em," she said. "Can you take me into town?"

"I thought you didn't like going to the big city?"

"It doesn't have to be Vegas. Just someplace I can buy some, uh, feminine products."

Emily smiled. "Sure," she said. "There's a Walmart about thirty minutes from here. I need to pick up some things myself. Give me a minute to clean up, and I'll be ready to go."

Bailey felt Emily's eyes on her.

"Are you doing okay?" Emily asked.

"Sure, I just need to do something to keep my mind off—you know," Bailey said as she walked over and took the trash bag from Emily. If she had her way, Senator Stevenson would be wrapped in a plastic bag himself just a few days from now.

———

Ahti hated what he was about to do but didn't see any other options. He was homeless, penniless, and a laughingstock amongst his fellow rebels. Things couldn't get much worse unless the United States reenacted Prohibition.

He knocked.

Daeva opened the door. She stood there in a black silk bathrobe, scowling at him. "I thought you were the masseur."

"No, but I do rub you the wrong way," he said, pushing himself past her and into the room.

"Hey!" she complained. "What do you think you're doing?"

"I was just kicked out of my theater by the Imperator. I've no place to go, so I thought I could bunk here for a while."

"Oh no, you don't! If you're on the Imperator's shit list, I don't want you within ten miles of me."

"But I saved you from—"

"The pit," she huffed. "Yeah, I know, but that story is getting old."

"That's the kind of story that never gets old," Ahti said, sitting on the corner of the bed. "How'd you get the money for a nice room like this?"

"I kept some of the cash Kim was paying me as the headliner, unlike some drunk I know."

"Well, I'm sure you've been looking for ways to pay me back for saving you."

Daeva crossed her arms and scowled. "So, what do you want?"

"A place to stay, room service, and some cash for gambling…oh, and I want to overthrow the Imperator."

He enjoyed Daeva's shocked expression until she raised her arm and pointed to the door. "Get out!"

"What?"

"You want to start a coup against the Imperator? That's been done before, and it's always turned out badly for anyone involved—as in, sent to the pit badly."

"This will be different."

"How's that?"

"All of the attempts before had one flaw."

"Really? What's that, Einstein?"

"Us."

"I'm not a flaw," Daeva said contemptuously.

"Not you per se," Ahti said, windmilling his arms. "Us, as in rebels."

"I don't get it."

"We always start united and then fall apart with bickering and backstabbing. The Imperator has the battle won before he even lifts a finger."

"Assuming I agree with your theory," Daeva said, "how would this be any different?"

Ahti fell back on the bed and gave a little laugh while kicking his feet in the air.

"Well?"

Ahti craned his head a bit so he could see her. "We work with loyalists and humans."

———

Masters trudged up a gravel road on the other side of the Falls. The path led to the top of an abandoned power plant. He gave Holly the assignment of staying with Ian until he could locate Edwin. Trudy seemed to think he'd be on top of the building, and sure enough, he was.

Edwin sat there on a concrete outcrop looking over at Horseshoe Falls.

"Beautiful, isn't it?" Edwin said as Masters approached. "Now that I have assumed a human likeness, I can truly appreciate the grandeur that He created here on earth."

"Yeah, water, rocks—it's great," Masters grumbled. "You missed out on the excitement. Brian Tannahill signed over his compound to the senator and then took a long walk off a short observation deck. Oh, and his wife was killed by demons in Arizona—in case you're interested."

"I'm sorry to hear that, but they have transitioned and have been reunited."

"That's a pretty blasé attitude, isn't it?" Masters said. "Personally, I'm mad as hell. Ian's a good kid. He didn't deserve to lose two parents in one day."

Edwin continued to stare at the falls. "These are dangerous times. Many will transition." He turned his gaze to Masters. "Eventually, even you."

"I don't have any plans of kicking just yet," Masters said. "I've got too much to do."

"What are you going to do?" Edwin asked. "You are but one human, one man against the demonic—against the Father of Lies."

"I thought *I* was the Father of Lies?"

"Seriously," Edwin said, "you can't take down the senator alone. You'll need help."

"What makes you think I want to take down the senator? He's my personal piggy bank."

"I see it in your eyes. Despite your protestations, you really do care about people other than yourself."

"Keep that under your hat," Masters said. "A demon has already been accusing me of going soft."

"Well, for once angels and demons agree on something," Edwin said with a smile.

"So, how long will it take to get some assistance from Calamity?" Masters said. His impatience was growing thin. For beings that could travel through time and space, angels seemed as slow as molasses.

Edwin stood up and walked over to him. "Do you trust me?"

"I wouldn't be asking you for help if I didn't."

"I didn't hear you ask for my help."

"Read between the lines," Masters grumbled. "Okay, I need some help to get rid of the senator once and for all. Satisfied?"

"That wasn't so hard, now was it?" Edwin said, adding: "Do you consider me your friend?"

"I'm not buying you flowers."

Edwin continued to look him in the eyes.

"Yeah, sure, whatever…you're my friend."

"Are you, my friend?"

"What is this, twenty questions?"

"Friendship between a human and an angel forms a bond that can never be broken. You learned this the first time I appeared when Uriel brought us together."

"Yeah," Masters said. "I think my response was 'hell no.'"

"Has anything changed?"

Masters sighed. As much as he hated to admit it, things had changed. He realized that Edwin was one of the few people in the world that wasn't trying to rip him off, take advantage of him, or use him for their own purposes. Edwin had no ax to grind, no hidden agenda. What you saw was what you got, which in Masters' line of work was oddly refreshing.

"Well, I guess I'm stuck with you," Masters said, and then he was blinded by Edwin's transformation.

The angel towered over him as he fell to the ground under the shaking of a hundred-year-old concrete roof that threatened to crumble to dust.

Masters was more annoyed than anything about Edwin transforming right next to him. He'd seen angels in their true form hundreds of times and wasn't all that impressed, but when they got close and crossed into his comfort zone he always felt a twinge of respect mixed perhaps with a small dose of fear. Seraphs like Edwin, with their six fiery wings, were the most unnerving.

He couldn't help but lower his gaze to the ground in submission.

———

Edwin looked down at Masters, who lay on the ground with his hands over his eyes. He hated to do that to the reverend, but current needs trumped subtlety. He had to be in his true form to summon a ladder.

Immediately, tourists from the passing Maid of the Mists boats started snapping photos of the awe-inspiring angel. Like almost all humans they would not be able to see what was transpiring just feet away from Edwin as space started folding in on itself. The view of the cliffs became muddled as the light began crossing between dimensions. Although humans could not see it, the earth reacted to the violence taking place on its surface—a deep rumble followed by quivering ground and rocks cascading down the cliff face, which the tourists would mistake for an earthquake as small waves rippled across the river.

The sky brightened as the ladder grew. Branches of lightning twisted out and away from the main trunk, rotating and flaring as they expanded. Edwin could feel the presence of the ladder, living and growing in its own way until the column of light was higher than the clifftop. It was the feeling of life.

———

Bailey planned how she was going to kill Senator Stevenson as she sat in the passenger seat of Emily's Jeep. With a handgun, she was sure she wouldn't be able to pull off a long-range shot like Ahti did in Vegas. She'd have to get close which might prove difficult, as she was sure the senator wouldn't allow a Tannahill near him after recent events.

Emily pulled the Jeep into the Walmart parking lot.

"I'm not feeling very well," Bailey lied. "Cramps are starting up. Can you go in, and I'll stay in the car?"

"Either cramps or I poisoned you with my bacon and eggs," Emily said, trying to lighten her somber mood. "I understand. Just sit here and rest." She patted Bailey's knee and looked at her with concern. "Are you going to be okay?"

"Sure, I just need to sit here for a while. Can you get me a box of Playtex Gentle Glides and maybe a Hostess lemon pie?"

"No problem," Emily said. "Look, I can't begin to imagine what's going through your head right now after seeing your father on television."

"God, give it a rest! I'd rather not talk about it," Bailey said, hoping her typically surly teenager response would make Emily stop asking questions she had no intention of answering.

"Sure," Emily said as she parked. "I'm here for you if you need to talk to someone."

"Thanks," Bailey said. "Oh, can you leave me the car keys so I can listen to the radio?"

Emily handed them to her. "Just don't drive off and leave me," she laughed.

Bailey smiled wanly. She watched as Emily made her way past the shopping cart return corral and into the store, then she scooted over to the driver's seat. She felt a little bad as she jerked the Jeep in gear and hauled ass out of the parking lot.

———

"Where is everyone?" Trudy asked Rachel as they walked into Emily's living room.

"I'm over here, Young Prophetess," Koda said as he rose from behind the kitchen counter. "My small stature sometimes causes people to assume I am not here."

"Where are Emily and Bailey?" Rachel asked.

"I have not seen them," Koda said, "but Emily's dishwasher was full, so I decided to put things away."

"We need to find Bailey and tell her that both of her parents are dead," Trudy sadly announced.

Koda looked stricken. "That is terrible news. Bailey is such a gentle soul; all the animals love her. She will be devastated."

"My fear is," Trudy said, "that gentle soul may try to kill someone."

Out of the corner of her eye, Trudy noticed the ladder flaring in Emily's backyard. Someone was coming through.

She was surprised when Edwin appeared. Opening the sliding glass door, she went out to speak with him. "Is my dad okay?"

"Yes," Edwin replied. "I left him on the rooftop of—"

"An abandoned power plant."

Edwin cocked his head. "You had a vision?"

"Yes," Trudy said. "A new ladder has opened, hasn't it?"

Edwin looked a little disappointed. "I wanted to be the first to tell you the exciting news."

"It's hard to get ahead of a prophetess," Trudy said.

Edwin noticed Koda walking out to join them. "Koda, your sacrifice has created new life. The Niagara ladder is alive."

"A baby ladder!" Rachel chirped.

"That is wonderful news, brother!" Koda grasped Edwin by the arm. "A ladder's life was given, but not in vain, as a new one has been created."

"How did it open?" Trudy said. "I thought it had to be through a bond formed between a human and an angel."

Edwin just stood there with a cockeyed smile on his face.

"No," Trudy said. "You don't mean—"

"Yes!" Edwin said. "Your father and I have bonded for eternity!"

"Uh," Trudy stammered, suddenly feeling sorry for her angelic friend. "Congratulations?"

Rachel gave Trudy's shoulder a gentle squeeze. "You should go and see your father. Edwin will protect you, and I'll stay here to speak with Bailey."

Trudy exhaled. "Thanks. Call me a coward, but I'd rather be around my father than tell a teenage girl that her parents are dead."

Rachel hugged her. "Go to your father. Tell him I said hi."

"I will take you," Edwin said. "The Niagara ladder is not like this one. It is just a thin strip of folded space-time. Finding its entrance is difficult, and it is still turbulent from its creation. It will settle down shortly, but for now the forces we will experience would be too much for you if I do not protect you."

Edwin transformed, causing Trudy to feel foolish for falling to the ground in submission while Rachel and Koda just stood there. The angel's burning figure towered over her until one of his fiery wings scooped her from the dirt and cradled her in the surprising coolness of his flames.

"I will take you to your father—and the father of the Niagara ladder."

CHAPTER ELEVEN

Masters had risen off the ground and was wondering where the hell Edwin had flown off to, when suddenly he appeared in front of him in his human form, along with Trudy.

"Hi, Pops," Trudy said. She surveyed her surroundings. "So, this is what Niagara Falls looks like." Then she turned around and gazed at Horseshoe Falls. "Wow…this is a lot better than my visions."

"So I take it we have a new ladder?" Masters said to her. "You told me that you could see the ladders, but I didn't know you could pass through them."

"It's your unborn grandson's talent. I'm just along for the ride."

"Do you have some time?" Masters said to her. "Come back to the hotel, we have a lot of catching up to do."

"Actually," Trudy said, "I'm grateful to spend some time away from Calamity. Bailey doesn't know that her parents have died. Rachel volunteered to tell her."

"Ian knows, but he's been so distraught I sent him to the hotel, hoping Holly could keep an eye on him," said Masters. "Even so, I'd be surprised if he hasn't called Bailey and let her know."

Emily didn't think buying tampons, frozen burritos, and a crescent wrench would take so long. It seemed like everyone in Las Vegas was at the

Walmart—everyone except for the cashiers, that is, as a row of unmanned registers stretched off into the distance. She wasn't in a huge hurry to get back to the Jeep. The news of the Tannahills' deaths was being broadcast on all the TVs in the electronics department. She wondered if it was appropriate for her to break it to Bailey, or if that should be somebody else's responsibility.

After finally making it through the checkout, she grabbed the flimsy plastic bag and headed out to the parking lot, only to find that her Jeep wasn't there. She knew that Bailey was upset and who could blame her, after seeing her own father on television being manipulated by a demon and signing away her inheritance.

"Well, shit," she muttered as she pulled out her phone. She tried calling Bailey, but it went to voice mail. Most of her other primary contacts nowadays were angels; she knew that Uriel, Koda, Nate, and Rachel weren't on the family plan for cell phone minutes.

She dialed Trudy.

"Hey, Emily," she heard Trudy say over a lot of background noise. "We dropped by your house, but you weren't there. Rachel is at your place, and I'm in Niagara Falls."

"Niagara Falls?"

"New ladder—my dad made it, with a little help from Edwin. I'm so proud of him." Her voice dripped with sarcasm.

"Listen," Emily said, "I'm in a Walmart parking lot. Bailey stole my Jeep and is probably heading in your direction."

"Stole it?"

"Well, I may have given her the keys…"

"I have bad news: Bailey's parents are dead. Rachel was going to tell her."

Emily sighed. "I know. I walked by the televisions in the electronics area, and it's all over the news. I didn't think she'd run off, but now that she did, I assume she's armed and therefore dangerous."

"Maybe not. After all, Bailey's just a teen."

"I know her type." Emily thought about it. "Hell, *I'm* her type. Military training and a need to make the world right can be a recipe for disaster."

"But still, she's only sixteen."

"And," Emily emphasized, "she's been studying survival skills since she was five. I had four years in the Army. She's had eleven years of combat training."

"Okay," Trudy said. "Call your house and ask Rachel to fly you back to Calamity."

Emily had heard what flights via angel were like. She didn't want to include nausea and vomiting into her already fubar day. "I think I'll call a cab."

Bailey ignored the constant ringing of her phone until she finally reached down and turned it off. She didn't want to have calls coming in from angels or humans telling her to turn around. She was barreling down I-40 towards Ash Fork, heading on to Flagstaff, Arizona. She didn't have a map of the off-the-grid Jeep trails, and her phone's GPS route wasn't helpful, so she resorted to taking the interstate until she could find a suitable map and go off-road.

Once she got to the East Coast, she'd have to try to locate the senator. Preferably he'd still be in Niagara Falls. She would avoid her brother, as she didn't want to drag him into this. Knowing the area helped; she might even be able to sneak back into her bedroom and grab her AK47, ammo, and some grenades. If the compound was too secure, she knew of several caches of guns, food, and equipment that her father had stashed throughout the woods around the area. But if the senator were in Washington, D.C., that would present a host of new concerns as she imagined he'd be heavily guarded. Bailey reminded herself that Ian's boss, the Amazing Ahti, killed the senator at a public event; she hoped to duplicate that feat.

As she passed a brown road sign that said 80 Miles to the Grand Canyon, she contemplated that she had never seen this incredible natural wonder. After what she was planning, she probably never would.

Glancing down, Bailey noticed she was getting low on gas. Using her turn signal and trying to remember every road rule to avoid any confrontations with police, she exited the highway and headed towards a Texaco station that sat forlornly by itself in the middle of the desert. At such a remote facility, there was less chance of her being identified. She also hoped they would have a trail map so she could get off of historic Route 66 and onto some backroads like her father had taught her.

Bailey started to tear up again as she thought of her father instructing her on backcountry survival skills. He was delighted that she, unlike Ian, was such an eager student. Bailey wanted to please him, and she loved the time they spent together. She wanted to learn everything but doubted that she'd ever need to use it—until now.

———

Ian sat on the couch in Masters' suite while Holly poured various little bottles of alcohol into a big glass. "Do bourbon and gin go together?" she asked him, cocking her head and then shrugging as she continued to pour.

He put his head in his hands. "I don't need a drink, and I'm not twenty-one."

Holly regarded him sympathetically. "Well, it's a good thing we're in Canada then," she said. "I can't imagine what you're going through. But Jay is going to make it right."

"How can I trust him? He didn't even tell me that Stevenson was a demon—and not just any old demon, but Satan himself."

Holly grabbed the glass and went over and sat down next to him. Putting the dirty dishwater-colored concoction on the coffee table. "I've known Jay for years," she said. "He's a lying, arrogant son of a bitch, but he's also a kind and gentle man once you get to know him. That being said, if I had a new pair of shoes for every time he's lied to me, I'd be a happy girl."

The door opened. Masters walked in, followed by Edwin and Trudy. "Speak of the devil," Holly said.

"Ian," Masters said, tossing his jacket on the bed. "This is my daughter Trudy."

"Nice to meet you," Ian said. He'd seen Trudy on television but didn't know she was pregnant. "How far along are you?"

"Four months more, give or take," she said.

"His name is Jay," Masters beamed.

"That's not written in stone," Trudy said. She looked at Ian. "Do you know where your sister might be?"

"What do you mean?" he said. "I thought Bailey was in Vegas."

"She borrowed Emily's car without permission and took off. We assume she's going to hunt down the senator."

Ian could feel his jaw hanging open. "She'll kill him."

"This isn't the senator we all knew and hated," Masters said. "This is Satan, and he's the one who will kill *her.*"

"Oh, my God!" Ian stood. "We've got to find her."

There was a knock at the door. Edwin turned around and motioned everyone back. "I feel something; let me open it," he said.

He approached the door cautiously and slowly opened it. Daeva and Ahti stood silently in the hallway. Ahti looked sullen, and Daeva was as red as her sequined miniskirt.

Nobody spoke until Daeva reached out and gave Ahti a shove.

"May we come in?" Ahti asked.

"Why?" Edwin asked.

"Oh, let them in," Masters said. "Daeva is on my payroll."

Holly and Edwin both turned to him and said in unison, "They're evil!"

"People are always saying that about me, yet everyone lets me in the door," Masters said as he waved them inside. "So, what can we do for you?"

They entered. Ahti looked at Ian and said, "Kid, I'm sorry for your loss. I had no idea that the Imperator was going to do that. I thought he was planning to seize the property, write your parents a fat check, and call it a day."

Ian tried to keep his anger under control. "I guess you were wrong."

"Ahti's wrong about a lot of things," Trudy piped up. "Like trying to kill my friend Emily—and my husband."

"Professional rivalry gone awry," Ahti said dismissively. "You may convey my apologies to both of them. It won't happen again."

"You seem to be doing a lot of apologizing," Masters said. "What do you want?"

Ahti looked around the room. "Simply put, I want the one thing every rebel wants: revenge."

"Revenge against who?" Edwin hissed. "God?"

"Not this time," Ahti said. "I propose that we unite forces and defeat the Imperator once and for all."

After hearing that, Ian decided he'd try the drink. When he touched the glass with his fingers, it disappeared. "Damn," he sighed. "I hope they need a drink in Calamity."

He looked up. Ahti had an astounded look on his face, and Trudy was staring at him with a big grin on hers.

"What?" he asked.

She turned to the demons and her father. "Let's do it."

———

Bailey was starting to yawn and lose focus as she drove Arizona's Route 15 North towards Dilkon in Navajo County. She had stopped in Flagstaff long enough to purchase a sleeping bag, a propane cook stove, a small tent, several hunting knives, and some easy to prepare rations.

The area was sparsely populated, with only a few houses and trailers dotting the landscape. Bailey was tempted to ask someone if she could park in their yard for the night but then found a solitary dirt road. Pulling off, she found a relatively flat and clear area to pitch her tent.

Being by herself didn't scare her. Despite her mother's protests, her father would test her by dropping her off in the middle of nowhere to see if she could survive off the land for several days at a time, all alone. He gave her a cell phone, but she had never needed to use it. Still, tonight she would sleep with the Beretta within easy reach.

She set the tent up next to the Jeep so the vehicle would act as a windbreak, and proceeded to cook up a can of Hormel chili. The night sky showed dozens of stars as the temperature began to drop.

Bailey sat on the ground, staring at the iPhone on her lap. She wanted to call someone, anyone, just to hear a human or angelic voice. She missed Emily and Rachel—even her mountain lion and Rachel's crazed shepherd. She especially missed her brother, and her heart ached from the hole put there by the deaths of her parents.

As she scooped a spoon of chili into her mouth, she saw movement in the darkness. She couldn't make it out but decided to act casually. She pulled the gun out of her belt and placed it on her lap alongside the phone.

Once her eyes adjusted, she could make out an animal no bigger than a medium-sized dog.

The critter came closer, and she realized it was a gray fox. It didn't seem afraid of her and proceeded to trot over to where she was sitting, spun around three times, and sat down next to her.

"Not another one," she grumbled as she stroked the fox behind the ear. "You guys are ruining my reputation as a hunter. Well, I appreciate the company. But at first light, you're on your way."

She scooped some chili into a bowl and set it down in front of the fox, which immediately started to lap it up.

Bailey sat with her back against the Jeep, looking up at the night sky. Ian would be seeing the same sky tonight: a link between them as siblings, even though they were separated by hundreds of miles.

A shooting star shot across the night sky. She remembered a Bible verse she had learned in Sunday school: "How you have fallen from heaven, morning star, son of the dawn! You have been cast down to the earth, you who once laid low the nations!"

Would she be able to kill a morning star? She had her doubts but had to try.

Bailey patted the fox again and wished she could live a simple life, like the animal beside her.

Another sound came from the darkness, the sound of footsteps—human ones. She chambered a round in her Beretta and took off the safety but otherwise didn't move. She wanted to see what kind of fight she was in for; only fools shoot randomly into the night.

She was surprised by the figure that walked into the light of the campfire. "Jonathan?"

"Good evening, Bailey. May I enter your camp?"

She re-engaged the safety. "Of course. But how did you find me?"

He came over and sat down cross-legged next to her. "You're a logical young woman. It was just a matter of thinking about what I would do in a similar situation. I knew you wouldn't stay on the highway long before trying to find a route that is a little more"—he looked around—"secluded."

"I guess I should be more unpredictable."

"Are you eating that?" He pointed to the pot of chili.

"Sorry." She grabbed a paper plate and shoveled some chili onto it. "I didn't expect visitors or I would have made cornbread."

Jonathan chewed thoughtfully on a forkful of chili. "My compliments to the chef," he said, taking another bite. "So, you're going to kill the senator—then what?"

"Probably be shot and killed. Maybe if I'm lucky, I'll get life in prison." She felt herself tearing up. "But why should I be alive when my parents are dead?"

"There are other ways," Jonathan said. "You cannot fight Satan alone and hope to win."

"I can try."

"And die. Let me suggest another way. You have certain gifts that you are just learning to use. In Calamity, you are surrounded by others with unique gifts as well. Gavin heals, Trudy sees visions and can move through ladders, Emily manipulates matter." He stopped for a moment and regarded her meditatively. "Your brother can transport things, and people, across great distances, and you can see what no other human can: the supernatural world that is all around us. Not to mention, you have a particular talent that terrifies demons."

Bailey patted the fox. "I'm an animal whisperer?"

Jonathan laughed. "I was thinking of another talent."

"The demons at the mall called me an exorcist."

The angel nodded. "And they are correct. What was their tone when they made this comment?"

Bailey couldn't shake the face of the old man as he shouted at her. "Fear. They feared me."

"As well they should. Why use the weak power of that pistol in your lap when you could use a power that is so much greater?"

Bailey thought about it. "My father used to tell me 'never bring a knife to a gunfight.' He got that line from *The Untouchables*; he just loved that movie. I understand now why he kept saying that to me."

"A gift is never given without purpose. There is a plan for everyone. Even you, but if you throw your life away on an assassination attempt that is doomed to failure, everything that is coming together now may be for nothing—and millions may die."

She stroked the fox that had fallen asleep next to her. "Am I that important?"

"If even one person is missing from our cause, then we will fail." He grasped her hand. "Yes, you are that important."

———

The sun was setting behind the mountains as Nate arrived at the convenience store that Tony and Josh had opened in Calamity. Sales were way higher than the rock shop Tony had previously owned; then again, the first customer who bought a pack of gum surpassed his previous sales record.

The FBI had stashed Tony in Calamity after he ratted out the mob. Having been the go-to priest for weddings and funerals, Tony knew all the wise guys that ran the casinos behind the scenes. The ordinarily quiet profession of priest turned deadly when his associates determined he knew too much. With a shallow grave in the desert looming, Tony negotiated a deal with the Justice Department. Renamed "Tom Ruxton" by the Witness Protection Program, he stayed mostly to himself in Calamity and viewed all strangers with suspicion.

Ever since Nate had befriended the crusty old curmudgeon, Tony had seemed happier and more engaged. Now, he wasn't afraid to speak to people, although when he did, his remarks were mostly critical. Tony never failed to remind Nate of his outdated fashion sense, or Uriel's Ethiopian complexion and accent, and the lack of gambling and prostitutes in Calamity.

Nate went inside. Walking up the stairs to Tony's musty bedroom, he knocked.

"Go away," came a gravelly croak from inside.

"Just visiting my friend," Nate said as he opened the door and entered the sparsely decorated room. Tony was in bed with the blankets pulled up around his neck.

"What's with the bowling shirt?" Tony said. "Aren't you cold?"

"Feels okay to me."

"Well, it's freezing. Close the door."

Nate complied and pulled up a chair to sit beside the bed.

"It's hell getting old," Tony said. "Of course you wouldn't know that, Mr. Disco Angel."

"I'm a lot older than you."

Tony gave a harrumph. "Only your clothes are older than me. Angels live forever."

"So will you, Tony."

"Yeah, in hell most likely. Although having lived in this shithole, it might be a step up."

"What makes you think you'd end up there?"

Tony laughed weakly. "I'm no better than the mob I used to minister to—worse, probably. At least they were honest in their crookedness. I was a phony from the start."

"Yet you have been working with Reverend Brustad and Reverend Salazar to bring religious services to the residents that have been flocking here. Reverend Brustad said that he is amazed by your knowledge of scripture and the way you can relate it to others. You're not the same Tom Ruxton that I met when I first arrived."

Tony managed a slight smile. "It's even better in Latin," he said, adding: "They're stand-up guys, them preachers. But the Vegas I'm from would have chewed them up and spit them out."

Nate said nothing, but only gazed upon his friend tenderly.

"Jeez, Nate, stop looking at me like that, wouldja?" Tony said; his eyes held a haunted aspect. "I feel like you're measuring me for a coffin."

"I'm sorry," Nate said softly. "I did not mean to upset you."

"That is why you're here, ain't it?" Tony said, a resigned note in his voice. "Will it hurt?"

"Sometimes it does, but only for a moment. Once you transition, you will look back on it like a needle prick on your thumb—nothing more."

"Sort of like getting slapped on the ass by the doctor when you're born?"

Nate laughed. "That's a better analogy, I suppose."

"It's just so damn scary." He looked away and said to the wall: "Disco… *Nate*, why does everyone ultimately die alone?"

"You won't be alone," Nate said, grasping Tony's calloused hand. "I'll be with you. You know a bond between an angel and a human can never be broken. I'll be with you every step of the way."

Tony turned his head and looked up at the angel. Nate could feel him weakly grasp his hand.

"Well," Tony rasped as he closed his eyes. "I'm down to the felt. I guess it's time I tap out."

Nate stood and put his hand on Tony's forehead. "I think when we get to the cage, you'll find your seemingly worthless chips have been transformed into gold."

Tony breathed his last as Nate vanished from the room. He couldn't wait to show Tony what his new life will be like.

———

Bill Stevenson was about to address the Senate and use his considerable oratorical skills to persuade the gathering of bickering mortals to back his plan for dealing with the angels. Co-sponsored by a backstabbing plutocrat from New York, his bill, which had already passed in the House, would in essence enact severe penalties on any human who knew the location of an angel and failed to report it to the authorities. The loyalists, of course, were impossible to contain, but this would allow him to always know where they were and perhaps have advance notice of their plans.

It hadn't been hard to convince the populace that, although the angels meant well, they were so high above *mere* humans as to not understand that they were destroying entire cities in a misguided attempt to "save" them. Creekside was an out-of-the-way town in the Wisconsin wilderness; the destruction of this insignificant Podunk didn't have the same impact as the devastation of the Vegas strip. People died, families were ripped apart, jobs lost, and for what? To combat an ancient evil that no one from this millennium had ever seen before? Some were even saying that the angels brought iniquity into their midst. Sensational grist like that made it almost too easy for Stevenson to lead the lambs to the slaughter.

The Nevada senator congratulated himself for being the igniter of the conflict that destroyed Vegas as he walked to the podium. Notes were not necessary, although he carried some blank sheets of paper in a manila folder to look the part.

As he stood there, he paused for effect. Looking around the chamber, he noticed the difference his presence made. Usually, the Senate was in constant motion with people coming and going and an abundance of empty chairs. Today it was full, and those in attendance were either seated or starting to take their seats. He continued to remain silent for an extended period. It was the same subtle form of domination that Hitler used during his speeches.

Finally, he cleared his throat theatrically. "We will all die!" he shouted to get their full attention. Another long pause ensued, punctuated by a sideways nod. "*Eventually*. But we do not need to die unnecessarily like those in my home state of Nevada: crushed under girders, ripped apart by swords of lightning, happy family vacations ending in death and destruction.

"No, we must not be trampled under-foot by beings that despite their good intentions, have no concept of frail humans such as ourselves. Obviously, we cannot control such spiritual creatures that would shrug off any weapons we might aim at them. Nor would we want to, as they are trying to help us, no matter how misguided their methods may appear.

"To assure the protection of our citizens, I propose that we monitor these divine beings. An 'angel preparedness system,' similar to Florida's hurricane warnings, would alert citizens to the presence of angels in a specific area, and outline the safety protocols they should follow, including, in some extreme cases evacuation. Yes, mass evacuations are disruptive, but far less so than the alternative. But it will depend upon everyone doing their part. Accordingly, I propose severe penalties to anyone who fails to report the presence of an angel. This may appear harsh, but it is the only way we can guarantee the safety of our citizenry.

"We must always respect and honor the angels that live amongst us, but we cannot let another cataclysmic battle destroy a major metropolitan area. My bill is restrained and yet comprehensive. It will allow us to monitor and, if necessary, interdict any actions before they escalate into a major confrontation."

He held up his hands. "I urge you to vote for our bill and save our citizens from the destruction I experienced in my state."

The standing ovation told him that he had won over the cynics. The first step towards world domination had begun.

———

"Is this a good idea?" Ian asked Ahti as they stood on a dirt road that bordered the compound.

"Sure, kid. We've got to get back into the good graces of the Imperator and see what they've been up to. Besides, Masters' spawn suggested it, so it has to be right... right?"

"If you say so," the boy sighed. He pointed to a gap in the woods. "This is the best way in. I know how to get around the surveillance—unless they've added more, that is."

"I don't know who they have running the place," Ahti said. "This is important, so I'm assuming that they have Corson overseeing the construction."

"He's the one who killed my father!"

"Hold it down," Ahti hushed him as they started walking into the forest. "He's a nasty guy for sure, but he also has the Imperator's ear."

"This way," said Ian, pointing. "It's a more difficult route, but if we go too far to the east we'll be in range of an automated machinegun nest."

"I'd rather sweat than get perforated," Ahti agreed.

After another ten minutes of trudging through the woods, Ian held out his hand to stop.

"Okay, the farmhouse is just up ahead," he whispered. "I'm not seeing any movement, but we need to be careful. There's a bunker entrance not far from here; we can probably scrounge up some weapons if they haven't moved them."

"No weapons," Ahti said, patting Ian on the back. "We're supposed to be on the same side—but I hope you're a fast runner."

As they approached the farmhouse, Ahti whispered to the boy: "I feel nauseous—that's a sure sign that a rebel is nearby."

They stood at the edge of the forest, a stone's throw from a home that Ian had known so well, but now looked so foreign. A figure in a dark suit stood on the porch, seemingly waiting for them.

"Ahti, what a pleasure to see my favorite comedian again."

"Magician, Corson," Ahti said. "Magician." He and Ian emerged into the sunlight.

"If you insist," Corson said as he came down the steps and walked over to them. "I've never understood the whole 'fascinate the humans with the occult' shtick."

Corson walked up to Ian and looked him in the eye. "Ian, I see you've recovered well from your father's death. You looked much more disturbed at the time. He must not have meant much to you after all."

Corson moved even closer until he was almost nose to nose with him. "As you know, I was the one inhabiting your father when he committed his so-called suicide. You might say that I put his best foot forward. Yet you stand before me?"

Ian attempted to restrain himself. He knew how he handled the next few seconds were critical. "I'm here for the senator, not for you."

"The senator?" Corson smirked. "And what would you want with the senator?"

"He's still the best hope for this world," Ian said. "This academy is the future, and I know this property better than anyone. I can be of service here."

"I thought you were working for Ahti?"

"The kid still does," Ahti interrupted, taking the pressure of Corson's stare off Ian, to the boy's great relief. "I plan to steal him back once I've found a suitable venue."

"I hear that Daeva is working for Masters now. Isn't one magic show enough around here? And let's face it when it comes to fascinating humans with the occult she's more apt to focus their attention."

"You don't—"

"Ahti," Ian broke in, returning the favor, "has a vast knowledge of the history of magic and the occult. He's not just a showman, he's an artist."

Corson laughed. "Well, boy, anyone who can lie as well as you deserves a chance to prove himself. I'll present your case to the senator. He'll either accept you into our academy or kill you. As for you Ahti," he added, "I would suggest you never again set foot on this property."

———

Emily was trying to clean up the living room. The angels who traipsed through the house were fastidious; the humans, not so much. She was picking up an empty cola can from behind a chair when Nate walked in.

"Hey, Nate, what's up?"

"Could you please call 911 and let them know there has been a death?" he calmly replied.

"What?" Emily stopped what she was doing and stared at him. "Who?"

"Tony transitioned last night. I would have said something, but I went with him to help him adjust to his new home."

"Oh, God. I knew he was having some health issues. I didn't think…" Emily said as she walked over to the phone. "Is there anything we can do?"

"His body is beyond repair, but he lives on," Nate said. "He wanted me to say thank you for putting up with his sometimes difficult moods. He thinks of you as the daughter he never had."

Emily sat down on the stool in front of the kitchen counter. She felt like the wind had been knocked out of her. So much had been going on lately that she sometimes forgot to check in on Tony and make sure he was doing okay. He was the oldest member of the community, and his crotchety personality sometimes made people think he didn't need—or want—the help and attention that someone his age usually required. Perhaps if she had been more attentive, she could have gotten him to the doctor, and he'd still be alive.

She felt herself starting to tear up. "I'm sorry."

"Don't be," Nate said. "He lived a full life and learned the lessons he had been given, albeit slowly. That is what he was asked to do, and he did it. If he didn't have neighbors like you, he would never have grown."

"He had been happier lately," Emily agreed. "Before you and the others arrived, Calamity was pretty depressing."

"He truly became a priest—not merely in name, but in fact."

CHAPTER TWELVE

Bailey and Jonathan were on the road and heading back to Vegas. The fox couldn't take the hint and refused to leave her side. It now sat contentedly curled up on the back seat of the Jeep. Jonathan said she had a way with animals, but right now they were getting pretty darn annoying.

"Let's stop at the wildlife park," Jonathan said, pointing at a roadside billboard as they made their way towards Williams, Arizona.

"I've seen enough wildlife, thank you."

"You need to be tested," Jonathan said. "It's part of the learning experience to see what you are now capable of." His face displayed the unbridled enthusiasm of a ten-year-old on the way to Disneyland. "It will be fun! I'll treat."

Shaking her head, she said, "Okay, we'll stop, but I'd better not get any claw marks on Emily's Jeep."

They pulled up to the wildlife park's phone booth-sized ticket booth. The female attendant took Jonathan's two twenties and held out a brochure chock-full of rules and liability disclaimers. Then she spotted the fox.

"Only domesticated animals are allowed in the park," she said, jerking back her hand.

"It's a dog," Bailey said.

"That's no dog."

"Oh, it's a dog, all right," Bailey insisted. "Uh, Rover—come here, boy!"

The fox obediently stood up, jumped onto the console, and nestled into Bailey's lap. "Good Rover," Bailey said as the fox licked her face "See, he's just a dog."

"Mm-hmm," the woman said. "Well, keep your *dog* inside the car at all times, and keep the windows rolled up."

The first set of gates opened, allowing them into the demilitarized zone between humans and animals.

"So, what are we supposed to see here?" Bailey said as the second gate opened. "Lions and tigers and bears?"

"Oh my!" Jonathan smiled. "Surprised I caught the reference? Rachel made me watch *The Wizard of Oz.* No lions or tigers, but we'll probably see bears. Let's see if they take a liking to you."

"Great..." Bailey mumbled back.

As they entered the compound, she wasn't impressed. "So far all I see are mountain goats and burros. I don't think I need any special powers at a petting zoo."

They drove through another set of automatic fences, the latter with the sign TUNDRA WOLVES.

"Okay, this is getting more interesting," Bailey admitted as she scanned the surroundings. "I'd like to see a tundra wolf; haven't had much opportunity, since they mostly live in northern Russia. I've never hunted a wolf, but I hear Federal Fusion makes a sweet 7mm round that works well. A tundra wolf can get to be well over one hundred pounds, so you need some serious stopping power."

To Bailey's regret, the large subspecies of gray wolves was keeping a low profile. "Guess I'm not going to see one today," she complained. "Bummer."

"Look behind us," Jonathan said.

Bailey was shocked to see in the rearview mirror a pack of about six white wolves following the vehicle.

"That's creepy," she said. One thing that hunters did not want to see was a pack of wolves closing in on them.

Exiting the wolf enclosure and moving past some bison, she hoped that one of those giant creatures wouldn't take a liking to her—they were as big as the Jeep. While possessing excellent hearing, they were known to have less than stellar eyesight. What if they thought the Jeep was another bison? She'd hate to have to explain that to Emily.

"We're coming up on the bear exhibit," Jonathan said.

Bailey wasn't sure why he was so excited to see bears. She figured angels had seen just about everything in the universe, so some stinky, flea-infested *ursus americanus* shouldn't be such a big deal. Her mountain lion's teeth and claws were scary enough. She crept along at the park's fifteen miles per hour speed limit, hoping the bears were taking a siesta.

"Over there!" Jonathan pointed. "Move to the side of the road and park."

"Is that a good idea?" Bailey said.

"They won't hurt you."

"But they may eat Rover for lunch."

"See," Jonathan said. "They're coming."

It looked like every black bear the wildlife park housed was heading in their direction. Soon there were eight bears—a mix of boars topping out at four hundred pounds, smaller but still intimidating sows, and their cubs— ringing the car from about ten yards away.

"Time for you to get out," Jonathan said.

"What! Are you crazy?"

"You need to prove to yourself what you are capable of."

"I'm capable of being eaten!" Bailey said as she double-checked that the doors were locked.

"Do you trust me?" Jonathan said.

"No."

Jonathan laughed. "I'll protect you if it looks like you are in danger."

Bailey could feel her heart beating out of her chest. She just hoped that it wouldn't soon be literally out of it as she undid her seatbelt and unlocked the door.

"Ian gets my AR-15 if I'm eaten," she said as she opened the car door and stepped out.

The bears had moved closer; they were now only about six feet away. Bailey was trying not to show fear but believed she may have peed herself as they circled around her. She could hear an alarm siren go off as the park personnel spotted her standing outside her vehicle.

A voice from a loudspeaker boomed into the enclosure: "Slowly get back into your vehicle. Do not make any sudden movements; we're coming to get you."

Bailey stood there, not knowing what to do. The bears had ringed her, so now it was impossible for her to run in any direction. She knew enough about bears to know that running would be the worst possible thing to do. Instead, she decided to sit down. If she was going to die, she might as well be comfortable.

A large female approached with two cubs behind her; Bailey lowered her head and looked away as she neared, in an attempt to be as submissive as possible. A female with cubs was about the worst-case scenario as far as her survival went. Feeling hot breath on her forehead, she assumed that it was the end.

The bear stuck out its tongue and licked the entire side of her face.

"Really?" she said, looking up at the bear with disgust. "Why does everything try to lick me?"

"She likes you," Jonathan said from the safety of the car.

Bailey stood up and brushed off her cargo pants. She could see several parked vehicles and a police cruiser coming towards them.

"Uh-oh," she said as one of the cubs waddled over and tried to climb up her leg. Bailey picked it up and held it in her arms. The mother didn't seem to mind and was instead focusing her attention on the cars that rolled up thirty yards away.

Several park rangers got out and pointed what she hoped were rifles loaded with tranquilizer shots and not lead. A policeman got out of the squad car and pointed what most likely was a rifle loaded with real ammo at the mother bear.

"Slowly put the cub down and get back into your car," a woman holding a megaphone said. "Don't make any sudden movements. We'll drive up, scatter the bears away from you, and escort your vehicle out of the compound."

The bears turned their full attention to the rangers as they got into their cars and started moving closer to them. The policeman continued to point his rifle in their direction, ready to deliver a fatal shot if necessary.

The mama bear started pawing the ground as her hackles rose, looking like she was going to charge the approaching vehicles. The other bears also seemed agitated and grouped in front of Bailey, as if they were trying to protect her or the cub she held.

She didn't know what to do; she didn't want the bears to be hurt because of some stupid angelic test of her powers—not to mention that she was in the line of fire as well.

Then she had an idea that seemed incredibly stupid, but deep down, she felt it might work.

"Wait," Bailey said to the mother bear. "Turn. Look at me."

She was surprised that the bear did stop and turn. She didn't know if it was the sound of her voice, or if the creature understood, but she decided to continue.

"Thank you," Bailey said as she put the cub down. "Thank you for trying to protect me, but it isn't necessary. Take your family and go to the trees over there." she pointed. "I'll be fine."

The bears, in unison, looked where Bailey was pointing and started to move in that direction.

She exhaled in relief as she saw the officer lower his rifle. "Hey, Jonathan," she said as the cars rolled up, "know of any angelic lawyers?"

But Jonathan wasn't in the car. The fox was looking through the back window at Jonathan as he circled around and stood ten feet in front of her. "No harm was meant, and no harm was done," he said to the rangers.

"That was a stupid stunt," the officer said as he approached. "Turn around and put your hands on the Jeep."

Bailey was about to obey when a bright light forced her to the ground.

Jonathan had transformed.

As she knelt trembling before him, she observed that he didn't resemble the protecting angels that guard New Creekside—the ones she had already grown used to. Jonathan stood twenty feet tall; his wings were not sharp swords like the protectors, but soft, feathery, white wings with lightning coursing through vein-like structures underneath. He held neither sword nor shield, but his right hand grasped a crooked staff of lighting that emitted a deep hum as it scattered sparks along the ground. He wore no armor but was draped in a robe of pure white that glowed of its own accord.

Slowly Bailey got off the ground while the officer and park rangers remained prostrate. The bears did not seem concerned and came back to stand next to her. They instinctively knew there was no danger here.

Bailey leaned her arm on the shoulder of the mother bear. "Hey, Jonathan," she called over to her angelic friend as he reverted back to his human guise. "Do you think Emily will let me borrow her computer? I need to check out GunsAmerica.com. I might have a few firearms to sell."

Rachel wanted to help Trudy, but she also didn't want to step on her authority as chief operating officer of Masters' Mysterium Entertainment Incorporated. When Trudy called, she was in a particularly sarcastic mood, mentioning how much she loved her new "cheap-ass job title." Apparently, her father bestowed the verbose title on her between rounds of bourbon with Ahti, toasting the demon's successful mission of deception.

Trudy was going to be staying a few days in Niagara Falls but had a critical meeting already scheduled for an initial walk-through of the Mysterium. Trudy's father had his helicopter pick Rachel up and bring her to the rooftop of Kim's conference center. She would have preferred just to fly over herself and suspected Reverend Masters insisted only because he knew how much she disliked riding in Terran aircraft.

Rachel was happy to see Kim and Bill waiting for her when she landed.

"Bill!" she chirped as she ran over to give him a hug. "I thought you were going to France?"

"I rescheduled so that I could see the Clunk and Grunt in the Mysterium."

"Bill's a perfectionist," Kim said as they walk to the elevator. "The Cluck and Grunt in the concourse was easy compared to trying to recreate Bill's original Wisconsin diner."

"I donated some of my pots," Bill crowed, "and my chili recipe."

"It was where you first transformed," Kim said to her, "right in front of a television crew. It was when the world knew we were not alone in the universe. We had to get it right.

"Since the government bulldozed it, we couldn't go there to examine the property. We had the video from when the battle started but not much else. The Wisconsin Historical Society had some photos of the building from the 1910s, and Bill found some photos from the 1970s."

"It hadn't changed," Bill said, "other than the Cluck and Grunt sign I put in. It had a couple different names over the years. What was the first one called Kim?"

"Joe's."

"Yeah, talk about no imagination!" Bill laughed. "Doesn't Cluck and Grunt sound a lot better?"

"Yes, Bill," said Rachel charitably, "it certainly does."

The walk from the hotel lobby to the Mysterium's entrance was via an elevated corridor that what would soon contain moving sidewalks, views of the asphalt parking lot, and a recorded welcome spiel in three languages. Ladders and pallets of acoustic tiles encroached on the central walkway as wires hung down like vines from the drop ceiling.

"Sorry about the mess," Kim said as they approached the concourse level entrance to the Mysterium. "Denise assures me we'll be ready by the scheduled opening."

As if on cue, Denise, holding a clipboard, appeared out of the shadows of the upper-level ticket area.

"Rachel, thank you for coming," Denise said. "I think you'll be pleased with our progress."

Rachel gave her a big hug, "Thank you for all your hard work under such difficult circumstances."

"Difficult?"

Rachel pointed to a poster on the wall featuring the Reverend Masters in a chic dark suit, holding a cigar and brandy snifter. His lips, thin and cruel, held his trademark condescending smile. Cunning and intelligence resided in his brooding brown eyes.

"Ah," Denise nodded knowingly. "I've had lots of practice dealing with his type. My ex-wife could give him a run for his money."

"Come on in," Kim said to her. "Let's give you something good to report back to Masters."

Rachel was impressed as they entered the central space of the building. The work lights were on; it was still rough, but it was beginning to look a lot like her old home of Creekside, Wisconsin.

Bill had already started to wander off towards the Cluck and Grunt as Denise spoke to some of her staff that had gathered around, presumably to see an angel for the first time.

"So," Kim said, "what do you think?"

"I wish Trudy were here with me," Rachel said as she pointed to the second floor of the building on her left. "Can we go see her apartment?"

Kim smiled. "I'm afraid it's only a façade. Since we're not letting guests up there, we never built it out. The plan is to use it for storage for the shop's merchandise."

Rachel put her hand on Kim's arm. "Would you do me a favor? Can you build it out for me—and Trudy. It would mean a lot to her."

"I'll check with Denise," Kim said. "We should be able to do that, but do we have any photos to work from? They bulldozed that building as well."

Rachel thought back to the claustrophobic, dirty, and slowly decaying room filled almost to overflowing with piles of dirty laundry, soda cans, and guitars. "I can explain to Denise's artists exactly how it should look. Oh, and one more thing," she added, "Trudy loves to play guitar but hasn't had a chance with everything that has happened over the last year or so. I would like for her to have a place for her guitars and amps, and let her come over and play whenever she wants."

She hoped she wasn't too pushy, but Trudy needed to rediscover that part of her. "Would that be okay?"

"She's the boss," Kim said. "She can play in the middle of the street if she wants. Actually, I think our guests would love that. Imagine a guest walking down Main Street with the interior environment set to a starry night. The streetlamps are lit; the recreation of the ladder glows off in the distance." She held her hands up in a viewfinder shape like she was directing a movie. "They see lights coming from the windows above the candy store. Music gently wafts down upon them, being played by none other than Trudy Masters-Young herself. It will be a memory they'll take with them and cherish forever."

Rachel thought of Trudy's love for full-volume metal, hard rock, grunge, and punk. "Yes," she agreed with a big nod, "it will be memorable, all right."

———

"Good news," Stevenson said. "You have your block of D-grade attractions."

"Really?" Masters said to the phone as he fought with the television remote, attempting to mute the shopping channel that Holly was fixated upon. "That was fast—even for you."

"Hey!" Holly screeched in protest as he muted. He only wished he had a mute button for her complaining voice as well.

"It is amazing how quickly someone will sell if you put the appropriate pressure upon them," Stevenson said. "The Travelodge was the most difficult, but they began to see things my way. My staff is working out the closing details and will be in touch with your lawyers by tomorrow at the latest."

There was a knock at the door; Trudy, Edwin, and Ian walked into the suite. Masters waved them in and motioned for them to sit.

"Thanks again, Senator," he said. "The Mysterium is the best way to spread the word about the supernatural."

"It's not the best," Stevenson corrected just before he hung up, "Or the greatest, but it is useful and probably will be for some time. This is a big opportunity for you. Don't fuck it up."

Trudy glared at him, "Okay, what scheme are you involved in with Satan now?"

"We just became the owners of an entire block on Clifton Hill. We even have a Travel Lodge."

"Jerk," Trudy said. "I had a vision of you doing something stupid like this."

"Yes!" Edwin grinned at Masters as he stood up, holding his right hand in the air.

Masters stared at him.

"High five," Edwin said as he continued to wave his hand. "Isn't this the way you do it?"

"I'm confused," Masters said while grudgingly slapping Edwin's palm.

180

"You have the Travelodge," Edwin said. "I assume by the name that it is some sort of lodge for travelers."

"Yes, Captain Obvious," Masters said as he went over to examine the mini-bar that was now mostly empty.

"We have hundreds of people moving to Niagara from Greenland and other ladders," said Edwin. "It's perfect."

"Hey, wait a minute." Masters' said. "I'm going to bulldoze the building."

Trudy stood up. "Eventually, but right now we have more than enough on our plate getting the Vegas Mysterium up and running. Oh, and I've heard about the Orlando property. By the time you're ready to start construction, the community will have found someplace else to live."

"We're family," Edwin said. "The ones arriving are your family as well. They need a place to stay."

"I said I was your friend," Masters said. "We're a long way from kissing cousins."

"But *I'm* family," Trudy said. "Plus, I'm also the chief operating officer."

"I knew that would come back to bite me in the ass," Masters said.

Trudy's phone rang. "Don't hold that thought," she said as she answered. "Hi, Emily," Trudy said.

Masters focused in on Trudy, who looked pale. Her whispered words came between deep gulps. "When's the funeral? Okay, we'll be there. Thanks for letting us know. Bye." She hung up.

"Funeral?" Masters said.

Trudy looked at him with tears in her eyes. "Tony died."

———

"What do we do with the young Tannahill?" Corson said.

Stevenson sat behind his large desk at his office in the Hart Senate Building. He hated coming to the office because the work was menial and beneath him, but it was a necessity at this moment in history. He hated the décor as well. The Hart Building was the subject of a nasty debate over cost overruns when it was constructed in the 1970s. To maintain the budget, they needed to slash some niceties, such as oak paneling for the offices, a gym, an art gallery, and penthouse level dining. Humans flaunted their supposed power through ostentatious displays of wealth and ornamentation. The fact that they cut back on such signs of prestige in the Hart Building irked him; he vowed not to cut corners with his new academy—or his future world capital.

"Senator?"

"I'm listening, Corson," he said irritably, glancing up from the voluminous notes on the academy's curriculum. "Do you expect me to have to look up at a subordinate? Sit down!"

"Sorry, Senator!" Corson took a seat.

"What is your opinion of the boy?" Stevenson asked.

"I killed his father. I find it hard to believe he could put that aside so easily."

"Yet, human history is filled to overflowing with filicide and patricide. If it is so easy for humans to kill their own, why should a boy trouble himself if you killed his father? Perhaps the boy desired his father's death. It wouldn't be the first time."

"There is also the matter of his sister."

"We know where she is. As long as she stays out of our affairs, I would not worry about her."

"But she's an exorcist." Corson's voice dripped with contempt. "She must be destroyed."

"An exorcist must have someone to exorcise. New Creekside is one of the few locations on earth were possession isn't being practiced by our kind." Stevenson wagged his finger at Corson. "If she stays there, she is of no concern."

"But—"

"When I first spoke to Ahti about finding a suitable location for my academy, he said the boy was on our side. He may be happy that he is free of his parents, but humans do not want to be alone in the world. Killing the girl would most likely turn him against us."

"But—"

Stevenson held up his hand. "We'll go with Ahti's judgment."

"Ahti's judgment?"

"Yes, I know how that sounds." Stevenson smiled. "Did you ever run into Ahti before the rebellion?"

"No, I'm happy to say."

"He was one of the seraphs who used to grovel before the Hated One's Throne." Stevenson held his hands in front of his eyes, mimicking a seraph's wings. "Always chanting that holy, holy, holy nonsense and covering their faces like they weren't just as worthy as the one they worshiped. I ignored him for the most part, until the rebellion, and then he became useful because of his proximity to the Hated One. Ahti was easy to turn. His weakness is that he has no ambition. He will always take the path of least resistance.

"How many rebellions have I put down since that first battle in heaven?"

Corson shrugged. "Tens of thousands. Perhaps hundreds of thousands."

"A fair estimate. The rebels all wish to topple me and become the greatest of all." Stevenson opened the cigar box on his desk and picked out a Gurkha Black Dragon. "They all have ambitions, desires for glory, and to be worshiped. Perhaps you do, as well. But Ahti has none. He will never be a threat to me."

"He's a drunk."

"And a drunk he will remain," Stevenson said as he clipped the end of the cigar and lit up. "But, a useful drunk. Still, let us watch the young Miss Tannahill a little more closely. We should know the full extent of the powers she has been given by the Hated One."

———

"This place doesn't feel right," Ahti said to Daeva as they stood on the stage of a recently vacated theater and imagined the possibilities.

"Because it's going to be mine and not yours?"

Daeva laughed openly at him. She didn't care what Ahti thought—or felt. Rebels cared little for others' feelings; sympathy wasn't in her repertoire. Actually, she found the now homeless and unemployed magician's pathetic expression humorous.

She had gone above and beyond to even invite him to join her in a new theater venture. At least now she held the upper hand and could shush any future comments about how he rescued her from the loyalists.

"It's available," Daeva said, "and it's on the Canadian side. It's going to be a couple years before Masters completes *my* theater. He told me to look for a venue while we're waiting."

"Our neighbors are a tattoo parlor and a 4D theater," Ahti said. "We can do better."

"Yeah, your choice was across the street from a wastewater treatment plant."

"Smelly neighbors, I admit. But tourists would hold their nose, turn away, and what would they be staring at: the Pantomime Theater."

"If they knew your act they'd be conflicted," Daeva retorted as she walked down the stage right stairs to the seating area. She pointed up. "And unlike your pathetic attempt at theater ownership, this one has a full set of stage lights."

Daeva sat down. She draped her shapely legs across the seat in front of her and crossed them at the ankles. Ahti remained on the stage. From his expression, Daeva guessed he thrilled to the deafening applause of an imaginary audience—the only kind the hack could draw.

"By the way," she said, "is that boy going to be working here—assuming that Corson doesn't kill him?"

"That's the plan," Ahti said, "but his main job is to get so embedded in the compound that they'll have to pry him out of Corson's ass."

"He seems naïve. I'm not sure he's that devious. Oh, and what *is* the plan, if you don't mind my asking?"

Ahti shrugged. "Beats me. Masters' brat said that we need Ian inside the compound and that they must trust him."

"I was there, I heard that part," Daeva said. "Anything else?"

Ahti stared blankly at her.

"So, you have no idea of what's going on?" she huffed. "I'm not surprised."

"I did the hard work," Ahti said, pacing the stage like he was already planning his act. "I made the introductions."

Daeva snorted. "Yeah, I admire your work ethic. So, are you going to work here with me, or live in the dumpster in back of the Burger King?"

"I did see a set of dressing rooms that would make a nice little apartment."

"It would be helpful to have an on-site security guard to protect my interests."

"Security?" Ahti stopped pacing and stared at her. "I'm not a rent-a-cop, I'm an artist."

"Yeah, an unemployed artist who is loathed by rebels and loyalists alike—although surprisingly, humans are just ambivalent towards you. Prove yourself, and I might promote you to popping popcorn." Daeva could see that Ahti was becoming angry as she sat there, soaking it all in. "Your choice," she added, knowing that he had no choice.

"I saved you from the pit," Ahti stammered.

"I'm saving you from the homeless shelter. I figure we're even."

She could see by Ahti's pathetic expression that she had won.

Ahti sighed. "How close are we to the nearest bar?"

———

Goodsprings Cemetery had been in use since the 1890s. Trudy found it to be a forlorn grouping of headstones scattered throughout the dust and dirt of the Nevada desert. She had flown back with her father, Holly, and Edwin to attend the funeral of Tony Abbadelli.

The veritable ghost town of Goodsprings, with a population of less than three hundred, was overwhelmed with three thousand New Creekside residents, all there to pay their respects to the gruff defrocked priest and rock shop owner.

"This is why we need to get married here," Trudy overheard Holly say to the elder Masters as they stood waiting for the hearse to finish backing up to the gravesite.

"Married so we can be buried in the middle of the desert?" Masters said. "Sounds kind of fitting. At least Tony gets a headstone. Lots of his former mob colleagues are buried in the desert without one."

Holly sighed heavily. "Because people care about others here. Look around."

"We were married in the middle of a desert," Trudy added while clutching Gavin's hand. "It's working for us."

"Vegas doesn't count," Masters said as the pallbearers pulled the casket out of the black Cadillac.

Trudy surveyed the scene and then walked over to Nate, who was nattily dressed in a wide lapel black tux that harked back to a 70s-era high school prom. Before he grasped the handle of the casket, she mentioned to him: "Aren't we forgetting something?"

"We are?"

"This isn't a managed cemetery. Where do you plan to plant that casket?" Trudy said as she pointed to the burial spot. "We need to get a backhoe out here pronto."

"No worries," Nate said. "Rachel!" He waved her over. "Can you dig a spot for Tony's remains?"

"Sure!" Rachel squeaked as if it was the most natural request in the world.

Rachel blazed brighter than the sun as she transformed. The residents of New Creekside were familiar by now with protecting angels but still diverted their gaze away from their friend. Meanwhile, the various media and tourists that ringed the cemetery bowed low under Rachel's commanding presence.

Spreading her massive wings of razor-sharp swords, she turned towards the burial spot. Using the tip of a wing, Rachel dug into the earth until it was six feet underground. With one powerful motion, she scooped tons of dirt and rock up and out of the newly forming hole and piled it neatly to one side.

———

Bailey walked up to the gravesite with Emily and Jonathan. She hadn't known Tony well and knew even less of his previous life as Tom Ruxton, the gruff former rock shop owner, who spent thirty years in the Witness Protection Program. He was a strange old bird, but everyone in Calamity seemed to like him.

She noticed that several of the mourners she knew to be angels turned in unison to look at her—no, behind her. She turned as well.

"Do you feel that?" Jonathan whispered to her.

"No," she said.

"But you see something."

Bailey looked towards the assembled news vans and tourists. A perceptible mist seemed to surround a bearded man wearing jeans and a leather vest. He stood next to a Harley, wiping his forehead with a bandana. The biker walked away, but the mist remained, clinging to another figure—a man in a pinstripe suit—like a shroud. The businessman adjusted the knot of his power tie and lowered his designer sunglasses just a tad, peering over the top of them and staring at Bailey. It wasn't the biker—the businessman in sunglasses and a power tie gave a little smirk in her direction.

"Demon," she said to Jonathan and Emily.

"Who? How do you know?" Emily asked, "Maybe someone's possessed?"

"The guy in the suit near the Harley," Bailey looked at Emily, "You can tell a Harley from a Honda, can't you?"

"Of course," Emily said in a tone that suggested it was the stupidest question ever asked.

"Well, that's the same way I know demons from demonic possession," Bailey said. "They're obvious."

"I can deal with demons," Emily said, "but make sure you're right. If he's possessed, I'll end up killing a non-combatant."

Jonathan put a hand on both of their shoulders. "Bailey's correct, he is not possessed. See the way he looks at you, Bailey? He's studying you to see how big of a threat you are to them.

Return his gaze! Use this experience to refine your senses. You'll need it in the days to come."

Bailey thought back to the old guy in the mall: how the mist was not settled, how it weaved in and out, as if it was always trying to find harmony with the body it possessed. It was the same with her dad. Even the senator's mist was not settled, as he was using a human body. This one covered the man like a well-tailored suit, not moving but firm in its hold.

"Emily," Jonathan said, "it is better to have no further angelic transformations to tantalize the press. Please deal with this demon quietly."

"My pleasure," she said, walking towards the man.

"Wait up!" Bailey called, following after Emily at a trot. "What are you planning to do?"

"What I do best."

———

Emily had no fear of demons or death. She'd been through human and angelic wars and found them both to be about the same. They, on the other hand, should fear her—and perhaps her junior assistant who followed along.

She flashed a big smile as she approached the man. "Hello there," she said. "I'm Emily Iverson, and this is Bailey Tannahill. Who might you be?"

"Corson," he curtly replied. "I am Senator Stevenson's associate. I replaced Alastor Hiisi, who now resides in a much warmer climate than Nevada. He was quite impressed with you, from what I hear."

"It was probably that time I chucked him into a mountain that got his attention."

Corson nodded as if tipping his hat to her. "We have no quarrel; I didn't come for you," he said while staring at Bailey. "I wanted to see the exorcist for myself. So far, I'm not seeing much."

Emily watched as Bailey's face turned as red as her hair.

Bailey reached out her arms and tried to grab the mist that she talked about so often. She presented a comical image as she flailed her hands in front of the demon, trying to grasp something invisible to all humans other than her. A knot of onlookers, oblivious to what was happening, laughed outright.

Corson, similarly amused, let out a slight laugh. "Exorcists can only remove spirits from the possessed, which I am not. I wanted to see if you presented any threat to us. Obviously, that's no longer a concern. In a way, you should find solace in your incompetence, as it will allow your brother to live a bit longer."

Bailey swallowed the lump in her throat. "What do you mean?"

"He has pledged his service to the Imperator. I had concerns about his sister having certain talents that could hinder our plans. Now I see that you are nothing."

"Nothing!" Bailey screeched. "Why, I'll—"

"You'll what?" Corson grinned. "You're an animated piece of meat—nothing more. Soon you will return to the dirt like your friend they're burying today."

"Why do demons talk so much?" Emily said. Her hands began to glow greenish blue. She spread her arms apart; the glow grew and sparkled in the Nevada sunlight. Making a tossing motion, the energy flew several feet to hit Corson in the chest and quickly spread around him.

Emily had the satisfaction of seeing Corson's stupid grin wiped from his face as the dimensional energy cocooned his entire body. She knew that her backyard was about five miles away, but she was now pretty good with her aim. She planned to chuck the demon at the ladder the same way she did rocks. Hopefully, there would be a pretty explosion of fireworks and sparklers when the demon hit. Tony deserved to go out with a bang.

She started to move her arms, only to be blocked by Jonathan. "If a demon touches the ladder," he warned, "it will be destroyed, along with part of the surrounding area. They are not allowed access to heaven—their darkness cannot coexist with light."

"And the ladder is in my backyard," Emily said. "That's bad for property values."

"The protectors around New Creekside would stop him before that happened, but it could cause an unnecessary battle at our town's perimeter." Jonathan pointed to the north. "Want to try a distance throw?"

Emily looked at him. "Are you thinking what I'm thinking?"

"It would be a stretch. You might not make it."

The demon started struggling, causing Emily to clamp her vice of dimensional energy down even tighter.

"Are you trying to motivate me?" she asked Jonathan.

He shrugged. "No, I really don't think you can do it."

"Oh, what the hell! It'd be fun to try, although I can't see the target. I just hope I don't toss him onto someone's house."

She wound up and attempted a distance throw that would be hard to beat, especially since she was the only one in the world capable of doing it. "Give my regards to the space aliens," she said as she let go, admiring her handiwork as the demon spun off into the distance.

"Well, do you think I made it?" Emily said to Jonathan as she slapped her hands together.

"We'll have to watch the nightly news to find out."

CHAPTER THIRTEEN

Trudy and Gavin sat together on the couch in Emily's living room. It was amazing to her that someone else's house had become more of a home for her than she had ever experienced before. Still, she couldn't wait to be with Gavin in their new home—albeit a crowded one, with a new baby, an angel, and a German shepherd.

The funeral had been sad, even though they all knew that Tony was far away from the remains they buried at Rachel's impromptu gravesite. Nate told them about the joy that Tony experienced as he transitioned and that first meeting between him and his Lord.

"Rachel," Gavin said, "please turn up the volume. I think this is Emily's demon toss."

Rachel, who was in a recliner next to them, obliged and upped the volume with the remote. Emily and Jonathan occupied the love seat. Masters sat on a barstool outside the kitchen, nursing a beer. All turned their attention to the TV.

"Reports have come in," the anchor said, "of an unidentified object that struck Groom Lake, the dry lakebed adjacent to Area 51. This may be connected to the event that took place at the funeral of defrocked priest Tony Abbadelli, the infamous 'Vicar to the Mob,' as he was known. The funeral in Goodsprings was well attended by the angels and human residents of New Creekside. Emily Iverson, a key figure in the Battle of Las Vegas, seemed to toss, for lack of a better word, a man through the air and out of range of our cameras. We are attempting to find out the details of what exactly transpired.

"At Area 51, almost a hundred miles away, several UFO researchers had their cameras on during the event. One captured this remarkable footage."

The scene cut away to a video depicting what looked like a meteor streaking across the sky and pounding into the lakebed, creating a plume of dust that sped across the tightly packed dirt.

"Estimates are," the anchor continued, "that the dust plume was at least fifty feet high and created a mile-long scar across the dry landscape."

"A personal best!" Emily shouted as she pumped her fist into the air.

"I never doubted you," Jonathan said.

"Yes, you did," Emily said. "You didn't think I had it in me to chuck a demon a hundred miles."

"Angels don't lie," Rachel corrected.

"Yes, they do!" Emily insisted. "Jonathan told me I couldn't do it."

Jonathan patted her shoulder. "I knew you could do it, but you didn't know you could do it, so I knew you couldn't do it."

Emily gazed dumbly at him, furrowing her brow. "What?"

"If I only had a dollar for every headache Rachel gave me," Trudy sympathized until she glanced at the television. "Look!" she shouted, pointing. "What's that?"

"The clip you're watching now," the anchor narrated, "was taken from a hill closer to the termination of the impact."

A twisted form got shakily to its taloned feet. The demon's torso seemed to be rotting away from the inside; it had to support its mangled body by clutching a bent trident. It spread its rusty wings of broken swords and flew off into the desert, its flight erratic and unsure.

"That's the demon," Jonathan remarked. "Human form would serve it no purpose at this time."

"Corson was once a protecting angel," Rachel said. "Now, his evil is consuming him."

"So why was he at the funeral?" Bailey asked. "I hope he didn't show up just to insult me."

"Be glad that you are not viewed as a threat," Jonathan said. "That works in our favor."

Bailey put in: "Corson said that my brother is helping some Imperator guy."

"Imperator is the term demons use to show respect to Satan," Jonathan explained.

"Ian's not helping Satan," Masters said. He took a swig from his Miller Lite and stifled a burp.

"You can believe him," Trudy said. "He knows what working with Satan looks like."

Masters shook his head. "I thought we were past all of that. Besides, he's there sucking up to Stevenson because of you."

"I never thought I'd say this, but you're right Pops." She turned to Bailey. "He's in danger because I directed him to pretend to be on the senator's side."

"Why?" Bailey said. "He'll get himself killed. He'll zap something to Emily's backyard when a demon is watching and they'll kill him."

"Ian's aware of the danger but wanted to help," Trudy said. "I haven't known him long, but I'm a pretty good judge of character." She scowled at her father and added: "Ian can do it."

Ian sat in the Bronco just outside of his parents' former compound. The phone call said that he should be there promptly at 8 a.m. Ian wasn't sure what to expect. If the senator didn't buy his request to help, he would most likely be dead at 8:01.

No sooner had he picked up the phone to call Bailey than it vanished from his palm.

"Fuck!" he shouted as he pounded the steering wheel. He had just lost his only form of communication with the outside world. If he did that with a demon watching, he was as good as dead. It was ironic that he at one time only wished for death, but now knew he must live—if not for himself, then for Bailey.

A voice from the intercom said it was okay to proceed. He started to drive down the entrance road, hoping that one of the machine gun nests he helped to install wouldn't turn him into Swiss cheese.

Corson was waiting for him in the gravel driveway. He couldn't tell from the demon's inscrutable expression what would happen next.

Pulling the Bronco over and getting out, he noticed that bulldozers were at work in the back forty clearing the land for Stevenson's academy. Several mobile classrooms were sitting on truck trailers waiting to be assembled. He prayed he wasn't too late.

"Tannahill," Corson said. "The senator has considered your request."

The pause was way too long for Ian's liking.

Finally, Corson continued. "He welcomes you to the academy. You will begin by working with our architects and contractors to transform this dilapidated compound into a facility that will be the envy of the world. After the academy is completed, you will be given a full scholarship in recognition of your services. Do well, and you may even become an advisor to the Imperator. As a young human of some intelligence, we could benefit from your counsel as to how he is perceived by the world's youth."

"Thank you," Ian was able to croak.

"It is an honor that you have received from the senator," Corson said, "one that may be retracted at any time."

"I understand."

"Grab your things," Corson said, extending his hand towards the farmhouse front door. "You have your old room back."

———

Bailey tossed a Frisbee to Maggie, who almost caught it. The mountain lion intercepted it in a prodigious leap and ran off towards the horse barn. Maggie stood there with a befuddled look before something caught her eye. She loped over to the item of interest and put a big white paw on top of it.

"What is it, girl?" Baily called out. "Bring it here."

The shepherd obediently picked up something in her mouth and brought it over, dropping it at her feet.

"Oh, God," Bailey said. "Jonathan!"

———

"So, we've lost contact with him," Trudy said as they all stared at the cell phone on Emily's kitchen table. She scanned the faces around her. Jonathan appeared troubled—or at least troubled for an angel. Bailey was close to tears; Emily had her hands balled up like she was trying to restrain herself, and her father looked...bored.

"What's the big deal?" the elder Masters said. "The kid doesn't know how to use a cell phone anyway."

"You!" She pointed at her father. "Come with me."

"So, are you going to chew me a new one again?" Masters said as Trudy led him out of the house.

"Not this time. We need to get to Niagara and find Ian. I'm to blame if something happens to him."

"I'll have Holly call the executive airport," he said as they walked into Emily's backyard.

"Too slow," Trudy said. "Emily and I experimented; I can take you through the ladder."

"Hold on!" Masters protested, halting. "I'm not going through that angelic death trap thingamajig."

Trudy groaned and held out her hand. "Okay, here's the deal: I know how to stop the senator; I've seen how to stop Satan."

"How?"

"I saw you and a young guy. I didn't know who at the time, but it was Ian. If he's hurt, then everything falls apart, and life is going to become very nasty for the human race."

"It isn't already?"

Trudy glared at him.

Her father blew out his cheeks. "So, I guess since I'm with him in this vision, I better start keeping better track of him."

"Exactly." Trudy continued to hold out her hand. "Take it!"

Her father did as instructed. He looked out of sorts, and she couldn't figure out if it were the thought of traveling through a ladder or some other bug up his ass.

"I remember," Masters said, "taking your hand at your wedding. Was that the first day we touched—other than you beating the crap out of me while I was trying to drive us back to Creekside?"

"It was an exceptional day," Trudy said. "I married my beau, told my father that I love him, got all painted up by Kris—and Nate didn't lose the rings." She smiled at him. "Yeah, a pretty exceptional day."

"So, how does this all turn out?" he asked. "Do I marry Holly, or am I killed first? Preferably the latter."

"Your shtick is getting old," Trudy said as she walked him towards the glow of the ladder. "Word's out that you care about people besides yourself."

"Do we have to go there?"

"It's obvious," she said. She stepped into the ladder, dragging her father along behind her.

His eyes grew wide as he saw the ladder for the first time. "No!" he shouted over the din. "Do we really have to go *here*!"

———

Ian surveyed his room, which was pretty much the way he had left it—other than the girl in camo who was lying on his bed.

"Excuse me?" he mumbled.

She looked up at him. "This is mine. You can have the cot over there." She pointed. "Try not to snore."

"But…"

"But what?" she said, rising up on her elbows. She was about Ian's age and had a fierce, no-nonsense look that reminded him a bit of Bailey.

"So," she said, "what brings you to the academy?"

He walked over to his foldaway bed and tossed his backpack down. "I live here. I'm Ian Tannahill."

He didn't know someone could go from prone to standing at attention so quickly. "Sorry, sir, I had no idea."

He was a bit flustered by her response. "What's your name?" he stammered.

"Susanna Higgins, sir! I'm here to support the senator, sir!

"At ease," he said, holding back a laugh. He realized then that his father's demon-inspired grant of the compound to the senator placed him above the mere students attending classes.

"So, Susanna Higgins," he said, sitting on the cot, "why are you here?"

"To serve the senator," Susanna said with a worried look. "Please don't tell him that I disrespected you. I didn't know who you were."

Ian waved her off. "Don't worry."

"Take your bed," she said. "I'll take the cot."

"It's really not necessary."

"But you're Ian Tannahill," she said in evident wonder. "*The* Ian Tannahill."

"And why am I so special?"

"Your father was on television giving the compound to the senator… You *know* the senator." She paused. "I'm sorry about him and your mother."

"Thanks, and I don't know the senator well," he confessed. "Mostly through Corson."

"That guy scares me," she confided.

Ian nodded. "He scares the crap out of me too. Stay away from him if you can."

"So, are you going to the academy?" Susanna asked.

Now that she had calmed down, he was starting to like the idea of having a roommate. Susanna had long auburn hair tied in a scrunchie and an upturned nose that might not be considered beautiful, but it definitely put her in the "cute" category.

"I will be," Ian said. "But first the senator wants me to help with the construction. I know this compound better than anyone, so I'll be an advisor to start with."

Susanna made no effort to hide her admiration. "That is so cool! You'll be one of the founders of the new world. History will be written by you—and about you."

Ian smiled embarrassedly. "I doubt it. So, what brings you to the academy?"

Susanna sat down on the bed. "My mother was killed in Las Vegas. She was there for a convention, and a demon's wing tore through the hotel that she was staying in. It went right through the walls like they were paper..."

Ian gulped. "I'm sorry," he said lamely.

She looked like she was about to cry. "She was cut in half."

"Oh, God."

"God had nothing to do with it!" she spat. "The demons only came out after the angels made themselves known. They're the ones who brought them here. They're the ones that killed my mother, every bit as much as the demon. I hate them all, and they can all go to hell for the death and destruction they brought to us. The senator has shown that he's above demons and angels. He can make the world right."

Ian felt his words choke him. He realized he was now exactly like the Reverend Masters as he said, "Stevenson's a good man."

———

Masters stepped out of the ladder and promptly threw up.

"The Niagara ladder is a little rough," Trudy admitted. "We need a larger community here so that it becomes more stable."

"How did you do that?" he coughed, still hunched over.

"I didn't," she said. "That was little Jay at work. He's a good boy, for a fetus—but he has started to kick me."

"So, he will be called Jay?"

"Can't go against a vision, I guess," she said, patting him on the back. "So, how do we get a hold of Ian?"

Masters straightened and wiped his mouth with his handkerchief. "Well, I figure that he's either at the compound or dead. So, I'd start at the compound because if he's dead, he could be anyplace."

"Thank you, Mister Sunshine," Trudy mocked. "Well, I can't go there, and you might be a little suspicious if you show up."

The ladder flared behind Trudy; she turned in time to see Rachel come through.

"Did I miss anything?" the angel chirped.

"Watch where you step." Trudy pointed to her father's lunch. "Just trying to find out how to get in touch with Ian. How do we get into the compound without attracting suspicion?"

"That's easy, silly," Rachel said. "But I wouldn't trust Daeva any farther than I can throw her."

Trudy looked at her father, then Rachel. "Like Emily's power," she said, "that phrase is better used when you can't throw someone very far."

———

Bailey stood in Emily's backyard as the wind kicked up dust around her. Ian wasn't stupid; he had the same training she had. What she knew, he knew, although she applied it better; he would find a way to communicate.

Everything that Ian had zapped to Nevada appeared within a twenty-yard circle in front of the ladder. She scanned the ground, looking for anything that didn't belong in the desert.

She was about to give up when a rock with a piece of paper rubber-banded around it hit her on the side of the head.

"Ouch!"

She ran into the house, waving the folded paper. "Ian's all right!" she shouted at Emily and Jonathan.

Emily walked over to her. "He sent it via ladder mail," she observed. "Your brother is a smart guy."

"Runs in the family."

"What does it say?" Jonathan inquired.

Trudy unfolded it and read aloud: "'In the compound, safe so far—I have a roommate, and she's very nice.'"

Emily laughed. "Sounds like your bro might have him a sweetheart."

"About time!" Bailey said as she sat down. "There's nothing after that and no way to get a message back to him. Guess he's not as bright as you thought."

"We'll keep an eye on the backyard," Jonathan said. "We don't want to miss any communications." He turned to Emily. "Can you contact Trudy and let her know that Ian is well, but we only have one-way communication?"

"Sure."

"I can't just sit around on my ass waiting for something to happen," Bailey said. "You're going to have one seriously tightly wound sixteen-year-old on your hands if I can't *do* something."

Emily looked at Jonathan. "She does have a point. I think cabin fever is already setting in."

Jonathan nodded.

"Look at her eyes," Emily said. "Aren't they beginning to cross?"

"Stop!" Baily said, punching Emily on the arm. "You know what I mean."

"I have just the thing to keep you busy," Jonathan said. "More practice."

"No thanks, I have enough animals already. I woke up yesterday and there was somebody's burro staring at me through the window."

"I thought that perhaps we should go demon hunting."

"Now, you're talking!" Bailey said as she gave a major fist pump. "Sweet!"

———

The alarm went off, and Ian slapped it to the floor. He managed to catch that it said 5 a.m. before it rolled out of view. Sitting up in bed, he rubbed the sleep out of his bleary eyes. He thought he was still dreaming as he took in the sight before him. His new roommate was stretching on her bed, fully clothed in shorts and a green top, but his imagination filled in the blanks. He decided that other than the constant threat of being torn limb from limb by demons, this wasn't such a bad gig.

"I have class at six," Susanna said, standing up. "When do you start?"

"I have no idea."

"Okay, I'll shower up first. They're serving breakfast in the mess tent behind the barn, but I imagine you know that already."

"Things have changed just in the short time I've been away. I have some catching up to do."

"Oh, and don't be surprised if people stare at you," Susanna said. "I may have told a few students that I'm rooming with Ian Tannahill."

As Susanna went to wash up, he changed and, despite feeling somewhat grungy, went down the stairs to the kitchen.

Upon arrival, a feeling struck him like a blow: the room that used to be the life of the house was empty. His father used to sit at the far end of the kitchen table reading the newspaper and drinking coffee before beginning the day's chores. His mother would be fixing bacon and eggs and talking about her next project for the garden. Bailey would have her baseball cap pulled down to almost cover her eyes that were buried in a dog-eared copy of *Guns & Ammo*.

It was the life he knew, and he missed it so damn much.

"Tannahill," a voice came from behind.

Turning, he saw Corson standing there in a suit and tie.

"We need your expertise in finding some of the bunkers and caches hidden throughout the compound," the demon said. "We'd like to have a full weapons inventory by the end of the day."

"Sure," Ian said, hoping that Corson hadn't noticed his sentimentality. "There are five underground bunkers and fifteen weapons and survival caches. I'm sure you'd never locate some of them without my help."

"Then it is fortuitous that you are here," Corson said without emotion and walked out.

———

Trudy sipped her glass of water as she and her father sat in the hotel bar waiting for Daeva to arrive.

"Hopefully Daeva will come alone," Trudy said. She still held a grudge that Ahti tried to kill Gavin and did not want to see him. It was for this same reason that she advised Rachel to stay in her room. She remembered Rachel tossing Ahti into the acrylic wall of Kim's enormous shark tank back in Vegas. If Kim was still mad about the flooded lobby, she didn't show it.

"For the bar owner's daily sales total, it'd be better if Ahti does come along," Masters said as he sipped an old-fashioned.

Trudy noticed that Daeva was heading their direction, stuffed into a way-too-small black miniskirt. She looked over at her father, who seemed about to drool, and shoved him with her elbow.

"At least," he said, "Ahti stayed home—wherever that is."

Daeva smoothed down her skirt and sat in the chair Masters pulled out for her. She had a big smile on her face, which somehow didn't seem to fit with her being a demon.

"Where's your loyalist pet?" Daeva asked.

"Beats me," Masters said. "Probably dancing on the head of a pin somewhere."

"Anyway, I found the perfect theater, and the lease is ready to be signed."

"That was fast," Masters said. He hoisted his drink at their server and held up two fingers, indicating himself and Daeva. "What does Ahti think about it?"

"Who gives a fuck what Ahti thinks?" Daeva spat. "He's going to be the theater's live-in security guard. I'm sure his breath will turn away any burglar."

"How much is this dump going to cost me?" Masters said.

"Don't worry, it's just under a million bucks. You should be able to reach into the Imperator's deep pockets for that."

"This time, that'll be your chore," Masters said.

Daeva's perplexed look said it all. "Excuse me?"

"Ian," Trudy interjected, "has lost his cell phone and we need to make contact. You'll meet Stevenson at the compound and give him your pitch. That way, you'll be able to check in on Ian and make sure he's okay."

"You'll also need to slip him a new cell phone," Masters said.

Daeva sat there for a moment. "You don't understand," she said. "Most rebels want to stay as far away from the Imperator as possible. Only bad things happen when you're in his presence. Ahti was told never to return to the compound, and I think he's happy about that."

"Why can't my father figure that one out?" Trudy said.

Masters waited while the server placed two brandy old-fashioned sweets on the table.

"Anything else, sir?" she asked pleasantly.

"I have a few ideas, but not in front of my daughter."

Scowling, the server stalked away.

"Okay," Masters said, "for this to work, we've got to keep Ian in one piece and not have his body parts scattered across the compound."

Daeva crossed her arms, not touching the drink. "Why would the Imperator listen to me? Why would he come out here?"

"This is why," Masters said. He pulled out his phone and dialed; the call went through instantly. "Senator Stevenson, I've just been talking with Daeva. She found the perfect theater for her..." He put the phone to his chest. "What the hell was it called again?"

"Theater of Depraved Delusions."

"Yeah," he said, putting the phone back to his ear. "Theater of Depraved Delusions, although I thought that was the United States Senate." He paused for a laugh that never came.

"Anyway, are you going to be out this way anytime soon? Daeva would like to discuss the theater with you personally, and I'll need to get a sign off on the lease before some country bumpkins from Branson, Missouri, beat us to it."

Masters listened to the senator's remarks, said goodbye, and hung up.

"Well?" Trudy and Daeva said in unison.

"The senator is going to the compound Monday to welcome the first batch of students to the academy. He said that you could drop by for a chat."

"The Imperator doesn't chat," Daeva huffed.

"You seemed kind of scary when you belted me with that fiery pitchfork thingy back in Vegas," Master said. "I guess it was all an act."

"Yeah, well, we all know our place in this universe," Daeva said. "I'm far above humans, but the Imperator was *the* Anointed Covering Cherub. There's a big difference."

"Well," Masters said, "you know that the old cure for stage fright is to picture your audience naked."

"You're trying to get me sent to the pit, aren't you?"

Masters raised his glass in a toast, even though Trudy and Daeva didn't respond. "May Satan be well-endowed."

CHAPTER FOURTEEN

"So, where are we going to find these demons that I can exorcise?" Bailey asked Jonathan as they drove through downtown Las Vegas. "We've already passed a used car dealership, the Clark County Detention Center, the Internal Revenue Service, and a couple suspicious crack houses."

She pointed out the window. "Oh, look, the Mob Museum! Emily' said they called to see if they could get some of Tony's stuff for an exhibit. I'm not sure if he should be remembered that way—it seems disrespectful."

"It was part of his past," Jonathan said as he turned the corner. "He tried being someone else, and it ate away at him. He was much happier after he acknowledged what he once was. He was then able to grow and become a better person."

"My mother always used to watch Dr. Phil," Bailey said. "You sound just like him."

Jonathan laughed.

"Ah, The Burlesque Hall of Fame," Bailey sighed as they passed another landmark. "They just have everything here."

Jonathan pointed to a white, vaguely Spanish-style building across the street. "That's El Cortez. Nate could tell you more about it. I believe that Bugsy Siegel owned it at one time."

"Who?"

"A famous mobster who was instrumental in the development of the Vegas Strip," Jonathan explained. "Tony may have met him."

"That's interesting and all," Baily said as she slunk down in her seat. "But where do we find the demons? This place is called Sin City; you'd think it would be chock-full of them."

"I'll sense their presence if they are close by," Jonathan said as he continued to drive around town.

"Can't we do this at night?" Bailey begged. "Maybe they're like vampires. Besides, we'd get to see all the lights. This place sucks in the daylight."

"Patience is required to be a demon hunter."

"What's that guy?" Bailey pointed to a man standing in front of the Heart Attack Grill whose tag line was "over 350 lbs eat free."

"Look closely."

She did and was disappointed. "That's just a demon pretending to be human."

Jonathan pulled the car up to the curb. "But he might know where we can find someone possessed. Go talk to him. I'll park the car."

"By myself?"

"You'll do fine."

Grudgingly, she got out of the Jeep and walked over to an ATM machine. The man seemed to be concentrating on panhandling the tourists and didn't even see her—or if he did, he didn't think she had any dough to spare.

Bailey reached into her pocket and pulled out what little cash she had. "Sir," she said, "let me buy you something to eat."

Suddenly the demon's eyes widened in recognition; he took a step back. "What do you want with me? I do not torture the living flesh."

"But you know those who do," Bailey said. "Lead me to one, and you shall be rewarded."

She counted the cash in her hand—$7.50—and held it out.

It seemed to be enough; the demon greedily grabbed it out of her hand. He pointed down the pedestrian street. "You'll find him in front of Binion's casino. He does a mime act on the hour."

"How many inhabit the man?"

"Just one," the demon said, walking away with his loot. "Most of our kind have no tolerance for mimes—they're way too creepy."

205

Ian stood near the warehouse, watching as the newly erected classrooms and barracks took shape behind the cargo container bunker. He was impressed at how fast construction was going. The first version of the academy would be a bit rough around the edges, but Corson had shown him some renderings of the final development, and he had to admit it was impressive.

His father, if he were looking down at his former home and compound would be swearing up a shit storm, heaven or not.

"Did you hear?" Ian heard as Susanna walked up next to him. "The senator will be here on Monday to welcome the first class to the academy."

"That's wonderful," Ian said without enthusiasm.

"Perhaps," she cooed, sliding up next to him, "you could arrange for me to meet him?" She moved even closer until he felt her soft, pert breasts poking his arm. "I'd be *very* grateful."

"I'll see what I can do," Ian gulped. He wasn't even sure if *he* would get to see the senator.

"You're a sweetheart," Susanna said. She stood on tiptoes and pecked him on the cheek.

He could feel himself blush.

"I'm off to class," she said with a wave. "Have a wonderful day, Ian Tannahill."

"You are becoming quite the Casanova," Corson said, walking up to him. "The benefits of being the son of a dead hero."

"Look," Ian said, "I know it was necessary to kill him. I have no problem with that...or with you."

"Really?" Corson said, taking a position in front of the boy, invading his personal space. "Didn't you love your father?"

"If I loved him so much, why did I try to kill myself in one of the bunkers?"

This seemed to give Corson pause. "You did?"

"He took me away from New York City, and the life I desperately wanted, to work at this shithole of a compound. Of course, I hated him, but it was either him or me. I couldn't bring myself to kill him, so I was going to off myself."

"And?"

"I failed, obviously. Just as I was about to pull the trigger, I received a call from Ahti, wanting me to come in for an interview. I saw my chance and haven't regretted it—although Ahti's a total ass."

He couldn't believe that Corson laughed at that. Then Corson patted him on the shoulder. Ian thought he'd pass out.

"I see we're on the same page," Corson said. "Continue with your outstanding work, and you will be richly rewarded in the new world to come. A kiss—and perhaps more—from a pretty girl is just the beginning."

As Corson walked off, Ian felt his legs wobbling and was deeply disgusted with himself. He hated to disrespect his father like that, but he needed to.

He knew his father would understand.

———

"There's the mime," Bailey said. She and Jonathan watched a man in the typical getup—black and white striped shirt, white gloves, black beret and tights, white-painted face and a single black teardrop under his right eye—attempt to extricate himself from an invisible box. The man looked on the pudgy side and could probably get a free burger at the Heart Attack Grill. Mist swirled around him as he moved his hands over the unseen container. A few tourists stopped to watch for a minute or two and dropped a buck in his jar.

"I see why he performs out on the street and not in a theater or on television," Bailey remarked. "If you ask me, all mimes should be sealed up in their invisible boxes and suffocated."

Jonathan couldn't disguise a slight smile. "Actually," he said, "mimes have a rich history going back to ancient Greece, although the Roman emperor Trajan banned mimes from the Roman Empire."

"Good for him," Bailey said.

The mime started to stare at them and then lost his balance and crashed through the invisible box.

"The demon senses me," Jonathan said. "You'll have to act fast."

"Crap," Bailey said.

"Go!" Jonathan commanded.

Bailey ran over to the man and grabbed hold of one of the cables of mist that moved around and through him. She could hear cries of pain, but she wouldn't stop. She had to free the man from his prison. She had to remove the menace that tortured him night and day.

Pulling as hard as she could, she felt the demon give way and fell on her back to the gum-covered sidewalk. The audience backed away from the scene, not sure what was happening. Bailey once again stared into the face of a mist-like apparition before it turned away and sped off under the canopy that covered Freemont Street.

The mime lay on the ground as his expression changed from pain to anger. "What the hell did you just do?" he shouted at her.

"What do you mean?"

"What did you do!"

Bailey stood up. "I rescued you from a demon."

The rotund mime rolled over and stood up. "Who gave you permission to do that?"

"I was helping you—"

"You just evicted the brains of the act!" he said, pointing an accusing finger at her. "I don't know how to do this without him. Now I'm going to have to go back to a forklift job at a broiling hot warehouse."

"You mean you want to be possessed?"

He looked like he was going to cry. "Of course! Who wouldn't?"

Bailey turned to Jonathan and shook her head. "I've got nothin'."

———

The limo ride to the Tannahill compound was a study in contrasts for Trudy. On one side sat Daeva in an understated (for her) burgundy miniskirt. Directly opposite sat Rachel, who was trying to stink-eye Daeva into the pit.

Her father sat next to Daeva and alternately looked bored or lecherous as Daeva's thigh hovered within arm's reach.

Trudy sat next to Rachel and put a hand on her friend's arm. She felt how tense she was.

"This is wrong," Rachel said, glaring at Daeva. "We shouldn't be here."

"Well, the original plan," Masters said, "was for Daeva to go alone, but apparently Stevenson wants us all there for his grand opening."

"We're doing Satan's bidding," Rachel said as she started to glow.

"Calm down," Masters said. "Maybe you'll win the door prize."

Daeva smirked. "Believe me, this wasn't my idea. I didn't ask for a loyalist to tag along."

"Hold steady," Trudy said, as they approached the compound.

Rachel shook off Trudy's hand, which startled her. Rachel had never done anything like that before.

"I'm sorry," Rachel said. "I can't do this. It's not right. I will not be a pawn for Satan: someone he can parade in front of the cameras to tell the world that angels are with him. We're not with him. We will never be with him."

"Stop the car!" Trudy shouted to the driver.

As they pulled over, a large crowd of protesters surrounded the compound's entrance. Many were holding signs proclaiming Stevenson the antichrist.

"They don't know how right they are," Daeva said.

Rachel opened the door. "Come with me," she said to Trudy.

Trudy wasn't sure what to do.

"I'm not commanding this as an angel," Rachel added. "I'm asking this as your friend."

Without another thought, she got out of the car. "I'm with her," she said. "Go do your damnedest, Pops."

"Don't I always?" Masters replied as Trudy slammed the door and the car crept towards the entrance road.

The parade ground boasted hastily installed sod rolls and a stage constructed at one end. Ian stood next to a couple dozen news trucks, their satellite dishes pointed up at some unseen craft 22,000 miles off in space.

The first class of Stevenson's Academy of Peace and Justice wore dress blue uniforms with decorative swords at their sides.

Ian was at the far end of the grounds, and behind him foundations were already being poured for the permanent structures. Rebar stuck up out of the concrete with little orange caps on top to prevent someone from being impaled should they trip. To the left and right of him were the makeshift mobile barracks and classrooms. Towards the cargo container bunker was an extensive mess tent and portable storage sheds; beyond that, he could see the roof of the farmhouse.

He had heard that Stevenson had arrived and was in his parents' house. This was the ultimate sacrilege: the desecration of everything his father believed in.

Yet, there he stood, doing nothing.

"Ian!" Susanna shouted across the parade grounds. "Wake up!"

He managed a smile as she walked over to him. He took a moment to inspect her uniform that fitted her like a glove.

"Whatcha doing there, Tannahill?" She grabbed him by the collar and pulled his face down within kissing range.

"Uh..." Ian managed to get out before receiving a very sloppy French kiss.

"People will see," he sputtered after she pulled her tongue out of his mouth.

"So? I want people to know that you're mine."

"I'm yours?"

"Well, we do sleep together in the same room. So, when do we see Senator Stevenson?" she asked. "He's supposed to be at the farmhouse, but they won't let me in. I can't even get into my—your room."

"Does it mean that much to you?"

He could see from her expression that it did.

"Okay, come on."

"Once we're inside," she said, grabbing his arm, "maybe we can sneak up to that room of yours for an hour or so."

Ian colored. "Uh, do you think it'll take that long?"

Susanna grinned. "Sure, big boy. Say, how'd you like a free sample?"

Ian nodded dumbly. He watched wide-eyed as she tugged at the Velcro on her tunic, easing the garment open to expose the tank top underneath—and an exquisite pair of nipples.

"Colder here than I thought," Ian deadpanned before Susanna laughingly took her leave.

———

210

"So, what do we do now?" Trudy asked as several hundred protesters began to surround her and Rachel. In front of the compound entrance, they could see a line of police cars and cops in full riot gear. "What's with all the people?"

"Humans can read the signs," Rachel said. "You see visions, but the truth is available for all who look for it."

"So, I'm just especially dense and need the visions is what you're saying?"

"Look!" someone shouted nearby. "It's Rachel the angel and Trudy Masters!"

"Masters-Young!" Trudy shouted back.

The crowd descended upon them. "What are you doing here?" one protester asked.

"Uh…"

"Rachel," another said, "is Stevenson the devil?"

Trudy knew that Rachel could only tell the truth and started to pull her away when a big guy in Levi's and a plaid shirt blocked her.

"Brian Tannahill was my friend," the man said, folding his python arms across his broad chest. "No one here believes that he killed his wife, then gave his pride and joy to Stevenson, then killed himself. Everyone here loved Brian and Linda Tannahill. We're going to do everything in our power to make sure their deaths were not in vain, and to protect their children from a similar fate."

He focused his steely gaze upon Rachel. "Tell us, little lady, is Stevenson Satan?"

Rachel took the man's calloused hand in hers and looked up at him. "Yes."

He turned to the others in the crowd and shouted: "It is as we feared!"

Others shouted out the message to those further away. The shouts turned to screams as tear gas canisters were lobbed into the protesters.

"Those aren't police, they're Stevenson's men!" the man said. Shielding them with his mountainous body, he pushed them towards a rickety Ford pickup parked off to the side of the road. "Let's get out of here!"

Ian, with Susanna in tow, approached the farmhouse. Several Secret Service agents in nondescript dark suits blocked their way.

One of them held up his hand and said, "No access at the moment."

"I'm Ian Tannahill."

"So?"

"It's okay," Corson said as he stepped onto the porch. "They are welcome inside."

The men backed off and let them continue up the steps and into the house. The sight of Senator Stevenson sitting in his father's recliner made him scream internally. Ian needed every ounce of restraint he possessed to keep from finding a loaded pistol and shooting the senator dead—again.

The senator stood. "Ian," he said, "it is indeed a pleasure."

Stevenson held out his hand. Ian knew there was no way he'd live through the day if he didn't shake it. The senator's grasp was bone-crushingly earnest; Ian expected no less from the reincarnation of Lucifer.

"Senator Stevenson, I'd like you to meet Susanna Higgins," Ian said, trying to shake some life back into his throbbing mitt. "She's a new recruit."

The senator gave a benevolent smile and shook her hand—far less aggressively, Ian observed. "It is indeed a pleasure to meet you. Young students such as you will reform the world for the better."

Ian thought that Susanna was going to melt. She didn't say a word, but her star-struck expression and goofy grin said it all.

Ian just wanted out of the room. "Well, Senator, I imagine you have a lot to do to get ready for the assembly," he said, taking a step backward.

"Oh, by the way, Ian," Stevenson said, "don't worry about your sister Bailey. Corson looked in on her, and she's perfectly safe in Nevada."

"Thank you," Ian said, not knowing exactly what the senator meant, especially the part about Corson looking in on her.

"Bailey's friend, though," Corson said as he walked into the room, "has quite the pitching arm. It made for a memorable experience."

"Glad you liked it," Ian said, clueless as to Corson's meaning. "Excuse me, I need to get something in my room."

"Go ahead, young man," Stevenson said. "After all, this is your home."

Ian grabbed Susanna by the arm and pulled her away from the senator. Halfway up the stairs, her eyes were still googly with idolatry for Stevenson.

"That was amazing!" she cooed.

"Okay, snap out of it," Ian said as he led her to his room. He wanted some time away from the event to think things through.

As soon as he opened the door, Susanna pushed him through and slammed it behind them. Pushing him onto his bed, she climbed on top of him, and he could hear the whoosh of Velcro being undone. Before he knew what was happening, she had her clothes off and was starting to unzip his jeans, which was fortunate since they were becoming much too tight.

Ian reached up and stroked the rosy bud of her right nipple with his index finger.

He felt her warm skin for a second...then she disappeared.

———

"Why is there a naked girl in your backyard?" Bailey asked Emily.

Emily looked out the sliding glass door. "Your brother must have touched her."

"Touched her...where?" Bailey scrunched up her nose. "Eww!"

Emily walked toward the bathroom. "I'll fetch a robe. Go out and greet her—she looks terrified."

Bailey wasn't sure she wanted to meet this new visitor. While she was happy that Ian was coming out of his shell, seeing his likely sole sexual conquest standing in her birthday suit in front of the ladder was a bit too much information.

"Hi, I'm Bailey Tannahill," she said. "I guess you've met my brother."

"Where am I?" Susanna stammered as she attempted to cover herself as much as possible.

"You're in Calamity," Emily said as she walked over and handed the girl a plaid robe. "Calamity, Nevada."

The girl quickly put on the robe. "How did I get here," she said, scanning her surroundings, "and where's Ian?"

"Ian has a nasty habit of making things, and people, disappear," Bailey said. "But they all end up here. Don't worry, it's perfectly safe. He zapped me here as well, and I haven't had any side effects—that I know of."

"I don't understand," Susanna said. "I was with him one moment, his zipper was stuck, then he touched me on my—"

"Stop right there," Bailey said, holding up her hand. "I don't want to hear about what my brother was touching."

She was starting to dislike the girl. Ian was in a dangerous place; he didn't need distractions like this. "Who are you, anyway?"

"Susanna Higgins. I room with Ian at the academy."

"Oh, so you're the one," Bailey said. "It's better you're here. He doesn't need you around him at the moment."

"And why is his little sister the expert in what he needs?" Susanna objected.

"Because I've always watched out for danger, and Ian's clueless." Bailey wagged a finger at her. "And *you're* danger."

"Perhaps we should take this discussion inside?" Emily said, pointing towards the house.

Bailey watched as Susanna realized she wasn't in Kansas anymore. Several protecting angels were visible in the distance, their glow, that of massive arc welders, difficult to look at for more than a moment. Susanna looked up; her jaw fell open as she gazed at the twisting, lightning-filled tornados and dark clouds that covered the town.

Then she turned her gaze back to Bailey. "This is that fucking town of angels, isn't it?" she said, visibly angry. "Get me the hell out of here!"

"Believe me, I'd like to get rid of you," Bailey said, "but it's safer for Ian if you stay here."

"I need to get back to the academy. I need to be there when Senator Stevenson blesses us."

Bailey was totally unmoved by her plea. "Ian's transporter only works in one direction, so we're stuck with you."

"Bailey," she heard Jonathan say as he opened the backyard gate and joined him. "You should extend hospitality to all that come our way."

"I've got a collection of critters to prove I'm hospitable. But Maggie's the only bitch we need around here."

Susanna moved closer to Bailey as if she wanted to fight, which was okay with her.

"Yeah, I said it," said Bailey, getting in the girl's face. "So?"

"Bailey!" Jonathan said, squeezing between them. "What is the first rule of a demon hunter?"

"We don't talk about demon hunting?"

Jonathan stared blankly at her.

Bailey shook her head at the ground. "Restraint—never show fear or anger towards them, as they will use it against me. But she's not a demon, unfortunately."

Uriel opened up the sliding glass door and walked out into the backyard. "Here you all are. Who's our new friend?"

"She's no friend," Bailey said. "She doesn't like angels."

"Perhaps she doesn't understand us," Jonathan suggested diplomatically.

"Oh, I understand you all too well," Susanna said. "You killed my mother."

"That's a lie!" Bailey said, trying to push her way around Jonathan. Then she noticed her nemesis was starting to cry.

"My mother is dead, and it's because of angels chasing demons down the Las Vegas Strip," Susanna spluttered. "She came to Vegas for a fun vacation and left in a coffin."

"I was there," Uriel said. "The demon was trying to cause as much damage as he could. He wanted to kill as many humans as possible."

"You brought them here," Susanna said. "You brought their destruction. I know the senator says you are just trying to help, but his mother wasn't killed."

"No, *he* was," Emily chimed in. "Look, I didn't ask for my backyard to become an angelic Grand Central Station. I didn't know what to make of these beings that could destroy entire cities, but at the same time caring about what chores they could help an amputee with. Archangels and war vets shouldn't coexist, but they do. They shouldn't be friends, but they are. I'm proof of that."

"She was a good woman—a good mother," Susanna said. "She shouldn't have died that way. Cut in two by a demon."

Uriel turned to Susanna. "Angels are not all powerful or all knowing," he said gently. "I was the one trying to stop the demon. I was successful, but not quickly enough to prevent many deaths, including your mother's. Do not hate everyone because of my failure. If you must hate someone, hate me."

"I…" Susanna sobbed. "I just miss her so much. It hurts so damn much… not having her here."

Bailey put her arm around her. "I just lost both parents to demons, Susanna. I know that pain. I'm so sorry."

She couldn't believe that she was hugging someone that, a few moments ago, she was going to slug. But it was like Susanna said: 'It hurts so damn much.'

———

"Well, hello, big boy," Daeva said as she walked into Ian's room and stared at his crotch. "And I do mean big."

"Sorry," Ian muttered. He sat up and tried to think of broccoli and puppy dogs. That didn't work, so he covered his boner with a pillow.

"Don't be sorry," Daeva said. She wet her top lip with the pink tip of her tongue seductively, which didn't help Ian's predicament. "It's a natural human reaction, but how did you know I was coming?" She tossed a cell phone on the bed. "Don't lose this one."

"Why are you here?"

"To check on you and make sure that Corson hadn't skewered you with a wing," Daeva said. "Masters is downstairs schmoozing the Imperator. Rachel and Trudy ran off to join some protest. And oh, yeah, I have a theater—with stage lighting. You'll love it. The Imperator just signed off on it."

Ian ignored her enthusiasm. "I don't know what to do. I think I just zapped my one and only almost sexual conquest to Nevada."

Daeva sat down on the bed next to him and put her finger to his lips. "Don't talk about that here. Don't even think it. If the Imperator finds out, then we're all dead. Well, not me, but I'll be sent to the pit, which makes death look like a day at Disneyland."

"I don't know if I can do this," Ian said. "I'm not the Reverend Masters. I can't live a lie. I can't pretend to go along with Stevenson and his academy. Sooner or later he or Corson are bound to notice my lack of enthusiasm and then the jig's up."

"Masters has no moral compass," Daeva agreed. "I think that's why he gets along with rebels so well. I don't have much experience with loyalty, love, or caring about someone other than myself. If I think back to before the rebellion, I can vaguely remember some of those feelings, but they are mostly lost to me—not that I'd want them again.

"Think about revenge, Ian. Remember who killed your parents. Hate is useful, and backstabbing is an art form you'll need to learn. No one here is your friend—not even me."

"Then how can I trust you?"

"You can't," she said as she stood up and walked to the door. "I live among humans but can't really stand them. After all, you were created in the Tyrant's image, after His likeness, as they say in the Book of Lies. I see His image in you, and it makes me want to kill you. I could snap your neck before you could scream."

"Should I be worried?"

"Nah, you're lucky. I hate the Imperator even more. Sometimes the necessities of life make for strange bedfellows. Speaking of which, is she pretty?"

Ian thought of his bare-naked roommate and sighed. "Very."

"Do you have the same beliefs and goals in life—does she love you?"

"I don't think so."

Daeva smiled. "Ah, young lust. Congratulations, you have a little bit of the devil in you."

———

Trudy and Rachel sat in the backseat of the pickup as the man who rescued them from the security forces pulled up to his home. It was a large, two-story brick house built in the 1890s, where multiple generations could have lived comfortably under one roof.

"So that wasn't the police?" Trudy asked, still amazed that Stevenson could already have a small army at his disposal.

"No, they're definitely Stevenson's private security," their rescuer said. "He's been bringing them in for the last week or so. Full SWAT teams at his disposal and answering only to him. They're stationed at the Tannahill compound. Many of the local police are on our side, and even the ones that aren't wouldn't lob tear gas at us."

He stopped in front of the house and reached a hand back towards them. "I'm Cyrus Miller, by the way," he said.

Trudy shook his big calloused paw. "You seem to know us already. Well, thanks for getting us out of there."

As they got out of the truck, she had to stop for a moment and lean against the passenger door.

"Are you okay?" Rachel said as she came over and put her arm around Trudy.

"Yeah, I think little Jay just kicked me. He's done that a few times now. Isn't it kind of early for him to be doing that?"

"He's a precocious child," Rachel said. "He already helps you to see ladders."

"I feel inferior, and he's not even born. He'll probably be asking for help with his algebra homework when he's three months old."

Trudy let go of the truck and started towards the house. "I'm okay now, but little Jay has quite the kick. I guess I'm going to be a soccer mom after all."

"Excuse the mess," Cyrus said, once they were inside. "I sent my wife and kids to Ohio to stay with her mother. Brian told me about what Bailey had seen on our property. At first, I didn't believe him, but then I saw the pentagram carved into my field and decided there was no way I'd let my family stay here with demons traipsing about."

Cyrus led them into the spacious kitchen. He sat on one of the farmhouse-style table's benches; Rachel and Trudy sat opposite him.

"Why are you staying here, Cyrus?" Rachel asked. "Shouldn't you leave as well?"

"A group of us from around the area have decided that we can't just run off with our tails tucked between our legs," said Cyrus. "If we don't fight evil, who will? You know the government won't. I bet they're working with Stevenson."

"They are deceived," Rachel said. "Satan disguises himself as an angel of light."

"Trudy," Cyrus said, "excuse me for asking this, but with all the news coverage the reverend has gotten, what side is your father on?"

"Mostly his own," Trudy said. "But he knows the stakes are larger than his own need and greed. He also has an angel buddy to keep him on the straight and narrow. So when you see him on television tonight kissing Stevenson's ring, it's not how it looks."

Cyrus laced his giant sausage fingers together on the rustic tabletop. "I don't know if my neighbors will be as convinced. Most of them despise your father, and a few wouldn't mind taking a shot at him."

"They'd have to get in line," Trudy said. "Look, I understand their feelings, but he's doing something incredibly brave right now, and I don't mean brave by his standards, but brave for anyone in his position."

"Fair enough," said Cyrus. "I'll spread the word to the others that the reverend is on our side."

"Cyrus," Rachel said, "this is a pretty big house for one person. Would you be interested in having some of my friends come and stay with you?"

"Friends?"

"Yes, both angels and humans from Greenland; they are relocating to this area. We need someplace for them to stay."

"Angels, you say? Living here?" Cyrus gave a big grin. "Well, sure, I can take some in. I bet a lot of the families in the area would be more than happy to have angels bunk with them. Most of the guys I know around here have sent their families out of state. They'll have room, too. Plus, they'll feel a helluva lot safer having an angel in the guest room." He glanced sheepishly at Rachel. "Pardon my choice of words, miss."

Rachel smiled. "That's quite all right. I'm getting used to colorful human expressions."

"Emily," Nate called out, "can you hand me that engine block?"

"Sure." Emily walked over and inspected the miscellaneous mechanical junk under the same shed that also protected her prized Harley. "Do you want the knucklehead?"

"No, that's too light." Nate pointed to her right. "How about the small block next to it? We need to challenge him."

Emily surveyed the mangled V8 block that she had at one time tossed from Robby's garage to the motel, an impressive throw of over a half a mile— not bad for a beginner. She was going to give it back, but it had a large crack running down from the second cylinder, and he told her to keep it.

Holding out her right hand, she felt the familiar prickling sensation as the greenish-blue light formed in her palm. Casting it towards the rusting piece of metal, she raised her hand, and the engine block followed along. Once it was about three feet off the ground, she walked it over to Nate.

"Where do you want it?" she asked.

"How about next to the rocking chair? I'm trying to go from lighter to heavier."

"That's my grandmother's rocker."

"It should be okay."

"Yeah, it's that word 'should' that worries me," Emily said as she gently lowered the engine to the ground.

"It took you a while to master your powers," Nate remarked, "but there were casualties along the way." He pointed to a twisted scrap of metal that sat on a card table nearby.

She frowned, looking at what used to be the front fork of her previous Harley. Now it was a half-melted pretzel of metal with only a few flakes of chrome remaining on its singed surface. "That was an eleven thousand dollar practice shot."

"We're going to lower the training costs with Ian," Nate said. He pulled a bowling ball out of a bag with a red and green swirling design that matched his bowling shirt and placed it on a blanket on the ground.

The sliding glass door opened and Bailey, followed by Susanna, walked over. "Hi, guys," Bailey said. "I just finished giving Susanna the grand tour of New Creekside."

"So, what do you think?" Emily asked her.

"Not much here," Susanna said, "but all the residents are very nice."

"How is staying with Kris?"

"She's nice too, but way too much pink!" Susanna laughed.

Bailey looked around. "What's with all the crap? Having a yard sale?"

"Hey!" Emily said. "These are my prized possessions."

"We're going to be doing some training," Nate explained.

"Guess it's not me," Bailey said. "I don't see any critters or demons in the collection."

"Actually," Emily said, "both of you will be very happy to see our train-ee—if he ever shows up."

Bailey and Susanna smiled hugely and said in unison: "Ian?"

CHAPTER FIFTEEN

Trudy watched as her father paced in front of the invisible (for him) Niagara ladder. When he wandered too close to it, a finger of lightning would emerge from the column and move towards him. Every so often it would even make contact causing him to flinch.

"Why do I feel someone is watching me?" he said.

Trudy turned to Rachel and inquired, "Why does the ladder do that?"

"Your father is also its father," she explained. "It's reaching out to a parent."

"So, do I have a kid sister or brother?"

"The ladders are asexual."

"If you say so, but I think I just saw it grab my dad's ass."

Masters looked at his watch. "Where are they? I don't want anyone to see us standing around up here. Couldn't we have a more secluded spot for the ladder?"

"No one can see it," Rachel assured him.

"But they can see us," said Masters, "and we're not exactly unknowns."

"Here they come," Trudy said, spying a pair of heads at the top of the ramp. Edwin and Ian walked over to join the group.

"What took you so long?" Masters complained.

"Ian was looking for his wallet," Edwin said.

"I did find it momentarily, but now it's in Nevada," Ian added. "Bailey will need to send it back. I need my driver's license."

Trudy smiled at him and offered: "How about we send you to Nevada?"

"I'd like to see Bailey," Ian said, "but I don't have of the luxury of time. They expect me back at the academy by tomorrow morning or there'll be hell to pay."

Rachel pushed her blonde hair out of her face as the wind kicked up. "It's important that you see your sister and strengthen that bond."

"I also hear," Masters said, "your roommate has a habit of traveling in the nude. I wish I had roommates like that."

Ian groaned. "She's going to kill me! Being blessed by the senator was important to her."

"I think she will come to find," Rachel said, "that the real blessing was not being blessed."

Trudy held out her hand for Ian to take. "Ready for your cross-country trip?"

"Come again?"

"Ladder travel," Trudy said. "You'll love it."

"Is it safe?"

"Not really," Trudy admitted, "but I'm the only Uber driver for angelic ladders around, so don't forget to tip."

———

Ian stepped out of the ladder and let go of Trudy's hand because he felt the sudden urge to vomit.

"It's a little rough right now," Trudy admitted. "It'll get better as the Niagara community grows."

"Ian!" Bailey whooped. She ran over and gave him a bear hug.

"Hey, little sis," he said, pecking her on the cheek. "I've missed you."

Bailey let go and wiped a tear from her eye. "Welcome to Calamity!"

Ian looked at the assembled group. "Hello, Susanna," he said when he spotted her.

Susanna walked over to him. Ian was pretty sure she was going to punch him—which he had to admit, he totally deserved.

"Ian," she said without emotion.

"I'm sorry—" was all he could get out before she jumped on him, wrapping her legs around his waist while forcing his mouth open with her tongue.

"Gross!" Bailey said. "Get a room!"

Susanna released her lip lock and said breathlessly, "Thanks for sending me here. I didn't want to be here at first, but now I understand."

"You do?"

"Thanks for protecting me from Lucifer."

"Well, I guess you do understand."

"Yeah, this place sort of jolts you back to reality, whatever that means in this day and age."

Nate stepped up and addressed Ian. "We're going to be on a tight schedule today. Then we'll have a little party to celebrate your reunion with Bailey this evening. Tomorrow you'll be back in Niagara Falls before anyone misses you. The reverend and Edwin will be waiting for your return."

Emily introduced herself to Ian, adding: "And this drill sergeant in bell-bottoms is Nate. You'll be staying with him tonight…although with all the catching up, you probably won't be sleeping much."

Ian looked over at Susanna.

"Uh," Emily said, "I mean all the discussions you'll be having with Bailey."

"Yeah, sure," Ian mumbled, mentally undressing Susanna and fairly salivating.

Bailey dealt him a sharp punch in the arm. "Snap out of it!" she said. "You're here for training, just like back at the compound. Dad's not here, but I am, and you're not going to screw this up!"

"I don't need any training," Ian said.

Bailey walked over and grabbed his wallet off the card table and chucked it at his head. Instinctively he caught it but felt it slip through his fingers as it disappeared. He then heard a thud as it landed twenty feet away in the opposite direction.

Before he could get it, a mountain lion cut him off, grabbing the wallet in its mouth and running off towards what looked to be a horse barn. "Shit!"

"That's Aslan," Bailey said. "I finally named him, and yeah I know Aslan was an African lion in The Chronicles of Narnia, but until I can get one, he'll have to do."

Ian went over to a picnic table and sat down. There was too much going on to process. He held out his right hand; it was shaking like a leaf.

"Are you okay?" Emily said.

"Should I be?" he answered. "Should I be okay with all"—he motioned with his shaking hand around the backyard—"of this?"

Bailey sat down next to him and patted him on the back. "I know what you mean, big brother. I've been through it as well, ever since you zapped me here. But we're here for a reason, and we have these gifts for a reason. Someone I greatly admired told me that, and I believe him."

———

Stevenson sat with his feet up on the desk in his Senate office. "Corson, I need to have some air time," he said, steepling his fingers in front of his mouth. "Can we arrange for a minor rebel attack in New York State, near my academy, so that I might come to their rescue?"

Corson sat in front of him, fidgeting with his power tie. "How minor are we talking about? How many dead?"

"Nothing too extravagant; perhaps a couple thousand—but try to avoid property damage. It may not be my home state of Nevada, but I do have business interests there."

"We should be able to do that with about twenty rebels, but if the loyalists are tipped off, all of them would most likely be sent to the pit."

"Do I care?" Stevenson thundered. "Send those who are currently imprisoned or disfavored by me. We will solve two problems at the same time."

"Certainly, Imper—Senator. I will start immediately."

"It will make for wonderful television," Stevenson said. "Oh, and on the list of rebels, make sure Ahti is included."

———

Ahti sat in front of the television in Daeva's hotel room as he absently shuffled a deck of cards with one hand. They were entering uncharted territory in doing business with humans and loyalists, but it was the only thing he could think of after his pride and ambition had been crushed under the Imperator's thumb.

He heard a key swipe at the door. Daeva walked in, tossing her purse on the bed and smiling at him.

"Hello, shit face," she said. "I have a theater. The papers are all signed and"—she dangled a set of keys from her fingers—"ready for move-in—as in you move in, so you'll get the hell out of my room."

"I haven't been here that long."

"Housekeeping is complaining about the number of bourbon bottles they have to remove every day. You're filling up their recycling bins."

"Have you watched the news lately?" he asked.

"Since when do you watch the news? It was better in the good old days thousands of years ago when you had to wait six months for news to reach you from Rome."

"All they're doing is replaying the ceremonies at the academy," Ahti said as he raised the remote and turned off the television. "He already has the world convinced that he's the best thing since fermentation."

"Getting cold feet?"

"No, it just makes me more convinced that we have to strike soon."

Daeva sat down on the corner of the bed. "So, what happens if we're successful?"

"What do you mean?"

"Rebels abhor a vacuum. Someone will want to assume power, and I know you're not the one."

"I never even contemplated taking power."

"Not even a little?"

Ahti thought about it. He was surprised that it had never even entered his mind. "No."

"Good, because when I take over, I won't have to destroy you."

"You?"

"Well, who else is capable? I started the coup—admittedly with a little help from you. I will have deposed the Imperator. I'm a natural choice."

"What about Corson and the other rulers of principalities, as the Bible so inelegantly put it?"

"Corson is nothing but a lap dog. Everyone will recognize that he is on the wrong side of history."

"I also think the loyalists will have a problem with that."

"Who needs them after the war is won? Now, humans are another matter. I can see Reverend Masters helping to promote me—after all, I'm on his staff."

"I think there is something in the contract about conducting business that conflicts with the Mysterium's business goals."

"Masters' only goal is to get rich, and I'll certainly provide that by the armored car full."

"I think you underestimate him."

"Then he'll be swept aside as well."

"So," Ahti said, "what's brought on all these feelings of superiority? I thought you wanted to stay out of the limelight other than at the theater?"

"Because I can create a paradise for our kind on earth," Daeva said. "This rock is all we've got, now that the Imperator caused us to be cast down. Even humans will benefit from my rule."

"And when did we start caring about humans?"

"They are just as rebellious as we are. We'll root out the ones that side with the loyalists, and the remainder can fulfill all their carnal delights while I rule over them."

Daeva walked over to the minibar and poured two shots of Maker's Mark; she handed him a glass. "Admit it, Ahti: wouldn't you want to keep the bars open for the next twenty thousand years?"

Ahti raised his glass. "I'll drink to that."

Nate walked Ian down the line of items they had assembled for his training. "We're going to start you out with small, lightweight objects and work our way up."

"I've already transported heavy objects," Ian objected.

Bailey and Susanna both glared at him and shouted in unison: "Hey!"

Ian waved them off. "You know what I mean."

"Well, let's start simple," Nate said as he picked up a roll of Life Savers from the card table. "Remember this?"

"Is that—?"

"Yes, it is," Bailey said. "I know you can transport that—even with me attached."

Emily took a spray can of orange construction paint and marked out several concentric circles in her backyard. "Everything," she said, "that you send our way appears within these circles."

She walked to the center and sprayed a big 'X' in the center. "This is your target."

"Take this and make it appear dead center in the target zone," Nate said, tossing him the Life Savers.

Ian caught the roll, but it didn't disappear. He held it between his thumb and forefinger. "It's still here."

"Try harder," Bailey said.

"Thanks for your instruction," Ian replied, and then he tossed it into the circle. "How's that?"

"We're missing something," Emily said as she walked over. "I had a similar problem at first. Ian, do you feel anything before something disappears?"

"Feel something?"

"Yeah." Emily cupped her hand, and a small ball of glowing energy formed. "Just before I do this, I feel pinpricks. It doesn't hurt, but I know that I can form the energy mass when I get that sensation. It took me a while to be able to form energy balls consistently."

She then waved her hand, and the ball of sparkling energy coated the bowling ball, encasing it a bluish-green glow. Raising her hand, she shouted, "Clear the range! Fire in the hole!" and tossed it towards the orange circle. It hit with force, shattering the bowling ball and embedding fragments into a crater about two feet deep.

"Oops, sorry, Nate," she said. "See, Ian, even the pros can make mistakes.

Ian looked forlorn. "I wonder if I'll ever get the hang of it," he mumbled.

Emily asked, "What did you feel when you made something disappear for the first time?"

"Disappointment…relief, perhaps."

"I'm not following."

"It doesn't matter," Ian said, thinking back to that day he almost put a bullet in his brain.

Walking over to the engine block he reached down, touching it with his finger.

It disappeared.

A fraction of a second later he heard a deep thud and looked over at the target area. A dust cloud appeared dead center in the circle, and when it cleared, he could see the engine block.

"Very nice," Nate said, "although my bowling ball has seen better days."

Bailey gave an appreciative whistle. "Wow, that's some serious shit," she said.

"What did you use? What facilitated your gift?" Emily asked.

"I thought about loss."

"Loss?" Emily prompted.

"My mom and dad, who I lost." Ian looked at his sister. "And Bailey, who I'm not about to lose."

———

Trudy took the opportunity of being back in Nevada to take Gavin to see the progress on the Vegas Mysterium. He'd spent most of his time in New Creekside, welcoming and then healing the new residents as they arrived. It was safer for him to be near the ladder, his source of power, but she didn't want him to end up as some crusty desert dweller, drinking moonshine and bathing once every fortnight.

"It's nice to be back in civilization," Gavin said as they walked into the lobby of Kim's resort. A massive wall of glass spanning the entire length of the concourse, and rising at least seventy feet above them, brightened the white marble floors. "So, you made a reservation?"

"You could say that," Trudy replied, on the way to the front desk.

"Can we afford it?"

Trudy turned to him. "I've got this. I'm making the big bucks now as the Mysterium's chief operating officer. Plus, as tenants, we get seven room comps a month. All Pops has to do is pay for the booze and hookers."

The woman at the front desk smiled at her and said, "Welcome to Kimberley Kali's Diamond Resort and Casino, Mrs. Masters."

"Masters-Young," Gavin corrected.

"Of course," the woman replied. "Your father's suite is ready. The bellman will be happy to show you to your room."

"Not gonna happen," Trudy heard a voice behind her say.

"Kim!" Trudy dropped her overnight bag and gave her a big hug. "Thank you so much for having us at your hotel."

"I'm thrilled to have you, but there's no way I'm letting you two stay in your father's suite—too much bad juju."

"I hope my father hasn't made it un-rentable. Bleach can do wonders, you know."

Kim gave a dismissive wave. "It was jinxed even before he moved in. A man from Germany rented the suite for a night. The next day housekeeping found him in the tub with his wrists slit. Apparently, he lost big—at someone else's casino. A double tragedy for me."

Trudy stared at her in disbelief. "I'm sorry. Did you tell my dad?"

Kim laughed. "Of course not. Honestly, I was hoping for a repeat performance." She looked apologetically at Trudy. "Sorry, guess I shouldn't have said that."

"Don't be," Trudy said. "You don't know how many times I've wanted to push Pops in front of a bus myself."

Kim gave a little snort of agreement. She scribbled something on a piece of paper and handed it to the front desk clerk. Receiving two key cards, she waved them toward the elevator bank behind the shark reef aquarium. "Let's take a walk."

Two security guards moved up beside them as they strolled through the lobby. Trudy had gotten used to it since she and her husband were well known, even without a diminutive blonde angel by their side.

"Where's Rachel?" Kim asked.

"She considered the risks and decided that our need to be alone outweighed her overprotective instincts," Trudy said. "But she does have Gavin's cell phone, and we can get her out here in about two minutes if needed."

"Obviously," Kim said, "she doesn't use the RTC."

"RTC?"

"Regional Transportation Commission—the bus system, that is. I hate to have tourists angry as they step onto my property, having already missed their restaurant reservation. It costs me money to calm them down and get them spending."

"I'm sure the busses are more comfortable than riding with Rachel," Trudy said as they reached the elevator bank. She gave the aquarium the once-over. "Looks like you've fixed up the tank."

"That poor aquarium has taken a lot of abuse," Kim said. "First, Rachel was tossing Ahti into it, and then it was Ahti's friend breaking it open so he could eat a shark. It's never boring around here."

"Ahti's friend?" Gavin asked.

"Yeah, a big guy in dirty jeans and a T-shirt from some whorehouse, dumb as a rock and stinking to high heaven—and that's in his human form," Kim said. "He continually tries to get into the Cluck and Grunt, mumbling something about the ribs."

"I've met that guy," Trudy said. "Several times, apparently. He likes banana splits."

"He told me how he was the star in one of Ahti's shows, and it wasn't hard to guess which one," Kim said. "It took two weeks to fix the damage to the theater and two hundred grand for the aquarium. Plus, PETA was on my ass for letting it eat a shark as if I put a bib around the demon's neck and offered a wine pairing."

Kim smiled like the cat that swallowed the canary on the elevator ride up to the east tower. Trudy wondered what she was up to. When the door opened, she realized what hallway they were on.

Trudy said, "You're just a hopeless romantic, aren't you, Kim?"

"Don't tell anyone," Kim said. "I'm supposed to be the tough casino owner."

"Your secret is safe," Trudy said as Kim guided them towards their room.

"You remember what room this is?" Trudy asked Gavin.

"Sure," he said. "It's written on the door."

He had already stepped back as Trudy wound up to punch him on the arm.

Gavin smiled. "I know what room this is. You can still see the sweat stains on the carpet where I tried to pick up my new bride to carry her over the threshold."

"Oh, you're just endearing yourself," Trudy said.

"Well," Kim said as she put the keycards into Gavin's hand and waved off security. "I'll leave you lovebirds alone. Come to my office tomorrow and we'll tour the Mysterium."

———

Bailey sat with Ian on a tack box in Emily's stable. "How's my big brother? Are you totally creeped out yet?"

"Pretty much," he said. "Things are just moving so fast I can't keep track."

"You did well today." Bailey patted his knee as the mountain lion and shepherd entered and sat down beside them.

"When did you learn you could do that?" Ian said.

"Do what?"

Ian pointed at the big cat. "That! I thought you liked *killing* animals."

"I never enjoyed killing," she said as a hawk flew in and landed on one of the stable gates. "I always felt bad taking a life, but that life helped us to live. People go to the grocery store and buy a steak, never knowing or thinking about what it was like when that animal died. I know very well what it's like."

"Still, it's odder than hell that God would pick someone like you to become a Dr. Dolittle."

Bailey watched as her fox came in and jumped up in her lap. "That's why God's in charge, and you're not."

"Listen, Bailey," Ian said, "I have something to tell you. It's about the first time I was able to make something disappear…"

"Yeah?"

"I told Emily that my feelings were of disappointment and also relief."

"I remember that. What did you mean?"

"It was when I was inventorying bunker three. I put the Beretta to my head and pulled the trigger."

Bailey's jaw dropped. "What? I don't understand."

"I wanted to die."

"Why?" Bailey said as she pushed the fox off of her. "What would make you want to do that?"

"I felt there was nothing left for me. My dreams were taken away, and all I had was the compound and Dad's paranoia."

"What happened?"

"I had the gun to my temple. It was cocked with the safety off. All I had to do was squeeze the trigger, nice and smooth like Dad taught us. It wasn't a light trigger, so it took some force to squeeze. During that process, it disappeared from my hand."

Bailey sat there, not knowing what to say. She couldn't imagine the pain that brought her brother to that point. She felt like a fool for not recognizing it and helping him before it got that far.

"When it disappeared, I didn't know what happened," he continued. "I looked all over for it, but it wasn't in the bunker. Then other things started to vanish when I touched them. It freaked me out. I climbed out of the bunker, not knowing what to do. Then Ahti called, wanting me to come in for an interview. The timing was so perfect, I assumed that Senator Stevenson had something to do with it."

"The senator is Satan!" Bailey spat.

"I know that now, but I didn't at the time. Now I realize that it was God using Ahti to protect me."

"Jonathan told me that all of us are needed to defeat Satan. I know that you'll play a big part in it."

Ian took her hand; he felt Bailey give it a warm squeeze. "I'm sure that's my purpose—why I'm still alive."

"I thought that after this is all over, I'll open a demon-hunting business."

Ian laughed. "Sort of like *Ghostbusters*?"

"Yeah, so I'll need to have a cool theme song—and a partner."

"So, now I have my little sister giving me job offers?"

Bailey stood up and swatted the straw off her butt. "Just something to look forward to, assuming any of us live through the next few weeks."

———

Trudy knew she was probably keeping Gavin awake as she kept tossing around in bed, but her mind wouldn't stop playing back every event of the last few months. Giving in, she sat up in bed.

"Anything I can do?" she heard Gavin say.

Trudy stood up and grabbed a hotel robe off the nearby chair. "I'm going to the living room for a while," she said. "No reason we both have to be awake."

Hearing no response, she assumed that Gavin had already returned to dreamland.

The living room of their suite was huge—bigger than what the entire first floor of their new house would be. She walked over to the floor to ceiling windows that looked down upon the city that never sleeps.

Her mind kept drifting back to the clouds that hovered over Calamity and New Creekside. How the desert towns were already becoming verdant under frequent rain showers, and animals were returning to drink from the spring and raise their young.

Trudy felt that there was something she needed to see, something that she was missing. She tried to concentrate like Rachel had instructed her. Ian, she admitted to herself, was already ahead of her in controlling his gift. Usually, her visions came upon her as unwelcome intrusions to her daily routine, either startling or scaring her.

She closed her eyes, and when she opened them again the hotel room was gone. Instead, she was in Emily's backyard, near the ladder. She stood in the circle that Emily had spray-painted to help Ian in his practice.

Nobody was around, only the ladder glowing off to the side, and above her, the clouds.

She had been so busy lately that she never stopped to study them. The four whirlwinds of lightning sat just outside of town, spinning up to the thousand-foot mark that she had warned her father about. After that, they spread out across the sky to cover the town.

They were unnatural formations, dark and churning with lighting flashing throughout. If they were over any other community, they might have signified the end of the world.

The clouds met and joined directly above her, forming a mini hurricane that spun over Emily's house. The ladder rose through the clouds, but it was slightly offset from the swirling center eye—just enough to be noticeable as it punched through the cloud cover and continued off towards the stratosphere.

She looked back to the ground. The rings that Emily had hastily spray-painted in the dirt, along with the crosshairs at the center, lined up perfectly with the center of the clouds.

At that moment, she realized this wasn't just Ian's target: it was also God's.

CHAPTER SIXTEEN

Ahti stood in the alley behind Daeva's new theater with a bottle of Jack tucked into a paper bag.

He had a lot to do to repair his reputation as a master showman and should have been inside preparing his act. Daeva had grudgingly given him the matinee performances so he could entertain school groups and the homeless seeking shelter from the harsh Canadian cold.

Ahti started to feel nauseous and knew a fellow rebel had to be nearby. Sure enough, he spotted a large man in overalls walking towards him.

"Pythius," Ahti sighed. "Don't you have the wrong alley? Last I heard you were impersonating a dead woman."

"Shut your pie hole," Pythius said.

Ahti could tell that his fellow rebel was in a foul mood and decided to back off. "So, what brings you here to the ass end of Daeva's theater?"

"You," Pythius said. "I'm supposed to deliver a message to you—a message from the Imperator."

Ahti took a swig from his bottle. Whatever message was coming from the Imperator was most likely bad. "Well?" he prompted.

"You need to be in Youngstown Wednesday morning at ten."

"I'm never anyplace by ten."

"You will be Wednesday," Pythius said. "We need to do some killing."

"What will we be killing?" Ahti asked, although he really didn't want to know.

"Humans, lots of them."

"I don't understand," Ahti said. He looked down the neck of his empty bourbon bottle, and then tossed it into the trash. "Isn't the Imperator all peace and kumbaya right now?"

"He's grown weak," Pythius said. "He plans for us to do the killing, then he'll show up and make a big show, and we'll disperse. It will look to the simpleminded humans as if he cast us out of the area."

"How many are to die?"

"A couple thousand, but what does it matter to you?"

"I'm jealous; I've never had that many casualties at a performance. Besides, they're all potential audience members for my show. It's hard to buy a ticket if you're dead."

"He leads us down a path to destruction," Pythius said. "Destruction for ourselves."

Ahti knew Pythius was an extremely rebellious rebel—too unruly to be confided with about the impending overthrow of the Imperator.

"I think you had a little problem last time you said something like that," Ahti said. "Be careful, or you'll be doing a repeat performance."

Pythius dismissed his warning. "We'll gather at the parking lot of the Presbyterian church on Church Street."

"So tell me," Ahti said, "which came first: the church or the street?"

Pythius flipped him the bird and started to walk off. He called back over his shoulder: "Be there, or I'll be looking for you."

Suddenly, Ahti was thankful his name didn't appear on the marquee.

"Do you have any idea how much this is costing me?" Masters groused as they stood in the concourse of Niagara International Airport.

"Sure," Edwin said. "Thirty-two humans needing resident visas, food, and hotel stays at their origination point, transportation to the airport, flights to JFK, then a commuter flight here; as well as bus rental, clothing stipend, English classes for those who do not speak it, set up of a kitchen and pantry… that comes to $750,000—give or take."

Masters sighed. "Mostly take—from me."

They walked towards TSA and the closest point they could stand to wait for arrivals.

"So, what are these new arrivals like?" Masters asked.

"I've never met them," Edwin said. "But Koda likes them."

"That's not reassuring me."

Masters looked at his watch as the second hand seemed to grind to a stop. There were so many things that he could be doing right now instead of standing in an airport looking like a lost chauffeur.

"You're Reverend Masters, aren't you?" a seventy-something woman asked, approaching him. Instinctually he reached in his coat for a Sharpie. Thanks to his newly minted celebrity, his autograph had become quite prized on eBay.

The septuagenarian came closer, into his personal space, which if she were fifty years younger he wouldn't have minded. She didn't smile at him or grasp his arm like some of the older women who treated him like their son or grandson. Instead, she was serious and poked him in the ribs with a bony finger.

"You shouldn't be here," she said.

"I agree," Masters said. "But he"—he pointed towards Edwin—"wants me to pick up some arrivals."

"Not *here*, the airport," she said, then leaned in and almost whispered to him: "Niagara Falls."

"Why not?"

"The Tannahills. Some hold you responsible. Say you're working for the senator. You pushed Brian off the observation tower. You're working with the government to destroy the lives of good people."

"Listen, lady," Masters said, "I had nothing to do with Tannahill's suicide."

"Doesn't matter; you come to town and bad things start to happen. You were there when he died. You're also friends with the senator, and a few smart folks have started to see him for what he is."

Edwin spoke up. "Who do you think the senator is, madam?"

"Why, Satan of course," she said, turning her gaze to Edwin. "Wake up, son! Don't be blind to heavenly things. There is a war going on, which you'd know if you bothered to look."

"Yeah," Masters said to Edwin, "get your head out of your ass."

Turning back to him, she said, "From what I've heard, you have a wonderful daughter and a son-in-law that heals the sick. Go back to them. Take joy in your family before the end."

"You're right," he had to admit, "I am a lucky man."

She waggled her finger in his face, like a stern teacher brandishing a ruler. "So go...before you're a dead man."

As she walked away, Masters looked at Edwin and said, "Was I just threatened by a blue hair?"

"She's right, you know," Edwin said. "It's becoming more dangerous every day."

Masters noticed a large group entering the concourse from one of the terminals. "Is that them?" he said, pointing.

"Yes, here comes more of our family."

"Great, a bunch of angel groupies here to save the day."

Edwin patted him on the back. "I could not have said it better."

———

"This is amazing," Trudy had to admit as she looked down the recreated streets of Creekside, Wisconsin. The lighting was set to evening; the streetlamps along what were now pedestrian walkways reflected off the shop windows, lending the scene a magical glow.

Gavin pointed to the far end of the street where a fiber-optic representation of the ladder glowed. "That actually is a fair representation of the ladder," he remarked. "What do you think, Trudy?"

"Don't know," she replied. "I never was able to see the Creekside ladder. Looks sort of like the ones I have seen, though."

They made a left turn onto State Street and walked towards the church.

"Remember when I dragged you to church that first time?" Trudy said.

"If I remember correctly," Gavin said, "I'm the one that stopped by your apartment and asked you."

She pointed to a storefront. "Do you remember Creekside having a fudge shop?"

Gavin let out a laugh. "No, but look at the church sign."

Trudy read it and shook her head. The sign, sporting the same flimsy plastic lettering Reverend Brustad used to place his outlandish calls to worship, now said: GOD WON'T MAKE YOU EXIT THROUGH THE GIFT SHOP.

"Somebody's been doing their research," she said as Rachel bounded into view with a welcoming chirp.

"Ready to go on the ride?" she said excitedly. "Kim said we could."

"Hey, missy," Trudy said. "Can pregnant women go on it?"

Rachel's mouth hung open. "I didn't even think about that."

"So much for having a protecting angel," Trudy said. "Why don't you and Gavin go on it? I'll just walk around and take in the sights."

Rachel grabbed her by the hand. "Go see your apartment. I think you'll be surprised."

"I don't like surprises."

"We'll tell you how the ride was," Gavin said. "Go see your place. We'll be over when we're done."

"Yeah, let me know," Trudy said. "It was thirty million dollars of the budget, so it better be good." She paused and added: "Damn, I'm starting to sound like an executive."

After Rachel and Gavin wandered off to be shaken and stirred by the Battle of Creekside attraction, Trudy ducked through an EMPLOYEES ONLY doorway that used to be an alley in the real world. A metal staircase led up to the second floor of a building that housed a candy store and photo studio in this version, but she had known it for years as an abandoned liquor store. The metal door at the top of the stairs had a large AUTHORIZED PERSONNEL ONLY sign posted. She assumed since it was her apartment, that she was authorized and turned the handle.

There was the same short hallway that she had known; it looked unpainted and worn, even though she knew that everything was fresh and new.

She opened the door to what was supposed to be her apartment, not knowing what to expect. A fresh springtime fragrance greeted her as the door opened, which didn't bode well for an exact recreation of her apartment.

She couldn't believe her eyes. Inside, her apartment just as she remembered it: a queen bed on the far wall of the studio apartment, her posters of various rock bands, her microwave, and an electric duel burner stove on the other. The only unrealistic detail was the absence of overflowing trash, piles of dirty laundry, and a mountain of empty Diet Coke cans. Then she saw them—four guitars and two Marshall amps sat in one corner.

She picked up the Arctic White Fender Stratocaster with maple neck and fretboard that, sadly, had gone to guitar heaven. Gavin had used the original to cave in the skull of the demon-possessed man who was trying to rape and kill her. He saved her life, but the Fender died in the rescue attempt.

Noticing an envelope on the bed, she gently put down the Strat and picked it up. Inside was a simple note. She sat down on the corner of the bed to read it.

Trudy, may you use this room to always remember who you are and what matters most in this world. Think back to the good times and also the bad but above all else, let your music inspire you as you move through this life. Love you! Your friend and sister, Rachel.

Trudy picked up the Strat and hugged it to her chest as she closed her eyes and cried.

———

Ian walked down the gravel road towards what he was told was Kris's house, where Susanna was staying. To find it, he was told to listen for the sound of multiple air conditioner units droning and a pink Cadillac in the driveway. Needless to say, the house was pretty easy to spot.

Susanna was sitting on a lawn chair on the front porch as he walked up.

"Hi, Ian," she said as she stood up to greet him.

"Hey, Susanna. Sorry I couldn't visit with you last night."

"Nonsense!" She grabbed him around the waist and gave him a peck on the mouth. "You needed to catch up with your sister. Besides, I learned the complete history of Mary Kay Cosmetics thanks to Kris's YouTube series and also what works with my complexion."

"Trudy should be back soon," said Ian. "She'll take us back to Niagara Falls via the ladder. It's quite the ride—I almost puked up my breakfast."

"I don't want to go."

"I'm sorry I didn't mean to scare you. Considering we'll be moving through a rip in space-time and through other dimensions, it really isn't that bad."

"It's not that." She took his hand and walked him out of earshot of the house. "I don't want to leave here."

"I thought you hated angels."

"That was before..."

"Before?"

"Before my eyes were opened to what is really happening. This is a war, and I almost joined the army on the wrong side of history."

Ian couldn't hide his pleased smile. "You need to go back," he said. "You'll be missed, and they'll start asking questions. They know you bunk with me, and I even introduced you to the senator. If you turn up missing they may start looking for you, and we don't want them to find you're here, of all places. It's bad enough that they know Bailey is here."

"There's no way they would know that I'm here. Besides, the community will protect me."

"I'm not worried about you."

Susanna cocked her head. "What?"

Ian realized he had just stuck his foot in his mouth. "What I mean, is you'll be safe here, but we have a mission to accomplish that could be jeopardized if you stay. No one must know that I can send people here with just a touch. If they find out, I'm dead, and we may lose an opportunity to fight back."

"Still—"

"Personally, I'd love to have you stay, but it's too risky. We need to play our parts; we need to return"—he raised his hand that was holding hers—"hand in hand like we snuck away as lovers."

"Play our parts?" Susanna let go of his hand.

"You know what I mean."

"Yeah, you keep saying that. I think I know exactly what you mean."

"Then, you'll do it?"

"Yeah, I'll do it, but I hate the whole idea."

He attempted to give her a kiss, but she turned her head away.

"Let me say goodbye to Kris," she said as she turned and walked back to the house. "Don't wait for me. I'll catch up."

———

"This should be interesting," Trudy mumbled to herself as she stood in front of the ladder. She would attempt to take Ian and Susanna back to Niagara Falls—through a still unstable ladder. She hoped little Jay was capable of some heavy lifting, despite his prenatal status.

"Stay safe, big brother," she overheard Bailey say to Ian. "If anyone tries to hurt you let me know, and I'll sic my mountain lion on them."

Trudy noticed that Susanna was standing off by herself, so she decided to walk over and see how she was doing.

"Bet you can't wait to get back to Niagara," she said.

"I don't want to go."

"I'm sure Ian made a trip through the ladder sound a little more intense than it really is. You'll be fine."

Susanna shook her head. "That's not it. I don't want to go back to the academy now that I know who the senator is."

"Did you talk to Ian about this?"

"I did this morning. He thought it would look odd if I didn't show up."

"Listen, there's one thing I know from hanging around my father: men don't know everything they think they know."

A smile formed on Susanna's face.

"You've got to do what your heart is telling you," Trudy said. "Lucifer isn't all-knowing, and he's got a lot on his plate right now. I doubt he even knows you exist or cares if you're there or not."

"That's not what Ian seems to think," Susanna said.

"How about this," Trudy said as she leaned in conspiratorially. "Tell him that I just told you of a vision that I had. You play a part in it, but in my vision, you were here in Calamity."

"What if he doesn't buy it?"

"Have him talk to me. Who would be foolish enough to question the word of a preggo? Besides, I'm driving this angelic Greyhound bus, and if I don't want to take a passenger, I don't have to."

Trudy pointed at Ian. "He's over there. Off with you!"

Gavin came up behind her and put his hands on her shoulders. "Inspiring the troops?"

Trudy reached up and patted his hand. "Sorry that I have another business trip," she said. "I'd rather stay here with my stud muffin."

"We have another group of residents moving here tomorrow, so that will keep me busy," said Gavin. "I hear that about a dozen are from Greenland."

"I wasn't there long enough to meet the community. I'm sure it's going to take some adjustment for them. It's a beautiful country but totally different from Nevada. By the way, how are they getting resident visas so easily?"

"Friends in high places, I guess," Gavin said.

"Well, time to be off," Trudy said as she turned around and gave Gavin a kiss. "Try not to get into too much trouble while I'm gone."

"Keep an eye on your father," Gavin said. "He's more likely to get into trouble."

———

Masters picked the keys off the desk in his hotel suite. "Come on, Edwin, my man, time to pick up my daughter at the ladder."

"Wait," Edwin said, holding up his hand. "I feel something in the hallway."

Sure enough, there was a knock on the door and Edwin opened it. Ahti stood in the hall, looking somewhat sober.

"What do you want?" Edwin demanded.

Ahti pushed past him. "Save some lives, do the right thing—some shit like that."

"Demons never do the right thing," Edwin said.

Ahti sighed. "There you go, using the D word. You are the bigoted one, aren't you?"

"Hey," Masters said to the both of them, "I'm over here. Speak to the grown-up."

"Okay," Ahti said to him, "here's the deal. The Imperator is going to become the hero of a little drama that entails a couple thousand human deaths—give or take. Normally, I wouldn't care, but I've been ordered to participate, and I hate losing potential audience members to unnecessary genocide."

"When and where?" Masters said. "Give me some details."

"Tomorrow in Youngstown," Ahti said. "Probably because it's a convenient drive from the compound and there's a Starbucks along the route. They're rounding up rebels in the area to participate. It starts at ten a.m. in front of the Presbyterian Church. It should be quite the show."

"Edwin," Masters said, "can you get an army assembled in that time?"

"That will not be a problem." Edwin looked at Ahti. "How many rebels are expected?"

"I haven't been told, but there can't be more than twenty rebels in the area that are on the Imperator's expendables list, which is more than enough to kill a couple thousand humans."

"So," Masters said, "I imagine the senator is going to show up to save the day?"

Ahti's lips curled in distaste. "Of course, he is. What a publicity hound! He'll rescue them, and the humans will become even more enamored of him. He'll lose a few rebels in the process, but he doesn't give a shit about us—or me."

Masters said, "So, you're on Satan's naughty list. Is that why you're being invited?"

"It appears that I'm of no further use, so I need to be careful. Needless to say, I will not be attending if the loyalists are going to show up, although Pythius told me he'll be looking for me if I'm a no-show."

Edwin nodded. "It would look suspicious if you are not there. We will protect you, and thank you for warning us of this."

"Well, that's the sweetest thing I've ever had a loyalist say to me," Ahti said. "Although you understand that I still hate your God and I'm not so thrilled with you either."

"Understood," Edwin said as he started for the door.

"Where are you going?" Masters asked.

Edwin opened the door to the suite. "To gather an army."

———

"Why do I have to be here?" Masters grumbled as he sat in a car in Youngstown. "It's not like I can fend off a horde of demons intent on death and destruction from a Hertz rental."

"Because we are friends," Edwin said. "And it's important that we share such moments of life together."

Masters sighed. "Or death."

"You are perfectly safe. I may not be a protecting angel, but I would not lead you into danger."

"Yeah, several thousand people may be killed, and I'm perfectly safe sitting in a car across the street from a church that is going to be the assembly point for a demonic invasion."

"Thanks to Ahti," Edwin said, "there will be no deaths. We are well prepared. Fifty angels have arrived from Las Vegas, Tasmania, Singapore, and India. Fifteen of those are archangels. We will end this before they can destroy this town. Our kind has been going around to the various houses and stores nearby, in human form, and asking them to leave the area."

"So, do you trust Ahti now?"

"He is a fallen one. He will never be trustworthy, but he has proven to be useful to God in the past, and I trust that God can turn even Ahti's evil into good."

"Jeez, Edwin, cut the Sunday school crap."

"You don't believe that God controls all?"

Masters dropped the sun visor and primped in the mirror. "What the hell do I know? I just see the world getting a clusterfuck without anyone seeming to control anything."

"That is an interesting observation, coming from someone who God has guided since he was a child."

"What do you mean?"

"I mean that your life is not an accident, that your daughter Trudy is not an accident, that your Mysterium is not one either. You have been under God's protection and guidance since the beginning."

"That's not true," Masters said. "I've made my own choices. Nobody has helped or guided me."

"Choices like Dieter Jaeger?" This was a reference to a big game hunter/gourmand of Masters' acquaintance who had met an ignoble end.

Masters felt like he had been punched in the gut. Not wanting to see his own image any longer, he slammed the visor shut. "Yes, like Dieter. I set him up to be killed. And how would you know about that, anyway?"

"We do not see all, but there is One who does, and who sometimes shares with us."

Masters thought back to the time in the Wisconsin forest when he willingly lured Dieter Jaeger to his death. He stood there emotionlessly as Dieter's guts were ripped out by a demon while he photographed the spectacle—the spectacle that made him famous.

"He was a friend of mine," Masters said, realizing how hollow that sounded.

"A friend of mine," Edwin remarked, "was present at the birth of Trudy."

"Really?"

"Yes, he was there to comfort your first wife, Elizabeth. She had gone through a lot, including the loss of the man she loved."

"She never loved me!"

"She did, and you were too blind to see."

"That's a lie."

"I do not lie. Elizabeth loved you and wanted you to be back with her, and with your daughter."

"Then why didn't she come with me?"

"She couldn't. You know that her parents would never allow it, and she wasn't strong enough to go against their will, yet you left anyway."

"I had no choice."

"Everyone has a choice, and you chose; the same as you chose to lead your friend Dieter to his death."

Masters sat there speechless.

"You could have stayed with her," Edwin said. "You could have loved her as your wife; you could have raised your daughter as a loving father."

"Shut the fuck up!" Masters bristled. "You have no idea what it was like. You judge me, yet you have no idea of what being human is like. You look human, but you're far *from* human."

"I do not judge, but my King and yours knows what being human is like," Edwin said calmly. "Do you think He would approve?"

Masters felt tears welling up and hated himself for it. "I couldn't stay. I couldn't live in that hicksville of Creekside. I couldn't live a life like that. I needed to be somebody."

"Elizabeth loved you, Jay," Edwin said. "You were going to have a daughter."

"I..." Masters' voice trailed off. With what little breath he had left after his protestations, he admitted: "I should have stayed."

"But God did not give up on you when you left," Edwin said. "Your life, your wife's, and Trudy's would have been better if you stayed, of course. But He never left you, and where you are today is the result of those choices you made so many years ago. As it is written in the Bible, in all things, God works for the good of those who love him."

"Even me?"

"Especially you," Edwin said. "Now you have a daughter that loves you, a son-in-law, a fiancée, friends, and a purpose. You have to admit that, despite yourself, you have a pretty good life."

Masters sat there in a Buick rental and thought about Edwin's sage words. He had to admit the angel had a point.

"It's almost time," Edwin said as he got out of the car. "Drive about a half-mile down the road and wait for me."

Masters started the car, grateful that he could at least get some distance from the impending battle. By way of parting, he said, "Go kick some demon ass, Edwin!"

Stevenson sat in the back of his limousine as it drove towards Youngstown. He was due to meet with local officials at 10:30 a.m. to discuss some volunteer work his recruits from the academy would be assisting with. The locals were more than happy to be receiving a soccer field for free and let him set the meeting time—one that coincided with his planned massacre. He imagined that the local kids wouldn't need the field after they were slaughtered, but it did help his philanthropic image. He thought perhaps he could donate to a new cemetery where the soccer field was going to be and score another publicity win.

Corson sat next to him in the Mercedes Maybach. "Make a note to do something nice for the people of Nevada," Stevenson ordered. "I'd hate for them to become jealous that their senator is more interested in New York than his own constituents."

"Another attack?"

Stevenson waved him off. "No, some public work or benefit given from my foundation. Help the homeless or some such nonsense. Ask around, you'll find something we can assist with."

Stevenson pointed out the window at a bright light over Youngstown. "Look, it's begun. In another five minutes we'll be there, and I can save what is left of the human animals from our despised kind."

"We should have invited the media to your soccer field meeting to provide live coverage of the event," Corson said.

"Nonsense. This way, it will be captured on countless civilian phones and uploaded instantly to all the social media sites. The news will be confusing at first and instill fear, but it will soon become known that I saved the poor inhabitants of Youngstown from certain death."

"Something's wrong," Corson said as the driver slowed to a stop. "The town should be fully destroyed, but all I see is a light—."

"The same one I saw earlier," Stevenson interrupted. "That's not coming from the rebels—it's the glow from multiple archangels. They knew we'd be here."

"Who would dare go against your wishes?" Corson said.

Stevenson's anger grew. "Driver! Turn the car around."

"Shouldn't we see what—?"

Pulling a pistol from his jacket, Stevenson shot Corson in the thigh.

"Argh!" Corson screamed. "Why did you do that?"

"Because I'm mad as hell and you're convenient," Stevenson said. "You'll heal. The one that did this to me will not be so fortunate."

"It looks a little worse for wear," Ahti said to Masters as he got in the back of the Buick.

"What does?"

"Oh, you missed all the fun?"

"Edwin told me to drive down here and wait," Masters said. "And why aren't you with the others getting smacked down by archangels?"

"There was no smackdown," said Ahti. "As soon as the rebels transformed, they were surrounded. They didn't even get to kill a single human. Several tried to fight but were no match for the loyalists. Everyone quickly disbursed, although not before the Presbyterian Church had a slight steeple malfunction. A rebel was tossed through the belfry by a loyalist. Hopefully, they're up to date with their insurance."

"Did you see the senator anywhere?"

Ahti shook his head no. "The bastard must have gotten wind of the failure and skedaddled. It just shows how weak he is. So, want to go get a drink?"

"I need to wait for Edwin."

Ahti shuddered. "He'll have us drinking unsweetened ice tea." He opened the door and got out of the car.

"Where are you going?" asked Masters.

"When I was out scouting for people to kill, I spied a liquor store over on Lockport."

As Ahti walked off, Masters pulled out his phone and dialed.

"Hey, Pops," Trudy said.

"Mission accomplished. No deaths and little damage, except to Satan's pride."

"That's good news."

"What state or country are you in now?" Masters said.

"I'm back in Nevada. We're going to have an informational meeting tonight on how to kick Lucifer's ass. Can you attend? I can bring you back through the ladder. Rachel's baking cookies."

"That's all right. I've got a few things to do around here."

"Sure. Well, talk to you later."

"Trudy," Masters said, and then hesitated. He closed his eyes and lowered his head.

Trudy waited, and then her voice filled the silence. "Yeah?"

"I love you."

"I love you too, Pops."

"I'm sorry I wasn't there for you growing up."

There was a pause, and then Trudy said, "Well, you're here for me now. Stay safe. Oh, and tell Holly you love her."

"Let's not go crazy," Masters said, hanging up.

———

Ian sat in his room, staring at the empty bed that once contained his—girl-friend? He didn't exactly have the best sendoff in Nevada as Susanna decided not to return with him. He should have been more understanding. Trudy was right: nobody cared if Susanna was here or not. The academy had been experiencing a number of defections due to parents cutting off their children's income streams, believing they had joined a cult. Although the senator was generally well-loved, an impassioned minority was starting to organize a resistance. Everyone on the compound had been cautioned not to wear their uniforms when venturing out to the neighboring towns, as some of the locals were so corrupted by evil that they didn't appreciate the good that the academy was doing in the world. They had explicitly been warned to stay away from places of worship because they were the ones creating the dissent.

He carefully tied a red bow around the box of chocolates he purchased at the Hershey's Chocolate World in Niagara Falls. He figured that any place that makes you walk through a four-story-tall imitation chocolate bar to get into the store had to be good.

Putting the card he purchased in a red envelope, he licked it closed and stuck it under the ribbon. Placing the box on the desk, he examined his handiwork. With rumpled corners and uneven folds, it looked like he'd wrapped it while wearing boxing gloves, but he'd done his best.

Extending a finger, he gently touched the box and watched it disappear.

Hopefully, Maggie wouldn't find it first. He would hate for the dog to get sick.

CHAPTER SEVENTEEN

Emily was using a wheelbarrow to transport a load of horse manure from the stable to a patch of ground outside her fence but still on her property. With the new and favorable temperatures, along with regular rain, she figured it was time to plant a garden.

She stopped and wiped her hands on her jeans as she spotted a new arrival near the ladder. This one had a pretty bow on it, and she could guess who it was for. She removed her work gloves and walked over to the spray-painted target area. Smiling at the sweet gesture, she bent down and tried to pick it up without coating it in horseshit.

Following extensive foot scraping on the back porch welcome mat, Emily opened the sliding glass door and gently placed the package on the kitchen table. "Hey, anyone here?" she called out.

After a minute with no answer back, she walked into the bathroom to wash her hands. "Well, this is a first," she said to herself as she squirted out the hand soap and turned on the water, "where's the normal living room traffic congestion?"

Drying off, she went back out to the living room to enjoy a few rare moments of peace and quiet before heading back to the wheelbarrow. Plopping onto the sofa, she casually cupped her right hand as a greenish-blue glow started to form. She sent the ball of energy to the refrigerator, where it opened the door and extracted a bottle of beer. Willing the ball and bottle back to her, the sparkling force popped off the cap just before it reached her hand.

Taking a swig, she leaned back on the sofa, let out a big, tension-releasing belch. "Now that's what superpowers should be used for."

———

Masters and Holly sat in a booth at the Tim Hortons restaurant on Clifton Hill. He purposely sat her facing the Ferris wheel, as he had something else he wanted to pay attention to.

Holly put down her Tuscan Chicken Panini long enough to ask him, "So, what's the plan? Have you heard anything?"

Masters stared past her and out the window to the chain-link fence on the other side of the road where bulldozers were starting the demolition on the new Mysterium property. Soon it would just be a flat plot of earth and ready to build. He wasn't thrilled that he had to keep the Travelodge, but it was a small price to pay for his daughter's happiness.

"Jay!" she screeched at him. "Are you listening to me?"

"Sure, what is it?"

Exasperated, Holly grabbed two handfuls of her hair and yanked—hard. "Do you know what's happening? Have you heard anything from Trudy?"

"Trudy says that everything is proceeding according to plan. Since she's the one with the visions, I'll take her word for it."

"Do we have to stay here, Jay? This place is worse than Wisconsin Dells."

"I admit the tackiness isn't up to our Wisconsin standards, but we're working on it." He watched the large laser tag building fall under the wrecking ball. "I'm glad we didn't bulldoze this side of the street," he added as he munched a ham and Swiss. "Tasty sandwich. I kind of like this place."

Holly reached across the table and rapped her knuckles on his forehead. "Earth to Jay! We need to go back to Nevada and get married. My biological clock is ticking."

Masters almost choked on his sandwich. "What are you talking about?"

"Don't you want kids?"

"I've got one. She's a pain in the ass."

"Maybe a little boy?"

He realized that he had unwittingly stepped into the quicksand of maternal instinct and couldn't think of a way out of it. "My grandson's going to be named Jay, so that works for me."

He knew immediately that was the wrong answer.

"Guess you'll be sleeping with Edwin tonight."

Holly tossed her napkin on the table and crossed her arms.

He avoided her gaze in time to see the Dairy Queen crushed under a bulldozer. "Yes!" he shouted to the packed restaurant.

All heads turned.

Holly stood up and walked out.

Masters watched her go. That pretty ass of hers always looked good when it was leaving. He hoped he wasn't seeing it for the last time.

———

Bailey finagled her need for some new T-shirts into an outing to the Vegas Bass Pro Shop with Susanna and Jonathan; she could tell Susanna was happy for the chance to get out of New Creekside.

"Do you like sporting goods stores?" Bailey asked her as they walked through the front door.

"I love them," Susanna replied. "I can't afford anything but it's fun just to look around."

"I'm going to take a look at the boats," Jonathan said to Bailey. "You two try not to get into any trouble."

Bailey batted her scanty eyelashes at him. "Trouble? Little old us?"

"So," Susanna said as Jonathan wandered off, "want to go look for those T-shirts?"

"Let's look around first, so I don't have to carry them all over creation."

"Okay."

"First stop"—Baily pointed—"the gun shop."

"How about the aquarium first?" Susanna suggested. "It's right over there."

"Sure," Bailey said, "although, I'm not much for fishing."

Bailey had never seen a Bass Pro Shop connected to a casino and a hotel before—only in Vegas. The anchor was the colossal saltwater aquarium that towered over her. She was impressed with the size of the tank.

"The sign," Susanna said, "says that it holds 117,000 gallons of water filled with 160 species of tropical fish, and also mermaids."

Bailey raised a skeptical eyebrow. "Mm-hmm. I've got a whale of a tale for you if you believe that."

"Uh, Bailey." Susanna sounded perplexed. "What are the fish doing?"

Bailey noticed that the fish in the tank were all swimming—towards her.

"Oh, crap—or is it carp," Bailey said. "Even fish? I better not start to have insects following me around."

"That's weird," Susanna said.

"That's my life," Bailey agreed. She tried walking to the far side of the tank. The fish were following her every move.

"That one fish, the sign says"—Susanna pointed—"is an emperor angelfish. He really likes you."

Bailey stepped up to the glass as the vibrant blue and gold angelfish moved closer as if trying to kiss her. "Of course it likes me—it's an *angel* fish," she said. "I've got to get out of here. Let's go see some of the Pro Shop's stuffed critters. At least *they* won't be following me around—I hope."

———

Ahti wondered why he was summoned to the academy after being told to stay away. He was present at Youngstown, so it couldn't be about that. Whatever it was it couldn't be good, but he dared not disobey. Besides, he had Daeva along with him to blame everything on if need be.

"Now what did you do, dumb-ass?" Daeva said, with more than a little contempt in her voice.

"Wasn't me, whatever it was."

Ian came out of the farmhouse and trotted over to them. "Stevenson's inside," he said.

"Does he look pissed?" Ahti asked.

"Hard to tell." Ian glanced over his shoulder towards the house. "Here, they come."

Stevenson, followed by Corson, who had a slight limp, came out of the house and walked down the half dozen steps.

"Ian, my boy," Stevenson said. "Why don't you go check on the construction of the firing range? I'm sure your knowledge will be invaluable. There's no need for you to be here for this discussion."

"Yes, Senator." Ian turned and gave Ahti a worried look before heading towards the back of the complex.

"Ahti," Stevenson said as he walked over, "I am so disappointed with you."

"With me, Senator?"

"Someone tipped off the loyalists that we would be conducting an operation in Youngstown."

"What?" Daeva said, stepping away from Ahti. "Why would you do such a thing?"

"I didn't have anything to do with it," Ahti insisted. "I keep my head down and do your bidding, nothing more. I was also present in Youngstown, ready to do my part in your service before those pesky loyalists showed up."

"Really?" Stevenson said. "I've been going over the roster of those who attended the Youngstown non-event. Every single one stood to gain from participating—everyone but you."

"I gain by serving you, Imperator."

"Also, you have daily contact with young Ian, who I imagine is also in contact with his sister Bailey. We all know where Bailey is living now."

"I would never tell the kid your plans," Ahti said. "I'm not that stupid."

"Yes, you are," Daeva chimed in.

"You may have mentioned something inadvertently that would have piqued his curiosity, and he then passed it on to his sister," said Stevenson. "Once that information was in the loyalist's hands, they would easily understand the importance of it."

"I do not divulge information to humans." Ahti protested. "Even accidentally."

"My concern is that Ian or the other students may recognize what is going on here. Look around, Ahti. Do you see anyone here at the moment?"

"No, Senator. Should I be concerned?"

"Tell me, Ahti," Stevenson said, "aren't you just a little bit upset that I gave you a theater, only to rip it out of your hands and toss you to the gutter to survive on whatever scraps Daeva decides to toss your way?"

"I—"

"He came to me and begged to be housed and fed," Daeva said defensively. "He kept muttering about destroying you, but I didn't think anything of it." She pointed at Ahti, her face an ugly scowl. "How could something that pathetic be a threat?"

"Still, you should have come to me, Daeva," Stevenson said. "Although I understand why you did not deem it a concern."

She bowed low. "I apologize and ask your forgiveness, Imperator."

"Forgiven," Stevenson said. "But you must be careful not to show mercy to others, especially one such as Ahti, as he would show none to you."

"He used me and the fact that he saved me from the loyalists in Vegas," she said. "He made me feel obligated to take him in."

Ahti glared at her. "Nice shove, I didn't even see that bus coming." He turned to Stevenson. "Imperator, Daeva instituted a plot to overthrow you. I was merely trying to save myself by agreeing to her harebrained scheme. You know that self-preservation is always at the top of any rebel's to-do list."

"Ahti, blaming others will not help you. Daeva is on Masters' staff, and she will perform perfectly as a purveyor of perversion to the populace."

Ahti was tempted to ask Stevenson to repeat that tongue twister ten times but decided it wouldn't help his cause.

Stevenson looked him in the eye. "You did as you were instructed in Las Vegas and you blew the senator's brains out as I wished. It saddens me that someone who was once useful must now be tossed aside. Perhaps after a few thousand years we will manage to release you, and then you may beg for my mercy."

"Imperator!" Ahti pleaded. "I beg for mercy now."

"Corson," Stevenson said, "send this one to the pit."

"Gladly," Corson said as he transformed. The human form covered in Armani morphed into a being as tall as the farmhouse and blackened with ashes. Its twisted torso turned as it looked down on Ahti, broken wings of rusted swords spreading out behind it.

"I beg you, Imperator," were Ahti's last words as Corson swung his trident and impaled him in the gut. With a sickening twist, Ahti's human form broke in two, splattering blood over Daeva's white miniskirt as his anguished scream reverberated between the buildings.

Ahti felt himself spinning out of his body and towards a fate he knew was worse than any death.

———

Daeva stood there in shock as she looked down on what was left of Ahti. It was hard to rattle a rebel, but Ahti's swift demise did it. It wasn't that Ahti was just sent to the pit; he deserved it. What shook her was that she came very close to the same fate. Now he lay on the ground with a stupid WTF expression on his face and his entrails spread for a good five feet in all directions. She also noticed that his liver looked all bumpy, which didn't surprise her.

Stevenson gestured at what was left of Ahti's corpse. "Corson, have someone we trust clean up this mess, then you can let the students back into this area."

"Yes, Senator."

"Daeva," Stevenson said, "go into the farmhouse and clean yourself up before our students see you."

She looked down at her dress, which was coated in blood and what may have been part of a cheeseburger at one time.

"Yes, Imperator."

"Here, I am identified only as senator."

"Yes, Senator," she repeated as she walked up the steps to the front door.

Once inside she went upstairs and found the bathroom. Judging from the hideous pink tile, she guessed the retro space hadn't been remodeled in about forty years.

She didn't bother undressing before turning on the shower and stepping into the tub. She stood there under the stream of warm water as she watched small chunks of Ahti's innards swirl around the drain. What looked like a piece of colon refused to go down, so she smushed it with her big toe until it finally broke in two and disappeared.

Having cleansed her dress somewhat, she stripped it off, tossing it onto the tile floor, and stood naked as the water cascaded over her. She needed to be away from the senator and Corson, and have a few minutes to think about what just happened.

Now was a dangerous time for everyone involved in the coup d'état—most of all her. Now that Ahti was gone, she would be the only rebel involved in this loyalist/human/rebel triad—not the most enviable or safest of positions. She also realized that Stevenson's suspicion of Ahti giving information to Ian would most certainly result in the boy's death.

She turned off the water and grabbed a nearby towel. Drying off, she grabbed her dress off the floor and carried it into Ian's room. His roommate might have left some clothing lying around that would fit her, as she was not about to wear her bloodstained miniskirt in public.

Opening the closet, she sighed. Although the sweat pants and baggy shirt would probably fit her, she was in total disgust by Ian's potential mate's fashion sense. Despite humans' lofty ideals, they were also biological animals whose sex drives were ingrained in their genes. She held up some ragged Levi's and decided that Ian's mate's faded jeans were in complete opposition to the drive of human genes.

"Hello?" she heard from the doorway.

Turning around, she gave Ian a nice full-frontal for him to contemplate.

"Oh, God!" he said and averted his eyes. "Sorry, I didn't know you were here."

"Come on in and close the door," Daeva said. "We have some things to discuss."

"Uh," Ian said, totally flustered.

"I'm just looking for something to wear," she said. "I know you've seen a naked female before."

"For a second."

"Well, here's a better look," she said as she held up a Stevenson's Academy of Peace and Justice T-shirt. "Do you think my breasts will fit in this?"

"Stop!" Ian said. He sat down on the bed and stared at the floor.

"You know, I'm not a human female. I put on this form as easily as you put on your pants. It helps me to get what I want." She sat down next to him. "I don't think you'd like the way I really look."

"Can you just put on some clothes? Please?"

"Sure." Daeva smiled and kissed his cheek. She stood and pulled the too-small T-shirt over her head and down her torso. Deciding to try the jeans, she was surprised that they fit so well. "Your mate must have nice hips."

"She's not my mate."

"Did you fuck it up?"

"Probably. Although I'm trying to make amends."

"Good for you." Daeva found some sneakers that appeared to be her size. "Human males are stupid creatures for the most part. I'm not sure what females see in you."

"I don't either."

"Well, I've got some news to cheer you up."

"What's that?"

"Did you notice anything when you came back to the house—perhaps some clotted blood or random pieces of bone or teeth?"

"No."

"Too bad," Daeva said as she laced up the shoes. "Ahti is now in the pit, and good riddance to him."

"What?"

"He's now a very long way from the nearest liquor store."

"You mean he's dead?"

"He's not human, so he's not dead." Daeva walked back over and sat down next to him. "He's on…extended vacation. Yeah, that's it."

"How did that happen?"

"Stevenson thinks that Ahti blabbed to you about the Youngstown massacre, and you told Bailey, and then the angels came and crashed the party."

"So he was killed, or whatever, because he informed me?"

"Yep." Daeva put a hand on his thigh and smiled. "You'll probably be killed next."

"Stevenson is going to kill me?"

She laughed. "No, probably Corson. Maybe not now, but he'll find the right time. Oh, and for you, it will be death."

"You're not cheering me up."

"It's actually fortuitous," she said. "It puts the Imperator off his game. He's not quite sure what's happening. Once he figures it out, of course, you're dead. But until then he's going to be keeping a close eye on you, so it's best if we skedaddle."

"So what do I do in the meantime, between now and when I'm killed?"

"We need to get out of here and talk to Trudy," Daeva said. "Everyone says she's the prophetess, so we might as well use her crystal ball and find out what the hell to do."

"I think she's back in Nevada," Ian said.

"Well, then, maybe I should take you on a little trip."

"I don't understand."

She smiled at him as she stood up and tried to adjust her breasts under the tight shirt. "Just remember, when I grab you and hold you close to my chest—try not to scream."

———

Returning from their excursion to the Bass Pro Shop, Jonathan, driving Kris's pink Cadillac, was just about to cross between the two protecting angels that guarded the entrance to New Creekside when he stopped the car.

"Why are you stopping?" Bailey asked as she looked over to Susanna, who was also puzzled.

"Something's not right," Jonathan said. "Both of you get out of the car."

When the girls got out, they noticed the protecting angels, who usually were as still as statues, bringing their shields up. The deep hum of the spinning disks of lightning cut through the desert calm as sparks spread across the ground. Raising their swords of lightning, they assumed a battle stance and moved closer to protect them, while spreading their wings of swords to shield the car.

Jonathan also got out of the car and transformed. "Move to the front of the vehicle," he commanded in a booming voice, "and stay hidden!"

Staying hidden was useful as a hunter, but since Bailey had given up that profession, she decided to peek her head up and see what was going on.

Off in the distance, she noticed an object moving through the air about fifty feet off the ground. She thought it might be a jet fighter due to the speed it was approaching. Condensation from the New Creekside's cloud formations formed a vapor cone around the object as it penetrated the sound barrier, sending a shockwave across the desert that pushed the car several inches forward and caused Bailey to duck.

Looking around the fender, she saw the object slow and was able to pick out some details. The glowing red mass of a torso suggested it had just re-entered earth's atmosphere from space; then she noticed the ashen blades of wings and a weapon that looked like a pitchfork in the creature's right hand. She had never seen this sort of demon before; it vaguely resembled the protecting angels that now moved forward to meet the adversary.

As the creature's wings fully extended, one arm moved forward, dropping something on the ground.

"Ian?" Bailey said in recognition.

"He isn't damaged," the demon said. "It is important that he speak with Trudy."

Bailey ignored the twenty-foot-tall demon and ran to her brother. He looked sick but was moving all his limbs.

"You must be Bailey," the demon said. "Ian's told me so much about you."

"He did?"

In a fraction of a second, the demon was no longer there, replaced by an attractive blonde woman in a T-shirt and raggedy jeans.

"Hey!" Susanna shouted. "Those are mine!"

"Why did you bring him here, Daeva?" Jonathan asked as he returned to his human form.

"Should I have left him for the Imperator to kill?"

"Kill?" Bailey said. "Ian, are you okay?"

"Yeah, I'm fine, except for probably a minor concussion when we broke the sound barrier."

"Sorry," Daeva said. "I was just showing off for the loyalists." She extended a hand and pulled the boy to his feet. "You did well, Ian. You didn't scream or throw up on me." She turned to Jonathan and added, "Could you tell your angelic goons to stand down?"

"It's okay," Ian said. "She's trying to help."

"Demons don't help," Jonathan said.

"Well, you've got me there," Daeva said. "But sometimes our objectives align, and I can bring my unique skill set into use. Now here's the deal. Ahti has a workman's comp case that might be resolved in a couple thousand years. Until then, he's out of commission. Ian was next in line to face the Imperator's wrath. Now that I have taken him, I'm sure to be on the list as well. We need to lay low until Trudy can tell us what to do."

"Ian can stay with us, of course," Jonathan said as Bailey walked Ian over to Susanna who was standing in front of the car.

"We're a package deal," Daeva said. "After all, he's seen me naked—we're practically engaged."

"What?" Susanna said, slapping Ian across the face. "Oh, and thanks for the chocolates, asshole."

"Hey!" Bailey said. "That's my brother."

Daeva clapped her hands happily as she walked over. "Isn't this just perfect! I'm not here five minutes, and look at all the discord I'm causing."

"You can't stay here," Jonathan said.

Daeva walked over and poked Jonathan in the chest with a manicured nail. "You need me, and you need me in one piece. Now, where is the one place that the Imperator will not be looking for a rebel?"

"Let her stay," Ian said, massaging his smarting cheek. "She did save me."

Jonathan looked uncertain. "This is against my better judgment."

"I promise to behave," Daeva said as she started walking towards the almost completed Welcoming Center. "Of course, what's the promise of a rebel, anyway?"

"Hi, everyone," Bailey said, opening the front door to Emily's house. "We have some guests."

"Guests are always welcome," Emily said. "Come on in."

"Well, some guests," Daeva said, entering behind her, "might be more welcome than others."

"What's she doing here?" Rachel said. She stood up from the sofa while *The Beverly Hillbillies*, in glorious black and white, played on the television behind her. Rachel found the show interesting primarily due to the Elly May character's affinity with animals, which strongly paralleled Bailey's newfound gift. Bailey herself thought the show was beyond insipid.

"Oh, fold in your wings," Daeva said. "I brought Ian here to see Trudy. Why don't you be a good little lap dog and fetch her, since you're the human's pet."

Rachel stood there silently, glaring at the demon.

Jonathan and Ian entered. "It is okay, Rachel," Jonathan said. "I gave her permission to be here."

"But so close to the…?"

Daeva smiled as she walked over and grabbed the television remote. "So close to the ladder, you mean? I have no intention of hurting your precious ladder, wherever it is. I assume there is also one in Niagara."

Daeva looked in disgust at the sixties sitcom and pulled up the channel guide. "Do you get Skinemax here?"

Rachel snatched the remote out of her hand.

"Rachel," Jonathan interrupted, "go find Trudy and Gavin and have them come over."

Not taking her eyes off Daeva, she walked over to Emily and handed her the remote. "If she tries to change the channel, toss her to Beverly Hills."

———

Masters sat in the suite going over some numbers on his laptop while Holly painted her toenails.

"Shouldn't you be doing this?" he groused. "You are the chief financial officer."

"If I were someplace that resembled a workplace, I would," she said coldly. "Since I'm in a hotel room overlooking Horseshoe Falls, I'm going to paint my nails."

There was a knock at the door. "Well, at least answer that!"

"I can't," Holly said, pointing to her toes.

Shaking his head, Masters stood up. "I can already see what married life is going to be like."

He reached for the doorknob, only to have the door fly open and hit him in the chest.

Corson, followed by Stevenson, barged into the room. Before Masters could protest, Corson hit him in the gut and threw him against the wall.

"Jay!" Holly had time to say before Corson walked over and punched her in the face.

Masters saw Holly fall onto the bed, blood streaming from her nose.

"Jay, Jay, Jay," Stevenson said. "You disappoint me so."

"I didn't do anything."

Corson reached down and pulled Holly off the bed by her hair, again punching her in the face. A feeble groan of protest escaped her lips; the left eye had taken the brunt, and a livid bruise was quickly forming.

Masters attempted to stand upright, despite the feeling that his spleen was now in his throat. "Leave her alone," he wheezed.

"I have found that Ian is no longer at the academy. Witnesses confirm Daeva stole him from me. Daeva is your employee, and therefore you are responsible."

"I have no control over what my employees do in their off-hours."

Still holding her by the hair, Corson gave Holly a vicious punch to the forehead. Masters winced at the sickening, fleshy thud the blow made. Holly went limp; her eyes rolled back in their sockets.

"Stop it!" Masters cried. "She didn't do anything."

"Innocents die in all wars, Jay," Stevenson said, "especially in this one."

"What do you want?"

"I suspect that Daeva has taken Ian to Nevada to reunite with his sister. Ian is nothing by himself, but he has probably given Bailey information that may be of use to her, as an exorcist. I expect you to go retrieve the boy and deliver him to me."

"And if I don't?"

"Then your fiancée will have a very similar fate to that of Brian Tannahill."

Corson punched Holly again, this time in the mouth, and dropped her unconscious body onto the bed.

"I'll do it," Masters said.

Stevenson tucked his hands into his vest pockets triumphantly. "I thought you'd come around. You know, once upon a time you occupied an honored place in the pantheon of most ruthless humans. Time was when you would have thought nothing about your fiancée having her face smashed if it advanced your station." He shook his head and lamented, "I'm afraid the rumors are true. You've gone soft, Reverend."

"Where do you want me to deliver the kid?"

"We're going to have a groundbreaking ceremony at the Niagara Falls Mysterium site on Saturday morning, and you will bring him along and turn him over to me afterward. I realize it is a bit premature, but we have cleared the site, and people are wondering what will be built there. Rumors are swirling that it will be a Mysterium; we'll confirm their hopes. We'll have to put a big 'coming soon' sign with a vague rendering of the building on-site for the next couple of years, but it will work. We must continue to present a business as usual face to the populace. Ian has notoriety as a Tannahill, so it will be useful to have him there for one last appearance."

Corson wiped his bloodied hand on a bedsheet. "I always enjoy the way human bones sound when they break. In this case, it was only cartilage—pity. And that kewpie doll mouth might never be the same again. Look on the bright side, Masters: beauty's only skin deep."

"Get the hell out," Masters growled.

"I hope," Stevenson said, as he motioned Corson to follow him, "that this doesn't in any way impact our future dealings. Your Mysterium is quite popular, and I would like to see more of them throughout the world. You still have a chance to become rich beyond your wildest dreams."

Corson nodded what would have been a cordial goodbye if he hadn't just knocked Holly unconscious.

Closing the door, Masters went over to Holly. She was still breathing but would have a nasty shiner and probably needed to have her nose set. He couldn't call 911, as he wouldn't have a reasonable explanation for how she was injured.

Pulling out his phone, he dialed.

"Hi, Pops," Trudy said. "Good timing. We have some visitors here."

"Yeah, I know, Ian and Daeva."

"Are you okay?" Trudy asked. "You sound funny."

"Corson just beat the crap out of Holly. I need you to get out here so we can take her back to Nevada so Gavin can heal her."

"Oh, God, is she okay?" Trudy said, concern rising in her voice.

"Corson busted up her face something awful. The son of a bitch punched her with all his might in the forehead. I'm afraid she might have a concussion—"

"You should call 911!"

"They would ask too many questions."

"Okay, I'm at Emily's so I can be there in a minute or two. Are you able to get her to the ladder?"

"Yeah, I'll find Edwin and have him take her," Masters said. "He's over at the Travelodge helping people move in. I'll give him a call and have him fly Holly over."

"I thought she didn't like angelic flights?"

"She's out cold, which is the best time for her to travel," Masters said.

"Okay, I'll let Gavin know to be by the ladder, and then I'll be right over."

———

Trudy held onto her father's arm as he carried Holly; Edwin followed behind. She knew by instinct now where the Nevada ladder was located and smiled at Gavin, who was waiting in the backyard.

Her father gently lowered Holly onto an aluminum and plastic lounge bed as Gavin bent down and inspected her.

"Has she been out all this time?" Gavin asked him.

"Yeah, Corson wouldn't stop hitting her."

"Stand back," Gavin said. He placed his right hand on Holly's forehead. They watched as a bright light traveled between his hand and Holly, indicative of his healing power at work. At one time he'd had a tendency to "over-heal" and accidentally bring dead things, such as Stevenson, back to life. But he was in control now; only a couple dead weeds under the chair started to turn green.

Like a cross dissolve transformation sequence from a quaint old horror movie, Holly's wounds healed before their eyes, and the beauty returned to her face.

Holly swatted Gavin's hand off. "Where am I? Jay, are you here?"

"I'm here," Masters said as he knelt beside her. "We're in Calamity. Gavin fixed you up, good as new."

"What happened? I remember Corson and Stevenson kicking in the door, and that's it."

"It doesn't matter," he said, kissing her on the forehead. "It's only important that you're okay."

Daeva shook her head. "Is that the cue for me to become nauseous?"

Masters stood and confronted her. "She was attacked by Corson only because you were stupid enough to remove Ian from the academy—in full daylight."

"I had just watched Ahti get skewered by Corson and figured the kid was going to be next," Daeva countered. "We didn't have time to be sneaky."

Masters registered surprise. "Ahti's dead?"

"No, but if you must put it in human terms: yes, sort of," Daeva said. "The important part is, we will not have his vast knowledge, superior intellect, or handsome good looks to enjoy any longer."

"My turn to gag," Emily said.

Masters continued: "Stevenson said that I need to return Ian to him during the—"

"Groundbreaking ceremony," Trudy broke in, "the one in Niagara."

"A vision?" her father asked.

"Yeah," she said, "but I don't know when. Have you scheduled it yet?"

"Stevenson said this Saturday," Masters said. "He's starting to treat the Mysterium as his own. He's bypassing us."

"You better start watching your back," Daeva said, "or you may be the late, unlamented founder of Masters' Mysterium."

"Okay," Trudy said, "we've got three days and all the key players here. It's time to start to put this together."

"Put what together?" Bailey asked.

Trudy looked at all the eager faces expecting words of wisdom from their prophetess. Usually, she would feel intimidated or inadequate, but now she knew what must be accomplished.

"The second fall of Satan."

CHAPTER EIGHTEEN

"What's on the schedule for the junior senator from the great state of Nevada, Corson?" Stevenson asked without enthusiasm while adjusting his tie.

"Senator Johnson wishes to have a lunch meeting with you to discuss the defense department budget request."

"No increases to the military," Stevenson said flatly. "We need to cut funding as quickly as possible. We need other powers to know that they can defeat us if they so desire."

"Unfortunately, you do not have much control over that," Corson said. "You are not even on the appropriations committee. Senator Johnson was merely consulting with you, as he recognizes your growing power."

"I need to be on the defense subcommittee, Corson. Make it happen."

"There are only thirty or so members of the appropriations committee, and those posts are highly coveted due to the pork-barrel projects they can introduce."

"Corson, do as I say, or you will return to North Korea in humiliation, and I will find someone more capable to assist me."

"Senator?"

"No!" Stevenson said as he turned on his assistant. "You will address me as Imperator."

Corson lowered his head. "Yes, Imperator."

"I do not wish to be stuck in this lowly position any longer," Stevenson said. "I must increase my status and power immediately. The loyalists seek to destroy my plans. I must crush them now."

"Yes, Imperator," Corson repeated.

"Use your contacts in North Korea," Stevenson said. "Let me bring them to the bargaining table. I will give them what they want—respect as a nation—then we'll bypass the president. And when I have a nuclear de-escalation agreement, I will be the hero, and he will be forced to sign it."

"I will start work right away—Imperator," Corson said.

"First, I want you to check the academy for Bailey's possessions. I need you to find one of her firearms, preferably a long rifle with a scope. As a hunter, I'm sure she kept the most powerful and lethal weapons for herself."

"Imperator?"

Stevenson smiled. "On Saturday, during our ceremony, you will shoot and kill her brother. After his betrayal, I can no longer allow him to live.

"Are you up to the job?"

"I have no qualms," Corson replied. "But should I make the boy suffer, or give him a quick dispatch?"

"He has been useful to us in the past, so blow out his brains in a similar manner to the way Ahti dispatched my host's body," Stevenson said. "No need to prolong the event. Besides we do not want Gavin to show up and miraculously heal him. It would detract from the terror we wish to instill."

"Oh, and Corson," Stevenson added, "the good reverend has outlived his usefulness. Make sure you kill Masters as well."

———

There was a turret-like structure on top of a pizza restaurant/bowling alley across the street from the ceremony that Corson considered the perfect spot for an assassination. It had easy access up a steel stairway that was well hidden by the dense forest of the park next door.

Corson had performed as instructed. He found a Savage Arms 11/111 Trophy Hunter rifle of Bailey's and attached a scope to it.

The turret was almost a complete circle, providing excellent cover. He unzipped the cheap, soft case, and pulled out the rifle. He had two, ten-round magazines ready if needed but doubted he'd use even one completely.

Climbing up several steel beams, he found a comfortable perch that would allow him to rest his rifle on the top.

He took a look across the street. The platform for the groundbreaking was up, along with the podium; to one side, a grouping of ceremonial gold-plated shovels stood gleaming in their display stands. From his vantage point, he knew he could hit anyone on the podium and still be hidden from any Secret Service agents that may be around.

Climbing back down the steel beams, he put the rifle and the case in a spot next to the plaster wall that would be difficult to see and willed himself to fade out of his current body and into a mist that no human would ever see.

Now all he had to do was wait.

———

Trudy waited in front of the ladder with the others. There were so many scenarios in which her plan could go sideways, she didn't even want to think about it. Gavin was standing near Emily on the other side of the yard in case his healing was required.

Bailey walked up to her. "Don't look so worried," she said. "This is just like trapping muskrat back home, only with a much ornerier critter."

"Yeah, you can't get much ornerier than Beelzebub," Trudy agreed ruefully.

"Looks like it's starting!" Nate yelled from inside the house, where he had been posted to monitor the groundbreaking ceremony on television, since Calamity's internet reception sucked, and pass updates to those in the yard.

"Guess I'd better get into position," Bailey said. She started walking toward the circle painted on the ground in front of the ladder.

Trudy let out a nervous sigh. "Guess I'll just stand here and look useless."

"Protect your baby!" Bailey called over her shoulder. "You did your job already."

"What's going on?" Trudy yelled back at Nate.

"Don't know," he said. "There's a commercial on about hiring a lawyer if you're in a motorcycle accident."

"That reminds me," Emily said. "Should I move my Harley? I don't want to get any sulfur or brimstone on it."

Uriel approached her. "I think it will be okay," he said, patting her on the back. "Unless we're not successful—then probably the entire town will be destroyed."

"Well, aren't you just the happy-go-lucky archangel today?" Emily responded.

"Okay," Nate shouted, "the ceremony's back on!"

"Well?" half a dozen people called out at once.

"Hold on," Nate said. "The senator just finished his speech. He's motioning for the reverend to come over."

"Is Ian there?" Bailey asked.

"Yeah, he's next to the reverend."

Nate held up his hand. "Get ready."

Everyone looked over towards the ladder.

"Stevenson is shaking the reverend's hand, and giving him a hug," Nate called out. "Ian has his hand out," he continued. "Stevenson's turning towards Ian… He's reaching out to shake…*Now!*"

Directly in front of the ladder, a man now stood—a man Bailey recognized as Senator Stevenson. He looked flustered, unsure of what had happened. If he were like the other demons, he wouldn't be able to see the ladder, but he would certainly recognize the community of angels.

Bailey casually walked over to the senator. "Hi there, welcome to Calamity," she said before grabbing onto the swirling mist that only she could see. She pulled back as hard as she could and Stevenson fell to the ground as the mist separated from the man.

"He's out of the senator's body!" Bailey yelled.

A greenish-blue light enveloped the senator's fallen body as Emily raised it off the ground and cast it into the ladder, whereupon the junior senator from Nevada was instantly immolated.

Bailey flew through the air as a being materialized where she had been standing and swatted her with a claw. She could see that Bailey's arm was severely broken, a compound fracture, with a bone sticking out of her forearm. Trudy was about to run over to help the teen, but Gavin was already there, looking after her.

"You dare to touch the Morning Star!" Lucifer roared.

Trudy gasped. Looking directly upon Satan was like gazing on the most treacherously beautiful star in the heavens. She fell to her knees under the sheer power of his visage. Lucifer stood taller than the impressive archangels and outshone them by far. She expected to see something resembling Uriel but was surprised that Satan was closer to Tomas—a cherub. His pure golden body looked smooth on the surface, but underneath, lightning coursed through veins just below the molten skin. Four massive golden wings spread out from his feline body. Teeth of diamond, claws of emerald, eyes of ruby; if he was degraded like the other fallen angels, what could he have possibly looked like standing before the throne—before his pride cast him down?

Lucifer turned towards her. "Trudy Masters, at least you are in the proper position of subjugation. I knew your father was cunning, but I never expected him to put love before his own greed."

"He has his moments," Trudy stammered as a sharp pain in her abdomen caused her to crumple face down in the dirt.

"He will soon mourn for his offspring and grandchild who will die this day."

"Do not harm the girl," Uriel said, looking small and weak even in his archangel form, compared to Lucifer.

"Her father's treachery means her protection has been forfeit. A single weak archangel will not prevent me from killing her and destroying all who live here."

"I will not fight you," Uriel said.

"Afraid, Uriel?" Lucifer scanned the horizon and laughed. "Wise, as I don't see an approaching army to assist you."

"You can see me," Rachel said as she walked around Emily's house and transformed.

This caused Lucifer to laugh even louder, rattling the windows of Emily's house. "Rachel, if I were to have respect for any loyalist, it would be you. You are indeed the fiercest warrior that remains in the Tyrant's grasp. That doesn't change the fact that you and Uriel will suffer pain beyond anything you have ever experienced. Then you may return to the Detested One and tell Him of how you failed His human pets, even as they return to the dirt from which they came."

"I think you have not paid attention to where you stand, nor the One you blaspheme," Uriel said.

Slowly and stoically, Lucifer revolved his massive golden, bejeweled visage to view his surroundings.

Then he looked up and cried out in rage.

Everyone's eyes turned towards the sky and the clouds that shaded New Creekside. The tornados at the far corners of the village began to rotate faster, their lightning intensifying and growing more prolific. The sound was deafening, like the apocalyptic rage of a thousand thunderstorms. Just when it looked like centrifugal force would spin them apart, the lightning traveled up all four tornados simultaneously and into the central cloud. They converged in the center, in the eye of the storm, directly over Satan.

Trudy couldn't read the fallen cherub's face but assumed his chief thought was *oh shit* as all the concentrated lighting held by the clouds rained down upon him. Paralyzed by the onslaught he stood roaring in pain, his wingtips turning black, curling and flaking off, as his body started to smoke. His skin of gold began to melt and disintegrate in the lightning storm.

Trudy had never heard such a wail of agony before; it sent a shiver down her spine and forced her to look away. When she regained enough courage to look again, the magnificent beauty that was Lucifer was gone. Instead, there was a shriveled, and near skeletal apparition, that would make the other emaciated demons she had seen seem robust by comparison.

Breaking free, and now the pale color of death, Lucifer ran several steps and vanished.

"I see him! He's heading that way," Bailey pointed into the desert. "Let's get him!"

Uriel transformed back into his human appearance and walked over to Bailey, who still sat on the ground, but thanks to Gavin, the bone had pushed back into her arm, and her skin was quickly healing. Bailey wouldn't even have a scar.

"We've got to get him!" Bailey cried.

"The senator is dead and will no longer deceive people," Uriel said. "Do you believe that God could have destroyed Satan just now if He wished it?"

"Yeah, sure, He's God and all, but why didn't He? You don't let rabid animals terrorize the neighborhood when you can stop them."

"How old are you, Bailey?" Uriel asked.

"Sixteen, why?"

"Satan continues to try to bring his reign to fulfillment through the evil of his human minions: Sargon of Akkad, Genghis Kahn, Tamerlane, Atilla the Hun, Ashoka the Great, Augustus Caesar, Ivan the Terrible, Adolph Hitler, Senator Stevenson. Each time he has been stopped, but he will persist. There will come a time when what we know of this world will end, and Satan and his demons will be forever contained. When that day comes, all of creation will rejoice. Because that time has mercifully been delayed, you now exist to join in that celebration—if that day had come seventeen years earlier, you would not."

"Well, when you put it that way..." Bailey said as she stood up. "But it still seems like a wasted opportunity to get the bastard."

"He has been marked now," Uriel said. "Forever condemned to see himself in ashes and not vainly parading his beauty before all. His pain may be short-lived, but the damage to his pride will sting forever."

"Do you think he will go back to Niagara Falls?" Bailey asked.

"Niagara Falls!" Trudy shouted. "What's going on, Nate?"

"Not good," Nate said. "Looks like a riot—hard to make out."

"Do you see my father?"

"No," Nate said as he poked his head around the open sliding glass door. His worried look said it all.

"Rachel, come with me," Trudy said, trotting as fast as a pregnant woman could to Gavin.

"I wish I could take you with me," Trudy said to him. "We might need your healing."

"I know," he said as he gave her a kiss. "Be careful. I'll be here waiting."

Turning, she headed towards the ladder and Niagara Falls.

The flight via "Rachel Airways" from the Niagara Falls ladder to the site of the groundbreaking ceremony took only a minute, but Trudy was afraid she would be too late.

Pandemonium reigned all around them as they landed near the stage being used for the ceremony. The gold-plated ceremonial shovels still sat in their display stands—never used for the groundbreaking. Trudy spotted her father standing near the edge of the stage just as a shot rang out.

Masters spouted blood from his chest and mouth as he fell off the stage to the ground.

"Rachel!" she shouted.

Her friend, who was still transformed, needed only a few strides to reach Master's motionless body. Rachel spread her wings of swords, creating a wall to protect him from any further danger, as she placed her shield near the ground to further deflect any projectiles.

Trudy ran around and reached him, as he sprawled like a bloody rag doll in the dirt. Sparks from Rachel's shield cascaded around them; the deep hum it emitted rattled the ground.

Masters was still conscious. "Hey, Pops!" she shouted as she knelt beside him and surveyed the damage. He was shot in the chest with a portion of rib protruding through his bloodied shirt. Her voice quaked with revulsion and raw emotion when she said: "Got any good stories for your daughter?"

"Ian saved the day," he coughed. "I was just the welcoming committee. Tell him thanks."

"You'll tell him yourself," Trudy said.

She looked up pleadingly at Rachel. "Can we do anything? Can you take him to the hospital or Gavin?"

"The flight would kill him. You've experienced the effect that I have on even a healthy person."

Masters arched his back in agony and threatened to crush her fingers in his grip.

"There is a demon nearby," Rachel said. "I must go."

Trudy watched as Rachel flew across the street and through the circular turret on top of the nearby pizzeria. The other side of the street exploded as a demon transformed, the weight of the two beings sending them plummeting down through the crumbling rooftop.

"What's happening?" Masters gurgled.

"Nothing," Trudy said. "Nothing at all."

She put her free hand on his chest to try to stop the bleeding, but most of the blood was coming out of his back, as the shot had gone clean through him.

Masters coughed; a bloody bubble formed on his lips and popped grotesquely. His words came out in a wet rattle. "Tell Holly I love her. I was always an ass to her."

"She's used to it."

"It's hard to see," he said. "Is it getting dark?"

Trudy couldn't help herself; she wanted to be strong for him, but she started to bawl. "Please, God," she whimpered, "don't let him go."

She put her head down close to his and said, "I love you."

"I love..." he managed to get out before he tightened up again and blood trickled from his nose.

Trudy felt her belly grow warm and heat move up towards her chest and through her right arm. Instinctively, she placed the hand upon her father's mangled chest. Her open palm started to sparkle with the same electricity that Gavin produced during his healing. It crossed into her father's chest; she saw him relax as the rib that protruded between Trudy's open fingers retreated into his chest.

"What's happening?" Masters croaked with slightly more strength. "What are you doing?"

"It's not me," Trudy said, kissing his forehead. "Now, hush for once and let your grandson heal you."

"Rachel is protecting your father-in-law," Nate said to Gavin as he came in to watch TV coverage of the aborted groundbreaking ceremony. "It looks like he's been shot."

Gavin saw the spectators moving away from Rachel as she placed her shield of spinning lightning in front of her to protect Masters.

"Have you seen Trudy?"

"Yes," Nate said. "She's behind Rachel."

Bailey ran in to watch as well. "What about Ian?"

"I haven't seen him," Nate said.

Gavin had known Nate long enough to realize something was wrong, despite the angel's matter-of-factness. "Shouldn't he be there near Jay? He was standing next to him before, right?"

"He should, yes."

"I don't like this," Bailey said. "I need to get there now. I need to find Ian."

"You can't," Gavin told her. "Trudy is the only one who can take someone through a ladder."

"Uh-oh," Nate said. "Rachel must have found something—either that or she doesn't like pizza; she just took the top off the pizza joint next door."

"I can't just stay here and do nothing!" Bailey protested.

"I can take you," Daeva said. They all turned around; she stood in the doorway in her human form.

"Not through the ladder," Nate said. "You would destroy it."

"Duh," she mocked. "But I am faster than anyone else around this dump."

Daeva looked at Bailey. "I can take you. I will keep you secure, but the forces at that velocity will be hard on your body—similar to what Ian experienced."

"I don't care!" Bailey said. She grabbed Daeva's hand and dragged her out into the yard. "I have to go—now!"

They watched as the demon transformed, so very close to the ladder, and lifted Bailey up to hold her against her chest. The force of Daeva's departure sent a shockwave through the backyard, blowing a barbeque grill off its stand and toppling Emily's prized motorcycle.

Emily sighed. "Shit! I knew I should have moved my bike."

———

Bailey passed out during the trip to Niagara Falls. When she awoke, she was lying on the ground as people fled from the sight of a demon towering over them. Bailey felt like someone had hit her shoulder with a baseball bat. Turning her head, she saw that they were at the site of the groundbreaking.

Daeva reverted to human form. "Don't try to move," she cautioned. "Your shoulder is dislocated."

"Nonsense," Bailey said. She got on her knees and put her right shoulder to the pavement. Bailey hoped she wouldn't pass out again as she pressed as hard as she could. After a long, agonizing moment, she felt her shoulder snapping back into place with a satisfying pop.

"That's better," she said with a groan of relief. "How long did it take us to get here?"

Daeva helped her stand. "About fifteen minutes," she replied. "I'm sorry that you were injured. Humans are so fragile."

Bailey snorted. "Spare me your sympathy. I'm made of pretty tough stuff."

Daeva smirked. "Oh, really? Remind me to challenge you to a good cat-fight sometime."

Just then there was a loud crunch on the other side of the street as the bowling alley caved in, creating a dust cloud that enveloped the nearby Ferris wheel.

"Looks like I'm not too late to the party," Daeva said before she transformed and sped off in search of a fight.

Desperate to find Ian, Bailey turned her attention back to the podium. She spotted Trudy and her father standing together and ran over to them.

Trudy held up her hands when she spotted her. "No!" Trudy shouted. "Bailey, stay back!"

"What? Where's Ian?"

She kept running until Masters grabbed her around the waist and brought her to a sudden halt. "Ian's dead," he said.

"No, I don't believe you."

Trudy moved close. "It's true; Ian was shot just moments before my father."

Bailey felt her legs turn to jelly as she started to collapse. Masters, still holding her waist, let her down gently onto the packed dirt.

"Where is he?" she demanded.

"On the other side of the stage," Masters said. "They shot him just after he shook the senator's hand."

"I need to see him," she said as she struggled to her feet.

"Bailey," Masters said gently, "you shouldn't remember him like he is now."

Bailey pushed him away. "I have to."

She walked around the stage and felt her heart sink. It was as they said. He was clearly dead. The bullet had hit him square in the forehead, most likely killing him instantly. He lay there in a pool of blood and brain matter.

She turned away and cried.

She felt a hand on her shoulder. "Bailey."

"Jonathan," she said, looking up at him. "How did you get here?"

"Through the ladder. I'm sorry for your loss."

"Let's take Ian back to Gavin. He can heal him just like he healed me!"

"Gavin, can't," Jonathan said. "he can heal the body, but the soul will not return once removed. Ian would become a vessel for demons similar to Senator Stevenson."

"Why did he have to die?"

"We all knew the risks when we started this. Your brother knew the potential cost; you did as well."

"That doesn't help," Bailey said, as she looked again at her brother.

"He died for a purpose. He died so that you could live your life with a purpose as well."

That was too much for her. She started to sob again as Jonathan wrapped his arms around her. "My mom and dad are dead, and now, my brother. Why am I still alive?"

"To help others live, Bailey," Jonathan said as he kissed the top of her head. "To help others live."

———

Rachel felt the pain of a trident being pushed slowly through her leg.

"You have no power over me, loyalist," Corson said to her. "I will torture you until I am satisfied, then I will cross the street to finish my work."

She brought up her shield, and the spinning disk cut cleanly through the pole of the trident, sending sparks across the shattered lanes of the bowling alley.

"It doesn't matter," Corson said as he spun what was left of the pole over his head and prepared to impale her.

"Corson," came a voice from the darkened lanes of the building. "May I join you in torturing this pathetic loyalist?"

"Daeva," Corson said, "how nice of you to drop by."

Daeva walked over and swung her pitchfork at Rachel's shield, knocking it out of her hand. "I've always wanted to do that," she chortled. She turned to Corson. "Look, Stevenson is no more; the Imperator is a mere shadow of himself—literally. Now is the time for us to take over and rule this planet."

"Surely you're not suggesting we share dominion, Daeva."

"Of course not, you would be supreme ruler. But you will need assistance."

Corson lowered the remnants of the trident. "I will give you this honor," he said, pointing to Rachel. "Make this one suffer like no other has since we were cast down."

"Gladly," Daeva said as she approached and raised her fiery pitchfork. Taking aim, she spun it around and struck Corson in the chest.

"What are you doing?" he cried out in pain.

"This is for Ahti," she said, twisting the pitchfork inside him.

She then rammed it in deeper. "And this is for making me have to babysit Ahti."

In one fluid motion, she hefted Corson off the ground and slammed him back down, ripping the demon in two.

"And that was for ruining my favorite white miniskirt."

CHAPTER NINETEEN

Creekside looked much the same to Masters, only now it was a sanitized Disneyland version. The streets were lined with the antebellum buildings he remembered, but the dirt and grime of decades were gone. Other than the time he spent there with Trudy, his only memory of Creekside was the year he'd spent married to one of its residents—a year of missed opportunities. Ironically, the town he once despised was now the central shopping district of the Vegas Mysterium. A screen covered the concrete ceiling as stars were projected onto it creating a night sky; fluorescent lighting bathed the sidewalk in front of the new Cluck and Grunt diner. Flashing lasers and LEDs simulated the ladder off in the distance over Morgan as large fans created an artificial fall breeze that gently swept down the street.

"Admiring your work?" Kim said as she walked down Main Street towards him.

"It's been a long time coming," he said. "It's hard to imagine we're opening after all we've been through."

"There were a few setbacks: construction delays, union issues, and a demonic war—nothing out of the ordinary for Vegas."

They took a leisurely stroll down the main drag. "Have you seen Holly?" Masters asked.

"She was in the office area, yelling at some poor employee. Your wife has quite the temper."

"Yeah, tell me about it."

"She did mention that she has the helicopter ready on top of the conference center for a quick getaway after the ceremony." Kim glanced up at Masters, adding, "I can't believe you're not staying after the ribbon cutting to revel in your success."

"We need to get back to Calamity. Little Jay is coming home from the hospital today."

She stopped and stared at him. "Who are you, anyway?"

"I hear you fucked up the VIP seating. You can't put celebrities with that much plastic surgery under the Vegas sun—they'll melt."

Kim laughed. "That's better! By the way, you do know they don't really use plastic, right?"

"Have you *seen* some of those monster pusses?"

"Touché," Kim agreed. "Oh, I almost forgot—there was a little delay with the tent setup. It's been handled."

"Good. And did you get the kinks worked out on the Battle of Creekside attraction? When I rode it yesterday, some of the 3D was off. It was giving me a headache."

"I spoke to Denise. She said it was a simple fix and she'd have it ready for opening."

"Who are you, anyway?" Masters mocked. "Where's my totally incompetent assistant?"

She frowned. "I should have kicked you out of *my* casino when I had a chance."

Masters made a grand sweep with his arms. "And miss all of this?"

He spied someone vaguely resembling Tony Manero from *Saturday Night Fever* exiting the food court.

"Nice place you have here," Nate said, making loud noises through a straw while he attacked a neon blue Slurpee.

"I see you put on your best paisley shirt and bell bottoms for the occasion," Masters said.

"That's right!" Nate shook the cup to get the last slurry of colored ice into position for his straw. "I'm going to be giving the first talk in the 'Lunch with an Angel' series here in Vegas. Good thing I have some experience."

"Ready for those tough questions from the little rug rats?" Masters asked. "Like, do angels shit in the woods?"

"Why, yes, I am, and yes, I do—at least in this form, if necessary," Nate said with evident pride as he slurped on his empty drink. "What goes in must come out. Oh, and I was quite impressed by the quality of the Mysterium's restroom facilities. You just wave your hands under the faucet and water comes out. It's like magic."

"I'm happy I impressed an angel," Masters said. "So long, Nate." He gave the angel a little parting salute and then offered Kim an open hand gesture to continue the tour.

"I've got some work to do," Kim said. "I'll catch up with you later."

"About time," Masters said. "If you see my wife, have her meet me in the lobby."

"Will do."

He continued down Main Street past several stores that never existed in the "real" Creekside—fudge shop, shooting gallery, glassblower—until he stopped next to what would have been an abandoned liquor store but now contained a photo studio with various angelic cutouts customers could pose with. He looked up at the second floor that was slightly reduced from life-size to force perspective and make the façade seem taller than it was.

That was where Trudy lived: the shabby apartment where she was almost raped and killed, where he was knifed and almost died, where Theodore did die, and Azael was sent to the pit. The recreation was accurate enough, if soulless; the plain windows and fiberglass brickwork couldn't begin to portray to tourists these monumental events that had changed the world. But Masters' memory of them was awful and indelible.

Holly walked up to him. She put her hand around his waist and looked up at the windows. "That was the place?"

"Yeah," he said. "That was it."

"To think I almost lost you there. Well, not *there* there, but in Wisconsin—you know what I mean."

He smiled and gently lifted her chin. Gazing into her eyes, he bent down and kissed the woman that now carried his child.

———

Knowing how much her mother had loved flowers, Bailey had scattered seeds and planted bulbs on not only her grave but also those of her father's and Ian's. Their plots were on one side of the house near the area where Linda Tannahill kept her vegetable garden. Thanks to Bailey's care, daffodils, snapdragons, and tulips were blooming in a riot of color.

It felt strange being back on the compound. Following the tragedies that had befallen the family, the courts ruled that Brian had been coerced into signing over the deed to the senator and the property reverted to the Tannahill estate. Bailey was the last Tannahill, but fortunately, she wasn't alone on the one-hundred-acre compound.

Violet, the chocolate lab had fully recovered from her injuries, was chasing Bailey's mountain lion around a tree. After about three revolutions, she would stop and lower her front end, raise her ass end, and vigorously wag her tail until the mountain lion turned around and started the chase in the opposite direction.

Jonathan walked up, wearing ragged jeans and a dirt coated T-shirt. "Hello, Bailey," he greeted her. "Can you put your coyote in the house for a while? He keeps trying to 'help' us while we're trying to plant the back ten acres."

Bailey smiled. "Sure, sorry about that. It's hard to keep an eye on all the critters."

She noticed a bald eagle on the rooftop that was watching several raccoons and a muskrat trying to figure out how to get into a trash can. Her menagerie had grown to include three gray wolves, a lynx, two moose, four white-tailed deer, and a black bear that liked to sleep near the chicken coop, which the chickens didn't seem to mind, oddly enough. She didn't even bother to count the dozens of smaller animals that currently called the compound home.

As a hunter, Bailey was a disgrace. Whereas before she had an unsentimental opinion of wildlife as a commodity, she now saw animals as furry friends to be protected. "Live and let live" was her new mantra. Her guns, knives, and traps had been mothballed.

She wondered how all the wildlife could put up with the constant activity. With a Niagara ladder open, angels had been making their way to the compound; construction was underway on what would become an angelic town of some size, hidden in the woods. The barn and several buildings the senator had started had been bulldozed; five new modular homes stood in their place. Construction was also underway on new houses for the constant stream of residents pouring in. Bailey stayed in the farmhouse and felt comforted by all the knick-knacks her mother had accumulated throughout the years. Jonathan slept in Ian's old room since he had the unenviable task of looking after her.

"So, would you like to go hunting?" Jonathan asked.

Bailey knew what he meant by hunting and that a rifle wasn't required: he meant demon hunting. She had become quite proficient in exorcism over the last months. After she cast out Satan, everything else was easy peasy lemon squeezy.

"I hear," Jonathan said, "that a demon named Pythius inhabits a buffalo chicken shop owner in Buffalo."

Bailey tapped her lip thoughtfully with her index finger. "I want to help the poor possessed guy, but it's kinda far away, and we have a lot to do around here."

"Let me give you a little background on Pythius," Jonathan said. "He rebelled against Satan and was punished by having to spend his existence in a railroad tunnel not too far from here."

Bailey smiled. "I've heard about that. In elementary school, the girls would try to scare each other with stories of ghosts and hauntings around the area."

"His profession of scaring tourists might seem trivial, but his heart is twisted." Jonathan paused. "He was let out right around the time of your mother's murder."

"You don't think—"

"I don't know for sure, but I do know that Corson, the senator's right hand and the demon who killed your father, had been close to Pythius. I need your help. I can't cast Pythius out of the human without it killing him."

Bailey could feel her hands balling into fists as her anger grew. She stood next to her parents' and brother's graves. Ian knew what he was getting himself into and died nobly to save others. But her parents—especially her mother, who had never hurt a fly—didn't deserve to die horrible deaths.

"I'm ready to go," Bailey said as she watched Jonathan transform in front of her. Sparks flew from his staff of lightning as ozone filled the air.

Just as he was about to reach out and pick Bailey up for a quick flight to Buffalo, Bailey held up her hand.

"Almost forgot." Bailey dug into her pocket for her iPhone. Putting on her earbuds, she smiled and gave Jonathan the thumbs up. "Let's go kick demon ass!" she yelled as "Mercy Me's Happy Dance" blasted in her ears.

The dusty and downtrodden town of Calamity never looked better to Trudy as she rode home from the hospital, with Gavin driving and her precious cargo snug in a baby seat behind her. Her father had given them a brand-new GMC Yukon as a present; no grandson of his was going to ride around in an old Jeep or borrowed pink Caddy.

They could see the ring of protecting angels from five miles down the road, standing sentinel over the town in unblinking silence.

"I'm glad the house is finished," Trudy said. "I'd hate to raise my son in a motel room."

"Rachel," Gavin said, "has finished decorating the baby's room. I've never seen her so excited."

Trudy grinned. "It's kind of weird having an angel as little Jay's godmother, but we were never going to be a normal family anyway."

"Are you up to visiting with the gang at Emily's? We can always postpone."

"We should go. They are all as excited as Rachel, albeit without the jumping up and down. Even my dad said he'd show up."

"Are you sorry you're missing the grand opening of the Mysterium?"

Trudy laughed. "Hell no! I worked nine months on my little excuse in the back seat just to get out of it."

They drove up to the Welcoming Center and stopped at the guard shack, which seemed entirely unnecessary with the entrance flanked by protecting angels. Typically, after being cleared, they would proceed to the parking lot next to Josh Barber's gas station and switch to their golf cart. But this time Gavin was informed that he could drive right over to Emily's, as this was a special day for the entire community.

"Baby perks," Trudy said, and then lightly punched Gavin's shoulder. "I'll have to get pregnant more often."

As they pulled up to Emily's house, they could tell by the racket that an overflow crowd of townsfolk had come over to welcome the new baby to Calamity. The celebrants had spilled out of the modest house into the backyard.

Trudy slowly slid out of the Yukon and stood on the gravel road. Looking off towards the way they had come, she noticed a black helicopter preparing to land.

"Dad's here," she announced.

"What's wrong with him lately, anyway?" Gavin said as he went around to help with the baby. "It's like he's almost human."

"He loves little Jay," Trudy said. "Plus, I'm his legacy, and you're the guy who had the good sense to marry me.

"Okay, deep breath," she said while holding Jay in her arms. "Let's do this."

Gavin opened the door to a packed house. At first, everyone just stood there, expectantly. Upon Emily's signal, they whispered a collective "Welcome home!" Only Maggie, the German shepherd, decided to break with the group and bark loudly at their arrival.

Emily came up and hugged the couple. "We didn't want to startle the baby," she explained, "but Maggie obviously didn't get the memo." The celebrants had gathered behind Emily and joined her in oohing and ahhing over little Jay.

"Let me see!" Rachel said, elbowing her way through the crowd. "Ooooh, he's adorable!"

"Finally," Trudy said, "someone smaller than you."

"You're so blessed," Rachel said as she softly stroked the baby's forehead. "He's got his father's eyes."

Trudy examined them. "He does. Hopefully, he won't have his mother's hair."

The elder Masters, followed by Holly, came into the living room. "Where's my namesake?" he bellowed "Where's my little Jay?"

He was met by a unison "Shh," by the assembled group.

"Sorry," he mumbled as he walked over to Trudy, "can I see?"

Trudy pulled the blanket back.

"He has my eyes," Reverend Masters proudly pronounced as he put a finger down for his grandson to grab hold of.

"Can we take him outside?" Emily asked. "I want to capture the moment with a group photo by the ladder I can't see."

"Sure," Trudy said.

The quartet of friends strolled into the backyard, where the overflow crowd descended upon Gavin, Trudy, and the baby. Emily took advantage of a lull in the congratulations to lead them to a quiet corner of the yard.

"Can you still see it, Trudy?" Emily asked.

"Yes, but I don't know if that's going to fade away now that Jay is born."

"Guess we'll find out," Gavin said. "Do you think he sees the ladder?" He looked down at his son. "Never mind, I think he just fell asleep."

"Hard to say," Trudy said. "Either way, it's awfully bright out here, even with the clouds. I'm taking him inside. We'll have to do the photo later when the sun isn't as bright."

Rachel pointed at little Jay and cried, "Look!"

Trudy glanced down at her baby. Gavin was correct; the little dude was fast asleep, but something else caught her eye. Little Jay's right hand was slightly cupped, and in it, he held a tiny ball of light as bright as the sun above.

She and Gavin said in unison: "What the...?"

Uriel came over and inspected the object in her baby's hand. "I have never seen this before." He beckoned to Jonathan, who was already moving closer. "Have you, Jonathan?"

"Never," Jonathan replied. "He's folding dimensions, but on a much smaller scale than the ladder. Other than size, however, it is the same."

"A baby's baby ladder!" Rachel chimed in.

"I can see it too," Emily said, "so it isn't *exactly* like the ladder in my yard."

"But what does it mean?" Gavin asked, curious about his son's new talent, as they all were.

"Perhaps it's a sign?" Emily suggested. "A sign that God is with him and will protect him, always."

Trudy reached down and touched the ball of light. It gave her little static shocks that didn't hurt but sparked with bright colors arcing between her fingers. The memory of a spectacular double rainbow from her girlhood flooded her mind.

She looked away from her husband towards the gathered friends that she had grown to love.

"No, it's not a sign," Trudy said. "It's a promise."

THE END

www.MastersMysterium.com

Named to *Kirkus Reviews'* Best Books of 2014: *Masters'*
Mysterium: WISCONSIN DELLS

"One of the best paranormal fantasy releases of this year…"
– *Kirkus Reviews (starred review)*

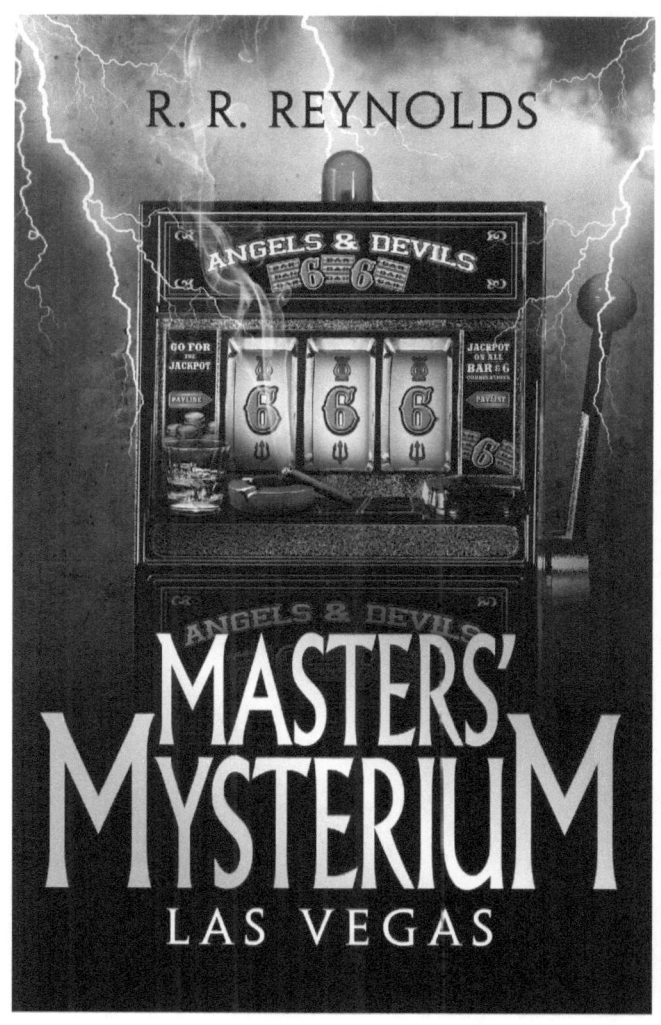

Named to *Kirkus Reviews'* Best Books of 2015: *Masters' Mysterium: LAS VEGAS*

"Like Charlaine Harris' Midnight, Texas saga this is cutting-edge genre fiction that will appeal to genre fans as well as mainstream fiction readers. It's a storytelling tour de force no matter the categorization."
– *Kirkus Reviews (starred review)*